To be a Soldier

JM Kearsley

TSL Publications

First published in Great Britain in 2022
By TSL Publications, Rickmansworth

ISBN / 978-1-914245-97-8

Front Cover image:
https://commons.wikimedia.org/wiki/File:British_Military_Short_La
nd_Pattern_Musket.jpg
https://en.wikipedia.org/wiki/File:Battle_of_Chiclana.jpg
https://imgur.com/gallery/iu7IOUo

For Karen

A fan of this book and sadly missed

1

London, England. Early September, 1811

The basket of apples flew up into the air, scattering the round fruit in all directions while the fruit seller tried in vain to stop herself slipping in the filthy refuse of the gutter. Her feet skidded out from under her and she sat down heavily in the muck, ragged skirt around her knees, screaming abuse at the boy who had crashed into her and at the laughing urchins nearby who were doing nothing to help.

The girl's indignant wails followed Will Tucker up the narrow street as he pelted between horses, carriages, and carts filled with produce, dodging the people who were everywhere. The noise was such that the yells of the girl were soon lost amidst the hubbub so Will paused for a second, panting for breath, and stole a glance behind him. Nowhere could he see the tall gentleman with the top hat and cane. From past experience Will knew that meant he hadn't noticed anything amiss. Good.

It had been an easy snatch. The gentleman, youngish, tall, and cleanshaven, wearing a forest green coat and tight yellow breeches, had been striding down the London street in high, black boots, picking his way carefully around the puddles and filth. Will had seen him coming from a shadowed doorway across the road, then had followed him, not too closely, for a quarter of a mile or more, keeping the bobbing top hat in view all the time. He wondered why such a seemingly wealthy man was walking and not riding in a carriage, thereby risking the well-being not only of his clothing, but his person as well. The streets of London were not healthy places in which to go on foot if you could ride. This man was strolling along as though he were on Richmond Common, and appeared to be unaware or oblivious of any possible danger. Will had kept the man in sight until he had finally stopped outside a jeweller's shop, old Manny Goldstein's Jewel Emporium, and there he had stayed, gazing in at the window, allowing Will to get close enough to pick his pocket.

The deed had been done in a flash. Still a few paces away from the gentleman, Will had waited for a woman who was walking towards them to come closer. The woman, towing a small child, and with a large parcel clutched in her arms, had come level with the man. Will had bumped into the child so that he stumbled against his minder who then dropped her parcel, spilling shiny blue satin material in the mud and falling against the man looking in the shop window. There followed a round of apologies, together with some loud cries and language best not heard in polite society from the woman as she cuffed the crying child for making her bump into 'the nice gentleman' and dirtying the bolt of cloth which her mistress would undoubtedly make her pay for. Unnoticed, Will had slipped a hand inside the man's tail-coat pocket and made off with his purse. In seconds he had disappeared into the crowded street, leaving the woman and child still wailing, and the man trying to extricate himself from their presence.

Now Will turned into a side street and walked until he came to the River Thames. He strolled jauntily along beside it, watching the barges and the ever-present seagulls flying and shrieking overhead, waiting for anything edible to be thrown overboard. The smell of fish was overwhelming as he passed fishermen gutting their catch and throwing it into baskets ready to sell. Will, used to the stink of the London wharves, hardly noticed. He was enjoying the feeling of the fat purse inside his shirt, next to his skin. He had not stopped to open it yet but could tell by the weight that this time he had struck lucky. He gazed above the rooftops at the tall masts of an East-Indiaman and a clipper in the docks around a bend in the river, and let his mind wander, thinking of the far away countries they had sailed from and what wonders the sailors might have seen.

He stopped to watch a cock fight on the dock-side, shoving his way to the front through the press of men. The two cocks snapped and bit in a flurry of feathers and squawks while the men who had laid bets shouted and urged on their favourite. Will kept a hand inside his shirt, not wanting to risk losing his ill-gotten gains. The fight was won to rousing cheers from some, curses from others, so Will wandered on until he came to a dingy alley, noisome and fetid, but empty of any drunk or layabout. He slid into the alley and crouched down behind a pile of refuse, unheeding of the rats that scrabbled in and out of the dirt.

Pulling it out of his shirt, he saw that the purse was made of pig skin, soft and supple, well used, and there was some sort of motif on it. Will could not read so he ignored the words, but he gazed at the rampant lion and the crossed swords which were embossed on a shield. A rich man's bauble. He hefted its weight in his hand and then opened the draw string and tipped the purse upside down. Coins fell out onto his lap. A shower of golden guineas. Will's eyes widened. He could hardly believe the pile of coins that shone in the dimness of the alley and rolled in the dirt around his feet. Never before had he seen so much money! Why, there must be ten coins! It was a fortune.

The money would buy him good clothes and a place to stay. A good place instead of the rat-infested hole he lived in by the wharf. And food. The thought of the food that the guineas could buy made his mouth water, for Will Tucker was always hungry, sometimes going without food for two days at a time, and then only eating other people's leavings. There were hundreds like him in the streets of London, all vying constantly for what slim pickings there were. Will did better than most. People, women especially, were taken by his looks; the thick straw-coloured hair, the merry blue eyes and the cheeky grin. He was a strong lad and sometimes managed to earn a coin or two by carrying bags for ladies, or helping out at the markets, shifting boxes of fruit and vegetables. Once or twice he had even been offered a more permanent job, but he was a vagabond, too independent and wilful to work for a master for very long.

However, there was a huge difference between working for someone and being financially independent. He wouldn't mind leaving the streets if he could have a big house, and servants and horses. Definitely horses. One of his dreams in life was to have a horse of his own because Will loved horses, though he had never ridden one in his life. And to be a soldier. That was his ultimate dream. He had seen the recruiting sergeants many times, trying to round up likely lads for the army that was presently in Portugal fighting Bonaparte's Frenchies, heard their patter that offered the king's shilling and more if the boys who listened to them would only sign up for king and country. Will had listened avidly to the patter, imagining the glories of battle, and had once tried to offer his services, lying about his age, but the experienced sergeant had seen through the lie and had told him to go home to his mother, that the army wasn't so hard up yet that it needed to take babes who were still wet-nursing. The comment had made Will angry. He had taken a swing at the sergeant, and nearly ended up in jail. He would have done so if not for a girl who had been standing nearby. She distracted the sergeant and, with a wink and a smile, gave Will time to make a quick escape.

So wrapped up in his daydreams of food and glory was he, that Will never saw the shadow creeping up on him until it was too late. A filthy, bony hand grabbed him by the shoulder and jerked him to his feet. Another hand wrapped itself around his mouth and Will felt the bile rise at the stink of the hand that was preventing him from shouting. He heard voices, saw another, larger shadow bending down and gathering up the coins that had fallen off his lap and he struggled, trying to shout, kicking and wriggling.

'Give over, yer little devil, you!' said the coarse voice of the man who had hold of him. ''Tain't your money!'

Will, angry, and cursing himself for his inattention that had allowed them to creep up on him like that, recognised the voice. Isaac Higgins, thief and murderer, curse of rich and poor alike. So the man picking up the gold coins would be his ally, Daniel Pots. He struggled harder. The bony hand on his arm let go while the hand around his mouth slipped down to his neck where it held him in a choking grip. He grabbed hold of the arm with both hands, trying in vain to loosen it, but the choke hold was rock steady.

'Now then, young Will. I don't know why yer strugglin' so,' said the voice lightly, and Isaac Higgins's face swam into view, ugly and scarred. The almost toothless mouth opened wide in a parady of a grin. 'Yer knows yer can't keep that money. A lad like you wouldn't spend it wisely. It'll be much better off wi' me.' There followed a short pause, then, 'Got it all, Dan?' There was a grunt from the other man.

'Well, we'll be off then. And don't try ter follow us, lad. Yer knows full well what the end'll be if yer do.'

Will knew only too well. Higgins and his henchmen lived in the filthy streets near St Paul's Cathedral and no one went there alone or at night if they wanted to survive. Many an unwary traveller, wanting to view the sights of London Town, had never been seen again after accidentally wandering into Isaac Higgins's domain.

Higgins let go of Will who coughed and wheezed, trying to catch his breath. By the time he had done so, the alley was empty. Will sat down on the dirty cobbles, despondent and angry. So much for his pipe-dreams. And what was worse, he had done it to himself. He should have been keeping a better eye out instead of gloating over his windfall. The streets were full of men like Higgins and it never did to keep anything valuable in the open for too long where others might see it.

Will felt something hard under his behind. Reaching underneath his ragged breeches, his hand touched the pigskin purse. With mounting excitement, he realised it wasn't quite empty and when he looked inside, he found one of the golden guineas.

Will smiled to himself, immediately feeling better. Daniel Pots had not been very thorough. Will pushed it inside his shirt. The coin represented a small fortune to one who had to rely on quick wits and a cheery grin for his supper. He walked out of the alley thinking he would go to Polly Frinton's place and get her to change the guinea for smaller coins because the minute he tried to buy something with it, he would be in trouble. Lads like him never had this amount of money, and the vendor would know at once that he was a thief.

So it was that late that night, Will sauntered into a seedy tavern lost amongst the backstreets of Holborn. The place was filled with noise and stank to high heaven of liquor, sweat, and more questionable odours. Men sat at tables or stood around, drinking, shouting, singing, arguing and cursing. Some had women; slatterns wearing low cut cheap dresses that left nothing to the imagination, and women threaded their way between the crowd, deftly carrying glasses of ale, parrying hands that reached out to their buttocks and bosoms, always ready with a pert remark for the drunken louts who owned them.

Will pushed unnoticed through the mass, searching over heads and between shoulders until he saw the person he was looking for. The owner of the tavern, Polly Frinton, was sitting on a bench at a table beside the wall. A tall, stringy man with a sharp beak of a nose and a black top hat perched beside her like a beady-eyed crow. Polly was conducting business. A portly, greasy man, red faced and sweating, sat on the bench opposite, fat thighs perched on the edge of his seat, cap clutched in nervous hands. He looked like a man who had come here as a last resort, as Will knew folk often did. For Polly Frinton was a money-lender, and people mostly came to her because they were in debt.

Will thought back to what he knew of Polly's past life. In her mis-spent youth she had been a looker, despite her up-bringing on the streets of London, and she had caught the eye of a rich gentleman from one of the big houses. Thwarting opposition from his family, they had married and Edward Frinton had showered Polly with money and riches until his sudden death, some sixteen months later, when relatives had come and taken the house away from her, declaring that the man must have been mad to so much as look at her, let alone take her for his wife. Thus Polly had returned to the streets of her youth, but with money that she had saved in her pocket and a baby in her arms. She had set herself up in business as a tavern owner and money-lender. Now, some fifteen years later, she was still fair-looking, and much richer because she was an astute business woman. Her interest rates on the loans varied for she had a kind heart. If she knew a man was really suffering and he had a large family to support, her rates would be low, but for someone like the poor devil in front of her at this moment, Will knew the rates would be high, for chances were that he had got himself into debt through gambling, and Polly abhorred gambling.

Sitting on the other side of Polly from the man with the black hat was Polly's daughter, Mary. Will stared at her and smiled, and was not the only person to give the girl a second glance. She was a redhead, as her mother had been before the grey started to take over, her figure voluptuous but not fat, and she bestowed her ready smile on Will as he approached the table.

'Will! Ain't seen yer for the longest time! Come 'ere now and sit yerself down by me. D'you want to see ma?' Mary laughed as she pushed up to make room for Will to sit on the bench beside her. 'No, 'course yer don't! What does the likes o' you need money for? Yer gets all yer need just by askin', don't yer?'

She pressed close to Will and he blushed. Mary Frinton was a fetching girl in a blowsy sort of way; a look that went down well with the customers of the tavern, though Will knew that Polly did not hand out Mary's favours lightly. She vetted every man who wished to bed her daughter, hoping that one day a rich man would want to have her. Mary's father had been a gentleman, and Polly had never given up hope that there might be one waiting out there for her Mary.

Polly Frinton concluded the business with her customer, handed over some coins, and the fat man went away, if not exactly happy, at least satisfied. She called for another bottle of gin in a voice that would have done credit to a fishwife on the wharf. When it came she took a swig out of it and passed it to Mary, who did the same, before passing the bottle on to Will. He took a long drink, gasping at the bite of the alcohol. It was a while since he'd had any strong liquor, and it would be a while more before he had too much of it. With so much money in his keeping, he needed to keep his wits about him and not risk losing the little he had managed to salvage. He would not make the same mistake twice.

'So young Will, is this a social call, or business?' Polly Frinton looked on the yellow-haired lad with a fond eye. Will was a good 'un, not like some o' them ruffians that roamed the streets these days. A handsome lad too with those blue eyes that didn't miss much, even if he was as poor as a church mouse. Growing into a fine young man, if a mite skinny, but then the lad never had enough to eat. Polly thought back to her days as a rich man's wife. Will's mother, Ellen, had been a maid in her household, a pretty slip of a thing who had fallen in love with the stable lad, and fallen into the family way as well. She had been dismissed by Polly's husband of course, poor thing, and the lad had refused to marry her. Polly, feeling sorry for her, had given her money and she had gone away to the countryside, to an aunt, and had the baby, Will. The lass had come back to London to find work but had died of a fever some months after arriving, leaving Will to the not so tender mercies of the poor house. Polly's husband had died in the meantime and she had been helping Ellen with money until she found a job, so Will was taken into her care and brought up with Mary who was then nearly a year old.

Will and Mary had thought of each other more as brother and sister until Will was around thirteen, when other feelings had started to intrude. He noticed Mary's swelling bosom and spreading hips, the way she flounced around in front of her mother's customers and the way they looked at her, mouths slack and wet, eyes admiring. Will began to get a hardness in his groin which he didn't understand at first until he and Tom Quirk, the man pres-

11

ently sitting with Polly, had talked one night when Tom was in his cups. The man who had become first Polly Frinton's admirer, then her partner and advisor, had described his first experience with a girl. It was then that Will realised what he felt for Mary was lust.

It did not escape Mary's notice either. She saw Will's broadening shoulders, the way muscles had started to ripple when he lifted the heavy barrels of ale in the tavern, and the way he looked at her, as if she was a different person to the one he had known all his life. By the time Mary was fourteen, her mother was selling her services to select admirers, and Polly also noticed the desire in young Will's eyes whenever he and Mary were together. It was only a matter of time before Will was seduced one night in a back room of the tavern and, for a time, he had thought himself in love. The need for Mary was so strong that Will found that he could not be in the same room as her without his lust being very much in evidence, and he could hardly bear the thought of her with other men. The feeling of jealousy got so bad it made him up and leave Polly's tavern and go and live on the streets, doing what Polly had taught him; thieving, picking pockets, and conning people out of what was rightfully theirs, except that now, instead of giving the proceeds to Polly, he kept it for himself. It wasn't much of a life, but he was free to do what he wanted and go where he would. It had been eight months before he had dared go back to the tavern, eight months of near starvation, and keeping one step ahead of the law and people like Isaac Higgins, but Will found he enjoyed it. He liked the spontaneity, the danger, the risk-taking. And the independence.

Polly had welcomed him back with open arms, though she could see how the eight months of life on the streets had changed Will. He had grown in more than stature and, at fourteen, was hers no longer. However, after that he visited quite often, and still regarded her, Tom and Mary, as the only family he had. Now it was two months since they had last seen him. At sixteen, he was tall and handsome. Studying him carefully, Polly saw his hair had grown. He probably hadn't had it cut since she had done it last and now it was well past his ears; shaggy and thick, falling over his eyes. His face had thinned, but then he was thin altogether, though it was more a leanness because there was muscle there. He looked well, she thought fondly. Those blue eyes that always had a twinkle of mischief in them, and that grin that could melt the hardest heart, were the same as always.

'Well?' she asked again. 'To what do we owe the pleasure of yer company tonight?'

Being careful not to let the tavern's patrons see, Will dug into his shirt and pulled out the purse, opened it and shook out the guinea. Mary's eyes rounded at the sight of it. So did Polly's.

'What did yer, do, lad? Rob the king?'

'No. I picked a pocket is all.' He didn't tell them the whole story, or how much he had lost.

'I suppose yer want me ter change it for yer, is that it?' asked Polly, still looking at the coin. Even now, rich as she was compared to others of her ilk, it wasn't often she saw a golden guinea.

'Yes,' said Will.

'Well I ain't got that much small change on me right now. It's in the chest out back. Go and get it, Mary luv. Count it out real careful now, and bring it 'ere, there's a good girl. Go with 'er, Tom. I don't need for 'er ter be done in carryin' so much coin.'

Tom Quirk stood up, and Will caught a glimpse of the pistol he always kept in his belt, under his coat. Dour and silent, he was tall, as tall as Will, and so much the opposite of Polly in character that some people laughed to see them together, but Will knew there was a strong bond between them, one that went beyond a mere business arrangement. They had never married but they lived together as man and wife, and Polly relied on Tom for security as well as comfort. Now Tom followed Mary across the crowded tavern to one of the rooms at the back where the three of them lived, where Will had lived until three years ago, to relieve the chest that was hidden there under the floorboards of some of Polly's hoarded wealth.

'Yer lookin' well, lad. Been 'avin' it good, 'ave yer?' Polly leaned towards him and Will caught a glimpse of a large patch of fleshy bosom.

'All right, Pol,' he replied. 'Can't grumble.'

Polly smiled and put a hand on Will's. 'Winter's comin'. If it gets too bad, yer can allus come back 'ere, yer know,' she said quietly.

Will smiled. 'I know,' he said, and the thought was comforting, but he wouldn't go back to living at the tavern. Not now he had been his own man for so long. He might stay for a day, even two, but the narrowness of the rooms and the closeness of the people would get to him after that and he would hanker for the streets again. Even though the streets teemed with people, there was an openness, a freedom there. It might mean sleeping in a cold door-way or hunched up in an old rowboat down by the river, but he would rather be alone than in company. Since leaving Polly's place he had found that more and more he wanted to be by himself, and sometimes he resented it when people tried to include him in things. There was a gang down by the Tower. Youths like himself, doing the things he did to survive. Somehow they had heard about him and one had asked if he wanted to join them, but he had said no. Not because he didn't want to share his pickings, but because he would rather work alone.

Mary and Tom came back with a bag of coins and Polly meticu-lously counted them out on the table. The amount correct, Will handed over his guinea and poured the coins into the pigskin purse which he tied around his neck for safety.

They talked some more, and Polly ordered him food; bread, cheese and pickled onions with ale to wash it down, the most food Will had eaten all day, and it was very late when he left. He had scarcely reached the corner of the street when he heard running footsteps behind him. Without turning round, he knew it was Mary.

'Don't go yet,' she said, slipping a hand in the crook of his arm and leaning her head on his shoulder. 'Yer know I miss yer when yer not around.' Will smiled to himself in the darkness. They walked arm in arm for several minutes in silence, then rounded a corner and Will paused near a pitch torch that had been lit outside an apothecary's shop. It never ceased to amaze him at the variety of life in London Town and the suddenness with which one could come upon an entirely different area in the space of a few streets. Here, after turning only three or four corners, they had come from a place of ill-lit streets, dingy slum tenements, taverns and broth-els, to a square of shops and eating houses. A closed carriage clattered by; some rake on his way home from a late night's gam-bling, Will supposed, but apart from that, the night was quiet.

'What d'yer want?' It was a question to which Will already knew the answer.

'Yer know what I want, Will Tucker,' said Mary pertly, looking up into his face. 'I want you.'

'Not 'ere,' he said. They walked on a little further until they came to an archway. The archway led into an alley that housed

14

stables. They could hear horses snorting on the other side of the wall. 'Come on,' whispered Will. 'I know a way in 'ere.' Taking Mary's hand, he went swiftly up the darkened alley until he reached a door. He pushed. It was unlocked and creaked as he opened it, the sound loud in the stillness of the night, but nothing stirred except a horse that was in a stall on the other side. This was the back entrance to the stables, with only a narrow passageway down the back of the stalls, ending in a pile of hay topped by a pitchfork. Will closed the door. It smelled in here, but no worse than the streets outside, and it was warm.

Will and Mary could hardly see each other, the only light coming from a lantern hung from a rafter a few stalls down but it didn't matter. Mary, her back to the door, felt Will's hands on her, playing up and down her thin dress, fumbling for ribbons and buttons. As usual, Mary was wearing no stays or corset, only bloomers. With practised hands, Will unfastened her bodice and her breasts tumbled out. She groaned softly at the desire he was arousing in her. She threw back her head, arching her back, then his hands were around her, in her hair and he was pulling her to him, his lips hungrily on hers, and she was drowning in that wonderful pool of desire she only felt with this boy. Her mother sometimes made her sleep with other men, but none of them roused her as Will did. Sometimes she thought she must be in love with him, but she wasn't sure about that. What she was sure about though was that when he did what he was doing now, she never wanted him to stop.

Finally, Will kissed her gently on the forehead and pulled away.

'Oh, Will!' she whispered. 'I...'

He put a finger on her lips, afraid of what she might say. Once upon a time he had thought himself in love with her but then, to his way of thinking, he had been just a boy. Now he was older, and wiser. His life on the streets had taught him many things, including the important fact that relationships were transient things. One took one's pleasures where one could and never made a commitment. He liked Mary. He liked her a lot. But he knew what her life was like, and he knew what his was like too. Heavens! He could be dead tomorrow. Life was for living, and Will Tucker had a lot of living to do before he settled down with any woman, that was for sure.

'I'll take you home,' he said, so, with a small sigh, Mary Frinton

15

adjusted her clothing and let Will take her back through the streets to the tavern where he gave her a swift hug and a kiss, told her he would see her again soon, and left. Filled with a curious mixture of elation because of their recent coupling, and sadness that their meeting had been so brief, she opened the door and went inside.

2

The next morning Will crawled out of the damp cellar he called home and greeted the morning, happy to be alive, despite the nip in the air and the cold wind that whistled round his bare legs. Yesterday had been a good day. He was a whole guinea richer and he had enjoyed the evening with Polly and Mary, especially with Mary. Walking along the street towards the bakery that stood between the pawn shop and the local tavern, and whose heavenly aroma of fresh bread was drawing him like a magnet, he smiled to himself, remembering the time spent with her in the stables. She was a good sort was Mary.

A pie-man shouted his wares on the corner of the street, selling pastries on behalf of the baker. The smell of hot meat was tantalising and Will stopped to buy one. He had money ready in his hand, not wanting to display his fat purse in public. Inside the shop doorway, the baker saw him and called him over.

'Mornin', Will! Come 'ere, lad. I 'ave somethin' for yer.'

Munching on the meat pie, which tasted wonderful, Will walked into the shop. The big brick oven made the place warm enough to bring out beads of sweat on the foreheads of the men pummelling the dough into cottage-loaf shaped lumps, and the boys who were sliding them onto long wooden paddles prior to baking in the oven. The baker, a large, red-faced man with forearms like pink hams, tossed Will a small loaf.

'There y'are, lad. The bloody apprentice left it in the oven too long and it got a bit burnt. No one'll buy it now but it'll be fine with the crust taken off.'

'Thanks, Sam.' Will bit into the crust which was indeed somewhat blackened but he didn't mind. It was food, and good food at that. Will hardly ever got a whole loaf to himself. Sam would sometimes give him a few crusts of bread or a broken pastry but not often a loaf. Will raised his hand in thanks and walked on towards the river, eating the bread and the pie with equal pleasure.

Several ragged boys were already on the river bank, examining it for anything interesting that may have been washed up overnight. One was exclaiming over a shoe. If one discounted the weed and mud with which it was encrusted, it looked quite new.

'You need two, yer fool,' said an older boy Will knew whose name was Harry Winston. 'Yer've got two feet, you silly bugger!'

The boys laughed at the younger one who ignored the jibes and paddled in the water, continuing to rummage through the flotsam and rubbish that rocked gently amongst the long grass and reeds. The pleasant aromas of the bakery and Will's loaf of bread had long since disappeared, to be replaced by the stench of foul mud and rank decay, but the boys were used to the smells of the river. Will and Harry Winston struck up a conversation. Basically in competition, they had a certain wary respect for each other's skills, though whereas Will preferred to work alone, Harry Winston was the leader of this small gang of urchins who relied on him for survival.

There was a sudden shout and the small boys ran to where the young one who had found the shoe was standing a few yards upstream. Will and Harry followed more slowly. Harry shoved his way through the gawping youngsters.

'Bloody 'ell!' he exclaimed.

'What is it?' Will pushed through the small crowd, to see a body partly submerged. It seemed the man was the owner of the shoe as its twin was still on his left foot. The body was bloated from being in the water, the clothes torn and stained. The face was waxen, bloodless, and the hair matted and tangled in weed. The boys stared, then the youngster who had the shoe began to tug hard at the other one until it came off, when he whooped with glee and capered around, holding the two shoes aloft. It was obvious to all that they were much too big for him, but the boy would find a ready buyer amongst the men in the taverns.

There followed a bitter battle as some of the boys tried to wrestle the shoes away from the lad until Harry Winston waded in and laid about him with the flat of his hand, sending the smaller boys cursing and cowering away, then grabbed the shoes himself. Will knew the way the gang operated. They shared everything, and

17

Harry would sell the shoes, then buy food and gin for them all. One of the boys was trying to pull the coat off the body, without much success, and he eventually gave up in disgust. Will walked away, wondering if he was the only one who was at all interested in knowing who the dead man was, and how he came to be in the river. Mind you, the Thames was awash with bodies sometimes. People were murdered and their bodies thrown into the water; sailors got washed overboard or they became sick and died and were thrown in; people drowned accidentally, and some even on purpose. It was no big deal and nobody cared very much unless it was some well-to-do person, but more often than not it was some riff-raff from the streets.

Forgetting the grisly find, Will pulled out the rest of the loaf from his shirt and ate it as he walked along. He sat beside London Bridge and watched the water traffic for a while, hearing the bargees calling over the water. Then he wandered back into the streets, now coming alive with tradesmen, clerks, business men on their way to work, and early morning shoppers, maids out for fresh bread and milk, boys shining shoes, even a chimney sweep on his way to one of the big houses in Bayswater. Will jumped quickly out of the way when a woman's voice shouted from above his head and the contents of a chamber pot came down and splashed into the gutter where he had been walking a few seconds before.

Deciding it was safer to walk in the street, Will heard another shout, from behind him this time. Looking round he saw a coach rumbling quickly towards him. He stepped to the side and the coach bowled past. Through the window he caught a glimpse of dark curls and a pretty face, then swore at the muck that splashed onto his legs from the wheels. Two days previously it had rained for most of the day and night and the streets were still thick with mud.

Will saw that the coach had stopped outside a milliner's just up the street. Ever watchful for an opportunity to make a copper or two, and remembering the pretty face, Will ran until he reached the coach. Before the ponderous coachman could get down from the seat, Will had wrenched the door open and pulled down the step. The young occupant of the coach looked down, trying to keep her dress out of the mud. She obviously expected the coachman to be performing this service because she said, 'Charles! I think...' then she stopped, realising suddenly that the hand helping her down from the coach was dirty, young, and not belonging to Charles.

'Who are you and what do you think you're doing? Let go of my hand this instant!' The voice was imperious and quelling, but Will just grinned, though he did let go of the gloved hand which was snatched away as if on fire.

'Beg yer pardon, m'lady,' he said with a grin, and bowed.

The brown curls shook as the girl tossed her head and walked past him as though he wasn't there. Meanwhile the coachman helped another, older lady, out of the coach and they both frowned at Will.

'It was a pleasure ter 'elp such a beautiful lady,' called Will to the girl's retreating back.

The girl turned round, and for an instant he thought he saw a faint smile and a slight redness touch her cheeks, then the haughty look was back as she said, 'I suppose I ought to thank you for the compliment, but I shall not. You have no right to speak to me at all. Good day!' And with that she stalked into the shop in such high dudgeon that she stumbled over the step and would have fallen but for the steadying hand of the older woman. Will bit back laughter and turned away. It didn't matter that he had made nothing out of the encounter, the remembrance of the girl's face was enough, for, despite her words, he had not missed the faint smile, and her face, on closer inspection, had not been merely pretty. It was beautiful.

As the milliner fussed around her, tidying her hair, and dressing her in hats that looked awfully dowdy and plain to her young eyes, Lady Megan Camberwell found herself thinking of the yellow-haired boy who had helped her down from the coach. She moved her head to look down at her hand where he had touched it – provoking a cry of, 'My Lady! Please!' from the milliner who was trying to pin a hat into place. She expected the grey kid glove to be dirty from the boy's grubby hand, but it looked no different than usual. The impertinence of him, to take her hand like that! He had probably been hoping for a few pence. Well, she was glad she hadn't given him any. If her uncle heard about it he would be furious. He had told her more than once that when she travelled to London she must never take notice of the street urchins or listen to their pathetic pleas because if she once gave in they would never

19

leave her alone. If he was with her, he would have probably whipped the boy with his riding crop. Lord Richard Camberwell was a man of short temper, easily given to vitriolic speech and sometimes even to violence. However, she could not help but remember the way the boy had smiled at her, as if he could see inside her head and, she thought ruefully, as if he did not give a fig for what she thought, or her angry words.

'This one looks lovely, my lady. It becomes you very well.' It was her maid, Martha, speaking. Megan looked into the mirror in front of her. She had taken absolutely no notice of any of the hats, and this one looked terrible, like a confection on a bird's nest of brown curls.

'It's dreadful!' She stood up. 'I will choose one for myself.' So saying, Megan stood up, and walked over to the array of hats on display, while her maid and the milliner glanced at each other and raised their eyebrows. Lady Megan was well known for her independent spirit and this was not the first time the two had had such difficulties with her. After some time, and finding nothing suitable in the shop, Megan told the milliner exactly what sort of hat she required, down to the shade and material, left her with instructions to make it up as quickly as possible, and notice that she would fetch it in a week's time.

On leaving the shop, Megan couldn't help but snatch a quick glance up and down the street, wondering if the boy was still around, but he was nowhere to be seen. Feeling somehow slightly disappointed, she let the coachman take her arm and help her into the coach.

As the coach rumbled away down the street, Will Tucker watched it go from a doorway a few shops down, half hidden by a stationary carriage. He wondered what had caused him to hang around until the girl came out of the shop. It was a pointless exercise but he wanted another glimpse of her, and he had seen the way she'd stopped and looked about her before climbing into the coach, when some impulse had made him shrink back into the shadows. Was she looking for him? He felt a pulse of excitement that she might have been, then chastised himself. What if she had been? She was a lady, he a street urchin. The likes of her were way out of his league.

She was beautiful though, he thought as he went on his way.

Will set about his daily business of survival in the busy London streets. Just because he had money, did not mean he would not take up an opportunity of making more if the occasion arose. Today pickings were lean however. The morning that had started off sunny, clouded over and the sharp wind that had been blowing in from the sea became a torment of cold gusts, bringing with it squalls of rain. The streets cleared of all but those who really needed to be outside, and those who had nowhere else to go. Towards the end of the day, Will, cold in his thin breeches, shirt and coat that had more holes than a moth-eaten curtain, decided to spend some of his precious guinea on a hot meal and warm mead, and to do so in a place he rarely frequented; the Jug and Bowl Inn on the southern outskirts of the town. He had been there only three times before. Twice Polly had taken him and Mary with her when she had business there, and the third time he had travelled to the inn with a foreign gentleman who had hired Will for the day to carry his considerable luggage around. Will had liked the place and, for once, felt in need of some cheery company.

The inn was not far out of the centre of London. It was a miserable walk in such inclement weather but Will could not face the thought of an equally miserable late afternoon and evening spent in his uncomfortable cellar. He supposed he could go to Polly's tavern, but two nights in a row would bring questions – even maybe some wishful thinking from Mary – and he was not in the mood for that today. The rain was a nuisance but he was soaked to the skin already and it was difficult to see how he could get any wetter. Besides, the thought of the comfort at the end of his walk kept his spirits up.

It was past seven o'clock when he eventually arrived at the inn, a large whitewashed stone building with a thatched roof that overhung the gables. Peering in at the windows, he saw that the place appeared to be full, a bedlam of noise, light, and bonhomie. It gladdened Will's heart just to see the cheerfulness of the patrons and to hear the laughter, it was so different from the depressing, rain-washed streets he had left behind. He even had it in mind to find somewhere to sleep tonight and just keep on walking tomorrow. What kept him in London? Nothing at all. He had money and he was free as a bird. Maybe he would walk all the way to the south coast. There were big towns there, so he had heard, including one where royalty spent a lot of their time.

Will found a dark corner and took the purse from round his neck, then counted out some pennies which he clutched in his hand before pushing the purse back into its hiding place. Then he lifted the latch of the inn door and went inside.

His first impression that the place was crowded had been right. People who might ordinarily have passed by, had come in to get away from the miserable weather. Travellers sat at tables, some eating, others talking, all drinking. The room he was in was large, with wooden benches and chairs, the light provided by candles in sconces around the walls and planted on the wooden tables. Will knew that this was the public room where the commoner ate and drank, but there would be private rooms where gentlemen and their ladies could eat in peace and quiet. Over by one wall a log fire roared in a large iron grate and Will sidled slowly towards it, warming himself in the welcome heat.

He squeezed into a small space by a window as near to the fire as he could get, sitting on the wide window seat. So far no one had taken any notice of him, and he had no desire to draw particular attention to himself, so he waited until one of the serving women came to a nearby table, then tapped her tentatively on the arm. She was a well built maid in apron and mob cap, who took one look at him and thought he was a beggar who had come inside to keep warm. She was about to kick him out when he smiled and said, 'I'd like a steak and kidney pie, 'taters, carrots, cabbage, bread and lots of gravy, please, and some ale.'

'Let's see the colour of your money, luv,' said the girl, standing with her arms folded. The mistress was very particular about not serving vagrants and this lad, with his dirty bare feet and ragged clothing, looked very like one to her.

Will opened his hand and showed the coins lying in the palm. He had been careful not to get out any silver. That would attract too much attention.

'Done well today, 'ave you, luv?' said the girl a little more kindly.

'Yes.' Will did not elaborate. He smiled again, and Rosy Jenkins smiled back, her motherly nature getting the upper hand. Shame, the lad must be cold in those thin clothes, and he was sopping wet from the rain. She looked around to see if the mistress was any-where about. No sign of her. In that case, she would see the lad got an extra big piece of pie, and a large mug of ale, or maybe even some mulled wine if there was any left. They had been run off their feet this afternoon because of the bad weather.

Will thoroughly enjoyed his meal, even though he had to sit with the plate on his lap. And it was so good to be warm. Steam wisped off his ragged coat as it dried and after Rosy had taken away his plate and brought him another mug of mulled wine which she whisperingly said was on the house as all his money had been spent on the meal, or so she thought, he leaned back against the wall in the corner and watched the patrons of the inn.

The unaccustomed warmth and the wine must have set him dozing because he woke with a start to a loud bray of laughter. It came from a short, round man who was coming down the stairs that led to rooms above. His companion, a much taller, dark-haired man wearing a wine-coloured tail coat, spotless white breeches, and tall black boots, said something to the man, and the short one laughed his braying laugh again.

'Lord Richard! You really do have a way with words!' said the short man in a loud voice that carried to Will's ears, just before they went through a door into another room. Will had caught just a glimpse of the two men but he was sure he had seen the tall, younger man before. Then it came to him with a suddenness that set his stomach lurching and his heart thudding wildly. It was the man who owned the pig-skin purse. The man he had robbed of ten golden guineas!

Will jumped to his feet, glad that the loud voice had woken him. He had to get out of there before the man came back and recog-nised him, but he was loathe to leave the cosy room. Rain was still spattering on the window. It was a filthy night, but he had to go.

Reluctantly he pushed his way through a throng of customers to the door and went outside. Immediately the cold stabbed at him and he shivered, huddled against the wall, wondering where to go next. It was too late to start walking home. He needed to find a place to sleep; a barn maybe, or stables would be good.

He was just about to brave the weather and go and look for somewhere, when the inn door opened and two men came out wearing long black coats, and wide-brimmed hats pulled down over

23

their faces. They were talking together in low voices and did not see Will, in the shadows by the wall. The men looked furtive and Will decided to stay where he was and not reveal his presence.

"E's 'ere, Bert,' said the taller of the two quietly in a deep voice. 'I seed 'im come in on that ruddy great 'orse of 'is. That was 'im just now, with the fella that sounded like a bloody donkey!'

'Are you sure it was 'im?' said the other, leaning towards the tall man. 'I ain't seen 'im afore.'

'That's 'im all right,' said the first man. He turned a little and Will saw, by the light from a nearby window, that he had a straggly black beard that covered his chin and reached halfway down his chest. 'An' 'e won't be 'ere long tomorrow. On 'is way 'ome, 'e is. We'll get 'im when 'e comes ter bed 'is 'orse down fer the night. Allus does that he does. Very fond've 'is 'orses 'e is. Then Lord Richard Camberwell'll regret the day 'e let me go. I was a damn good 'un with the 'orses, I was. Pity 'e found the silver I stole and stashed away in the stables. It was that bloody niece of 'is. 'Twere all 'er fault. Got eyes like a bloody 'awk, she 'as. Always poking 'er nose in where it's not wanted.'

The two men walked away towards the back of the inn, leaving Will in a quandary. Lord Richard Camberwell. Was it the same Lord Richard whose name he had heard just a few minutes ago? If so, the man who had been Will's pick-pocketing victim was in for trouble when he went to his horse later that night, and only Will knew and could do something about it. He supposed he should rush right back into the inn and tell Lord Richard about the two men, warn him that he was going to be attacked. On the other hand, if he did so, there was every likelihood that Lord Richard would recognise him as the boy who had stolen his purse, and have him arrested. What should he do?

There was no choice. His conscience would not let him walk away. With a heavy heart, Will pushed open the door and went back inside the inn.

The warmth was like an enveloping blanket after the cold outside. Will threaded his way between tables and people until he reached the door he had seen the two gentlemen walk through. Taking a deep breath, and pulling his coat collar up around his chin as far as it would go in an attempt to disguise himself, he knocked on the door, but there was no reply from within. They probably couldn't hear him with all the noise, thought Will. He tried again, with the same negative response so, diffidently, he turned the knob and opened the door a little.

The room was dim, lit only by an oil lamp The two men he had seen coming down the stairs were seated at a table, talking earnestly, a bottle of brandy and two glasses between them. They both looked up, frowning, when the door opened. The stout man put a finger under his nose at the smell that had come into the room with Will. The filth of the London streets had a stink all of its own, which was only worsened by sweat and damp.

'What is it?' The tall gentleman's voice was cold, his expression stern. 'I gave orders that we were not to be disturbed!'

'I'm sorry, sir,' said Will, keeping his head down and eyes averted, relieved that the man's first reaction was not one of recognition, and he launched into his short tale but, to his dismay, Lord Richard Camberwell did not believe him.

'Stuff and nonsense!' he said, rising from the chair, highly annoyed. 'You're trying your luck, you young scoundrel! Hoping for some coppers, I don't doubt! Someone who used to work for me, you say? The only man I've dismissed in the last month was Amos Wilkins, and he's long gone to Cheapside. My housekeeper, Mrs Proudfoot, told me she saw him there not a week ago!'

'But, sir...!' Will tried again to convince the man, but to no avail. Lord Richard Camberwell took a menacing step towards Will, mouth set in a grim line.

'Get out of here right now, boy, or I'll call the landlord and have him remove you. Go and do your begging elsewhere!'

Will went, knowing it was useless to argue. Bugger him, he thought angrily. Serve the bastard right if he does get done over!

He went outside again, to find that the rain was pouring harder than ever. He decided to find the stables. Maybe the men had changed their minds and had gone. He would go and see.

Stealthily he went around a corner of the inn, then another. Now he was at the back of the building, in a beaten earth yard. A small closed carriage stood there. Apart from that it was empty, but there was a long stone building, and the large straw and manure heap standing beside the wall told Will it was the stables. A lamp hung beside a wide arched opening that led into the building. Will crept in the shadows until he was near the door, then crouched under the eaves keeping in the darkest places, his bare feet cold in the rain water, but content to wait. He was good at waiting. And watching. Usually his survival depended on it, and it was what made him successful at what he did. Of the two black-garbed men, there was no sign. Perhaps they had changed their minds and gone away after all. Then again, maybe they were waiting as he was, but inside the stables.

It was nearly an hour later when Lord Richard Camberwell strode into the yard, alone, wearing hat and cape against the rain, and carrying a lantern. He walked through the archway and Will followed.

Will had not even reached the inside of the building when he heard a thump and a muffled cry. He ran onto straw-strewn cobbles. Horses were behind low wooden fences, shuffling and snorting at the sudden noise. By the light of another lamp that hung from the rafters, and the one the gentleman had dropped, Will saw Lord Richard lying on the floor, groaning. The two black-coated men were standing over him and the one with the beard had a heavy wooden club in his hand. He had his leg back and was about to put the boot in.

Without a conscious thought, Will flung himself at the man and sent him flying with a head butt in the ribs. Black Beard let out a startled cry which made his friend turn and lash out wildly at the surprise attacker. His arm hit Will on the cheek. The blow hurt but somehow Will kept his balance, though the man did not. He slipped on the dirty straw and went down onto the legs of Lord Richard who was moaning but still flat on the floor. Will wondered momentarily if Lord Richard was seriously hurt as he was showing no real signs of recovery, but then his attention was taken by the bearded one who had scrambled to his feet and was reaching for the club that had fallen from his hand and was now lying on the ground nearby.

As Will scrambled away, he heard a growl of anger behind him and a meaty thud. His spirits rose when he realised that Richard Camberwell had recovered sufficiently to begin getting some of his own back on the thug who had slipped, but his own eyes were on the grim man who held the heavy piece of wood in a large fist and, with a loud cry of rage, was rushing towards him. However, Will was quick and agile and he had been brought up on street brawls.

26

He ducked under the arm and pushed hard with his bony elbow, knocking Black Beard off balance, sending him tumbling. Will kicked hard at the sprawling legs and arms. The man dropped the club again, and Will quickly picked it up, then swung the piece of wood as hard as he could. It was not well aimed but caught the tall, would-be-murderer on the arm. There was a sickening crack and Black Beard let out a scream that set the horses neighing and skittering in fright while Will crouched with the club gripped in both hands, ready to have another go if the tall man looked like attacking again, but he just sat on the mucky floor, clutching his injured arm and moaning.

'I think we'll end it there.' The voice was hard as granite, and Will heard the sound of a pistol being cocked. Lord Richard Camberwell was standing next to the groaning body of the smaller of his two attackers, aiming the weapon at the man Will was covering with the club. Blood trickled from a cut on Lord Richard's forehead, just above his left eye.

'Get out of here, Wilkins, and take your pathetic friend with you. If you ever try anything like this again, I'll damn well have you arrested! I gave you a chance once. I won't do so again!' Lord Richard's eyes glittered in the dim light of the lantern and the stare he gave the tall, bearded man was as hard as his voice.

Amos Wilkins flashed Richard Camberwell a look of pure hatred as he stood up slowly and helped his partner up off the floor with his uninjured arm. 'Don't think you've seen the last of me, Camberwell, because you 'aint,' he sneered. 'Mark my words, I'll get the better of you yet, see if I don't.' He turned to Will. 'And you. If I ever set eyes on your damn face again, you'd better run or you'll be dead!' With that, he and his groggy comrade stumbled out of the building and into the rain, leaving Will with a sharp knot of fear in his stomach that he tried to ignore.

Putting the pistol in an inside pocket of his coat, Lord Richard said, 'Are you all right, lad?'

'Yes, sir,' Will answered. 'Are you?'

'I'll live.' Lord Richard put a hand to his cut forehead where the bleeding had slowed to a trickle. He pulled out a handkerchief and wiped his face. 'Thank you. That was a great service you did me, and I'm sorry I didn't believe you when you warned me of it earlier.' He raised blue eyes and took his first good look at Will since the fight began. His eyes narrowed, and his hand suddenly streaked out to snatch hold of the pigskin purse that had fallen out of Will's shirt during the fight and was dangling from his neck for all to see. Will drew a sharp intake of breath. In the excitement of the fight, he had forgotten all about it.

'Where did you get this?' The voice dared Will to lie.

There was a moment's silence as Will's defiant eyes locked with the angry ones of Lord Richard Camberwell. Will saw recognition stir, and knew that lying would do him no good at all.

'I've seen you somewhere before.' Camberwell yanked the purse hard and the knot on the thong gave way. He stared hard at Will again, then light dawned. 'You're the little bastard who stole this from me, aren't you?' Suddenly he was shaking Will so hard his teeth rattled. 'Aren't you?'

'Yes.' He could hardly get the word out.

Richard Camberwell paused in trying to make Will into a bag of bones and loosened the drawstring around the purse. Will took a step away, ready to run, but the man's hand whipped out and grabbed his shoulder, stopping him dead. 'This is copper and some silver!' he snarled. 'Where's the money that was inside? You can't have spent that much already. Where the hell is it, you little thief?'

Will struggled to get away but the man's grip was vice-like.

'It were stolen off me,' he grudgingly admitted at last. 'The bastards missed one coin. A friend of mine changed it for me.'

For a moment Lord Richard glared angrily, then he seemed to see the irony of the situation and a faint smile crossed his lips. 'So the thief was robbed, eh?' he said. 'If it wasn't so damned annoying, it would almost be amusing.' He let go of Will who truculently shrugged his damp coat back onto his shoulder. Lord Richard stepped back, and stared at him speculatively.

'What's your name, lad?'

'Will. Will Tucker.'

'So, Will Tucker, what am I to do with you?' pondered Lord Richard Camberwell. 'My first inclination is to send for a constable and have you arrested.' Will felt the hard knot in his stomach growing but he continued to stare back defiantly. The tall man was a handsome fellow; straight nose, long, lean face, brown hair pulled back onto the nape of his neck, but the blue eyes bored into Will's like gimlets, and the generous mouth was set in a thin, straight line.

28

'On the other hand,' the man continued, 'you owe me nine guineas and some change, and if you're incarcerated in Newgate I'll never get it back, now will I? So how do you intend to repay me, Will Tucker? I don't suppose for a minute that you've got that kind of money stashed away anywhere, have you? Or any money at all for that matter?'

Will shook his head.

'No, I didn't think so. From the look of you, I'd say you live on the streets. Am I right?'

Will shrugged.

'Half starved, I suppose,' mused Lord Richard. He paused, continuing to study Will who shifted uncomfortably under his gaze. 'I'm not generally known for having much of a conscience, Will, but I don't know that I could send you to your fate at the hands of London Town's dubious justice system. They'd throw you into Newgate Gaol as soon as look at you, and there you'd probably stay for the rest of your days, which wouldn't be many if I'm any judge. From what I've heard, you might as well get the death sentence as spend more than a few months in there. Besides, if you did somehow survive, all you'd learn from the experience was how to become a better thief. No, I don't think that's the answer. But you did steal from me.' He rubbed his chin, seeming to Will almost as though he was talking to himself. 'On the other hand, you probably saved my life just now for which I feel I owe you something.' He looked Will up and down. 'You seem like a strong enough lad. Can you ride?'

'No, sir. Never 'ad the chance to learn. But I likes 'orses.' Will said this last eagerly, sensing a glimmer of compassion in the man's voice and a slight change of attitude.

'Hmm. Maybe there's a chance for you to pay me back what you owe then, Will, and for me to repay you a little for saving a life that doesn't mean much in the general scheme of things, but of which I am inordinately fond. That man you saw just now, the one with the beard, was Amos Wilkins, one time stable hand at my place of residence. The scoundrel also tried to steal from me, Will. Maybe you could take his place.' He laughed suddenly and it transformed his face, making the eyes suddenly full of warmth and good humour, so that Will smiled too. 'That's very funny. I'm thinking of replacing a thief with a thief!' Richard Camberwell shook his head at his own foolishness, then the smile went and the grim look

29

returned. 'So, Will, you can see my dilemma. Do I hand you over to the constables, or do you come and work for me until your debt is paid?'

There was no choice to be made. 'I'll gladly work fer you, sir,' said Will.

'But...and this is a very big but, Will...if I catch you thieving so much as a spoonful of sugar, there'll be hell to pay, do you understand?'

'Aye, sir.'

'And I will be keeping a very, very close eye on you, lad, as will the rest of my staff. In return for work, and my life, you will have regular food and a roof over your head, plus the chance to learn an honest trade. And I will not tell my staff of our agreement, so no one need know you used to be a thief.' Lord Richard stressed the words 'used to be' and glared at Will again. 'Is it a deal?'

'Yes, sir! Thank yer, sir!' Will was overwhelmed with relief, at the same time wondering what it was he had got himself into. He had a feeling that Lord Richard Camberwell would be a hard task master. And it would ruin his independence. Still, the thought of not having to go out in all weathers to find food and shelter, especially with a hard winter approaching, was an incentive not to be sneered at, and Will thought he could put up with a lot of grief for that, at least for a while. Long enough to repay the money anyway.

'Good. It's settled then.' Richard Camberwell put a hand on his forehead again. 'I have a head that's thumping like a hammer on an anvil, Will, but time is getting on, and if I'm not back home by mid-morning, I shall have my niece and my mother worrying themselves silly. I only came in here to see that Hades was all right, and I can see he is, so we'll get some sleep now and leave before dawn.'

'I don't 'ave money ter stay 'ere, sir,' said Will.

Camberwell smiled wryly. 'No, you don't,' he said. 'However I have grave misgivings about letting you out of my sight for the next few hours. So instead of sleeping in the stable as I suppose you should, and not wanting the possibility of my horse going missing during the night, you shall sleep on the floor of the room I have taken.'

Thus it was that Will spent a dry, warm night on the rug in

front of the fire that burned in Richard Camberwell's room, and was sound asleep when he was shaken awake at four in the morning. Sleepily he downed a bowl of porridge served to him by the tavern keeper's wife. Soon afterwards, saddling Hades, he noticed Richard Camberwell wince and put his hand to his head, so he asked for some money to buy something. Reluctantly Lord Richard gave him some and Will ran back into the inn and bought a small bottle of brandy which he gave to Lord Richard, then exhorted him to drink it to relieve his headache.

'This may make it worse, but thank you,' said Lord Richard dryly, and took a good swig from the bottle, then handed it to Will. 'You'd better have some too, lad. It's a long way we have to go, and the weather's still bad. It'll warm you up.' Will drank some of the harsh liquor, felt it hit his stomach and spread warmth around his body. Richard Camberwell mounted his big black stallion, then helped Will scramble onto the horse's broad back behind him.

As the horse trotted out onto the wet road, Will thought that this was not at all how he had expected his trip to the Jug and Bowl Inn to end. However, his stomach was full, he was riding a horse, and he had spent the night in relative comfort.

His future could not be all bad.

3

As Richard Camberwell had said, the journey to his home was long and tiring, so much so that sometime near dawn, and despite the fact that he had slept well the previous night, the movement of the horse lulled Will into sleep. As night became morning the rain finally stopped, and a watery, cloudy grey sky met the faint tinge of dusky pink on the horizon. The horse stepped into a rut in the road, jolting Will awake to find himself leaning his cheek against the firm back in front of him. He was immediately embarrassed, but Richard Camberwell said nothing.

In his sixteen years, Will had hardly ever ventured into the country before, certainly no further than the Jug and Bowl Inn, so he took great interest in the scenery which was mostly green fields and woods. They rode along leafy lanes edged with stone walls over which hawthorn and blackberry brambles poured in wild profusion, and passed orchards ripe with apples.

Eventually Lord Richard said, 'We're nearly there. Just a few miles to go.' They left the road and travelled along a barely discernible track that wound its way between low hills. Gazing about him as the horse climbed up a grassy slope, it struck Will that the most amazing thing about the countryside was colour. All around him were hues of green, orange, yellow, and brown. Not vibrant colour, the sky was too grey for that, but certainly more colour than he was used to seeing in the drab streets of London where everything was dull greys and browns except when the gaudy clothing of the gentry brightened the scenery a little. Now, from the top of the slope as far as the eye could see, were rolling green hills, wide fertile valleys and fine views of distant villages and farms. There were copses of chestnut, sycamore and oak; woods of silver birch and ash, the leaves just beginning to change colour and, around the farms, stone-walled meadows of hay, some already cut. Wheat and oats stood thickly in other fields, ripe and heavy, a dull yellow, the drooping stalks waving in the small breeze. Swallows swooped and dived over the fields, gathering for their yearly migration to warmer climes. The only sounds were the birds, the lowing of cows down in the valleys, and the occasional bleat of a sheep on the higher pastures. From this high point, Will saw a river a long way below him, silver in the early morning light, wending a smooth, unhurried passage towards the sea.

Although appreciating the beauty of such vistas, they made Will feel uncomfortable. Used to the narrow, close streets with their endless bustle and noise, the comparative silence and the enormous space of the countryside was disconcerting. Will felt small, insignificant, and out of his depth. He wondered again what Richard Camberwell was leading him into, but then thought of the alternative, and shivered. Anything would be better than Newgate.

Soon the track led them down again and became heavily rutted. It wound between the hills and valleys until, rounding a bend, they came upon a small village consisting of a few thatched cottages, an inn, a small church, smithy and one shop, clustered together around a village green and pond. Will stared with interest, glad to see houses again, albeit very different from the squalid tenements of London. These picturesque cottages spoke of comfort and peacefulness, nestled as they were at the base of the hill, and Will tried to imagine what life was like inside them, but found it very difficult. For sure, though, it would be quite different to that which he had experienced to now. He sniffed the air. Smells here too were quite alien to him. Newly scythed grass overlaid by the perfume of flowers in the cottage gardens, but there were three smells Will recognised; fresh baked bread, stagnant water from the pond and horse manure.

Richard Camberwell heard Will sniffing behind him and wondered if the rain had given him a cold, then he realised the boy was only sniffing the air. He smiled to himself as he let the horse take them along the pathway across the green. Hades did not need guidance. He could sense his stable was near. Camberwell thought again of his companion. This must all seem very strange to a lad who had lived all his life on the streets, never having seen the sky hardly, let alone the sun or a blade of grass. On the long journey from the inn, he had wondered more than once if he had made the right decision in bringing the boy with him. He probably ought to have left him to his fate at the hands of the law, or even just let him go back to his life of crime. After all, what was another thief amongst the hundreds on London's streets? His mother would have words to say and she would tell him he was a fool, that the boy would most likely steal everything not tied down and that he would come to regret his magnanimous gesture. She would most likely be right, he thought ruefully.

The village was quiet at this early hour. Ducks waddled and pecked on the green, inhabitants of the small pond beside which two boys were sitting with home-made fishing poles, hoping to catch minnows on this cool and cloudy morning. One of the boys called out `G'mornin', sir,' in a thick but not unpleasant accent, to which Camberwell replied, 'And to you, Robbie. Good morning, Jacob.' The smaller boy just giggled, and they heard Robbie admonish him as the horse passed by on the edge of the green. Both boys stared after Will, curious to see a stranger.

The track carried on up a steep hill and around a bend, away from the village, until it stopped at a pair of large, rusty iron gates which stood open and looked as though they had not been closed in a very long time. Will noticed that both gates had a shield with the rampant lion and crossed swords wrought on them; the same coat of arms that decorated Lord Camberwell's purse. The gates leaned drunkenly against a high wall that ran along on either side, and were overlooked by two huge horse-chestnut trees. The ground was thick with strange round, green, spiky balls and Will asked what they were.

Camberwell chuckled. 'Those are seed cases from the trees, Will,' he said. 'Inside are hard brown seeds. The children thread them on strings and hit them against one another to see whose will break first. They call them conkers.'

Will thought it sounded a very peculiar thing to do, and wondered that children had time to play such games. His own childhood had given him very little leisure time, consisting as it did of looking out for suitable victims for his pick-pocketing skills, and running errands for Polly.

Lord Richard Camberwell turned his horse into the gateway and cantered along a rutted path that carried on where the track left off. The landscape was wild at first, long grass vied with tangled bushes and ancient shrubbery but suddenly they came to a gap in an old stone wall, much lower than the first one, and Will stared in amazement at the green lawns, huge hedges of rhododendrons and towering trees that studied extensive gardens. He had never seen so much tamed land before. Could all this be owned by one person?

Will's wonder at the gardens was nothing compared to the shock of seeing the house that was the central feature. It stood resplendent before them. Made of local stone, it stood grey and solid amidst a stand of oak trees. A square building reaching up three floors, the third with dormer windows in the roof, it reached out to Will as if welcoming him home. It was the strangest feeling, yet it struck Will like a blow in the face. He felt as if he belonged here, almost as though some unnatural force had brought this house into his life for a reason. Usually much too practical for such fanciful thoughts, he shrugged them away and studied the house more closely as they rode up to it.

The windows were mullioned, small panes of glass glinting in the weak sunshine that was trying to break through the clouds. Will could see that the house was old; lichen and moss were growing on the stone, and the roses and ivy that rambled around the doorway and stonework had stems as thick as small trees. Judging by the raw wood showing, the ramblers had recently been cut back.

The front door was wooden, sturdy, and braced with iron, almost like a castle door, thought Will who had listened eagerly to stories of knights of old told him by travelling peddlers when he was younger. Despite its size, the big house looked as comfortable in its way as did the cottages around the village green, and Will felt a small thrill of pleasure, the first since meeting the man sitting on the horse with him. Somehow the house emanated a feeling of security and well-being, as if it was satisfied with itself and its inhabitants, and would welcome a stranger.

Will shook his head in wonder at himself and his imagination. Inactivity must be affecting his thinking. However, he did not have much time to consider his thoughts because Hades was trotting round to the back of the house. Outbuildings surrounded a cobbled yard; a long stable block, a dairy and, judging by the steam that emanated from the doorway, a wash-house.

The horse's hooves sounded loud on the cobbles, noisy enough to bring an elderly man out of a lean-to next to the stables. Grey-haired and red-faced, the man beamed when he saw who it was.

'Lord Richard! Welcome back!' he said delightedly. 'Did yer 'ave a good trip, sir?' He noticed Will. 'And who's this yer've brung with yer, sir? A new stable lad?'

'That's right, Ben,' said Richard Camberwell, dismounting and steadying Will who slipped awkwardly from the saddle. 'This is Will Tucker. Hopefully, he'll do a deal better than the last one we had.' He stared hard at Will who lowered his eyes in embarrass-ment. 'Show him what needs to be done, Ben, and make sure he does it. He can bed down in the hay loft. I dare say it'll be an improvement on his usual abode. Oh, and tell Lizzie to inform cook that she's to send over two plates of food at meal times. He can eat with you. And if you have any lip from him, Ben, you have my permission to beat his backside black and blue.'

'Aye, sir.' There was a faint smile of amusement on the old man's face.

'Do as Ben here tells you, and I'll see you later,' Richard said to Will sternly.

'Yes, sir,' Will replied.

The old man took the horse's reins and bade Will follow him into the stables while Camberwell strode away to the house.

Once in the stables, Ben looked Will up and down, in much the same way that Lord Richard had back at the inn. 'Hmm,' he said, hands on hips. 'Yer look a mite scrawny, but I dare say yer used to 'ard livin' so yer've probably got stamina. 'Ow'd you meet up with yon master then, lad?'

Will was silent for a moment, wondering what to say. In the end he said lamely, 'I met 'im at an inn. 'E said 'e was lookin' for someone to work in the stables.'

Ben Hover nodded. He already had the saddle off Hades and was taking off the bridle. 'You worked with 'orses afore then, lad?'

'Yes,' said Will, unwilling to reveal his lack of experience which was limited to holding horses for gentlemen while they kept secret assignations with their mistresses or gambled the night away at the gaming tables, though once he had spent a few days helping out at a coaching inn. That was when he had discovered he actually liked the animals.

'Well, get that curry comb over from over yonder and groom 'ades while I sees to 'is feed,' said Ben. ''E's more full o' mud'n a ploughed field.'

Will spent what was left of the morning in the stables, following Ben's orders. He found the work enjoyable and not too arduous, and he was a quick learner. Ben Hover was a talkative fellow and Will said little, not able to get much of a word in even if he had wanted to, but he was content to listen. His lonely life had not made him the most gregarious of people but he was a good listener.

It was after a welcome lunch of bread, cheese and an apple, brought to the stables by Lizzie, a stick-thin, greasy-haired girl of about twelve, that Will was summoned to the 'big 'ouse' as Ben called it.

'It'll be yon mistress wantin' to meet yer,' declared Ben. 'Allus wants to meet new staff, she does.'

'What's she like?' asked Will anxiously. The thought of meeting a grand lady was rather frightening.

'Oh, 'er's not so bad.' Ben was taking a break, perched on a low wall and puffing at a briar pipe. 'So long as yer does yer job and stay out o' trouble, she'll pay yer wages right enough.' Will did not mention that he was getting no wages. 'It's yon master yer've ter watch,' Ben continued. 'Can charm the flies off the wall when 'e wants ter, 'e can, but 'e's got a mean temper on 'im.'

'Is the mistress 'is wife?'

'No, 'is mother. The master's not married, though I 'ear tell 'e's quite a man fer the ladies. Anyways, you'd best be off, lad, but first wash yerself at the pump there. Then go ter the scullery door and ask one o' the maids to show yer the way ter the mistress's rooms. And mind yer act polite now. She can't abide bad manners.'

At the pump Will took up a bar of hard soap and ran some cold water over his dirty hands and face, then dried them on an old towel, before walking to the open scullery door. Inside, Lizzie was scrubbing the floor. Wiping her hands on her apron, she took him as far as the door that separated the downstairs from the upstairs and found one of the maids there to take him further.

Will followed the maid, a pretty girl who kept giving Will backward glances that he ignored, thinking she was only checking to make sure he was keeping up with her. Down hallways they went, past numerous rooms, up stairways and along more corridors until they finally came to a closed door upon which the maid knocked and a voice bade her enter. She opened the door, bobbed a curtsey to whoever was inside and said she had brought the stable boy, then she told Will to go inside.

The room he entered was large, furnished with comfortable chairs, a chaise longue, small tables and, near the window, a writing desk. A woman sat at the desk writing busily, and Lord Richard Camberwell stood with his back to a log fire that burned in the hearth. He gave Will a glare before turning his attention back to a book he held in his hand. A faint perfume emanated from a bowl of roses on one of the tables, making the room smell fresh and clean.

'Is this the boy you found to work in the stables?' The woman at the desk put down the pen with which she had been writing, and turned to look at Will.

'Yes, Mother,' said Richard Camberwell without looking up.

'Come here, boy. Let me take a good look at you.' The middle-aged woman peered over her glasses and stared hard at Will though he thought the gaze not unfriendly. In fact Lady Helen Camberwell looked kindly, her face wrinkled with laughter lines, the blue eyes quizzical rather than stern. Her skin was quite brown, as though she was used to the outdoors and did not keep herself shut up inside the house all the time as Will understood gentlewomen to do. When she spoke it was in a cultured, refined voice but the tone was mellifluous and pleasant on the ear. Will decided there and then

37

that he liked her.

'What's your name, young man?' Lady Helen asked him.

'Will Tucker, ma'am...er...my lady,' answered Will, uncertain how to address her.

'Ma'am will do, Will. And how old are you?'

'Sixteen last birthday, ma'am.'

'My son tells me he found you at an inn. What about your parents? Won't they wonder where you are?'

'I've no parents, ma'am.'

For a brief second, a sympathetic look passed over Lady Helen Camberwell's face, then she said, 'Well, I hope you enjoy working here, Will. You'll find that we are not demanding employers so long as you do your work to our satisfaction, and if you do, you will find us not ungenerous in the matter of wages. However, should you hurt one of my horses, be lazy, or steal from us, Will, then you will be out of the door very quickly. Do you understand?'

'Yes, ma'am.' Will was glad the lighting in the room was dim. It helped to hide the flush of embarrassment that reddened his face. He stole a quick glance at Lord Richard who seemed to be concentrating on the book. Will looked at Lady Helen who was smiling.

'You may go, Will,' she said. 'Behave yourself and we shall get along tolerably well.'

'Yes, ma'am,' said Will. He wondered what he should do next. Would he be able to find his way out of the house, down those endless corridors? He was saved from further thought by Lord Richard who suddenly flung the book down on a table and said, 'I'll see him out, and let you get on with your writing, Mother.'

'As you wish, Richard. Dinner's at eight,' said Lady Helen, adding in a voice only a mother would use, 'And don't be late! You know how I abhor tardiness and you've been at least five minutes late every evening since you came home from Portugal. It means the soup is always cold. Oh, and get the boy some boots, Richard. His feet'll freeze when winter comes.'

'Yes, Mother,' her son replied before hustling Will out of the room and along the corridor, walking so quickly Will had a job to keep up without running. Richard Camberwell led Will to the west wing of the house and into a room that was obviously his own. It was furnished plainly, with no fripperies; a bachelor's room, comfortable enough, the furniture solid and practical but lacking a

38

woman's touch.

Lord Richard closed the door and turned Will to face him. 'You will have judged from that conversation, Will, that I have said nothing to my mother of the manner of our meeting, nor of your previous lifestyle. It would upset her to know that I was careless enough to be robbed by you, and set upon by those two scoundrels at the inn, and I do not want her upset. Let us keep it that way. If she learns of your... profession, shall we say, I doubt she will let you stay as she cannot do with vagabonds and thieves. However, I am determined to retrieve the money you stole from me, if not in coin then in kind. Just remember one thing, Will. You are here for that reason, and that reason only. It is to be hoped you will make an adequate stable boy but if you do not, I shall find you other employment that may not be as agreeable, so I suggest you listen, learn and tread the straight and narrow. Is that clear?'

'Yes, sir,' said Will. The lecture had been forcefully given and Will could tell that Lord Richard would be very capable of clearing his conscience with regards to handing him over to the law if he jeopardised his situation. Richard Camberwell opened the door and bellowed for the upstairs maid. When she came scurrying along the corridor, he told her to show Will how to reach the scullery door again and once outside Will made his way to the stables.

That night was the most comfortable Will had spent in a long, long time, even better than the floor of the inn. He was glad that he had the hayloft to himself and did not have to share sleeping quarters with Ben who slept in the lean-to. Lying on his back under blankets with hay as his mattress, he crossed his hands behind his head and thought back to the events of the last couple of days. He wondered at the fate that had led him there. So far he had nothing to complain about. His stomach was full again, he was warm, and the people here seemed pleasant enough, even Lord Richard most of the time, though he wasn't quite sure how to take the master of the house. Ben had told him the man had a temper. Well, he had already seen some of it, hadn't he? He wondered what Lord Richard did all day. Had he a job or did he just look after his estate? He had mentioned a niece, but Will had seen no children about. Still wondering, Will drifted off to sleep.

He was woken the next morning by Ben clanking a bucket around below him.

'Come on, lad! Rouse yerself, now. It be mornin' already.'

Will rubbed the sleep from his eyes and stood up, then winced as he bumped his head on the low beams. Kneeling, he struggled into his jacket and ran a hand through his hair, dislodging hay and dust. He clambered down the ladder.

'Go to the pump, lad, and no pissin' against the wall or shittin' in the bushes. Use the out'ouse privy back o' the laundry, same as I showed yer yesterday,' said Ben cheerfully. He had dealt with town riff-raff before and knew that their personal habits were not always those favoured by the gentry. He handed Will the bar of soap and the old towel.

Will performed his ablutions, thinking as he did so that he had washed his face and hands twice in two days – something unheard of in his life before. Then, under Ben's instruction, he started to feed the horses. He was in the lean-to filling nosebags with oats when he was startled by a shrill voice, a girl's voice, talking to Ben outside.

Peering out of the door, he had a shock that nearly matched that of his first sight of Richard Camberwell back at the inn. Standing beside the horse trough, wearing a riding habit and carrying a crop, was the girl he had helped out of the carriage in London two days before.

Will slipped back inside the lean-to and nibbled on a finger nail. What on earth was she doing here? Was this her home? A thought came to him with a shock. Was this the niece he had heard about? If it was, his only thought was to keep out of her way. She had been so pompous and haughty during their brief meeting in London, her reaction upon seeing him again would surely not be good, but his intentions were thwarted by Ben Hover who shouted, 'Will! Where are yer, lad? Get Dinah out of 'er stall and bring 'er 'ere!'

Will sidled out of the lean-to and walked slowly to the stable door, fortunate that the girl had her back to him and was not looking his way. But there was no avoiding her when he brought the horse out.

The girl was chatting to Ben, but on hearing the clip-clop of hooves on the cobbles, she turned – and stared. Her mouth dropped open and she said, 'You! What are you doing here?'

At the sight of her gawping at him, Will couldn't help but smile. Now she had seen him, he decided there was nothing he could do

40

but brazen it out.

'I work 'ere,' he said.

'What? I don't believe it! How on earth...?' She turned to Ben. 'This boy is street scum. How does he come to be working in our stables?'

'Yer uncle brought 'im 'ere, m'lady,' said Ben. 'Yesterday.'

'I shall speak to him at once. It's absolutely preposterous!' The girl started to walk away but was stopped when Richard Camberwell himself strolled into the yard.

'What's all the shouting about, Megan?' he said lazily. 'You sound like a washer-woman, child.'

'It's this boy, Uncle Richard,' answered the girl, 'And I'd be pleased if you would not liken me to riff-raff, nor call me a child! I'm sixteen!'

'Well, don't sound like a washer-woman or act like a child then,' said her uncle, amused at the girl's tone, 'Now what's the matter?'

'I saw this boy in London when I went to buy a hat,' said Megan Camberwell. 'He touched me as I left the carriage.'

'Oh he did, did he?' The amused look on Lord Richard's face vanished, to be replaced by a frown. 'How did he touch you? If it was in any way indecent, I'll thrash the living daylights out of him!'

'I only 'eld 'er 'and to 'elp 'er down the step, sir,' said Will quickly.

'Is that true, Megie?' The glare bid her tell the truth.

'Well...yes. But his hand was dirty. And he smelled,' said Megan. She wrinkled her nose. 'He still does.' Will blushed and shifted his feet uncomfortably.

Lord Richard's blue eyes twinkled but his voice was still stern as he said, 'Is that all he did? Just took hold of your hand?' He was wondering if Will, being the thief that he was, had not taken the opportunity to steal something from Megan. It still rankled that the young scoundrel had stolen his purse so easily.

'Yes...No. He shouted something.'

'Something rude?' The frown was back.

'No.' Lady Megan had the grace to blush too, which she did very prettily, Will thought. 'He said it was a pleasure to help such a beautiful lady.'

Richard Camberwell laughed. 'You should be flattered, Megan. It's not every day a girl scarce out of school gets a compliment from a vagabond.' He turned to Will. 'Fetch the saddle and bridle that

41

are on the left hand side in the tack room, Will, and saddle Dinah while I speak to my niece.' He put a hand on the girl's shoulder and walked with her a little, talking quietly. Whatever he said seemed to put the girl in a slightly better humour because when Will came back she was smiling, though not at him. She ignored him as he held the reins while her uncle helped her into the saddle, then she said goodbye to Lord Richard and trotted the horse away round the side of the house.

Ben went to fetch the nosebags for the stabled horses and Lord Richard said, 'It seems you made an impression, Will, albeit not a very good one. I have to say, Megan was probably only acting on my instructions. I've told her many times to avoid street urchins because they pester like flies. And she's right. They are dirty. And so are you. Ben!'

At his master's shout, the old man came hobbling quickly out of the lean-to. 'See that this lad has a bath before I get back,' said Richard Camberwell. 'The stink of carbolic is a damn sight better than the stink of the gutter.'

'No way!' said Will, stepping backwards, getting ready to run. He had never had a bath in his life and did not want one now. Lord Richard's arm whipped out and a firm hand gripped him as it had back at the inn. 'You will have a bath, lad. If you don't, you know what's to become of you!' The threat was delivered in a low tone so that Ben would not overhear. Will scowled but nodded as Lord Richard let go of him and said in a normal voice. 'Now saddle Hades for me. I'm going out for a ride.'

Will grudgingly did as he was bid and watched as Hades galloped away with Lord Richard on his back.

'That there girl is a problem right enough,' said Ben later when the two of them were mucking out the night straw from the stalls. No more mention had been made of a bath for Will and he was hoping that Ben would forget Lord Richard's injunction. 'As prickly as a gorse bush, she is, an no mistake. 'Er father were Lord Richard's older brother; a gambler through and through. Lived in London most o' the time 'e did, an' left the runnin' o' this estate ter Lord Richard and 'is mother. There weren't a thing 'e wouldn't take a bet on. I 'eard tell as 'ow 'e only managed to stop short o' gamblin' away this land and the 'ouse by shootin' 'isself 'cos of 'is bad debts. 'Is wife were a sickly woman and she died soon after.

42

Pretty lady. Foreign lookin'. Never took to our weather. Yon Megan was, what...about ten at the time. No parents, no brothers and sisters, and no 'ome, so 'er granny took 'er in and the lass 'as 'ad a chip on 'er shoulder about it ever since. Crabby as 'ell, she is. Worse 'n a nagging wife an' 'aughtier than the King's mistresses. The lass's got nothin' to be mopin' about neither, 'cos 'er granny's a kind soul. I does me best to be civil to 'er, but she barely gives me the time o' day. The master's really the only one who can 'andle 'er, but then, as I said, 'e does 'ave a way with women.' Ben leaned on his pitchfork and smiled. 'There's a tale or two I could tell yer about 'im and women, lad, and maybe I will one day if yer stick around. In the meantime, if it were me, I'd keep out o' Lady Megan's way as much as yer can unless yer want yer ears blasted off'n yer 'ead!'

Will nodded in agreement, thinking it very sound advice, and carried on pitchforking the dirty straw into a heap, but he couldn't help picturing that lovely face, and what it might be like with a sunny expression on it instead of the petulant look Lady Megan seemed to favour.

Will's heart dropped when the job was done and Ben said, 'Right, me lad. Time for that bath now. I told Lizzie a while back ter 'eat water in the copper. It should be warm enough. So go on. Get yerself to the scullery, sharpish.'

'Aw, Ben, must I?' whined Will, hoping to get the old man on his side. 'I ain't never 'ad a bath. Maybe I'll drown!'

''Course yer won't,' Ben laughed. 'It bain't be no worse'n a dip in the stream.'

'I ain't never done that, neither' said Will. The thought of immersing his whole body in water scared him. Yesterday and this morning were the only times he had washed his face in months, not since he had last stayed a couple of nights with Polly who insisted on a modicum of cleanliness.

'There's nothin' to be afeared of, lad. I 'ad a bath meself last June,' said Ben. ''Ave one every mid-summer, regular as clockwork, I does.'

Very reluctantly, Will walked to the scullery where a zinc bathtub filled with steaming water awaited him. There was no one in sight so Will stripped off his clothes, shivered naked for approximately thirty seconds, then decided that the warm water might be better than exposing himself to anyone who happened to come in.

43

He sat down gingerly in the tub, but it felt very strange to have water coming up to his waist. He saw that someone, probably Lizzie, had left a bar of soap and a scrubbing brush beside the bath, so he started to work the hard soap into a lather and wash himself. He was just beginning to think that maybe it wasn't so bad after all when the door to the scullery opened and the laundry maid, a girl named Nell, walked in, bold as brass.

Will was mortified, and splashed a lot of water out of the bath and onto the stone floor in an attempt to cover his nakedness, though Nell could see nothing in the dirty, soapy water anyway.

'You must be the new stable boy,' she said, standing with her head on one side, giving him an appraising look. 'Hmm. Better'n the last one if a mite too skinny. Now don't you fret none. I ain't lookin'.' She gave him a cheeky grin as she flounced to his few clothes and picked them up gingerly between finger and thumb. 'The master gave orders I'm ter burn these.'

'What?' Will was aghast. 'I ain't got no others! What'll I wear then?'

'Don't yer worry, I'll bring yer some as the mistress sent down. She collects clothin' fer the poor, yer know, an' yer seem poor enough. There's some as'll do yer a turn.' Nell pulled a face at the pile of rags dangling from her fingers. 'Can't say as I blame, 'er. These are only fit fer the fire.'

Without further ado, she hurried out and Will sank back into the water. Good food. New clothes. He was beginning to think that stealing Lord Richard Camberwell's purse had been one of the best things he'd ever done in more ways than one. And having a bath actually felt...well, if not exactly right...not as bad as he'd expected.

Unfortunately, his embarrassment was to get worse. He had just stepped out of the bath and was reaching for the thin towel that was on a shelf, when Nell again waltzed unannounced into the scullery. Red-faced, Will quickly grabbed the towel and wrapped it around himself, but he knew from the girl's round, laughing eyes and broad grin that she had seen things she shouldn't have. However, she said nothing but merely handed him a small pile of clothes and walked out, still smiling.

Will told himself that he would do his utmost never to see Nell face to face again. It would just be too embarrassing. Hurriedly, he pulled on the cotton shirt, cloth trousers and soft leather jerkin, which, although not new, were better than any clothing he had ever had. There was even underwear. And boots. They fit snugly, but felt very strange and uncomfortable. Will thought that maybe he would wear them only on special occasions, like when he had to see the mistress. He was sure he would never be able to work in them.

In his bed that night, he went over his first full day at a proper job and decided that it hadn't been too bad. He had seen the Lady Megan again, even though he might as well be a peck of dirt under her feet for all the pleasure she seemed to have gained from the encounter; he was properly clean for the first time since the mid-wife had washed him at birth and he had new clothes.

It had definitely been a good day.

4

Will saw little of either Lord Richard or Lady Megan over the next few days. Lady Megan arrived each morning to exercise her horse and ignored Will completely, though he could not help but cast surreptitious glances at her from the stable doorway. He thought this action was not completely lost on her because he could have sworn that he saw her eyes swivel his way once or twice. Somehow she contrived to bring her horse back while Will was eating his lunch, and as he liked to wander the estate during the half hour he was allowed for this purpose, he always missed her return.

Lord Richard left for Winchester a week after Will's arrival. No one told Will where he had gone, but he was adept at gaining information by using his eyes and ears and he overheard Ben telling Lizzie that same day. It did not escape his notice either that the house maids were paying him an uncommon amount of attention, a fact that led to him striking up a conversation with one of them during his lunch break the day after Lord Richard left.

Connie, the upstairs maid who had taken him to see Lady Helen, was on her way back from the wash-house when Will literally bumped into her, rounding a corner by the scullery. Connie stepped back with a small cry of shock and dropped the pile of clean linen she was carrying.

'Now look what you've made me do, you big oaf!' she said crossly, bending down to pick it up. Apologising, Will bent to help her and their eyes met as they both tried to retrieve the same sheet. Will could not help admiring the fair curls under the mob cap, rosy cheeks and cornflower blue eyes that blazed with indignation. Connie straightened up, holding out the sheet that now had a streak of dirt across one corner. 'Look at this! The mistress'll 'ave me pay for a week, 'an no mistake!'

'I'm sorry,' said Will, handing her a pillow case. He brushed ineffectually at the mark on the sheet with his fingers but the girl snatched the sheet away. 'Don't be stupid! Yer'll just make it worse. Yer 'ands are filthy!'

Will looked at his hands. They didn't look that dirty to him. He shrugged. 'Sorry,' he said again, and prepared to walk on, but the girl's hand on his arm suddenly stopped him.

'Listen,' she said with a sudden change of heart, 'I'm sorry too. It was just as much me own fault as yours, and I suppose I can wash the corner of the sheet, so's Nell don't 'ave to do it all over again.' She saw Will was carrying his lunch, a Cornish pastie and an apple. 'You goin' to 'ave yer lunch?'

'Yes, I was goin' to go and sit on the wall over there.' He pointed to the low wall that separated the lawn from the wild undergrowth that grew beyond.

'Mind if I come too? Look, I've just got ter take these ter Mrs Proudfoot. The 'ousekeeper,' she said when she saw Will's blank look. 'Then I can have me lunch. It's a nice day, I'd rather eat outside than in.'

So it was, that a short while later, Connie Preston joined Will, sitting on the old stone wall in the shade of a gnarled crabapple tree.

'Mrs Proudfoot weren't 'alf cross,' she said, 'but she calmed down a bit when I promised ter wash the sheet meself.' She bit into her pastie. 'Where d'you come from then?'

'London,' said Will through a mouthful of food. The pie was excellent.

Connie looked suitably impressed. 'I ain't never been there,' she said. 'Is it as big as they say it is? 'Ave yer seen the king? I 'eard tell there's buildins there bigger'n this 'ouse. Is it true?'

For the next fifteen minutes, Will found himself telling Connie about London. He laughed at some of her notions, such as her thoughts on the cleanliness of the place, that most of the people lived in grand houses such as the Camberwells' and that the King preened and paraded in front of his subjects every day. Will told her nothing of his life there, keeping the conversation general, but she listened absorbedly until there was a shout from the direction of the big house and she suddenly recollected what she should be doing.

'Oh my, I'm late!' she said. 'And I've a million things to do before tea, and that bloody sheet as well!' She started to run, then looked back swiftly. 'Bye!' she called, and was gone.

Will walked slowly back to the house. Ben wasn't a particularly good timekeeper and didn't bother if Will took a few minutes longer over his lunch than he should. So long as he did his work all right, that was all that mattered.

Talking of London had made Will realise how much he missed it and he suddenly felt a great pang of home sickness. This came as somewhat of a surprise, because Will had always thought that his battle to survive had precluded any love for the town in which he had lived all his life but now he understood that the hustle and bustle of the teeming streets was in his soul and could not be discarded like an old hat, or forgotten after a few days in the country.

All that afternoon he was morose and miserable, preoccupied with the thought that he would have done well not to have stolen Lord Camberwell's purse after all. If he had left well alone, he would not be here now. He would be back amongst the streets he knew. His mood was so far removed from the pleasant one he had shown thus far that after the horses were bedded down for the night Ben Hover was forced to comment on it. Will just grunted a reply but Ben was a canny man and guessed that his new friend was missing his home.

'You got family back there then?' he asked, thinking that was the reason for Will's sombre mood.

'No,' said Will.

'Friends?'

'Some.'

'A girl?'

'Not really.' Ben didn't press the point and Will didn't feel like telling him about Mary.

He said nothing further, and Ben got bored with trying to lighten his mood and went into his lean-to. Will decided to go for a walk. He had been told that he was allowed to walk about the estate as much as he liked in his spare time, what little there was of it, but Lord Richard had impressed upon him in a short talk before he left for Winchester that he was not to go further afield. Will guessed he was on some sort of probation. If he proved trustworthy, then maybe Lord Richard would give him more latitude. He would like to see the village and the surrounding hills. Despite missing the streets, Will felt the countryside calling to him and longed to explore. Perhaps the enforced restriction was part of the problem and he needed more freedom.

So, that evening, in the hour before the sun was due to set, Will walked away from the stables, past the kitchen garden and on towards an old orchard. The grass was long and chickens pecked amongst it, clucking contentedly. Red apples on the twisted trees were ripe, ready for picking. Will plucked a fat one from a branch and bit into it, savouring the sweetness of the juice. Apples didn't taste this good in London.

He walked past the wall and into the tangled undergrowth, finding an overgrown pathway that wound between brambles and blackberry bushes, ripe with juicy fruit. Soon Will's hands were smeared a dark purple as he picked and ate the sweet berries. He walked on, past a small ornamental pond that had a birdbath in the middle of it. The water was scummy and green, the stonework dappled with lichen.

It was a fair autumn evening, and Will felt better for being alone. Silver birch and ash trees led up a slope, the ash keys rustling in the faint breeze. There was no other sound and one would never have known a mansion with its coterie of servants and family was only few hundred yards away.

Will started to climb the slope, then was startled by a humming close to his ear and the sound he recognised as a gunshot. He dived to the undergrowth and lay there, heart pounding, wondering if he had imagined that he was being shot at. All sorts of thoughts winged their way through his head. Had someone followed him from London? Had his thieving past followed him here? Was someone trying to kill him?

He was still lying amongst the dead leaves when he heard footsteps and he looked up to see Lady Megan glaring at him and holding a smoking pistol.

'What do you think you're doing here, street scum? Don't you

48

know I could've killed you?' she said crossly.

'I know,' said Will, getting to his feet and brushing leaves from his leather jerkin. Anger was replacing the fear. 'I wasn't expectin' to be shot at just goin' for a walk, my lady.'

The glare faded a little from Megan's eyes. 'I suppose not,' she said ungraciously. The incident had frightened her more than she would care to admit. Now the stable boy was standing there, looking at her with those bright blue eyes, a grim look on his face, all fear seemingly evaporated. Suddenly flustered, she dropped her gaze.

Will wondered what she was doing firing a gun, and the thought arose that her uncle probably knew nothing about it. Curiosity got the better of him. 'If yer weren't shootin' at me, what were yer shootin' at?' he asked.

Megan pointed to a dead branch on a tree about five yards from Will's head. 'That branch,' she said.

'Yer missed,' Will said pointedly.

'So, what if I did? I haven't been practising long.' She turned her back on him and walked on up the slope. He started to follow her but she rounded on him. 'Go away. You have no business here.'

'Yer uncle said I could go where I liked in the grounds,' he said amicably. 'Anyway, perhaps I'd better stick around. Yer might hurt yerself.' He pointed. 'With the gun, I mean.'

'No, I won't.' She carried on walking. Not to be outdone, Will followed her. At the top of the slope the ground dipped down into a glade, thick with dead leaves and grass. The setting sun flickered redly through the few leaves still on the trees, infusing the wood with a rosy hue.

'There are bluebells here in May,' said Megan. Trying to steer the conversation away from herself, thought Will, but he was not so easily diverted.

'So what d'you want ter learn ter shoot for?' he asked.

'None of your business.'

Will shrugged. 'Does yer uncle know yer shoot 'is gun? It is 'is, ain't it?' The pistol was a fine piece of craftsmanship, with a polished walnut grip and long barrel. Much too heavy for a girl, he thought. He wondered how she ever managed to fire it at all.

Megan Camberwell was silent, and her silence told Will that Lord Richard knew nothing of her secret use of the weapon. 'You won't tell him, will you?' She glared again. 'If you do, I'll have him dismiss you.'

She was startled to hear Will laugh out loud at the outrageous statement. Lord Richard would not dismiss him until he felt that Will had paid off the debt of nine guineas, and that would be a long time coming. He stared at the girl whose curls framed her pretty, stubborn face like a chestnut halo and whose eyes held surprise at his reaction and...yes, a little fear as well. Suddenly, mischief welled up inside him.

'What will yer give me if I promise not ter tell?'

She was outraged. 'Nothing, of course! Why should I?'

'Because I think Lord Richard would be very upset ter know that 'is niece is playin' with guns and puttin' 'erself and other people in danger.'

'Uncle Richard won't believe you. He'll think you're lying.' Tough words, but Will was a good judge of character and he could tell she wasn't entirely sure that would be the case.

'Maybe. Maybe not. Are yer willin' ter take that chance?'

Megan Camberwell turned away from him and appeared to be thinking. Will marvelled at his own cheekiness but he knew what he wanted from this girl who liked to appear so haughty and refined. Perhaps he felt he deserved a little from her for the scornful attitude she showed towards him whenever they were in each other's company.

She turned to face him again. 'What is it you want?' she asked coldly. 'If it's money, I...'

He smiled at the thought. 'No. It's nothin' like that.'

'Well, what is it then?'

'A kiss.'

'What?' Amazement in her voice.

'A kiss. That's my fee fer not tellin' yer uncle.'

'I will not kiss you!'

'It's up to you.' Will started to walk slowly backwards, still looking at her. 'I'm sure Lord Richard would love to know that 'is niece is stealin' 'is gun, and shootin' at poor, unsuspectin' stable boys.'

Megan saw the twinkle in his eyes. 'You wouldn't dare tell him!'

'Try me,' he said, and stopped walking.

Megan looked at the maddeningly impertinent smile on Will's

face and knew that she could not take a chance on her uncle believing him. Richard Camberwell would be furious if he knew what she was doing behind his back and she couldn't risk this irritating boy telling him.

'All right,' she said, grudgingly. 'If you promise not to tell, you can kiss me. But only once mind.'

She stood there with her eyes closed and Will gazed at her. She really was very pretty. It was a pity about her condescending and patronising manner. He walked closer and gently lowered his lips to hers.

Megan felt a touch, light as a feather on her lips, then a slight movement of his mouth. A sudden tingle ran all the way down to her toes and she nearly gasped aloud but the lips were pressing harder now until, with no conscious thought on her part, her mouth moved against his.

Her eyes flew open, anger, and something indefinable that might have been surprise in them as she backed away hurriedly and fought for words. Her expression changed to one of disgust but Will had felt her response and knew that he had kindled desire. He grinned. 'There. That weren't so bad, eh?' he said lightly.

'Oh! You!' She lashed out at him with the hand holding the pistol, but Will caught her arm and held it in a firm grip. For a long moment they stared into each other's eyes, then Will let go of her and deftly removed the gun from her hand.

'Give it back!' Megan grabbed for the pistol but Will held it high.

'No. I'll tell yer what we're goin' ter do.'

'Give it to me at once!' The girl made another furious grab for it but Will lifted it out of her reach.

'Tell me why you want it, and I'll teach yer 'ow ter use it properly.'

That stopped her. She stared at him in astonishment. 'You? You can shoot?'

'Aye, I can.'

She looked disbelieving, then scowled. 'How can street scum like you have learned to use a pistol?'

'Don't yer believe me?'

'No.'

'Give me powder and a ball and I'll show yer.'

Will could see her thinking, then she reached into a pocket in the fold of her dress and brought out ball and powder. Will carefully loaded the pistol then found a broken stick and placed it in the cleft of a nearby tree before walking back twenty paces. 'Move away,' he called. Megan backed swiftly to the other side of the glade. She hadn't even reached it when a shot rang out and she looked back. The stick was no longer there. She stared at Will, open-mouthed and, for the first time, with something other than disdain.

'How did you learn to do that?' she asked again but Will said nothing whilst walking over to her.

'I'm goin' to give this back to yer so's yer can return it to wherever Lord Richard keeps it but yer must promise me not to practise on yer own any more. I'll meet yer 'ere tomorrow after I've finished me work and I'll teach yer. All right?'

'What if I don't keep my promise?' There was a faint touch of bitterness at being outdone in Megan's voice. The spoilt child who was cross at not getting her own way, thought Will.

'Then I shall exact payment again,' he said mischievously. 'Another kiss.'

'Never!' she said, though Will saw that she blushed.

'Besides, I keep my promise, you keep yours,' Will said as he handed her the gun. 'Tomorrow?' She nodded slowly and watched as he walked out of the glade and disappeared through the trees.

It wasn't until he was lying on his bed of hay that night that Will realised that he still didn't know why Lady Megan Camberwell wanted to learn how to shoot.

And Lady Megan, lying in her silken sheets behind the curtains of her four-poster bed, realised that she still didn't know how that dirty ragamuffin had learned to shoot so well.

† † †

It became obvious to Will at noon the next day that Connie Preston had intentions as far as he was concerned. She was waiting for him by the stables when he knocked off for lunch and they walked together to the wall where they had eaten the previous day. Connie sat very close to him and shared an orange she had been given by the cook.

Will decided to take the opportunity of this new friendship to elicit some information.

'So when's the master comin' back, then?' he enquired.

'Oh, probably not for another week yet,' said Connie, carefully breaking the peeled orange into two halves and passing him one.

This was good news. It would give Will time to teach Megan a little about shooting. 'I 'ear 'e went to Winchester,' he said.

'Yes. 'E's gone to see 'is new Company.'

Will looked at her sharply. 'New Company? What d'yer mean?'

'What I said. 'E's goin' to take back some new recruits when 'e rejoins the regiment in Portugal.'

''E's a soldier?'

She looked at him strangely. 'Yes. Didn't yer know?'

Will shook his head. This was news indeed. If Lord Richard was about to go back to war, was he going to let Will return to London?

'Why's 'e 'ere then? If 'e's a soldier, I mean?' he asked.

Connie wiped juice off her mouth with her sleeve. 'Because 'e was wounded, silly. Got a ball in 'is side and another in 'is shoulder. Nearly died from loss of blood and fever, 'e did. Came 'ome to get better near three months ago. Got the papers t'other day, sayin' as 'ow 'e 'ad ter go ter Winchester and pick up some new lads and take 'em back with 'im.'

Will brooded on this for a few moments, then he said, 'When's 'e got to go to Portugal, then?'

'End o' the month, I think.'

''Ow did you find all this out?' asked Will, smiling at her.

'Oh, I 'ears things,' said Connie airily. 'Lady Megan and the mistress talk a lot and sometimes they sort of forget I'm there, tidyin' up and whatnot.' She tapped the side of her nose and gave him a mischievous grin. 'There are things I could tell yer an' no mistake!'

'What regiment's Lord Richard in?' asked Will.

Connie frowned at him. If it were her, she would much rather know what gossip had been overheard but all this lad wanted to do was hear about the master. 'My, but you're a nosy one, ain't yer? Fourth Kent Infantry, if yer must know. 'E's Captain o' the Light Company. Why?'

'Just wondered.' What wouldn't he give to go to war! Listening to the recruiting sergeants, Will pictured war to be a glorious charge of horses and men, over-running and cutting down the enemy like a scythe for king and country. He'd give anything to go himself.

'Will!' Connie was shaking his arm. 'Yer dreamin'. Come on. It's time we got back ter work.'

Will roused himself and walked with her back to the house. Passing the wash-house, from which issued clouds of steam, a raucous voice shouted, 'You keep yer thievin' 'ands off that one, Connie Preston. 'E's my lad. Ain't that so, Will Tucker?'

Nell the laundry maid, her arms and hands red and raw from scrubbing the dirty washing, leaned on the damp door jamb to let the air cool her down a bit. She grinned at Will and he had the awful feeling she was going to say something about his bath. To his eternal relief, she didn't. Instead, she said, 'Come by 'ere after supper, Will. There's somethin' I'd like to show yer.'

'Sorry, Nell. Got other business,' he replied, grinning. He knew exactly what it was Nell wanted to show him. Ben had already warned him against her.

'You leaves that 'un alone, Will, lad,' he had said one day soon after Will's arrival. 'Goes after everythin' in britches, she does, and my guess is she'll make a bee-line for yer, bein' as 'ow yer a good-lookin' lad. It's a mystery as 'ow she's not got 'erself in the family way already. She's a grand laundry maid but the mistress 'as told 'er that if she gets 'erself pregnant she's as good as gone, though it don't make no difference, she still runs after the lads, and 'er with six brothers and sisters to 'elp feed. 'Er ma and pa are the scourge of the village. Good for nothin' 'cept drinkin', the pair of 'em. They both works fer old Farmer Ridgley, but if it weren't for the fact that 'e's 'alf blind and can't see what they're up ter, they'd've got the sack long ago. Nell was damn lucky to get this job so don't help 'er ter lose it, lad.'

Will had assured him that he would not give Nell any encouragement, though she was not easy to discourage. So far he had managed to keep their relationship on a fairly friendly basis but it was difficult to avoid her suggestive looks and pointed comments.

'What business?' Nell wanted to know now, pouting at his refusal to accept her invitation.

'None o' yours,' countered Will.

Nell scowled at him and went back inside the laundry.

'Bye Connie,' said Will.

'See yer, Will,' said Connie who then shouted something to Nel as he walked towards the stables. Ben was swilling the yard down with water from the trough so Will picked up a bucket and went to help him.

† † †

That evening, Will managed to finish his chores quickly and so it was still very light when he went to the glade. He sat down on a fallen log to wait for Megan, wondering if she would actually turn up. While he was waiting he thought about Polly Frinton and Tom Quirk. Tom it was who had taught him how to use a gun.

Before becoming involved with Polly, Tom Quirk had had a chequered life. In his youth he had worked with his father, a gamekeeper on an estate in Dorset, but he had poached and sold so much of the game he was supposed to be protecting that, once found out, he had run away before he was arrested. Handy with a musket and pistol, he had joined the army but had deserted before a month was out. From there he had tried his hand at several jobs, mostly illegal, until falling in with Polly. He had taught Will to shoot with an old but serviceable pistol, telling him that it was a necessary skill to learn, especially since Will hoped to join up one day, though, having experienced three weeks of the army himself, he strongly advised against it. They had practised regularly, shooting at empty kegs behind the tavern, and Will had become quite proficient.

Will was brought from his reverie by the sound of footsteps crunching on the dead leaves and Megan appeared. He smiled a quick smile.

'I decided you may give me instruction,' she said pompously, as though she was bestowing a great gift on him. Her severe expression and pretence that she was only willing to accept his offer because she wanted to, and not because of the possibility of him revealing her secret to her uncle, made his smile widen.

Will set up a primitive shooting range by upending some logs and standing them in a straight line. He wondered aloud whether the noise would attract curiosity from the big house but Megan told him that the villagers and farmers round about sometimes shot rabbits, deer and ducks for meat, or a fox that was getting at the chickens. As long as they didn't shoot too frequently, it would not attract much attention.

Megan already knew how to load the pistol from secretly spying

55

on her uncle when he cleaned it but her accuracy was appalling. The stance she adopted meant that the recoil nearly knocked her over. Will asked her to fire the gun so that he could see what she was doing wrong, and in her haste to show him, she stepped backwards and fell over a log half hidden in the undergrowth, whereupon Will caught more than a glimpse of bare thigh and frilled petticoats, a sight that set him laughing. Highly indignant, she was so annoyed at his laughter and having to be helped up from the ground, that she pummelled his chest and shrieked her displeasure but Will easily caught hold of her arms, then stopped her noise with a kiss.

For a moment there was utter silence in the glade as Megan Camberwell fought against emotions she had never felt before, then she pulled away and slapped his face hard.

'How dare you!' she spat, angry with Will who, despite his red cheek that showed the imprint of her fingers, still had that wicked grin on his face. She was angry with herself for being exhilarated by his kiss. The feeling had come as a great surprise. Will was thinking how marvellous she looked with her curls dancing and her hazel eyes blazing. He felt not the least repentant.

'I'll tell Uncle Richard you kissed me, and he'll have you dismissed in an instant!' said Megan.

'No, yer won't.'

The angry look gradually faded as Megan Camberwell realised that she couldn't tell her uncle at all. Unless she lied about the circumstances, she would have to reveal what she and Will were doing with the gun.

'Well, maybe I won't,' she said huffily. 'But you'd better not do it again! Now show me how to use this thing properly.' She handed him the gun and for the next half hour Will tried to educate her in the proper use of it. But Lady Megan Camberwell was a very difficult pupil, sulky and unwilling to be told. In the end, Will unloaded the pistol, laid it on the ground in disgust, and started to walk away.

'Wait! Where are you going?' Megan called after him, but when he didn't stop she ran and caught up with him. 'I demand that you come back!'

'Demand?' Will turned to face her. 'Let me remind yer, m'lady, that I offered ter do this and am free ter decide whether I continue ter do so or not. And yer obviously don't want me ter 'elp yer anyway, or yer wouldn't be makin' it so difficult.'

'In what way am I making it difficult?'

He shook his head in mild amazement that she really didn't know.

'Every time I tells yer to stand straighter, yer grumble. When I tells yer to 'old the pistol still, yer grouch and wave it around like it's a parasol or somethin'. I touch yer ter straighten yer arm and yer tells me ter keep me 'ands off yer. Yer shout and scream and stamp yer foot. Yer not a lady, Megan Camberwell. Yer a spoilt child.'

Leaving her with her mouth open wide with shock that he could address her so, Will turned and strode away through the wood. Let the girl do what she would with the pistol, he was buggered if he was going to put up with any more of her nonsense, though he had to admit he had enjoyed the kiss and, if he was any judge, so had she.

He missed seeing Megan the next morning because he was letting some of the horses loose in the fields to graze when she came to fetch her mare. He was glad he had done so. On reflection he was actually quite surprised that he had not been hauled before Lady Helen to explain his tart words but then he remembered that Megan was practising with the pistol illicitly and would not want anyone to know about it, though he supposed she could have made something up with which to disgrace him. Her grandmother would be bound to believe her niece over a stable boy any time. But nothing was said and Will was tempted to go back to the glade that evening and see if she turned up.

Nell had another go at tempting him to do things of another sort later that day when Will was currying one of the carriage horses. She brought him another shirt.

'Lady 'Elen says as 'ow I 'as to wash the one yer 'ave on,' she explained.

'Why? I've only been wearing it a while.'

''Er ladyship's very particular about keepin' clean,' said Nell. 'You 'as to change yer shirt and yer drawers regular.'

Will was astonished. He'd never heard the like. The clothes he'd worn in London had been on him for so long he'd actually grown into them, since they'd originally come from Tom Quirk who at that time had been at least one size larger than he.

'Regular?' he said in amazement.

Nell nodded. 'We 'as a clean apron and work dress every week,' she said proudly. 'And underdrawers as well.' She said this as if it was something of an uncustomary event in her life too. 'She's real good to us, is 'er ladyship. Now, take off yer shirt and let's be 'avin' it.'

Will took off his jerkin and pulled off the shirt. He saw Nell staring at his torso so he grabbed the clean shirt out of her hands and put it on quickly. 'And the drawers,' she said, mischievous eyes gleaming.

'I'll bring yer those later,' said Will hurriedly.

Nell moved closer to him. 'I could 'elp yer take 'em off,' she said, in what she probably thought passed for a seductive voice but only made Will want to laugh.

He was saved from having to decide how to respond to that offer of help by a loud shout from the direction of the wash-house; the housekeeper suggesting that it was time Nell put in an appearance because the copper needed emptying and refilling with clean water.

Nell pulled a face, then smiled. 'I'll 'ave yer yet, Will Tucker,' she said cheekily. 'And don't forget to bring me yer drawers.' She tossed him the clean ones and went.

Will was unable to go to the glade that evening after all. One of the hunters had developed an abscess on its foreleg and Will had to apply a hot poultice every two hours in the hope that it would burst. As it was one of Lady Helen's favourite horses, Ben was vigilant, and Will was unable to creep away to see if Lady Megan had gone to the glade or given up on him. Ben took over from him somewhere near midnight, leaving Will to fall into an exhausted sleep.

The next evening he slipped away after supper. The weather had turned again that day bringing squalls of light rain, the usual mix of an English autumn, and Will was glad of his new jerkin as he walked to the glade with clouds overhead, though the showers had stopped for the moment.

To his surprise, Megan was already there, aiming with what he hoped was an unloaded pistol, at Will's makeshift target range.

'Where were you last night?' she snapped as he approached. 'I waited for half an hour.'

Will told her about the horse and she thawed a little, knowing it was one of her grandmother's favourites.

'Did yer practise without me?' he asked.

'No,' she said. 'But I heard today that Uncle Richard's coming home at the end of the week so try and get here earlier tomorrow night.'

That would be difficult. The only time Will could only get away without arousing Ben's suspicion was after they had eaten their supper, and he told Megan this. She pouted, but seemed to accept the situation and said nothing about their argument the last time he had seen her.

Will was a good teacher, and despite the fact that Megan was not an easy pupil, he had her hitting the target, a thick log, twice that evening from a distance of ten yards, an achievement that made her clap her hands with glee and brought a smile at last to her pretty face. Will grinned too, and thought how the smile transformed her often petulant features. The first time a ball hit the log she even went so far as to grab him around the waist and do a little jig. Will leaned forward as though to kiss her again but she pulled away and said, 'Oh, no, Will Tucker. You're not going to take advantage of me again,' but it was said in a light-hearted manner, quite unlike her vehement anger of before and Will's heart leapt. The change didn't last long, however, and Lady Megan was soon back to her old self because she ran out of powder and there was still daylight left.

'Won't Lord Richard miss the powder and ball?' Will asked.

'I doubt it. He's got lots and I only take a few balls and a little powder at a time,' she replied. 'He keeps it all in a drawer in his study. Bother! I should have taken more. Now we're wasting daylight!'

'We don't have to.' Will busied himself setting up more logs and branches, then ferreted in the undergrowth for pebbles and stones. He made Megan stand about thirty feet away, then handed her a stone. 'See if yer can hit that branch there, the one ter the right of the log,' he said, pointing. She looked at him quizzically. 'Ter get yer eye in,' he explained.

He had her throwing stones at the branch until it was dark, and was gratified to see that her aim was definitely improving.

Later, when Will was rounding the corner of the big house on his way to the stables, he saw a movement in the shadows. He stopped, alarmed, then the shadow moved into the light of the lamp that always burned at night by the stable doorway, and he saw it was Nell, shrugging a shawl around her shoulders to combat the chill.

'What are yer doin' 'ere?' he asked grumpily, pushing past her through the doorway.

'Waitin' fer you,' she said pertly, following him inside, apparently unperturbed by his surly greeting. The light from another lantern hanging from the rafters cast long shadows and the horses shuffled uncertainly. Ben Hover was nowhere to be seen. He was probably in the lean-to, smoking his pipe and reading by the light of a candle. He had told Will that he was a stumbling reader, but liked to persevere with some books that Lady Helen lent him. She was keen to help anyone on her staff better themselves, and Ben pored over the difficult words for a while each evening.

Realising he wasn't going to get rid of Nell easily, Will turned to her. 'What d'yer want?' he said.

'I think yer know,' she replied, her eyes and mouth holding an invitation Will could not miss. He swallowed hard and turned away from her again, busying himself unnecessarily by rewinding some halter ropes that hung from the wall.

'Go away,' he said. 'The mistress'll 'ave yer guts and mine if she knows yer 'ere.'

'The mistress won't get ter know,' said Nell airily. She was very close to him now, and he caught a whiff of the lye soap she used to wash the clothes. She pressed up against him and he felt the softness of rounded breasts against his chest. Unbidden things started happening around his groin area.

Nell traced a finger along his cheek. 'Come on, Will,' she wheedled. 'We could 'ave a lot of fun together, you and I.'

'No,' said Will, remembering what Ben Hover had told him about Nell's large family.

She pouted. 'Why not?'

'Because I don't want to,' he said, though it was a lie.

She sighed and pulled away. 'I think yer lyin',' she said and glanced at his crotch, then grinned slyly. 'In fact, I know y'are.' He breathed a silent sigh of relief as she moved towards the door. 'But I won't press yer now. There'll be other times. There bain't been a man who worked 'ere yet that I've set me cap at what 'asn't given in eventually. I'll be seein' yer, Will Tucker.' With that she went out of the door. Thankful that temptation had gone, Will took the lantern with him up the ladder to the loft and went to bed.

5

It was pitch black when Will was woken from a deep sleep by something stroking his cheek. Thinking it was a rat crawling over him, he yelped and sat up with a jerk, brushing his hands across his face.

'It's all right. It's only me.' The harsh whisper belonged to Nell, and Will's pounding heart beat even harder.

'Nell! Go away!' he hissed.

'Why? What's the matter? Are yer worried we'll get found out? Don't be. It'll be our little secret, Will. Just yours and mine.' Nell's voice was soft and, this time, really seductive. Gone was the brash, loud speech she normally used and Will was beginning to understand what Ben had warned him against. He tried to make out her face in the darkness but even though his eyes were adjusting to it, he could only see her as a darker figure against the black background. Outside was cloudy, and no moonlight came in through the small glassless window under the roof.

However, what his eyes couldn't see, his body could surely feel. Nell was ignoring his command to go. Her hands were wandering all over his naked chest and she was pressing herself against him and the blankets in such a way, there was no mistaking her intentions.

He pushed her away. 'Stop it, Nell! I told yer, I'm not interested,' he said.

'I don't believe yer.' There was a scuffle as her hand suddenly darted under the blankets and his moved to stop it. Will's thankfulness that he had his breeches on was short-lived. 'You do want me, Will,' she said slyly. 'I can feel it.'

What did the hussy expect? He was only human. Will rolled away from her and got onto his hands and knees. The loft was not high enough for him to stand.

'Get out of 'ere, Nell,' he said. 'I don't want yer.'

'Why not, Will?' A thought suddenly struck her and her voice lost its seductive allure and changed back to it's usual caustic tone.

61

''Ere! Yer not a virgin, are yer?'

'No. I'm not.'

There was a pause for a moment, then, 'I know, it's that bloody Connie Preston, ain't it? I've seen you and 'er together. If it is, I'll tear out 'er bloody curls one by one!'

'No, Connie and me're friends, that's all.'

There was another pause and he heard Nell shift closer again, so he crawled further away. This was ridiculous, he thought, playing cat and mouse in the dark.

Still trying to find a reason for his rejection of her advances, Nell said, 'Yer not bad lookin'. I 'ope it's not boys you like, Will Tucker.'

'Course not!' Will was offended she could even think it.

'Then it must be Miss 'Igh and Mighty 'erself, I suppose,' said Nell petulantly. ''Cos for sure it can't be Lizzie, an' the others are too old. It's Lady Megan yer like, ain't it?'

Will didn't answer, glad she couldn't see his face, which was hot with embarrassment. Yes, he was attracted to Lady Megan but he wasn't about to admit it to anyone. He was only now admitting it to himself.

Suddenly Nell was beside him again and this time she was pressing his head to her ample chest. He realised with a start that she had undone her bodice and that his cheek was lying next to soft, bare skin, with a nipple tantalisingly close to his mouth.

'A sample of what yer missin', Will,' she said, then lifted his head and found his lips with hers. Every sexual nerve in his young, virile body was crying out to him to take what this slut was offering but...

'No!'

With an effort, he managed to extricate himself and push her away. 'Nell! Go away!' he said with as much firmness as he could muster.

Another pause. 'Yer really mean it, don't yer, yer bugger?' She sounded surprised.

'Aye, I do.'

'Bloody 'ell!' It was obvious from her tone that Nell was not used to being turned down. In some ways, she reminded Will of Mary. They both had the same blowsy look, fresh, open face and well endowed and ample body, but whereas he and Mary saw occasional sex as part of their friendship, he was quite sure in his mind that he didn't want to have sex with Nell, even though his body might be doing its best to tell him differently.

'Well, I ain't about to give meself where I ain't wanted,' said Nell huffily, drawing back from him. 'But I'll tell yer somethin' for nothin', Will Tucker. Yer'll never get the iron maiden to take 'er bloomers off for yer, and yer'll probably get the sack if yer even try.'

With that piece of unwanted advice, and to Will's fervent relief, Nell went down the ladder and back to the house, leaving him with his thoughts and an extremely uncomfortable bulge in his breeches. Nell's physical closeness had affected him a lot more than he had let on. When he was sure she had gone, he crawled back under his blankets and groaned aloud. Lying there, fantasizing about Megan and remembering the feel of Nell's soft breasts, only made matters worse. With a great effort he turned his mind to other things, until at last he fell asleep.

The next morning, Nell's nocturnal visit was forgotten when the news flashed around that the master would be home that day, earlier than expected. In a way, Will was not looking forward to it. Ben Hover was a lax task-master and Will suspected his work load would be increased with Lord Richard around. Not that he particularly minded working with the horses. It was not difficult work, and he seemed to have a way with them. There was another reason he wasn't eager to have the master of the house close by. It would mean his evening meetings with Megan would cease and would probably not be resumed. Surely when Lord Richard went back to the war he would take all his pistols with him and there would be no weapons for Megan to 'borrow'. The hunting muskets she had told him were on the walls of the study would be much too heavy and cumbersome for her to handle. Will also wondered what would happen to him. Was there a chance he would be sent back to London? He doubted it.

It was late morning when Lord Richard Camberwell rode into the stable yard, dusty, tired and irritable after a long ride. He had barely dismounted before he was shouting for Ben and Will. When they appeared he gave a string of orders regarding his horse before striding towards the house.

'By Gaw, but the master's in a black mood,' said Ben, starting to unsaddle Hades. 'Ne'er even a greetin'! Wonder what's up.'

Will was curious too, and it wasn't until later that afternoon

63

that he found out. Lizzie was the bearer of supper and news. Nothing much that went on at the big house escaped the servants' notice and any gossip soon reached all ears. Now Ben and Will listened avidly as Lizzie told them the reason for Lord Richard's irritability.

'Connie told me 'e ain't got enough men to take with 'im to Portugal,' she confided. 'Seems as 'ow 'e was supposed to take an 'ole Company, that's an 'undred or so, and there's only about forty. On top o' that, 'e 'ad some bad news while 'e was at Winchester. 'Is man as kept 'is uniform clean and looked after 'is 'orse 'as been killed, an' his best 'orse too.'

'I didn't know that soldiers 'ad servants,' said Will.

'Lord, aye,' said Ben. 'All the gentlemen officers 'as their own man to see ter things for 'em. Can yer imagine someone like the master washin' 'is own clothes?'

Will couldn't.

'When's 'e off ter war then?' he asked Lizzie.

'Next week 'e 'as to go to Portsmouth an' meet up with the recruits who's meantime goin' there with a sergeant, so 'e'll be gone from England by the end o' the month.'

Will's mind was suddenly filled with a vision of a sailing ship carrying soldiers across the sea to war. What glories awaited them on the far shore! More than anything, Will wished he could go too.

He was brought back to earth by Ben telling him to bed the horses down for the night. But all the while he was working, his imagination worked overtime too, and carried over into his dreams.

† † †

After his return, Lord Richard said little to Will until he came to the stables early one morning specifically to talk to him.

He caught Will swilling his face at the pump having only just woken up, and the boy blinked damply at his benefactor who leaned nonchalantly against the stable wall. Lord Richard waited for Will to finish before tossing him the towel.

'Good morning, Will.' The tone was friendly and Will was glad to hear that Camberwell appeared to have got over his grumpiness.

'G' mornin', sir.'

'How are you?'

'Well, sir.'

'I must say it's gratifying to hear that you haven't been up to any mischief while I've been gone.'

Will thought guiltily of the shooting practices in the wood, but said, 'No, sir.'

'In fact Ben says you're doing well. And my mother seems to have taken quite a shine to you.'

This news surprised Will. He had not seen Lady Helen since the first day of his stay at Camberwell Hall, but she had obviously had her spies out.

'Yes, she says it's a long time since we've had such an efficient stable lad. Did you know that she asks for reports from the housekeeper and Ben every week so that she can make sure things are running smoothly?'

'No, sir.' Will had no idea he was being so closely scrutinised.

'She wants me to give you an increase in wages. That, of course, is impossible, given the circumstances, and she fortunately did not ask what I was paying you already, but as I shall be away and she will have to pay the staff, she is going to have to know why you are being paid nothing for your work. I thought it only right that you should know this, as it may alter her attitude towards you. I think I mentioned to you the fact that she has no time for a thief or a scoundrel, both of which you are, Will Tucker. However, I shall, of course, insist that she not terminate your employment. Not until the debt is paid. Now, saddle Hades for me. He's coming with me to Portugal, so needs the exercise.'

Lord Richard's words were food for thought, but Will did not let them worry him. His job was secure, at least for the time being, though he had rather hoped that Lord Richard might have released him from his debt, and sent him back to London. Back home. But was it really home? His dank cellar by the wharf would have been taken by someone else long since. On reflection, he was probably better off here where at least he had decent shelter and food.

He had no more problems with Nell while the master was at home. Whether the girl was afraid of what might happen if she was caught flirting, or whether she had given up on him, Will had no way of knowing, but he was pleased nonetheless. He was not at all sure as to how long he could maintain his noble celibacy when presented with such temptation. He only saw Connie once too during those few days, and then only in passing. She told him she had a lot of work to do and had to eat her lunches in the kitchen. It seemed that Lord Richard's return had put the whole household into a state of bustling activity.

Megan visited the stables daily. Her attitude towards Will was as sour as ever, and she gave no sign that they had shared any time together. At first he was mildly miffed but then he thought that maybe she was ignoring him deliberately in front of others so as not to arouse suspicion about their clandestine meetings. It was a reason he preferred to believe because the only other one that sprang to mind was that she was merely treating him as the servant he was and had forgotten all about the stolen kisses. Will's admission to himself, during Nell's midnight visit, of feelings for Megan Camberwell, had come as perhaps not so much a shock, more a revelation. That first meeting and the first kiss in the wood had provoked only mischief from him; a street boy trying to make a pretty girl smile, and he still thought her arrogance was laughable, but now he was aware of stronger feelings. Although he was secretly glad to admit these feelings to himself, he almost wished he hadn't because there was absolutely no hope that their relationship would prosper, no hope at all. He was way out of her league even if she liked him, which she obviously did not. It was something he would rather push to the back of his mind and forget altogether before his feelings had time to develop any further. It was with this in mind that an idea came to him, something that might help him make a better impression with Lady Megan and give him other things to think about. An idea which he proposed to put to Lord Richard the following day.

So it was that when Richard Camberwell came for Hades the next morning, Will had the horse already saddled. Lord Richard said nothing, just took the reins that Will held out to him.

'Could I speak to yer fer a moment, sir?' asked Will, nervous yet determined.

'I suppose so. What is it?' Lord Richard did not seem in a particularly good mood again this morning and his voice was cold. He swung himself into the saddle.

'Sir, I was wonderin'. When yer go ter Portugal, would yer take me with yer?'

For an instant Lord Richard looked startled, then he laughed out loud, making Hades skitter sideways on the cobbles. 'Whatever for, Will? Don't tell me you want to become a soldier?'

'Yes, sir. I do.'

The laughter subsided and Will felt the older man's keen gaze upon him.

'Now why would that be?' Richard Camberwell was genuinely curious. In his experience, it was hard going to find men willing to join the army and most would do an awful lot to get out of it, yet here was someone who actually wanted to go to war. Or thought he did.

Will didn't know how to answer. He couldn't tell the master the real reason why he wanted to join up, neither did he want to lie. In the end he said nothing.

Richard Camberwell smiled condescendingly. 'I know the army's made up of rogues and thieves, Will, but I don't think they need you just yet. You're only what...sixteen? Much too young to be laying down your life for king and country.'

'I'll be seventeen soon, sir. I know other lads my age who've taken the king's shillin'.'

'Well, they'll be the stupid ones then and probably did it to get out of a life of misery, only to find another that was much worse. And they're probably dead by now. There's nothing those damn Frenchies like better than blasting young lads like you to bloody ribbons. No, I will not take you to Portugal, Will. You must pay your debt to me right here in England. You might be a scoundrel, but having your death on some battlefield on my conscience would be somewhat worse even than sending you to rot in Newgate.' He gave another of his rare smiles. 'I may be a hard-hearted bastard but I haven't sunk that deeply yet. You've got a good berth here if you did but know it. Appreciate it while you may.'

With that, Lord Richard kicked his heels into the horse's flanks and trotted Hades out of the stable yard, leaving Will feeling somewhat let down, yet relieved. One part of his brain might be telling him it would be better to be far away from Megan Camberwell, a much bigger part was saying it would be nicer to stay as close as possible. And it was rather heartening to hear that, despite everything, Richard Camberwell thought enough of him not to take him up on his suggestion and risk his life, though it hadn't blunted Will's ambition to be a soldier one day, maybe when his debt was fully paid. If he wasn't too old to hold a musket by then.

67

He looked up at the sudden sound of hooves, and Lord Camberwell was back. 'Oh, by the way, Will, I almost forgot. Good news. I told my mother the reason for you being here and she took it very well. In fact, I don't think she believed me. Said you couldn't possibly be a thief because you haven't the face for it! I had the devil of a job to persuade her not to pay you!'

With those words, he was gone again. Will laughed. He laughed so hard that he didn't hear Megan come into the yard until she said, 'Don't you think you should be getting on with your work?'

Her sharpness couldn't flatten his good mood. 'Of course, m'lady,' he said, still smiling. He could see that Megan was wondering what had caused the laughter, but he wasn't about to give her the satisfaction of knowing.

She sniffed. 'I think it's about time you had another bath,' she said. Not even that caustic remark could dent his well-being.

'I'll remember to stand out in the rain next time we 'ave a shower, m'lady,' he said mischievously, and was gratified to hear the noise of disgust that signified she knew she was being made fun of. Refusing his hand, she stood on the mounting block and, once in the saddle, wheeled her horse around before galloping away without another word.

Ben Hover, carrying bags of oats from the lean-to, had overheard their brief conversation and he chuckled. 'You're a rum 'un an' no mistake, young Will,' he said. 'I ain't never seed anyone 'ceptin' the master get the better of 'er ladyship's tongue afore. She's got an acid one on 'er, right enough. Keep at it, lad. You never know, she might even get ter like yer after a few years!'

Laughing, they both went into the stables to start their day's work.

Riding across the pastures that surrounded the village, Megan Camberwell found herself thinking about the stable boy. His flippant attitude was extremely irritating. No one in her admittedly narrow acquaintance had ever spoken to her like he did. It didn't seem to matter what she said, or how demeaning she was, he just didn't care, and even sometimes gave back some wise-crack remark that she was unable to answer. It was very vexing. And he'd even kissed her! That she would never live down. It was dreadful. Disgusting even. And if she had not been going behind her uncle's back with the shooting practice, she would have told Lord Richard, and then the street brat would have been dismissed.

But a sneaking little part of Megan Camberwell did not want to see Will Tucker dismissed. She remembered the funny feeling his kisses had given her. Was it normal, she wondered? She only vaguely remembered seeing her parents kiss, and then it had been a chaste peck on the cheek. No one she knew kissed on the lips like that, though she had heard rumours about Nell and that boy who came to clean the chimneys. Mrs Proudfoot had caught them kissing behind the wash-house and the boy had gone in a great hurry, without sweeping all the chimneys. Then there was Amos Wilkins. He was much older than Nell but there had been talk about them as well, and the stable boy who had been there before Wilkins, when Nell had been only twelve or thereabouts. Had Nell tried to get Will to kiss her too? Everyone knew she went after anything in breeches. Suddenly Megan felt a stab of what could only be jealousy and she knew she didn't want Will to kiss Nell like he had kissed her.

Pitch-forking clean straw into the stalls, Will was thinking about Megan. She was his own age, he thought, though judging by the response to his kisses, had never been kissed before. But then one wouldn't expect a lady of her breeding to have done so. He wondered if he would ever be at liberty to get through that refined veneer. It was doubtful. Young gentlemen would be lining up to marry Lady Megan Camberwell when her grandmother thought it time. She would probably be presented at court. Wasn't that what young ladies like her did?

It was the one and only time in his life that Will felt envious of the upper classes.

Lord Richard duly left for Portsmouth. It was said around the house that his mother had wanted to give a farewell soiree for him and invite the gentry from the nearby villages, but her son had declined, saying he would much rather rejoin his regiment with the least possible fuss. Connie who, the day after his departure, resumed her lunches in Will's company, said that Lady Helen had shed tears. Not many came back from the war unscathed and she was naturally worried about her son's welfare but would never have suggested he not go. Sons of the gentry were expected to go to war as officers. After all, said Connie, if it weren't for them, who would the rank and file have to look up to?

Three nights after Lord Richard's departure, Will had a dream. He dreamt he heard a horse whinnying and the sound of a voice bidding it be quiet. He was dreaming he was in Portugal, listening to the sounds of a picket, keeping watch against the French, then the sounds came again. He awoke and realised that it wasn't a dream. Someone was in the stables talking to a horse.

Quietly, he crept to the ladder and looked down into the stables below. A dark shape came out of one of the stalls, leading a horse. The figure moved into the beam of light shed by the moon through the open doorway and he saw, to his surprise, that it was Megan. She was leading her horse, Dinah, and carried a saddle awkwardly under one arm.

'What are yer doin'?' His loud whisper made her jump so much, she dropped the saddle and the horse shied away.

'Oh my goodness! You scared me!' she said.

Will jumped down the ladder, barefoot and wearing only his breeches. Seeing him like that, tousle-haired and half naked, Megan felt her chest tighten suddenly.

'What are yer doin'?' Will asked again.

'I'm going for a ride,' she said, turning away from him to heave the saddle onto Dinah's back then tighten the girth strap.

'At this time o' night? Are yer mad?'

'I am neither mad nor unaware of the time,' she retorted.

Will noticed that Megan was wearing travelling clothes; a woollen dress, stout boots, jacket, cloak and gloves. His observant eyes also took in a bundle of what looked to be clothes wrapped in a blanket, and a carpet bag.

'Where are yer goin'?' he asked.

'None of your business,' she replied.

He did not intervene as she saddled the horse, nor when she struggled to fasten the carpet bag and bundle onto the horse's back but once she was mounted he caught hold of the bridle.

'Let go!' Megan yanked on the reins, trying to make him release his hold, but he held fast.

'Not until yer tell me what this is all about,' he said.

Seeing he meant what he said, and knowing she had nothing with which to bribe him, she capitulated.

70

'If you must know, I'm going to Portugal,' she said.

'What?' Will was stunned, then it came to him. The reason she had wanted to learn to shoot.

'Yer want to go ter the war?'

'Yes. I hear there are women there.'

'The only women are nurses and those who follow their men. I don't think yer either.'

'Maybe not now, but I can learn to be a nurse.' There was a determined lift to Megan's chin, though Will was not at all sure she had the right temperament to minister to the wounded.

'Yer uncle will never let yer go,' he said.

'Uncle Richard won't know until it's too late to do anything about it.'

'Megan, yer can't go by yerself! For a start I bet yer don't even know the way to Portsmouth.'

'I'll find it. I have a map.'

'But it's dark. Anythin' could happen to yer. There're plenty of men on the roads, men discharged from the army with no work, just waitin' for someone like yer ter come along so's they can rob 'em.'

'I'll be fine.' Megan tugged on the reins again but Will still had a firm grip. 'Now let me go and promise you'll say nothing when I'm missed in the morning.'

'That I won't do,' said Will. 'It's insane. In fact...' Suddenly he let go of the bridle and pulled her down from the saddle, his arm around her waist.

'Let go of me!' Her voice rose almost to a shriek as she struggled in his arms.

''Ush! Someone'll 'ear!' Will knew that should Ben Hover or anyone see them like this, they would assume the worst.

Megan quietened down. She did not want to be discovered either. Will half dragged her to a pile of straw bales and sat her down on it.

'Listen,' he said, standing over her. 'Yer can't go by yerself. 'Ave yer any idea what a long journey is like without a carriage or servants? Yer'll be wantin' to come 'ome after one night, I promise yer. Besides, somethin' might happen to yer. It's not safe fer a girl like you to travel alone.'

Megan looked at him for a long minute, then said, 'Well, you come with me then.'

Will blinked in surprise. 'Me? I can't take yer. Lord Richard'll thrash me dead for 'elpin' yer.'

Megan pouted. 'I thought you had more about you, Will Tucker. I thought maybe you had a spirit of adventure and the courage to use it. I heard tell you wanted to be a soldier but if you're so afraid of my uncle what are you going to be like when you meet up with the Frenchies?'

She was goading him and he knew it. He wanted to impress this girl, and she thought him a coward. Now might be the time to tell her how he came to be working for Richard Camberwell, and why he was not able to leave Camberwell Hall, but he couldn't do it. He was sure such an explanation would demean him even more in Megan's eyes.

'Well, if you won't come with me, I'll have to go by myself,' said Megan and stood up, then marched across to her horse.

Will was in a quandary. He had to make a decision. And fast.

'All right,' he said. 'I'll come with yer as far as Portsmouth.' Her uncle would most definitely send her home once he found her there anyway. He only hoped that he wouldn't get into a great deal of trouble for leaving his job and helping her go that far. A picture of the Newgate gallows flashed in front of his eyes.

He went up the ladder and put on all his clothes, even the hated boots. 'You do know I can't ride,' he said when he came down again. He was looking worriedly at the stalls, wondering which horse to take.

'Lord God above!' Megan exclaimed. 'Don't tell me you've never ridden a horse before?'

'No, I 'aven't!' he said angrily. 'When the 'ell would I 'ave 'ad the chance ter. I'm street scum, remember!'

She had the grace to look a little abashed. 'Take Lightfoot,' she said. 'He's gentle enough.'

Lightfoot was ill-named. He was a sturdy grey Welsh cob, slow, plodding and heavy footed, bought for Megan's use some years before, but Will was glad enough to have him for his first attempt at riding because, of all the Camberwell horses, he was certainly the one least likely to mind having a novice on his back. Will fetched a saddle and bridle and followed Megan's instructions as to mounting, which he did with only a modicum of difficulty. The instruction continued in hushed whispers as they rode out of the stables at a slow walk, keeping to the grass after that as much as possible, and leaving the estate the back way which led past the ornamental pond and the wood where the shooting lessons had taken place. The house was dark except for a faint glow of light in the east wing which Megan said was a lamp her grandmother kept lit all night.

The small gate in the outer wall of the estate did not pose a problem, for Megan had taken the key. Will wanted to say that she was taking up his profession but resisted the temptation. Staying in the saddle was taking up much of his concentration and he was just glad that the night was more or less cloudless so that the horses could see where they were going. Once out of the gate, the way led onto the rutted track into the village and the horses would have been in danger of falling if there was no moonlight.

There were two roads into and out of the village, one from the north which is the way Will had come with Lord Richard, the other heading south. That was the one Megan led them onto. It was not a road as such, more a wide beaten track, rutted and used by farm carts and wagons. Will had no knowledge of where Portsmouth was at all, except that it was by the sea. He didn't even know where he was now. He wondered if Megan knew, but then she had said she was in possession of a map, so he assumed she had some idea.

Will began to find the steady gait of the horse fell into an easy rhythm, but not so when they came to a long flat stretch of road and Megan said they would have to make better time. She urged her horse into a trot and then a canter, expecting Will to follow. The change of pace when Lightfoot followed suit, rocked Will perilously close to falling but he clung onto the reins and the cob's mane, and listened to Megan's shouted commands. Whatever else could be said about her, Will had to acknowledge that she was a very good horsewoman and he found that if he did as she instructed, it wasn't all that difficult.

Megan had obviously memorised the map, at least for the first part of their journey, because she seemed to know the roads to take when they came to the first few villages but then the clouds came up and hid the moon and it started to rain. Soon wet and bedraggled, she slowed to a halt under a tree and shouted to Will that they should look for somewhere to shelter.

Starting off again, they passed an inn but it was dark and unwelcoming, and Will was beginning to doubt whether they would ever find anywhere. He was wishing he'd stayed in his snug, dry loft when Megan pulled up again and pointed. There, in a field, was the dark shape of a barn.

They found the gate to the field half off its hinges, which they took to be a good sign that the barn might be unoccupied. It was, though it smelled strongly of cows, mice, and other odours neither could identify. It was also falling down. One side was completely open to the weather and half the roof had holes in it, but there was a corner that seemed dry enough, and they were just glad to get out of the rain which fell with uninterrupted persistence.

Not being able to see a thing inside the barn once they had dismounted, Will grabbed Megan's arm and whispered that she should be quiet. They stood in silence for a couple of minutes. As well as his pick-pocketing enterprises, Will had sometimes entered the houses of the well-to-do and stolen trinkets and jewellery, mostly on Polly Frinton's behalf. Stealth, and the ability to discern the smallest sounds, were part of the job and Will listened now for signs of habitation. Apart from the rustling of rats in old hay, there were none, though Megan shuddered when he told her what the slight sounds were.

Will tied the horses' reins to one of the remaining upright poles that supported the roof, unsaddled the animals and, holding Megan's arm, led her to the inky blackness at the rear of the barn. He felt around with hands and feet until they touched hay and mounded some up to make a cushion for them to sit on.

'What about the rats?' Megan whispered, even though there was no need for lowered voices.

'I doubt they'll bother us,' said Will. He was used to them. 'Sit down.'

Megan did so, gingerly. Will sat next to her. They said nothing, but leaned against the wall and listened to the sound of the rain pattering on the roof. Both cold and wet, they huddled together for warmth, and Will tentatively put his arm around Megan to warm her. Surprisingly, she didn't object.

Like two lost babes, they finally fell asleep.

6

Will awoke to grey daylight. It was still raining. Cold and stiff, he tried to sit up from the slumped position he had fallen into during the night but Megan was still asleep, lying on one of his arms which had gone numb. Carefully he managed to extricate himself without waking her, then shook his arm vigorously, trying to get the blood flowing properly again. Looking around, he saw that the barn was in even worse repair than had been obvious in the dark. There were cracks in all the walls, the roof was leaking in several places, and the pile of hay they had slept on was dank and musty. In fact, he thought they were lucky the wind was not gale force or the place might have fallen down around them in the night. He looked at Megan whose hair was tangled around her face and threaded with grass stalks. She looked very innocent and gentle in sleep, much nicer altogether, he decided.

Shivering, Will walked to the open side of the ramshackle building, patting the stoic horses on the way, and looked out at the weather. It wasn't very inspiring. The outlook was bleak and windy, gusts blowing the rain past his face. He needed to relieve himself but the thought of going outside to do it was not appealing, so he stood where he was and peed into the rain. This natural function was less easy for Megan to accomplish a few minutes later, when she woke with a bladder fit to burst and had to blushingly appeal to Will to keep his back turned while she did the necessary in another corner of the barn.

The thought of travelling further was not one either looked upon with much enthusiasm but they were hungry and needed to get to the next town or village to buy something to eat. Will's questions illicited the information that Megan had brought money with her, saved from the allowance she was given every month. Before they went on though, they stood in the doorway and had a look at the rudimentary map, trying to figure out how far they had come in the night. From the barn they could see the track they had been travelling along, but elsewhere was just fields and trees. Will decided their best bet was to just keep on going. The first village they came to would give them an idea of where they were on the map.

Will gave the horses some of the old hay to eat, and a puddle of rainwater provided them with a drink. He saddled them both while Megan attempted to tidy herself up with a hairbrush and comb. They were neither of them very communicative, Will because he was afraid of provoking her temper, Megan because she was viewing the morning with very mixed feelings.

They started off with clothes still damp from the night before, and were soon wet again, though Megan was the drier, having a cloak. As she rode, she wondered what Lady Helen would be thinking this morning when informed that her grand-daughter had gone missing. It was possible she might not even be missed until later in the morning because it would be assumed she had gone for an early morning ride as she often did. Megan suddenly felt a pang of guilt. Up until now she had not given a thought to Lady Helen and whether or not she would worry. She knew her grandmother loved her, but it only occurred to Megan now, how much she loved her too. The pang of home-sickness that attacked with the remorse almost made her stop the horse and turn back, but she resolutely sat up straighter and determined to carry on, though she vowed she would somehow get a message to Lady Helen just as soon as they reached Portsmouth, to tell her she was safe.

Beside her, and already soaked to the skin, Will was thinking that Megan was taking the discomforts of the journey a lot better than he thought she would. He had fully expected to have to put up with tantrums and endless complaints this morning, especially after such an uncomfortable night, perhaps even an abandonment of the journey altogether, but Megan kept silent about any distress she might be feeling. The rain, the cold, lack of comfort and hunger were all things he was used to, but Megan belonged to a more privileged society and had never before experienced them.

Truth to tell, Megan Camberwell was mentally gritting her teeth as the horses plodded through the mud and the puddles, bearing the discomforts only because of her noble purpose, which was already beginning to pale, and because of Will. Casting a sideways glance at him she marvelled at his patience, and indifference to the weather. Hatless, his thatch of yellow hair was plastered darkly to his head and his clothes were sodden, yet he rode as though the sun was shining. He caught her glance, turned to her and smiled and she found herself smiling back, somehow unable to ignore him or make some scathing remark as she probably would have done back home. It was strange, but she felt quite comfortable with him; surprising given their difference in backgrounds and the fact that it was the first time she had spent more than an hour or two with a boy her own age. She also had the feeling that despite the two kisses he had already bestowed on her, kisses that she thought about with both shame and secret pleasure, he would not take advantage of her. Maybe he was just easy to get along with. She spared a thought for him, wondering if he really wanted to travel with her, or whether he had agreed simply because she had goaded him into it. Or was he being chivalrous? The thought was appealing, but she doubted very much it was the reason he had agreed to come along. More likely he had wanted to get away from having to do any work for a while, but for whatever reason, having initiated the journey herself, to back out now would be both cowardly and falling right into Will's hands. She was almost sure he was expecting her to give up and return home.

Wet, uncomfortable and hungry though she was, longing with every fibre of her being for the comforts of home; the log fires, good food, clean clothes and a hot bath, she could not – would not – give in. Not with Will along. She had practically coerced him into accompanying her, in truth a little afraid to travel alone, especially at night, though she would never have admitted it and had hid her fear from him. But this morning, waking up knowing that a street urchin had slept close to her all night, having to relieve herself in some old hay with him in the same room, and probably looking like the worst scarecrow ever – well, it was enough to make anyone relinquish the most grand enterprise. Her grandmother would have an attack of the vapours for sure if she knew. And now the rain and the hunger that gnawed at her belly were making her miserable and cross, but she was determined not to complain and give Will Tucker the satisfaction of being proved right.

Little did she know, but Will was guessing her thoughts as the two horses splashed slowly along the wet and muddy track. He rightly supposed that Megan's silence was due to misery and bad-temper this morning and that she was hiding her feelings from him. He was amused rather than sympathetic. The whole thing was a fool's errand and he had been persuaded along only to provide protection, not support. He had every reason to believe that her

77

uncle would order Megan home immediately he saw them. He himself could very well be in Newgate Gaol a few days hence. The thought was not attractive and he made up his mind that if Lord Richard blamed him for Megan's foolhardy venture, then he would run away. He could easily lose himself in Portsmouth's streets which he imagined to be similar to London's. He might even take a berth on a ship as a cabin boy. The more he thought about it, the more the idea began to take root. He had a notion he would like to see far away places.

He was brought out of his reverie by Megan who said she was starving and suggested again that they should stop at the next village they came to. If it didn't have an inn, there would at least be a shop where they could buy some food. Will agreed. His stomach too had got used to being full lately, and was missing breakfast.

At last they reached the outskirts of a sizeable town and stopped at the first inn they came to. The rain had slackened off to a persistent drizzle. Tying the horses to a convenient rail outside, they went through the open doorway of the inn to find a man busily sweeping the floor. The dim room smelled of stale ale and tobacco smoke, but overlying it was the smell of bacon; an aroma that set both their mouths watering.

'My, but you be up early, young 'uns,' said the man, stopping his work and staring at the two from under bushy white eyebrows. They matched a long beard that tapered off somewhere near his waist. 'Do you be wantin' some breakfast?'

'Indeed we do,' said Megan. Will noticed she was using her hoity-toity voice again, as he liked to think of it, the voice that talked to servants who were on a rung far below her on society's ladder. It made Will's face burn, made him feel ashamed, and he wished he could say something to her about it, but he had the feeling she would never understand.

'We would like a full breakfast, my man. And tea. Lots of tea,' Megan demanded.

'Yes, ma'am.' The old man put a finger to his white forelock, as though tipping an imaginary hat, realising at once that, despite this girl's dishevelled appearance, she was gentry. And the man probably took him for her servant, thought Will wryly.

Breakfast was served by a cheerful woman, so round and fat as to waddle around the room like an oversized duck. She was seemingly the old man's daughter. The plates were piled high with bacon, sausages, eggs, and hunks of soft, new bread, dripping with butter. The woman poured them mugs of milk from a large jug.

'Fresh from the cows this mornin', me dears,' she said before going back to the kitchen to fetch a large pot of tea. Then she left them to eat.

The two said nothing, but ate like starving orphans. They obviously intrigued the woman who watched them from the kitchen doorway. She lumbered over to them once the plates were empty.

'So what brings you young 'uns out so bright and early on such a damp day?' she asked, curiosity getting the better of her.

Will glanced at Megan, hoping she would say nothing incriminating. 'Oh, we're just out for a ride,' she said.

The woman obviously didn't believe her. 'You bain't be runnin' away to get wed, I suppose?' she said, glancing slyly at Will.

Megan looked horrified, and opened her mouth to speak but Will said quickly, 'That's right, ma'am. 'Ow did you guess?'

The woman smiled, her small eyes almost lost in her fat cheeks. 'Aw, it's the way you look together, lad. Two such 'ansome children as you must be made for each other. I'm a-guessin' 'er pa says yer too young, am I right?'

'That y'are, ma'am,' said Will, warming to his theme. He lowered his voice as if not wanting to be overheard, though there was no one else in the room. 'We're goin' ter get married, then when the deed's done, we'll go back 'ome. It'll be too late ter do anythin' about it, 'specially when I've put a bun in the oven.'

Out of the corner of his eye, Will saw Megan's eyes grow rounder with shock, and he nearly burst out laughing. Instead, he lowered his voice still further. 'Could be there's one there already,' he said.

The woman said, 'Aw, now ain't that nice. So romantic. 'Ere, I'll put yer up a little somethin' for yer journey. Where did yer say yer was goin'?'

This stumped Will, but only for a second. 'We ain't made up our minds yet,' he said. He could see Megan's face was getting redder and redder.

'You wait there, dearie, an' I'll fetch yer a bite to take with yer,' said the woman, and she shuffled off back to the kitchen. When she was gone through the door, Megan leaned her face close to Will's.

'How could you?' she hissed. 'Bun in the oven indeed!'

'Well, yer wouldn't want 'er ter know what we're really doin' now, would yer?' he whispered back. 'Besides, now she thinks we're lovers, she's givin' us food for free, and that'll save us money.'

'Still, you could have thought of something else!' whispered Megan, then drew her head away swiftly as the woman came back into the room carrying a parcel which she put on the table.

'There y'are,' she said. 'Some bread and a nice cheese and a couple o' pasties. Oh, and some apples.'

'Thank yer, ma'am,' said Will, all smiles. ' 'Ow much does we owe yer fer the breakfast?'

'It's on the 'ouse, dearie,' said the woman kindly. 'It's not every day I gets to feed nice young folk such as yerselves. Now just yer take care along the road, yer 'ear?'

'Yes, ma'am. Thank yer kindly,' said Will.

Outside, the weather had improved and, although cloudy, the rain had stopped. This, and full stomachs, cheered Will and Megan. They pored over the map before riding on and decided their course lay more to the south west. There did not appear to be a well-beaten track but they found a country lane that wound its way between fields and stone walls and seemed to head in the right general direction.

They were only a short distance from the inn when they saw two men coming down the lane. Dressed in homespun breeches and woollen jackets, Will took them to be farm workers, especially when he saw they each carried a rake. Probably on their way to hay-making, he thought. As they closed on the two men, he saw one bend his head and say something to the other, stockier man.

They were nearly level when the men suddenly straddled the narrow lane, effectively stopping Megan and Will who had no room to pass. They stood there like two soldiers on guard, holding the rakes out in front of them.

'Well, now,' said the taller and bigger of the two, a deceptive smile crossing over his coarse features. 'Where would you two be off to this fine mornin'?'

'That's none of your business,' said Megan spiritedly, 'and I'll thank you to get out of the way!' She urged Dinah forward, intent on knocking the man down if need be. 'Come on, Will!'

'Now then, missy. There's no cause to be like that.' The man glanced sideways at the other, then suddenly dropped the rake he carried, reached out a hand, and grabbed the bridle of the horse as she tried to push past, pulling her to a halt.

'Let go!' Megan yanked at the reins but the man kept a strong hold.

Will kicked his heels into Lightfoot's flanks and the horse lumbered forward. The stockier man, who had the ugliest pock-marked face Will had ever seen, and a nose that had been broken more than once, dropped his rake too, and put a thick arm around Megan's waist, lifting her easily down from the horse, kicking and screaming.

'Let go of 'er!' Will shouted, trying to force Lightfoot between Megan and the man. The tall one caught hold of Will's leg and yanked hard, trying to pull him out of the saddle, but Will grabbed Lightfoot's plentiful mane and hung on tightly, twisting his leg in an attempt to make the man let go.

'You stay out o' this, boy,' growled the man with a sneer. 'Yer too young ter know what ter do with a pretty maid like this.'

'Will!' Megan's angry yells suddenly became a frightened scream and Will turned to see her struggling fiercely, and being carried towards the grass that sloped up to the stone wall at the side of the lane.

With a cry of anger, Will gave one almighty kick and succeeded in planting his booted foot in the tall man's midriff. The ruffian gasped and let go of Will's leg long enough for him to jump from the saddle and run after the stocky man then fling himself onto the other's back.

All three went down, Megan's yell cut off to a grunt by the sudden weight of the man and boy on top of her. The man in the middle heaved up onto his hands just as Will felt himself being lifted bodily by his breeches and the scruff of his neck and being thrown towards the stone wall. His head hit it and he lay stunned for a moment then was brought to his senses by Megan screaming blue murder.

Staggering upright he saw her lying on the grass on the other side of the lane, her skirts halfway up her legs, pinned by the shorter man who was kneeling astride her and fumbling for the string that held up his breeches. The big man was standing nearby with his back to Will, watching, hands on hips, shouting encour-

81

agement over Megan's yells.

Will shook his head, dizzy and wobbly, and started towards the girl, then stumbled over something. Looking down he saw it was one of the discarded rakes, and suddenly his head was clear. He picked it up and charged.

The head of the rake caught the ugly man right in the small of his back so that he fell on top of the struggling Megan who screamed even louder. Will swung the rake again and this time the tines clanged against the man's head, making him groan and fall sideways off the girl. Will turned, just in time to avoid the second fellow who was coming at him with the other rake. The two wooden staves clashed together, but Will was the first to bring his away and he jumped neatly over the other that swished under his feet, a massive swing that would have broken his legs had it connected. The missed blow threw the tall man off balance and Will shoved the rake's head into the other's stomach, causing air to explode from his lungs. The man clutched his belly while Will brought the rake round one more time and cracked it across the man's head. He went down like a scythed sheaf of corn.

'Will! Watch out!'

Megan's cry came as Will was grabbed from behind and pulled over backwards by Megan's abuser who had recovered sufficiently to resent Will's interruption. Will dropped the rake and fell, and a punch landed on his ear. He screamed in agony then felt another blow on his forehead. Through smarting eyes he saw the stocky man, blood running down the side of his face where the rake had hit him, draw back his fist to deliver another telling blow. With his last vestige of sense, Will rolled, and the blow missed his face but clipped his ear again. Through a fog, Will heard a thump and a cut off scream.

Then there was nothing but silence.

'Will! Will! Wake up! Tell me you're not dead! Oh, please tell me you're not dead!'

He was being shaken hard and the voice was coming from far away. Will opened his eyes to see Megan, tears running down her cheeks, shaking him so hard he felt like he was going to be sick.

'I'm not dead.' he croaked thickly. He couldn't be. There was too much pain and wasn't the pain supposed to stop when you died?

'Oh, thank God!' she said, and stopped shaking him.

Slowly he sat up and looked around. His ear was still ringing and felt twice as big as the rest of his head which pounded like the worst hangover. Megan was kneeling beside him, her bodice torn, her cloak and dress muddy, and her hair in an even worse tangle than when she had woken up that morning. The two farm workers were lying still, unconscious.

'How...?' he asked, gesturing weakly towards the man who had been thumping him.

'I hit him with the rake like you did,' she said proudly. 'It made him fall against the wall and he hit his head on it, I think. Anyway, he didn't get up again.'

'Thanks. Are yer all right?' To Will his voice sounded like he was in a cave, and he could hardly hear it over the ringing in his ear.

'Yes. And thank you too,' said Megan. Her voice was quiet, and serious. 'If you hadn't been here, that man would have...well, he would have raped me. Wouldn't he?' The realisation sobered both of them. 'You were right, Will. It's dangerous for a woman to travel alone. I was just a stupid girl trying to be too clever. And I thought you were dead!' The tears that had stopped when he recovered consciousness, started again.

Will said nothing but carefully stood up. His head spun and he gripped Megan's arm to steady himself, then put his arms around her. They stayed like that for some minutes while she cried on his shoulder.

'We must get you some help,' she said, pulling away at last, sniffing and fumbling in her dress pocket for a handkerchief, a flimsy piece of lace that Will privately thought too small to even mop up one tear properly. 'Your head's bleeding. So's your ear.' Will had thought the wetness on his head was dew from the grass, but now he put fingers there and they came away bloody.

'I'm fine,' he said but then the feeling of sickness that had persisted since his faint suddenly became overpowering and he fell to his knees and vomited up his breakfast.

'What a waste,' said Megan, her face wrinkled in disgust. She was already beginning to regret the moment of weakness that had induced her tears.

The injured men were beginning to stir so Will and Megan

hastily mounted the two horses that had spent the time calmly plucking at the grass growing beside the lane, but not before Will had picked up one of the rakes. It would make as good a weapon as any and he carried it under his arm when they rode on.

Nothing was said about the aftermath of the fight but both were thinking about it. Will was thinking that it was worth a sore head to have held Megan in his arms for a few minutes, and Megan was thinking that it had felt good to have Will's arms around her even though her dress was now spotted with blood and the hug had been rather weak. She also wondered at the absolute terror she had felt when she had momentarily thought that the farm worker had killed him. Did she really care that much for him, or was it just that she did not want to be left alone in a strange place? Something to ponder on. And worry about, because Megan Camberwell was very conscious of the distinction between their two classes and still considered Will little more than a filthy brat from the gutter. That he was the family's stable boy did not elevate him at all in her estimation. Class distinction was ingrained in her and Will was definitely down there below the peasants. No. Thinking about it, she was sure that her fear had been induced solely by the fact that Will's company was useful to her at present and had nothing to do with him as a person. She stole a glance at him. He did look pale. Maybe they had better get help. It would not do for them to be held up in any way.

In twenty minutes or so, they came upon a farmhouse near the side of the road, and Megan said they should go and enlist aid for Will, though he insisted he was all right. He maintained that they only needed to find a stream so that he could wash the blood off his head. However, Megan's strong obstinacy had by now reasserted itself and she over-rode his feeble protests, went up to the door, knocked peremptorily, and demanded that her friend be assisted. Fortunately for her, the farmer's wife who answered her knock was overawed by the sight of a haughty, if somewhat grubby, young lady who told her that she was the niece of a Lord, and a Lady herself. The woman was only too willing to help. Will's head was bathed, a bandage applied and Megan allowed to wash in water heated on a large range. The two were given strong tea and scones while Megan told the sordid tale, making Will out to be something between Sir Lancelot and Ivanhoe, an exaggeration Will found not totally unappealing. The farmer's wife advised them to stay a while, believing that with all those bruises, Will could probably use some rest, but neither he nor Megan were keen on the idea. Megan, having recovered her natural ebullience, wanted to get on to Portsmouth, fearing that her uncle's ship would sail without her, while Will just wanted the fussing to stop and be out in the fresh air again.

So it was, that after thanking the farmer's wife for her kindness, they headed for Ashton Forest. At around mid-day they stopped to eat the food the innkeeper's wife had given them for the journey and, nearly two hours later, came to the forest itself. Riding through it they got lost, and it led to their first real argument.

After riding in what appeared to be aimless circles for an hour or more, Will stopped Lightfoot. The weak sun sent pale rays through the trees and from its place in the sky, he tried to work out in which direction they were heading.

'I think it's that way,' he said pointing west.

'No. We just came from there,' said Megan, brushing the hair from her face irritably.

'No we didn't. We came from that way,' said Will, jerking his thumb north.

'Poppycock!' said Megan. 'Well, I'm going that way.'

Will reached out and held Dinah's reins. 'Bloody 'ell, Megan! When will yer stop bein' so bloody stubborn! It's the wrong way, I tell yer!'

'If you don't let go of those reins right now, Will Tucker, I'll tell Uncle Richard this was all your idea!' said Megan. 'And mind your language when you speak to me. Besides, I'm not Megan to you. You're supposed to say, "my lady".'

'Your uncle'll probably blame me anyway,' said Will philosophically, not letting go, and ignoring her demand that he address her properly. 'I told yer before, yer don't behave like a lady, so I won't treat yer as one. And if I think yer need swearing at, I'll bloody well swear!'

Megan was so cross that she yanked the reins suddenly and Will yelped as they whipped through his hands, burning the palms. With a yell of delight, she cantered off through the forest.

'Bloody 'ell!' muttered Will. He kicked Lightfoot into motion and went after her, brushing low thin branches out of his way as the horse blundered through the trees.

85

He kept the girl in sight for only a few minutes before she was lost to him because Dinah was able to go much quicker than the stolid Welsh cob. He stopped, wondering what to do, listening for the sounds that would tell him where she was. There was nothing, then suddenly a thud and a cry. Will's heart dropped and he kicked Lightfoot hard to get him moving faster.

'Megan!' he shouted. 'Where are yer?'

'Here, Will! Over here!' The call came from his right. Will turned Lightfoot towards the sound.

He came upon Megan kneeling beside Dinah who was standing awkwardly.

'What's wrong?' he asked, dismounting.

'She stumbled on a tree root. She's hurt her leg. I nearly fell off.'

The look of distress on her face called out to him to comfort her, but some little demon inside made him say instead, 'Yer shouldn't've ridden off like that.'

She looked up at him and scowled. 'It's your fault for arguing with me. If you hadn't made me cross, I wouldn't have.'

Will resented being blamed for something that was not his fault. He dismounted, saying, 'So, Miss Know-all. What do yer suggest we do now? I'm tired, my 'ead 'urts, and I'm fed up of bein' yer scratchin' post. And I'm 'ungry and thirsty. Why didn't yer think to bring some food with yer? At least then we wouldn't be looking fer somethin' ter eat all the time.'

'What did you expect me to do. Steal it from the kitchen?' she asked.

Will shrugged, thinking that was exactly what he would have done had he been given warning of the enterprise, but now he didn't much care. He had spoken the truth. They were lost, stuck here in a forest with only a little food and nowhere to get any more, and his ear was aching so much it was making him feel nauseous again. He sat down on a pine-needle covered bank and put his bandaged head in his hands.

Megan stared at him and the anger that had flared briefly suddenly disappeared. She went over to Will and sat beside him. Rather surprisingly, she laid her head on his shoulder.

'Oh, Will, I'm sorry,' she said. 'Does it hurt much?'

'I'll live.' He lifted his head and looked at her. 'I'm sorry too.' He stood up and went over to the horse. 'Can Dinah walk?'

Megan joined him. 'I think so.' She smiled. 'We'll go your way.'

They set off again, leading the horses. Dinah was limping and they had to go slowly. 'When we get out of the forest, we'll 'ave ter find someone who knows how ter fix 'er leg,' said Will, 'otherwise we'll 'ave ter leave 'er and both ride Lightfoot.'

'I won't leave her behind, and Lightfoot'll take ages to get there!' Megan scowled again. 'Uncle Richard will sail without us!'

Privately Will thought that wouldn't be such a bad thing, but for now they needed to find help for the horse, and the way out of the forest.

The afternoon wore on. Will wished he could ride, but the tree branches hung too low. As it was they had to keep twisting and turning to get around them and he was no longer sure they were going in the right direction. His headache was, if anything, worse, and he sometimes found his vision blurring, but he said nothing to Megan, fearing she would either have another tantrum or be frightened.

At last he imagined the trees were beginning to thin and he felt a leap of hope that they had found the edge of the forest. Peering ahead, he suddenly stopped.

'What is it?' asked Megan, alarmed.

'Look there. Through the trees.'

Megan looked where he was pointing and saw a splash of colour. 'What is it?'

'Caravans,' he said. 'Gypsies.'

'Gypsies?' Megan stared at him. Sometimes the Romany bands came to their village but were not usually well received. Often they were accused of any petty thieving that went on while they were around. From what she had seen they were tinkers who tried to make a living selling pegs and colourful shawls, or mended pots and pans and told fortunes for a penny. She grabbed Will's hand, suddenly scared.

'Can we go around them?'

'I don't know. Maybe they're friendly.' Will's eyes were hopeful as he looked at her. 'I bet yer they could fix Dinah's leg.'

'Do you think so?'

'They 'ave 'orses ter pull their caravans. They probably know a lot more about 'em than I do.'

So saying, he pulled on Lightfoot's reins and Megan could do nothing but follow as Will walked into the clearing.

7

There were three caravans in the clearing, wooden, with large spoked wheels, painted in gaudy primary colours, though the paint was faded and peeling in places. Steps led up to their doors, and lace curtains graced the windows. Three sturdy ponies stood cropping the grass under some trees. At first there seemed to be no one around, but then one of the caravan doors opened and a bent, thin old woman stepped out. She didn't seem surprised to see them.

'I saw you coming,' she said in slow, thickly accented English. Will wondered how she had done so when the caravan windows faced the other way.

'Come,' she said, and beckoned them. Warily, the two led the horses over to the steps.

The old woman watched them keenly, with little black eyes like a bird's that flitted from one to the other. She was small and bird-like herself. Her hair that lay long and white down her back, was partially hidden under a red scarf, and her face was a wrinkled nut-brown. She wore a long, multi-coloured skirt, a black blouse, and a wide paisley patterned shawl. Her feet were bare.

'Your horse. She is hurt,' the woman said.

'Yes,' said Will. 'Can yer 'elp 'er?'

The woman said nothing but came down another step until she stood only a little higher than Will and put a gnarled hand gently on his head. 'You are hurt too.' She lifted his chin and stared into his eyes. 'I see it. You need rest.'

There came the sound of a baby's cry from inside the caravan and the old woman called something over her shoulder in a language Will didn't know. The crying subsided.

Suddenly there was a shout and an angry voice snapped quick words in the same language the woman had spoken. Will spun round and tightly clasped the rake that he had held in his hand all the time they were walking, using it as a walking stick and to brush aside tangles of undergrowth.

Coming towards them were five adults and six children. All

carried something; wood, skins of water, or bowls of blackberries and raspberries, and two of the three men had dead rabbits dripping with blood, fastened to sticks. The man who had shouted ignored Will's battle stance and spoke to the old woman and there followed a quick-fire conversation which, Will presumed, centred around himself and Megan. There was much pointing at Dinah and Will, until eventually, whatever the old lady said, calmed the man down a little and he stamped off to one of the other caravans. A woman Will assumed was his wife, went with him, and then sat on the wagon steps and started to skin the three rabbits with quick strokes of a sharp knife.

Will glanced at Megan who was taking it all in with wide eyes. So far she had said nothing and he was glad, because he was very afraid that she would say something derogatory and make the gypsies angry.

The old woman hobbled down the steps and ran a hand over Dinah's foreleg. She said something to one of the children, a girl a year or so younger than Will, and the girl ran into the caravan and fetched a bowl of salve that the woman applied gently to the horse's bruised limb. She then instructed a boy of about ten to tether Dinah and Lightfoot to a tree nearby.

'Now you,' she said to Will. 'Come.'

Will glanced at Megan. The old woman, as if reading his thoughts, beckoned and said again, 'Come. She will not be harmed.'

The other young woman and most of the children were gazing at Megan with suspicion, but then the smallest girl, a pretty child with long black hair tied in braids, went shyly up to her and took her hand. Megan smiled rather anxiously, but the old lady spoke sharply to the others and then they clustered around her and took her to a log near the remains of a fire that one of the men was feeding with wood, so that the flames suddenly flared up hungrily. They sat her down and one of the children brought her a wooden bowl containing some of the blackberries.

Seeing that Megan would be safely looked after, Will followed the old gypsy up the steps and into the caravan. He was surprised to see it was just like a little house inside, with wooden bench beds against the walls that seemingly became cushioned seats during the day. In the centre was a table and, in one corner, a small unlit iron stove with a narrow chimney that went up through the roof. A baby gurgled in a basket on one of the beds and all around the top of the walls were cupboards, and parapeted shelves that held all sorts of gaudy knick-knacks, jars and bottles. Bunches of herbs, onions and spices hung from the roof and walls. The caravan was a mixture of aromas from them. In the middle of the table was something covered with a cloth, round in shape. Will wondered what it was but then the woman spoke to him.

'Sit.' The matriarch indicated a bench and Will sat down. Gently she removed the bandage and examined the swollen and cut ear, and the bumps on Will's head. She waved a finger in front of his eyes. 'Follow,' she said. Will tried, but the finger went out of focus. 'It hurts much,' she said, touching his ear lightly. Will nodded. He was beginning to feel rather odd, as though this was not really happening to him but to someone he was watching. The smell of herbs and spices was overpowering. The woman busied herself for a few minutes with herbs and mortar and pestle, poured some water over the herbs in a bowl, stirred the mixture, and handed it to him. 'Drink,' she said. It was a bitter brew and Will grimaced at the taste. Then he felt the gypsy plastering some sort of salve on the side of his head and heard her call to someone outside. The door opened. Will was finding it impossible to keep his eyes open, and his limbs were great weights. He tried to lift an arm and was hardly able to, then he felt someone pushing him gently down onto the cushions. The woman was telling him to sleep. His eyes closed.

He awoke to flickering light and the sound of music. Momentarily forgetting where he was, he sat up, and winced as his head reminded him. Had he fainted again? Or had the brew given him by the old gypsy made him sleep? He touched his head and discovered that it had been bandaged again. He was still in the caravan, on the cushioned bench, and the light and music were coming from outside. Slowly he stood up. The pain was much less and he felt a good deal stronger.

He opened the caravan door and went down the steps, then stopped in surprise at the sight that met his gaze. The two young women and the older girl were dancing, swirling round the fire, stepping in time to music from a violin and a guitar played by two of the men. He stared at Megan. The girl actually looked as though she was enjoying herself, laughing and clapping her hands, trying to imitate the steps of the dancers with the small girl clapping excitedly by her side. Will grinned, and suddenly felt great. The wild music, the darkness of the surrounding trees, the flickering flames and the wood smoke lent the scene an aura of mystery and excitement that sent a thrill through his young bones.

'Come, come! You feel better.' The old gypsy called to Will from her place by the fire, seeming to take it for granted that her potion had cured Will of his aches and pains. He wondered how she knew everything, but then his mind was taken off that thought by the older girl who stopped dancing and picked up a bowl that stood on a stone near the fire. She came across to him, caught hold of his hand and led him to a log next to the old gypsy, then pushed the bowl and a spoon into his hands. Will saw it was rabbit stew. He tasted it, then ate ravenously. The girl filled his bowl again from a huge cooking pot that hung over the fire, and he ate that too. Replete, and with a wooden mug of elderberry wine in his hand, he sat back to watch the dancers and listen to the music.

The matriarch told him, in broken English, that they were Romany gypsies, come many years before from Hungary, a far-away country Will had never heard of. The three men were her sons. Two had wives, the youngest did not. The children belonged to the two married couples. For the most part, they were a solitary people and some, including her eldest son, did not like mixing with folk who were not their own kind, hence his harsh words when he had first seen Will and Megan. But she was the leader of the group so the younger ones obeyed her wishes, and she had felt a strange compulsion to help them.

While the old lady spoke, the eldest girl sat on Will's other side staring at him until her father, the matriarch's eldest son, who still flashed dark looks at Will, said something sharply to her making her blush. Quickly she went and sat beside her small sister. However, Will could still feel her eyes on him. Later, the girl danced with the youngest man, her uncle, her skirt flaring out close enough to the fire for the draught to send sparks leaping into the sky.

Will, with Megan beside him, drank more of the heady wine and could see that the gypsies drank it too, so that the music played faster and livelier, until the girl's partner dropped out of the dance, exhausted, and only the girl danced on. She watched Will, smiling an enigmatic smile, until he couldn't take his eyes off her, mesmerised by the vibrant colours of her dress, the sweeping, swirling movements as she seemed to dance just for him. It was as if everyone else was blotted out and there were just the two of them. Her black eyes never left him, drawing him in, until he realised with a shock that the music had stopped and so had she. He shook his head, as though to rid himself of dizziness, and felt Megan tugging on his arm, asking him if he was all right. He nodded and forced himself to take note of his surroundings again.

The dancing went on until late, even the girl's father thawing eventually, due, Will suspected, to the potent elderberry wine, then the matriarch saw Megan yawning and told one of her daughters-in-law to show her to a bed. Having slept for a long time earlier, Will sat up beside the fire, trying to make conversation with the unmarried son who was only a few years older than himself. It was a conversation carried on in halting English and mime, but he found out that his life in London wasn't so different from the gypsy's. Both lived on a subsistence level, though Will found his food and money in the streets, whereas the gypsy found his in the countryside and villages. The night grew colder and the young man brought blankets. The two sat beside the fire until Will's head began to nod. The gypsy led him to the caravan he shared with his brother's family and Will slept there on the floor until the family stirred in the morning.

Will and Megan were getting ready to leave when the old lady beckoned them to go into her caravan. Curious, they did so, and Will saw that the strange object which had been covered with a cloth the evening before was now uncovered. It was a large glass ball.

'A crystal ball!' gasped Megan. She had heard of such things but never seen one. Will frowned. He had never even heard of one before. 'It's supposed to tell the future,' Megan whispered.

'It can, child,' said the old woman. 'I wish to tell yours.'

'But aren't we supposed to cross your palm with silver?'

'Yes. But you have little money. For you it is free.' The gypsy studied them keenly. 'You interest me.'

She made Megan sit on one side of the table while she sat on the other and looked closely into the ball. Megan too gazed into the milky white glass but could see nothing.

'What do you see?' she asked impatiently.

'Be patient, child,' said the gypsy. There was a pause, then, 'I see mountains and a river and smoke. A lot of smoke. A town, maybe a castle or a fort.' The old woman paused again. 'I see a man. He is handsome. But cruel. So cruel.' The old lady gasped and looked horrified for a moment.

'What is it?' Megan leaned forward anxiously, but the old woman's expression was normal again.

'I see another young man. And you, smiling.' After a moment, the gypsy looked up. 'There is confusion and danger in your life but you will find your destiny and come to know what is truly important. That is all.'

Megan gave her place to Will, wondering what it all meant. The old woman closed her eyes and rested her hand on the ball for a few seconds before peering into it again.

Will watched her face, and was disturbed by the expressions that flitted across it; first worry, then horror and alarm before, finally, a smile. He met her gaze questioningly.

'I see guns and fighting and two men who will be a great influence on your life,' she said. 'And two women.'

'What are they like?' he asked, hoping that one might be Megan.

'That I cannot say. The ball is too misty.' The old woman lied. She had seen the women clearly but was not going to tell him. Now her small black eyes stared into Will's blue ones.

'Your face will attract people, but I see hatred too and great danger. Your life will greatly benefit another but it will be hard and there will be times you despair, but you have courage and you too will find your destiny.' she said. She stood up and put out her hands, touching each of them on the shoulder. 'Now is time for you to go.' Before they left the caravan, she gave Will a small bottle of the potion and a pot of the salve she had smeared on his head. She wondered whether to tell him that her gaze into the crystal ball had foreseen a use for such things, but decided not to. If what she had seen was true, he would have plenty of other important things to occupy him.

Will saddled the horses and they left the gypsies, thanking them profusely for their kindness, especially the old woman. The girl who had danced for him pressed something into Will's hand as Megan was saying her goodbyes and when he looked, Will saw it

93

was a stone, shiny, round, and grey in colour, perfect except for a small hole in the centre. On the one side was the imprint of a leaf, a fern. Will didn't know it, but the stone was a fossil, possibly thousands of years old.

'It is good luck,' whispered the girl, looking around warily to make sure her father wasn't watching. Her accent was so thick, Will could hardly understand her, but he nodded. He would keep the stone as a memento of his night with the gypsies.

Dinah walked with scarcely a limp now, and Will's head ached not at all. It turned out that the gypsies' camp was very close to the western edge of the forest. Following their directions, the two only had to travel for a short distance through ever thinning trees before they reached the open air again.

They made good time that day, stopping briefly around noon to eat some food given them by the gypsies. Finding their place on the map was easy now because the forest was marked. They crossed a bridge fording a river and followed a well-beaten track that took them to Horsham where they decided to stop for the night. They had a minor argument over whether to use some of Megan's money and stay at an inn. Megan was desperate for a few home comforts, longing for hot water and a soft bed, but Will, who was more used to roughing it, said they should save the money for food as they still had a long way to go. In the end they compromised because it was cloudy and chilly. If it did not cost too much they would stay at an inn, but only in its cheapest room which would probably not have the luxury of a feather bed or the services of a maid. Megan grouched, but Will was adamant.

Horsham was a bustling town compared to the sleepy villages they had passed through, and the two caused no comment as they rode down the main street. The first inn they came to was a coaching stop and a poor prospect for cheap accommodation, so they carried on, Megan beginning to despair, until they saw another, smaller place down a side street.

The inn was tiny, tucked away between a pawn shop and a grimy building that housed several families in cramped discomfort. They tied the horses to a broken railing and Will pushed open the door.

The room inside was dingy and empty except for a hunched figure in the corner by a cold fireplace. Will was wondering how to attract the attention of the landlord when the figure stood up and hobbled towards them.

'Can I 'elp yer, young sir?' The voice was cracked, the manner obsequious. Will could not see the man clearly in the darkened room, but the smell of drink was strong enough to fell an ox. Megan shivered with a sudden chill that did not entirely emanate from the cold room, and touched Will's arm.

'Let's go somewhere else, Will,' she whispered.

Will also felt uncomfortable and he turned to leave, but quick as a lizard's tongue the man's gnarled, clawed hand flashed out and clung to Will's sleeve.

'Come, come, young sir. I've a nice room upstairs'll do well fer yer and yer doxy...'

'Doxy?' Megan's voice was loud with righteous indignation and her hand swept out, connecting with the landlord's thin shoulder and making him let go of Will's arm. She took hold of it instead and pulled Will towards the door. 'I have never been so insulted in all my life!'

The man wheedled and whined but the two went swiftly outside to the horses, Will shooing away a small crowd of barefoot children who had gathered round them.

'That man's creepy, and has the manners of a pig!' said Megan, still smarting from the insult as they rode away.

Will agreed. 'We'll look for somewhere else,' he said.

They finally found an inn on the edge of town that looked more suitable for Megan's sensibilities and, although it offered only enough hot water for her to wash her face and the mattresses were stuffed with straw instead of the feathers she craved, the food was hot and plentiful and they started out early the next day rested and in good heart.

That day they had some more good luck and were able to hitch a ride on a farmer's cart, giving their own horses a rest by tying them onto the back of the cart so that they followed behind. When they reached the coast, their spirits were raised even more. They delighted in the sound of the waves crashing to shore and the cries of the gulls wheeling overhead. The sight of the sea was something of a revelation to Will who had only seen it before from London's wharves where the water was dark, dirty, and sluggish. Now the vistas from the cliffs and beaches made his heart light and filled him with a sense of excitement he had never felt before. Somehow he was sure that his destiny lay beyond the sea-filled horizon. Once they stopped on a headland and stared at the tall masts of a frigate patrolling the channel, helping to keep Bonaparte's navy at bay, a navy that had been nearly destroyed by Nelson at Trafalgar six years before. Megan told him there must be other ships out there with the frigate, but they could see no more masts or top sails and Will wondered why, when the sea seemed so flat. So then Megan told him that it was because of the curvature of the earth. Although he had heard that the world was round, Will had never before seen evidence of the fact and was fascinated. He could have stood and watched the horizon for hours, waiting for more ships to appear above it, but Megan was eager to get on, so they trotted the horses back to the path and headed steadily westwards.

Their journey was easier now and they did not have to look at the map. All they had to do was keep the sea to their left and even when the tracks and pathways took them out of sight of it, the smell, and the clear view of the sky over it, kept them heading in the right direction.

They bought food at a fishing village; smoked herrings and winkles, and slept that night on a bed of fishing nets in an abandoned rowing boat, not realising until they rode on the next morning, how close they were to their destination.

They had been travelling barely half an hour and rounded a headland before the sight of masts and the shouts of people told them they were nearing a large town and at eight-thirty on the morning of the 27th of September 1811, Megan and Will entered Portsmouth.

Immediately they entered the streets, Will felt at home and excited, despite the fact that they must now be wary of discovery. Lord Richard Camberwell was somewhere in this town. For a time they wandered the streets, but although they saw red-coated soldiers amongst the many naval personnel and merchant seamen, they did not see any sign of Megan's uncle.

Will wondered how Megan was going to go about getting a berth on the ship that was taking soldiers to Portugal. A small niggling part of him wished her uncle would see them and send Megan back home to safety, but he knew that he would be in loads of trouble himself for bringing her to Portsmouth, and for that reason did not wish them discovered.

They found a small tavern near the docks where they stabled the horses and stowed their small belongings. Megan was now used to Will sleeping in the same room as her, and she never made a murmur when he asked for only one room to save them money. But she might have said something had she noticed the sly look the woman gave Will, a look that plainly said she was thinking much the same thoughts as other people had on their journey; that the two were lovers.

Later, sitting on the one bed in that room, Will asked Megan what her plans were now they had reached their destination.

'We have to find out which ship the soldiers are going on and I must board it without being seen,' said Megan blithely, brushing her hair vigorously, trying to get rid of tangles put there by the sea breezes. 'Once the ship's under way, there'll be nothing Uncle Richard can do.' She made it all sound so easy.

'What about Dinah?'

'You can take her back with you. And I'll give you a letter to tell my grandmother I'm safe.'

Will was thinking that should he do what she wanted, it would mean instant dismissal for having assisted in her adventure, despite the debt he still owed Lady Helen's son. He had done a lot of thinking during the last couple of days, thoughts that revolved around himself and his future, and Megan's welfare. It had been obvious on their journey that a girl alone was considered fair game for some unscrupulous scoundrels, and Will had come to think of himself as Megan's protector. Also, he was eager, now that the journey was started, to finish the job and become a soldier. He had a feeling that in the unlikely event he was allowed to stay on at the Hall, life there without Megan would become tedious and boring, despite the attentions, welcome or otherwise, of Connie and Nell. Tentatively he put forward the idea that he accompany her all the way to Portugal.

Megan frowned. She had become used to Will's company and he made a useful servant, yet his plan annoyed her.

'How am I to get the horses back home, and a message to grandmother if you come with me?' she asked, vexed.

Will shrugged. 'Pay someone?' he suggested.

'I don't have enough money left.'

'Don't yer 'ave anythin' yer can sell?'

'No. Yes.' She held up a finger. 'I have this ring but it was my mother's. I don't want to sell it.'

'Pawn it then.'

'And how am I to redeem it if I'm on a ship, you stupid boy!' Megan was getting really annoyed now. Why couldn't Will just stick to their original plan?

Will saw her point. They sat in silence for a while, then he heaved a big sigh. 'There is another way to get money,' he said slowly. Even if it meant Megan would hate him even more, to help her he would have to reveal the truth about his past.

'How?' Megan was sceptical.

'I'll steal some.'

She stared at him. 'What?' she said. 'You can't do that! It's...well...it's stealing!'

'I know,' said Will, his voice resigned to the inevitable. 'I've done it before.'

An expression of astonishment crossed Megan's face, quickly followed by realisation, and her eyes widened.

'You're a thief?'

'I suppose so, yes. But mostly only so's I could eat,' he hastened to add, purposely forgetting the times when he was much smaller and Polly had made him sneak into the mansions of the rich to steal jewellery and expensive trinkets which she had then fenced herself. He had not done that in a long time, not since he'd got too big to squeeze through narrow window spaces.

'Does Uncle Richard know?'

'Yes.'

She put her head on one side and studied him silently. Somehow, after the first shock of his revelation, it excited her that Will was not just the street urchin she had thought him. His profession, however unlawful, elevated him in her eyes. Another rung up the ladder. Will, who thought her silence was because she was shocked beyond words, sighed again.

'I stole yer uncle's purse,' he said.

'You did?'

Then Lady Megan Camberwell did something that came as a complete surprise to Will. She started to laugh. She laughed so hard she fell back onto the bed they were sitting on. Will stared down at her in amazement.

'Yer don't think that's bad?' he asked.

'I think it's priceless!' she said. 'That Uncle Richard could let himself be the victim of a pickpocket! After everything he said to me about the bad streets of London!' She laughed again. 'But he caught you,' she said, sitting up.

'It's a long story,' said Will.

'Tell me,' she demanded.

So Will told her the whole story. Megan listened avidly until he had finished.

'So you're supposed to stay at Camberwell Hall until you've paid off the debt,' she said thoughtfully. For the first time Megan realised what Will had done by coming to Portsmouth with her. Not only would he be in trouble for encouraging her recklessness, but he would have made things much worse for himself by leaving the Hall.

'What would have happened to you if Uncle had had you arrested?' she asked.

'I would be rottin' in Newgate Gaol,' he said. 'I might even've been 'anged by now.'

'Hanged?'

'They 'ang thieves yer know.'

Megan considered this. 'Were you ever caught before?'

'No.' Will said this proudly. He had been good at his trade. 'And I wouldn't've been this time either if I 'adn't gone to yer uncle's rescue.'

'Then he should have let you go,' declared Megan. 'I shall tell him so when I meet up with him.'

'Which won't be too soon, I 'ope,' said Will fervently. It was one meeting he was not looking forward to.

'I can't ask you to steal again. You'll have to go back with the horses.' Megan sounded determined.

'No. I can't leave yer 'ere alone.'

She rounded on him. 'I don't need you, Will! You have to go home with the horses!'

'Yer can't make me!' he countered. He wondered if she was concerned for his welfare or just being stubborn, and felt put out that his company obviously meant so little to her. He had rather hoped that their enforced togetherness might have made her like him a little more but it would seem not to be the case.

They sat in silence for a while, neither willing to give ground, then Will asked her how she was going to find out which ship was taking the soldiers to Portugal. For either of them to go walking about town was to risk discovery.

'I don't know,' she said, not having thought that far.

'I'll find out,' said Will. 'I'll go down ter the docks this afternoon.'

'No. It's my job,' said Megan.

'I'm better at goin' places without bein' seen,' Will pointed out. 'I'll go.'

Megan had to concede that he was probably right so, without too much argument, he left her resting on the bed that afternoon, and walked down to the docks.

Will felt right at home mingling with the hawkers, urchins, shoppers and business men who populated Portsmouth's streets that day. No one took any notice of him. After days on the road his new clothes were dirty, and he had discarded his boots so that he looked like any other street urchin. The wind blew off the sea, bringing with it the smell of fish and the pungent odour of ships at anchor. A long sea voyage made a ship smell worse than a midden, and the bilges, rotten with stagnant water, dead rats and algae, were an overwhelming stink that the fresh breeze was blowing to shore. Will felt happy. There was no way he was going back to Camberwell Hall, despite what Megan might say. Tonight he would steal her enough money so that she could pay a man to take the horses back home, and he would go to war and become a soldier.

Although enjoying the noise and bustle of the town, Will was ever watchful for Lord Richard Camberwell. Though he saw a small group of redcoats being marched along the street by a vociferous sergeant, he saw no sign of his employer.

He came to the docks and stared at the ships moored there. Right at the end nearest him was a brig whose sailors were loading a cargo of wool to the accompaniment of shouts from stevedores on the dockside. A fishing boat swayed on her mooring ropes, her seamen busy on deck, mending nets torn at sea. Looking between the two vessels, Will could make out a third-rate British warship of the line standing out to sea, its lion figure-head shining in the sun. Walking along the dock he came to a great East Indiaman unloading tea, spices, and silks from the Orient. Anchored away from the dockside was a frigate waiting for one of the ships to put to sea so that she could come into port. Will was mesmerised by the noise and activity. He had loved to go to London's docks and dream of the places the great cargo ships had come from and now he stood on the corner of an alley between a ship's chandlers and a grog shop, and watched.

Suddenly his attention was taken away from the ships by an educated voice close by, talking loudly. Turning, he saw two men strolling down the alley towards him. He caught his breath when he saw that both wore the red jackets and gold braid of officers in the British infantry, but then he breathed again, realising that neither was Lord Camberwell.

'Three more days and we'll be away from here, James, back to that Godforsaken place.' The voice was petulant.

'At least it'll be a little warmer there,' said the other.

'Only for another month or so,' grumbled the first. 'The winters in the Peninsula are colder than charity, especially in the hills, and that's where we're going.' The speaker came to where Will was leaning on the wall and, although there was plenty of room to get by, shoved past him, knocking him against the brickwork.

'Get out of my way, brat!' he said with a sneer. 'Can't you see I'm an officer?'

Will rubbed a shoulder that had been roughly bumped on the wall and stepped back, but he said nothing. The two men rounded the corner, and Will saw that the one who had pushed him walked with a limp. They stopped walking and stood looking at the frigate. Will stayed where he was, listening, hoping to glean information.

'That's her there,' said the first man, who, now he was out of the dark alley, Will could see was tall and heavy-set. His red jacket tails flapped on thick thighs as he lifted a hand to point to the frigate out at sea. 'That's the heap of wood and canvas to which we must trust our lives, James.'

'I quite enjoy the sea,' said the other man whose attention was briefly taken by two young women strolling slowly along the wharf. Judging by their painted faces and coarse language in response to comments from the dock workers, they were whores touting for early trade.

'Well, I don't like being afloat at all,' said the grumbling officer. 'Give me the earth under my feet any day. Though not the earth of the Peninsula.'

101

'If you didn't want to go to war, Robert, you shouldn't have become a soldier.' The young officer leaned on the wall facing the sea, only a few feet away from Will, who still stood at the corner of the alley, listening to the conversation. The man took a small cigar from his pocket and proceeded to try and light it, though the wind kept blowing out the flame in the tinderbox.

'Going to war was not my idea, James. Second son and all that,' said the heavy-set man peevishly. 'My brother Edward was the heir. My legacy was a damn war wound.'

'At least you were allowed to come home. Most men with a wound like that would have stayed behind.' There was a scathing note in the younger officer's tone.

'And ended up losing the leg,' retorted the man called Robert who obviously had no faith in the army's doctors. 'Privileges of rank, James. I'm a Major and I demanded to be sent back to England to recuperate. If that blasted man Camberwell could be sent home, then so could I.'

'Richard's wounds were a lot worse than yours, Robert,' said the other man mildly, giving up on the cigar and putting it and the tinderbox back in his pocket. 'And he has to see that the recruits are brought from Winchester too. You've been sitting on your arse since you got here.'

'What if I have? Doesn't a man who's been in Portugal for nearly two years deserve a rest?' The Major was annoyed. 'Two damn years of poor food, too much sun, freezing winters, poxed whores and lice-ridden beds.'

The other officer, a Captain, laughed. 'We do much better than the men, Robert.'

'And so we damn well should! I'm the son of an earl, damn it! The rank and file are nothing but criminals and peasants. They don't deserve anything better.'

The Captain said nothing. He had heard the same litany many times before and Major Robert Underwood was a man it was best not to argue with too loudly. He shivered in the cooling air.

'I'm going back to the lodgings,' he said. 'Can't even get a damn cigar lit in this wind.' So saying, he started to walk away along the wharf and the Major, realising he had lost his audience, followed him.

Will came out of the alley into the weak sunlight and stared at the frigate wallowing on the small waves. So that was the ship that would take him to Portugal. It was big, but smaller than the man-o'-war that stood further out to sea. He supposed that one of the cargo vessels in port at the moment would leave shortly and then the frigate would come alongside.

He determined to be there when it did.

8

It was past midnight when Will opened the door slowly and winced as it creaked. He cast a swift look at Megan, but she slept on, warmly wrapped in blankets on the bed. Will had been sleeping on the hard floor and it had not been difficult to stay awake. He had heard a church clock strike the witching hour, then one o'clock, before he slipped out of the room.

Megan had tried again that evening to persuade him to return to Camberwell Hall with the horses, but Will had just as adamantly refused. Now he was going out into the streets to do what he did best; find a suitable candidate for his thieving skills, and steal enough money to send the horses home without him.

After his visit to the wharf, Will had scouted the streets for the gentlemen's whore houses and gaming dens. These, he knew, would provide his best chance of stealing a good amount of money. He had known from his childhood that the gentry and the army's officers spent their evenings in such pursuits, and usually ended up drunk, therefore making easy prey.

One such place was Fanny Blake's, a large house in what had once been a fashionable neighbourhood on the outskirts of the town. From his observations that afternoon, it appeared to provide all the necessary pleasures a rich young man could desire. Will had watched gaudily dressed females entering and leaving the house, and had seen carriages and phaetons bringing elegant gentlemen. One young man had brought out a purse, paid the driver of the carriage he had arrived in, and then poured a glittering shower of gold and silver coins from one hand to the other in anticipation of the evening ahead.

So it was that Will crept through the streets towards Fanny Blake's establishment in the dead of night, with only flickering street torches and a fitful moon to guide him. The few people he saw were drunks and beggars and none stopped him. Probably they were unaware of him, because Will moved as stealthily as a cat. On barefeet he kept to the shadows and made no noise. Within ten minutes of leaving the inn, he was outside the house.

Trees grew on the pavement beside the road, and the double-storey house itself was partially hidden behind discreet shrubbery. Lights shone at all the windows, and voices and laughter carried into the cool night air. Will shrank back into the shadows as a carriage trundled up the street and stopped outside the gate. The coachman looped the horse's reins around his hands, then sat back to wait for his customers.

They were a long time coming. The coachman had fallen asleep, and Will was shivering with cold, by the time the door of Fanny Blake's establishment opened again. Two men stepped into the sudden shaft of light caused by the door's opening and Will caught his breath for they were the very same two officers he had encountered that afternoon. Mischief welled up in him. What a chance this was! He would pay back the grumpy Major who had knocked him against the wall, and he knew just how to do it.

The two men swayed down the short driveway towards the road, both very drunk, the Major claiming in a loud voice that the night had been a good one, that the cards had been charmed, and the lady he had entertained had promised him more delights the next evening.

So intent were the two on trying to stay upright, they at first did not comprehend the sudden commotion by the gate. The patient horse suddenly reared up and pulled the reins out of the sleeping coachman's hands, making the poor man nearly fall off his seat in surprise. The horse skittered sideways, then cantered off down the street, to cries of distress from the driver who desperately tried to regain control of the frightened animal.

The two officers made it to the gateway to see their transport halfway down the road. Reeling against each other they tried to make some sense of the situation, and never saw Will who crept silently out of the shadows afforded by the trees, to neatly pick the Major's tail-coat pocket that bulged with a fat purse.

Will left the two men sitting disconsolately on the pavement bemoaning their fate and wondering how to get back to their lodgings when neither was in a fit state to walk. Luckily for them, one of the regulars at Fanny's gave the two a lift to their abode just as dawn was breaking, but it cost Captain James Shaw more than two night's winnings for the favour.

It was not until he awoke with a hangover second to none the next afternoon, that Major Robert Underwood missed his purse and, when he did, he blamed the coachman who, having finally brought the horse under control, had not dared go back to Fanny's for fear the officers would blame him for the whole fiasco.

† † †

When Megan Camberwell opened her eyes that morning it was to see Will sitting cross-legged on the wooden floor, counting out a pile of money. She shrieked, 'Will! What have you done!'

'Ssh!' Will put his finger on his lips. He tipped the coins back into the purse and handed it to her, 'Here. Twenty-five pounds and six shillings.'

'Dear God!' Megan held the heavy purse in her hand and stared at him. She wasn't sure whether to be pleased or angry. 'Where did you get it?'

'From an officer,' he said.

'Not...?'

'No. Not yer uncle. I wouldn't be that daft now, would I?' Will grinned. 'No, this was one sour bugger who 'as no manners and even less charm.'

'Tell me how you did it?' Megan's eyes were shining. Instead of being horrified as Will had feared, the idea of being an accessory to him breaking the law seemed to excite her.

He told her how he had spooked the horse by pulling its tail hard and Megan laughed at the mental picture he conjured, of the sleepy driver trying to stop the runaway animal, and of the two officers sprawled on the pavement, both too drunk to do anything about it.

'I wonder how they got home?' she said.

'Probably waited for the next carriage ter come along and begged a lift,' said Will. 'So now will yer let me come with you?'

'Yes, and this morning we'll find someone to take the horses home.' She gazed again at the purse, hardly able to believe that Will had stolen it and wondering why she felt no guilt.

Finding someone to take the horses back to Camberwell Hall

proved more difficult than expected. Risking the streets together, they went first to a coaching inn and asked there, but the only coach going in the right general direction was travelling as far as Horsham. A groom, overhearing the conversation, offered to do the job, but Will saw the greed in his eyes when Megan mentioned payment, and he decided the man was not to be trusted. Like as not, he would make off with both money and horses. It was a problem, and once back at the inn with a wasted morning behind them, Megan was in a thoroughly bad mood and tried once again to persuade Will to go back to her home.

'You see, Will, it's the only way,' she said.

'Yer could sell the horses,' said Will.

'No! Dinah's my favourite, and Lightfoot is a darling. He was my first horse.'

Will sat thinking and an idea suddenly came to him. Maybe there was a way out of the problem after all. 'Yer could sell 'em ter the army,' he said. 'From what I've 'eard they're always on the look out for good mounts and pack horses.'

'That's it!' Megan was smiling again. 'How could someone like you come up with such a good idea?' She stood up and flung her arms around him. Will preferred to ignore the oblique reference to his ignorance because the feel of Megan's arms around his neck more than made up for it. 'Yes,' Megan said, letting go of him. 'That way the horses get to come with us, and we get even more money!'

'Greedy!' laughed Will, pleased that he had made her happy again.

They discussed ways in which they could find out who was in charge of buying stores and equipment for the army in Portugal. Any ship carrying soldiers to the Peninsula would undoubtedly be taking ammunition and other necessary items for the war effort. It was decided that Will would have to do some detective work on his own again that very day, because the following day they would have to somehow get on board the frigate.

So it was that Will sauntered down to the quayside again that afternoon and was just in time to see the frigate coming closer to the wharf, intent on berthing in the large space left by the East India merchantman and the brig, both of which sailed with the tide early that morning. Will watched and marvelled at the seamanship that enabled the sailors, swarming like cats up and down the ratlines and across the decks, to bring the three-masted ship safely into port. Will counted the gun ports on the side of the ship facing him, a single row of them, fifteen in all, and knew there would be the same on the other side. Thirty cannon with which to blast the enemy, though Will had heard enough down by the London docks to know that frigates were usually not big enough to be part of the battle line-up. They were used mainly as patrol vessels, for carrying despatches, or, as now, to transport the army. He listened to the shouted orders and watched the men following them, knowing exactly what to do, until at last the heavy anchor went down with a loud rattle of chain, lines were tied to the bollards, and the ship stood wallowing gently up and down, only feet from shore.

The gangplank was lowered and the port's officials went aboard to talk to the ship's captain who now stood on deck ready to receive them. Then Will's attention was diverted by a short, red-coated man striding along the dock with a much younger soldier following close on his heels and carrying a large notebook and pencil. Will thought that maybe the short one was the soldiers' quartermaster and the other his clerk.

The two soldiers walked up the gangplank, and Will sidled closer to the ship, hoping to overhear something useful. He picked up a bundle of old fishing net, and squatted crosslegged at the bottom of the gangplank, listening all the while to the conversation above him. No one took any notice of a grubby, barefoot boy seemingly trying to unravel an old piece of netting.

Judging by the men's talk, he had been right in his supposition that the soldier was in charge of stocking the ship with the army's stores. He was discussing with the captain how much space would be available for casks of gunpowder, cartridges, guns, cannon balls, and canister shot. The ship was also to carry boxes of fuse wire and flints as well as tea, salt, sugar, flour, vinegar, boot blacking, items of uniform, buttons, rope, candles, whitening and a host of other requirements for the army already in Portugal. This then was the person he would have to speak to, thought Will as the two men went below to inspect the holds. He knew that Richard Camberwell would be taking Hades on board ship, and probably some of the other officers would be taking horses too, so he was hopeful that Dinah at least would be wanted. Lightfoot was another matter. He was not officer horse material, but then they might be glad of anything. Will would put forward the cob's case because Lightfoot was certainly a hardy beast and well trained to the saddle.

Will waited until the ship's captain and the two soldiers came back on deck. The older, squat man, a sergeant, came down the gangplank in deep conversation with his clerk who was scribbling feverishly in his book. Will followed them to a dockside tavern where both sat at a table outside, intent on slaking their thirst while continuing the discussion. Boldly Will went over to them.

'Pardon me, sir,' he said humbly, 'but I wonder if I might 'ave a word?'

The sergeant stopped in mid-sentence, thanked the tavern girl who placed two frothing tankards of ale on the table, and frowned at Will. Taking in the dirty face, untidy clothes, and bare feet, he said shortly, 'Bugger off, lad. Can't you see I'm busy?' and dismissed him with a terse wave of the hand then carried on talking to the young soldier.

Will didn't move. 'Pardon me, sir. I was wonderin' whether yer'd like to buy some 'orses. For the army like.'

The sergeant looked up again. The frown was not quite so fierce. ''Orses?' he said.

'Yes, sir. I 'ave two to sell and I know the army's mighty short of 'orses, sir.'

'Well that it is, lad, that it is,' agreed the sergeant, his ruddy face half covered by a large brown moustache and beard that almost hid his mouth. He frowned again and stood up. He was shorter than Will, but broad as a barrel. He leaned towards him giving him a frosty look. 'Tell me somethin', lad. 'Ow does the likes o' you come to 'ave two 'orses to sell? Tell me that now!' His voice rose as he suddenly grabbed hold of Will's shirt under his chin and almost yanked him off his feet. 'Are they stolen?'

Will shook his head rapidly. 'No, sir. No,' he managed to say.

The man let go of him. 'Are yer sure?' he said, his eyes still glaring fiercely. ''Cos I ain't got no truck with stolen beasts. The Major wants everythin' above board. We 'as to pay for everythin' we takes with us.'

'Yes, sir. The 'orses ain't stolen, sir,' said Will.

'Then 'ow did yer come by 'em?'

Will's fertile imagination came to his rescue. 'They was me

master's, sir. 'E was a doctor and died just last week, sir. Of the apoplexy. 'E left me the 'orses in his will, but I don't want 'em, sir, 'cos I fancy ter go ter sea, so I won't need no 'orses there, sir.'

The sergeant nodded his head, seeming to consider his story.

'Are you certain they're yours to sell, boy?'

'Oh, yes, sir. The master, 'e didn't 'ave no relatives, sir. We used to go round the villages tendin' the sick, and 'e knew as 'ow I liked the beasts. Looked after 'em, see, so 'e said as 'ow I could 'ave 'em.'

'Hmm.' The sergeant sat down again. 'What d'yer think, Trim?'

The young soldier doing the writing, a bright, cheerful lad, smiled and said, 'We could do with more, sir, and I don't suppose the lad'll want much for 'em.'

'Oh, no, sir!' said Will. 'Just enough ter buy me some togs and the things I'd need on board ship, sir. And a telescope, sir. I've a real mind ter buy a telescope. So's I can see things from up the mast,' he explained, pleased with his inventiveness.

The sergeant laughed. 'Well, lad. Yer a good salesman right enough. I tell yer what I'll do. I'll come by and see these 'ere 'orses tomorrow mornin'. Where are they?'

Will told him the name of the inn where he and Megan were staying and a time was agreed upon. Will left the inn well pleased.

Major Robert Underwood sat in front of a coal fire in the parlour of the officers' lodgings, his sturdy legs stretched out in front of him, and a glass of French brandy in his hand. He pondered on his task of seeing that the forty-seven new redcoats and supplies reached Wellington's army in Portugal before the winter set in. The frigate had brought a despatch from the regiment's Colonel, requesting that Underwood put himself in charge of the undertaking that, so far, the Major had lazily left to Captain Richard Camberwell. The despatch had told him to get the whole thing under way and to hurry up about it because Wellington was in a lather. The Colonel had used that exact word to describe the army commander-in-chief's temperament after the ups and downs of the summer. The army had suffered losses during the battle for Fuentes de Oñoro back in May, though the British had won the battle to prevent the French bringing fresh supplies to the fort of Almeida, currently in French hands. The French casualties had been more than the

British, but Wellington needed every man he could get to further his campaign and he had set his sights on Ciudad Rodrigo and Badajoz – those massive fortifications that blocked the roads to Spain.

Underwood turned his head briefly when the door opened and his two captains entered the room.

'The loading's going well, Robert,' commented Captain James Shaw, walking to the sideboard and pouring himself a glass of brandy from the decanter.

Underwood grunted, and Shaw cast a wry look at his companion. Lord Richard Camberwell raised his eyebrows. It was obvious that Underwood had not yet recovered his vigour, nor his temper, after the previous night's debauchery and its aftermath. Camberwell too poured himself a drink and the two officers joined the Major at the fireside.

'Who did you put in charge?' Underwood sat up straighter in his chair. His stomach still felt sour but the brandy was helping. If he had not had to hold a parade that afternoon, he would have had some hair-of-the-dog before now, and maybe he would not still be feeling like a fiddler's bitch. That Shaw, who had imbibed easily as much wine and brandy as himself the night before, looked so chipper, grated, and deepened his already dark mood.

'Sergeant Readman. And I gave him young Trim to do the counting,' said Richard Camberwell.

Underwood nodded.

'No sign of your purse, I suppose?' James Shaw knew he was taking a chance by bringing up the subject that had done much to put the senior officer in such a foul mood, but being an optimistic soul, he thought that it might have been found and returned to its owner.

'Of course not!' Underwood drank another mouthful of brandy. 'Damn thief! Never even saw the bastard! One minute the purse was a nice hefty weight in my pocket, then by the time that damn horse had run off with the carriage, it was gone! There must have been twenty pounds or more in it! I'd be willing to bet it was the damn pickpocket who spooked the horse and that the bloody coachman was asleep!'

'It would seem that Portsmouth has its share of thieves,' agreed Richard Camberwell, warming his legs by the fire. A cold wind had

110

sprung up outside and the clouds had spread over the town, a harbinger of rain to come. 'The same thing happened to me in London a few weeks ago. Except that I didn't even have the excuse of being drunk at the time.'

Underwood forgot his own misery for a moment and stared up at the younger man. 'Do tell, Camberwell,' he said with interest.

'There was some confusion with a small boy and a woman carrying a parcel. When it had been sorted out, my purse was gone and ten guineas with it,' Lord Richard said ruefully. Then he grinned. 'Caught the little bastard, though.'

'Well done, man. I hope the constables hanged him,' said Underwood grimly.

'Not exactly.' Lord Richard poured himself another drink. 'The scoundrel saved my life later, so I spared his. He is now in my employ, working to pay back what he stole.' He smiled wryly. 'The money was stolen from him by an even more unscrupulous rogue.'

There was much exclamation from Lord Richard's two listeners. Captain Shaw demanded he tell the full story. When it was told, Major Underwood said, 'I hope you haven't made a grave error of judgement there, Richard. Once a thief, always a thief, my old mother used to say, and I happen to agree with her.'

'Maybe not,' said Camberwell, putting his glass on the mantelpiece and lighting up a cigar. After seeing it well lit, he continued, 'Maybe it was his way of life that forced him into it. The lad has no home, no family, and no one wants to employ street riff-raff. He's doing well at the Hall. I actually have high hopes of him.'

'Uncommonly good of you, Richard,' said Shaw.

'Me, now, I would have sent the bugger packing,' said Underwood emphatically. 'Saved him from Newgate maybe but not risked the safety of my family and belongings by employing him.'

Richard Camberwell had been bothered by the same misgivings many times, especially since he was not at the Hall himself to make sure that Will trod the straight and narrow but he hoped that his mother would be keeping a good eye on Will, and that the boy would have plenty to keep him occupied and away from his previous trade.

'So are you totally bereft of coin now, Robert?' he asked, to take the subject away from his own misfortune.

'Not quite, though I could've done with those winnings. I shall

111

have to gain some more at the tables tonight.' Robert Underwood put the brandy glass down on the table rather harder than necessary. 'Damn the bastard! Now I shall have to forego that pretty wench at Fanny's who's been so obliging of late. She's damn expensive and I know Fanny won't agree to a discount.' The thought made him gloomier than ever, so Richard Camberwell left James Shaw trying to and lighten the man's mood, and went in search of something to eat.

The lodgings were owned by a well-to-do merchant who was pleased to accommodate the three army officers for a quite substantial fee. The family had given over their front parlour and two of the bedrooms to the officers, forcing the merchant's two daughters to be accommodated in a tiny storage room behind the kitchen. As Richard Camberwell made his way to the kitchen to roust the cook, one of the daughters, a girl of some nineteen years, came into the hallway just as he was passing the storage room doorway, and bumped into him.

'Oh, I'm sorry, Captain,' she said, smiling a wide smile and blushing prettily.

'Pardon me, miss.' Richard Camberwell was not wearing his shako, or he would have politely removed it. He stepped hurriedly to one side of the narrow corridor and indicated that the girl should pass him. She thanked him and he watched as she entered the kitchen, appreciating the slim figure and wanting suddenly to touch the feathery strands that fell from her upswept hair onto the back of her slender neck. The officers had been staying at the house for less than a week and he had said scarcely a word to any of its usual inhabitants, leaving Underwood to mediate between them, but he had noticed that this eldest girl always blushed when they unavoidably met and he, a connoisseur of women, knew that she was attracted to him. As, if the truth be told, he was to her, but he knew that any contact between them was out of the question. He sighed deeply as he followed the girl into the kitchen. It had been too long since he had been with a woman and he refused to risk the pox by sleeping with one of Fanny's whores as his colleagues did. One day he would meet a woman who would be more than a passing fling, but until that day came, he would just keep on looking. And hoping.

Sarah Harvey, the girl Camberwell had just seen, suddenly

112

stopped her conversation with the cook when she became aware that the Captain had entered the room behind her. Tongue tied, she blushed a deeper red, and fled the room. The cook looked surprised, but turned her attention to the tall officer who was looking equally surprised. A woman of mature years, she smiled to herself. She knew exactly what was going on here, even if the two of them did not.

Sarah shut the door of the small room she shared with her sister, and leaned on it, breathing heavily. Why did that man have this effect on her? Every time she saw him, her heart would pound, her skin would become clammy, and the strangest tingling would attack her nerves from head to toe. Surely he must notice and think her a complete ninny! Just the thought of his tall, graceful body, so handsome in its captain's uniform, was enough to set her swooning. And that face, so hard and unyielding and oh, so masculine, yet she was sure that he was not hard inside. His eyes belied the fact. She had seen him laughing with his friends and then his eyes had been full of warmth and good humour. Sarah Harvey was sure this must be love.

Having ascertained from the cook that dinner would be served shortly, Richard Camberwell left the kitchen musing on the fleeting glimpses of the eldest Miss Harvey. It was a great pity there was no time to further their acquaintance. He felt strangely drawn to the girl yet he knew nothing about her, nothing except her name. Sarah.

Realising there was no future in wishing, he went to tell his colleagues that dinner would soon be served.

† † †

The next morning Sergeant Readman and Private Trim went round to the inn where Will and Megan were staying and had a look at the horses. Readman rubbed a hand over Dinah's withers and opened her mouth to look at her teeth.

Will stood by and listened to the Sergeant exclaiming over Dinah's attributes. He would definitely buy her. He ummed and aahed over Lightfoot but Will told him what a strong, willing horse he was, and after much discussion, Readman said he would do as a pack horse. Will haggled over the price and eventually the Sergeant found that he had agreed to a lot more than he had originally planned to spend.

'I'll bring yer the money when I fetch 'em,' he said gruffly. 'The ship sails in the morning.'

'I'd like the money now, sir, if yer please,' said Will who knew that tonight he and Megan would have to stow away on that very same ship and would not be at the inn the next morning.

Readman rubbed his bearded chin. 'I dunno about that, lad,' he said. 'Dunno whether I can get it for yer right now.'

'Please try, sir. There's a fishing boat leavin' first thing and I've been taken on as a deck 'and,' Will invented.

'Well all right, lad. I'll do my best,' said the Sergeant kindly. He liked the look of this boy, even though he was obviously poor. He put his head on one side and studied Will. 'I don't suppose yer'd like ter join the army instead, would yer?' he said. 'We could do with a few more enterprisin' lads like yerself.'

For a moment Will thought of taking the sergeant up on his offer and joining up legitimately, but then there was the problem of Megan, and if Richard Camberwell saw him before they actually left port, there would be hell to pay and he would be sent back to Camberwell Hall. No, he must stick to their original plan so he said, 'No, sir. I've still a mind ter go ter sea.'

'Pity.' Readman patted Dinah on the back. 'I'll go and speak ter Major Underwood now. 'E's in charge o' the money. Trim, you stay 'ere.'

'Yes, sir,' said the young private.

The sergeant left and Will took down the saddles and bridles. 'Yer might as well 'ave the tack,' he said. 'No use ter me.'

'They're nice 'orses. What d'yer want to get rid of 'em for?' The boy, who was not much older than Will, sat himself down on the wooden partition between the stalls.

'Like I told the sergeant. I'm going to sea.' That part at least was true.

'Sometimes wish I'd gone to sea,' said the boy. 'I've only been in the army for two months and it's bloody 'ard work and we 'aven't even got to Portugal yet! The name's George, by the way. George Trim.'

'Pleased ter meet yer,' said Will. 'Will Tucker.' They shook hands. Trim was a cheerful looking fellow with a shock of brown hair. He was well built and red-faced, and looked as though he came

114

from farming stock but his next words belied the thought.

'Used to be a clerk.' He held up the notebook. 'That's why I'm followin' the Sarge around. We 'ave to start loadin' today and I 'ave to count everythin' that gets put on board.'

''Ow'd you get to be in the army then?' asked Will. He decided he liked the young man and wanted to befriend him. If things went according to plan, then they would soon be in the same regiment.

'Stupid really. Was on an errand for the master at the countin' 'ouse when I 'ears this man shoutin' his 'ead off. There's quite a crowd around 'im, see, so I pushes me way through to see what all the fuss is about, and there's this sergeant, 'im as was 'ere just now, Sergeant Readman, tellin' all the lads 'ow great the army is, an 'ow they'll give yer a guinea just for joinin' up. Well, I ain't never 'ad a guinea in me 'ole life, not all at once like, so I tells the master I'm off to the army an' I goes an' signs up. Five other lads from the town did too. Bloody pack o' lies they told us about that guinea, though. Once they gets us to the barracks in Winchester they tells us we 'ave to pay for food, boots, uniform, laundry, boot black, whitenin', and a dozen other things, an' all we end up with is ninepence! Ninepence! I ask yer! I could make more'n that at the counting 'ouse, and for a bloody sight less work too! An' we ain't even seen that ninepence yet! Still, I suppose if yer don't mind bein' shouted at all the time and not 'avin' any time to call yer own, then some might not think it's a bad life. At least yer gets fed regular.'

'If yer don't like it, why don't yer run away?' asked Will.

George Trim smiled a wide, ingenuous smile. 'I didn't say I didn't like it, did I? Plenty of fresh air, better food than I'm used to, so far anyways, and the officers don't get on yer case if yer do as yer told. I'm used to takin' orders. Old Milton, me master at the countin' 'ouse, 'e was a far worse task master than Major Underwood, and Sergeant Readman's bark's worse than 'is bite. No, I'll stay in the army.'

The two continued to talk, Will warming to the young man more and more as the morning wore on, until the sergeant came back, carrying, to Will's great delight, a bag full of money.

'Yer in luck, lad,' he said. 'The Major did all right at the gamblin' last night and was in a good mood this morning so 'e was prepared to part with some o' the army's guineas. 'Ere's yer money.'

'Thanks.' Will took the bag.

'Aren't yer gonna count it then?' asked Trim.

'Are you sayin' as 'ow I'd cheat the boy, George Trim?' said the sergeant testily.

'No, Sarge,' George answered with a disarming smile. 'But I'd sure count it if I were 'im.'

To please George, Will tipped the coins out and counted them. Satisfied, he tucked the purse inside his jacket. 'When'll you be wantin' the 'orses then?' he asked.

'No use takin' 'em now,' said the sergeant. 'They'll be loaded last tomorrow and there ain't no more stablin' where the officers' mounts are.' The sergeant's eyes narrowed. 'If I leaves them 'ere, 'ow'll I know you won't run off with 'em, or sell 'em again to somebody else?'

'Yer can trust me, Sergeant,' said Will, giving the man his most winning smile. 'They'll be 'ere tomorrow.'

'Hmm. If they're not, lad, then I'll 'ave the damn constables waitin' when yer fishin' boat docks!' said Readman. 'I'll speak to the landlord and ask 'im if I can put a soldier in with 'em tonight. It's not that I don't trust yer, lad, but I'd 'ate anything to 'appen to 'em. Not now they's paid for. Come on, Trim. The lads're takin' the stores to the docks as we speak and there's countin' to be done.' He shook Will's hand. 'Good luck, lad.'

'Same ter yer sir,' said Will, wondering how the sergeant was going to react when they saw each other again. This was probably the best terms he and the non-commissioned officer would ever be on. He shook Trim's hand too. 'Nice ter meet yer, George,' he said. 'Go well.'

'Thanks, Will. Maybe we'll meet again some day.'

'I'd like that,' said Will, meaning it, and knowing it was very likely.

That night Megan, wearing as many layers of clothing as she could, packed the rest of her belongings into the carpet bag, and walked with Will through the dark streets to the wharf. It was time to set the next part of their adventure in motion and stow away on the ship that was to take them to war.

Neither noticed someone else close by who had that same purpose in mind.

9

Boarding the ship proved to be easier than either Will or Megan had expected. Night time found the frigate with only a skeleton watch. As the soldiers had not boarded yet, there was no possibility of desertion, and the captain of the ship, Elijah Ross, had allowed his off-duty tars to have a final sample of the delights the dockside taverns had to offer. The excessive noise from the taverns and brothels took away any attention that might have come their way as the two neared the moored ship.

Will told Megan to hide in the shadows near the gangplank while he scouted around. He sauntered past the ship, hands in pockets, and glanced up at the deck. Lanterns cast beams of light and deep shadows but the nearest man on watch was on the quarterdeck, and he was leaning against the main mast, seemingly unconcerned with what was happening on the dock below him. However, Will was well aware that there would be other sailors below deck, and, once on the ship, he and Megan would have to find somewhere to hide. An obvious place was one of the longboats fastened to the upper deck. They had weatherproof sheets tied over them and would be a good hiding place but for the fact that they were a long way from the galley. Will had a fancy to stow away somewhere close to the ship's kitchen so that he could steal some food from time to time, though his pockets bulged with bread, cheese, and cold potatoes that he had bought, and inside the carpet bag was a skin of wine. Unfortunately, he had no idea where, in this huge ship, the galley was situated.

Suddenly Will saw a man, an officer by his uniform, walking the deck, approach the sailor on watch, so he crept along in the shadows towards the prow where the name of the ship, *The Painted Lady*, stood out in bold lettering, and the figurehead that gave the ship its name, jutted out above him. There he came upon something that made him smile. A rope-ladder was hanging conveniently over the side, the bottom rung level with his head, and it appeared to go all the way up to the deck. Quickly he ran back to Megan who was waiting anxiously.

When she saw the precariously swinging rope-ladder, Megan vowed she would not be able to climb it.

'D'yer want to get on this ship, or not?' hissed Will in her ear.

'Yes, of course I do,' she whispered back.

'Well this is the only way. Now I'll 'eave yer up onto the first rung. Climb up, but when yer get to the top for God's sake look around carefully before yer climb over the rail. There be two men by the main mast and more could come on deck any minute.'

'What about the bag?'

'I'll bring it. Now 'urry afore somebody comes.'

Megan stared up at the ladder swaying gently from the deck. It looked so high, and the prospect of climbing it was daunting. Nevertheless, she allowed Will to hoist her up onto the bottom rung, grasped the rope firmly, and started to climb. Will followed, the carpet bag a bulky nuisance slung over one shoulder by the handles. The climb was a lot harder than it had seemed from the dock. Although he was nimble, Megan was not, and she was going so slowly he was sure they would be seen by someone on the wharf. The ship was moving alarmingly in the dockside swell, the timbers creaking, and the ladder swinging from side to side.

''Urry up!' he hissed.

Megan said nothing but he could hear her laboured breathing. Suddenly her foot slipped and she trod on his head, uttering a small cry. Will held his breath as she regained her balance, but there was no sudden shout to show that they had been spotted.

With her heart in her mouth, Megan slowly clambered on, her hands chafing on the hard tarred rope, until at last she reached the rail. Peeping over the top, all she could see were piles of rope and miscellaneous shadowy lumps of she knew not what. But no people. With a breathless heave, she swung a leg over the rail, wishing she could wear trousers like a boy when her dress snagged momentarily on the railing. She landed in an unladylike heap on the wooden deck. Scrambling to her knees she leaned over and watched Will climb quickly up the last few rungs. He passed her the bag, then swung himself over the rail.

There was no one near this end of the ship and all was quiet. Will told Megan to stay close and made for the nearest hatchway. It was very dark and Megan clung nervously to Will's jerkin. They reached the hatch and Will could just make out the start of a steep companionway below his feet. 'I'll go first,' he whispered in Megan's ear. 'Throw the bag when I tell yer.' He gave her the bag again and went backwards down the steps. Megan crouched at the top, her nerves taut, expecting to hear a shout from one of the crew at any moment. But the noise from the dockside taverns and the creaking of the ship's timbers were the only sounds, until she heard a loud whisper from below and she let go of the bag.

Will caught it, and told Megan to come down. 'But be careful. It's steep,' he said quietly. Even with that warning, it was steeper than Megan expected and she lost her footing near the bottom, but Will was there to catch her.

'Take off yer shoes, it's easier,' he said, setting her on her feet.

The part of the deck they were on held some of the crew's hammocks, and as they walked nearer the middle of the ship, ducking to avoid bulkheads and wooden beams, they came upon the galley, and, near it, a small space that contained nothing at all. Will felt around in the darkness and his hands touched a wide, round length of wood that reached up to the low ceiling and beyond. The foremast. Behind it would do as a place to hide.

In darkness, he and Megan settled down as best they could, leaning on the mast. Their efforts had made them hungry so Will broke a piece of hard bread in two and they nibbled it, making it last. Megan shuddered as a scuffling sound told that a rat was nearby, attracted by the crumbs, and she shuffled closer to Will who willingly put his arm around her. Sometime later, caught up in his own thoughts, he became aware of her even breathing and knew she was asleep, but he couldn't sleep himself. Their hiding place was precarious and they were almost certain to be found, but he hoped they could stay undiscovered until the frigate had left port. Once the ship was at sea, there was nothing Richard Camberwell could do to stop them reaching Portugal. However, meeting Megan's uncle in these circumstances was not something Will was looking forward to. The night wore on, and he listened to the sounds of a ship at anchor; the water lapping at her sides, the shifting timbers, and the rats.

Alert for footsteps or voices, he hugged Megan closer and dreamed of war.

✝ ✝ ✝

So pleased had Will and Megan been to think of a plan that would mean the horses could travel to Portugal with them, and give them

119

some more money, they had rather put out of their minds the fact that Richard Camberwell was going too, and that he might well recognise two horses from his own stable.

The morning dawned cloudy, with a small breeze that ruffled Lord Camberwell's dark hair as he stood on the wharf and idly watched Sergeant Readman helping to supervise the loading of last minute supplies for the army and the ship's crew; fresh fruit and vegetables, barrels of fresh water, and forage for the officers' horses. It seemed to Richard Camberwell that as much forage went on board as food for the men but then they might be on board ship for a couple of weeks and horses could eat a lot of hay in that time, even though there were only two going to Portugal with them. Major Underwood's horses were already with the army in the Peninsula, but Captain Shaw had bought himself a second string horse with his winnings at the card tables. That horse had already been hoisted aboard by means of ropes and slings, and Richard Camberwell wanted to make sure that Hades suffered no damage when it came to his turn. It was not a pleasant experience, and he wanted to help by reassuring the stallion whose reins he held loosely in his hand while standing by the chandler's wall.

He wished he did not have to take Hades to war and regretted keenly the loss of Sable, the horse that had carried him through two years of warfare. He wondered how she had died. The message he had been given at Winchester merely said that the horse had been killed. He hoped that her death had been quick.

Good mounts were scarce now that the war was old. Too many had been killed in battle and the cavalry took the best of what was left. Spanish horses were fast and sure-footed, but those that had not been already commandeered by the army, were used by the Guerilleros, the Spanish and Portuguese partisans who hated the French even more than the British did, and fought their own war against them in the hills and valleys. Officers were obliged to buy their own horses and those who returned to England for whatever reason, and if they could afford to, usually took one or two spare mounts back with them. Richard Camberwell still had one horse in the Peninsula, or at least he hoped he did. He wondered now what had become of his stallion Dragoon after his man, Jeremiah Todd, died. Hopefully someone had looked after the horse in the intervening months.

Camberwell stroked Hades on his shiny black neck and the horse whinnied gently, turning his head to nuzzle at the hand. Hades would have to be trained to battle, to learn not to shy away from the terrible noise of the guns, from musket balls that would whip around his ears, and to evade charging bayonets. He would have to learn to do battle himself, to rear up and kick out at the enemy, to bite and snap, and to carry his rider swiftly out of danger. There had been no time to teach the stallion any of these things, and it worried Richard Camberwell that he might have to take an untrained horse into battle. He hoped that, with winter coming, there would be no serious battles to be fought and that he would have time to teach his young and intelligent stallion the ways of war.

Thinking it would soon be the turn of Hades to be loaded on board the ship, he was rather surprised to see a private leading two more horses towards Sergeant Readman, and then putting the sling around one of them, a grey cob. At first he stared without seeing, then recognition slowly dawned. He looked at the mare standing next to the cob and recognised her too.

Flinging Hades's reins around a bollard, he strode across to the sergeant.

'Where did those two horses come from?' he demanded. Now he was closer, there was no mistaking Dinah and Lightfoot.

Sergeant Readman stopped shouting at the sailors helping to load the horses and turned a cheerful face to Camberwell. 'Bought 'em yesterday, sir. The brown mare's a fine saddle horse. The cob'll make a good pack horse.'

'I know, damn it! They're from my stables!'

'What? But that's impossible, sir! I bought 'em 'ere, in Portsmouth.' Sergeant Readman's bearded face took on a look of disbelief.

'Who sold them to you?' Camberwell's dark eyes pierced those of the sergeant.

'A boy, sir. A boy. Said 'is master'd died and left 'em to 'im.' Readman tried to placate the officer. These horses couldn't possibly belong to the Captain. Didn't he live in Kent? It was miles away.

The sailors had stopped what they were doing and were listening to the exchange.

'This boy. What did he look like?' Richard Camberwell was afraid to hear the answer, though he had a horrible feeling he already knew.

'Nice enough young lad. Sixteen, seventeen years old. Tall, thin. Good lookin'...'

'Yellow hair?'

'Aye.' For the first time, Sergeant Readman realised that he might have made a dreadful blunder. His voice trembled a little as he said, 'Are yer certain they're yours, sir?'

'I'm sure,' said the Captain grimly. Will! It had to be Will! The bloody boy had run off with his horses! Stolen them! Rage made Camberwell pace around in front of the wary sergeant. The brat had run! After everything he had done for him. Stolen the horses so that he could sell them. He should have listened to those niggling inner voices that had told him he was being stupid to take him to the Hall. But why had he come here? Camberwell stopped pacing for a moment to ask, 'Did this boy say anything else to you?'

'Only that he didn't want the 'orses because he was goin' to sea, sir,' said Readman. 'Mentioned a fishin' boat pullin' out this morning.'

Was that the truth, or had Will been lying? Richard Camberwell remembered that Will wanted to join the army. Was that why he had come here? To catch a ship that was going to Portugal? And he probably guessed that the army would be willing to buy any horse-flesh to replace the horses lost in the war. He had a feeling that the fishing boat story was a lie.

'Where did you meet him?'

Readman told him the name of the inn. Lord Richard looked again at Lightfoot, and patted him on the back. The grey cob whinnied and swished his tail, recognising his smell. 'If only you could talk, you could tell me what's going on, old chap,' Camberwell said quietly to the horse. He came to a decision.

'You'd best carry on, Sergeant,' he said, reluctantly. There was nothing to be done about the horses now. It was too late to arrange their transportation back to the Hall or to go through all the paperwork that would revert their ownership back to him. The ship was due to sail in two hours. The horses would just have to travel with him.

In the meantime, he would do his best to find Will Tucker. He left Hades in the care of a corporal, exhorting the young man to see that the horse was safely put on board the vessel, then he walked to the soldiers' camp just outside town where the men were packing up ready to leave. A brief look around elicited the fact that no one answering Will's description had joined up since they had come to Portsmouth, so he went to the inn Sergeant Readman had told him of. There he met with some disturbing news. The landlord told Richard Camberwell that there had indeed been a young lad staying there for the past couple of days and there had been a lass with him too. Hearing the description, Richard Camberwell knew it could be no one else but Megan.

Coming out of the inn, he didn't know what to think. Had Will abducted Megan? Unlikely. Had he persuaded her to come with him for the adventure? Not so unlikely. Richard Camberwell would be the first to admit that his niece was a spirited girl, but if that were so, what would Megan be doing while Will was off in a boat, or joining the army? It was worrying in the extreme, and Lord Camberwell set off to search the town in the hope of finding the two before the ship set sail.

It was a fruitless search. No one he spoke to at inns, shops, or hawking wares on street corners, had seen either of them and taking out his pocket watch he saw it was nearly time for the ship to set sail. He made his way disconsolately back to his lodgings to fetch his baggage and then went back to the wharf where the soldiers were already trudging up the gangplank and onto the ship. Hades had been loaded on board and he felt a pang of guilt that he hadn't been there to help him through the experience, but Sergeant Readman said that the horse had been a model of good behaviour.

'Did you find the lad, sir?' he asked.

'No, Sergeant. Tell me, did you see a girl with him?'

'No, sir. He never mentioned one neither.'

Richard Camberwell was in a ferment of worry. What was he to do? How could he go, knowing that his niece was in the town and might be in trouble? His anxious thoughts were interrupted by a shout from above and, looking up, he saw Major Underwood's fleshy face peering down at him from the deck as he leaned over the railing.

'Ah, there you are, Richard! Come on, man! The Captain wants to leave with the tide.' The sailors were already making for the mooring ropes, getting ready to cast off.

123

'Robert, I need to...'

'No time, Richard, no time! Come along, man, or we'll go without you!'

For an instant Richard Camberwell was tempted to let them do just that, but three of his horses were on the ship and he had been ordered to return to war, so he walked up the ramp and onto the deck. A few minutes later he was standing by the ship's rail, watching as the gangplank was drawn up, the mooring ropes were cast off, and the sailors climbed the rigging to unfurl some of the sails. The ship sailed slowly away from the dockside, and Richard Camberwell watched the receding shores of England. Once into the Channel, wind caught the sails, making them flap and billow out with a huge cracking sound, and they were on their way.

Richard Camberwell stayed at the rail, staring morosely at the distant shoreline. His niece was in Portsmouth with a thief for company and now he could do nothing at all about finding her. A sudden thought struck him. What if the two had fallen in love? Then just as suddenly the thought disappeared. Surely not. They were too young, and anyway Megan had always shown nothing but disdain for Will, although Camberwell had to admit the boy was extraordinarily handsome and Megan was a pretty lass. But why else would she have agreed to run away with him, if that was indeed what had happened?

He sighed and turned away from the rail. There were just too many unanswered questions. Megan was his ward and under his protection. Richard Camberwell knew that this voyage would now be one of constant worry, yet there was nothing to be done.

At noon the army officers, together with those of the ship's officers who were not on watch, gathered around the Captain's table for lunch. To make conversation, and because it still smarted, Major Underwood told once again the story of the loss of his purse, though he left out the fact that he and Captain Shaw had been four sheets to the wind at the time of the theft, and James Shaw did not enlighten the listeners who were hearing the story for the first time. After receiving commiserations on his misfortune, his lack of funds set Underwood to complaining about Lord Wellington's insistence on the British army paying for everything they commandeered from the Portuguese peasants.

'We have to pay for every damn chicken and drop of wine,

124

Captain,' he said, his mouth full of succulent flesh of the bird that was the officers' lunch. 'I've even seen officers hang perfectly able soldiers for stealing bread! Half the damn army's made up of thieves, so what the hell do they expect? The French take provisions without payment all the time, which is why the damn peasants hide all their harvests and tell us they have nothing. And we go hungry!'

It was true. The French were not under the same instructions as the British soldiers, and stole more than they bought, yet Wellington insisted the British commissary and his men pay for their food. That was why, a lot of the time, the soldiers went hungry as Robert Underwood said. Yet in one way it helped the British army. The Portuguese population appreciated the fact that the army paid for what it ate, and most of the time helped the British, whereas the French had earned their everlasting enmity.

Although he had done well at the gaming tables since, it irked Robert Underwood that the dispossession of his winnings that fateful night meant he would now have less money with which to buy the little extras that made life at war somewhat more bearable, and he kept harping back to his unfortunate loss.

'Damn it! If I'd managed to catch the thief, I'd have killed the bastard!' he said angrily, helping himself to another chicken leg.

'Why, Robert? You grumble that someone stole from you, and yet you would condone the army stealing from Portuguese civilians,' observed Richard Camberwell wryly. 'It seems contradictory to me.'

'War is different, Richard, and well you know it,' said Underwood, brandishing the chicken leg to make his point. 'We have thousands of men to feed and we're doing the peasants a favour, damn it, by trying to rid Spain and Portugal of the French. You'd think they'd give us the food for nothing! Stealing food and stealing money are two totally different things. Anyway, I know you seem to think thieves need no punishment, whatever they take. I still can't countenance the fact that you actually employ the scoundrel who stole from you!'

'You employ a thief, Captain?' asked Elijah Ross, supping a great mouthful of wine. The ship's Captain was a big man who was obviously going to match Robert Underwood's appetite for food and drink.

'Yes, Captain. I do,' said Camberwell, whose thoughts had been constantly of Will since seeing the two horses, though not tempered with any of the benevolence he had shown when first relating the tale to his friends. Now he was forced to tell the story of his meeting with Will all over again. The general consensus was that he should have had him up before the magistrate.

'Or forced him into the army. Then in all probability, he would've been killed and your unfortunate conscience would be clear,' said Underwood savagely. It was a fact that most of the men in Portugal would not see England's shores again, and the Major's comment set Camberwell to thinking once again of Will's desire to be a soldier. Suddenly something occurred to him, and he startled his companions round the table by thumping it hard with his fist, making the crockery jump, and exclaiming in a loud voice, 'That's it!'

'Richard?' Major Underwood frowned at his subordinate curiously but Richard Camberwell was on his feet and, with a hasty apology, rushed out of the door.

The thought that the boy had wanted to become a soldier and not a fisherman, had been nagging at him since discovering the horses. If Will wanted to go to war, then this was the ship that was going there. Might not the boy have stowed away? Richard Camberwell went up the nearest companionway and onto the deck.

'Can I help you, sir?' A young midshipman, sent by the ship's Captain, had followed him up on deck.

'Yes, you can. I have reason to believe there's a stowaway on board this vessel,' said Richard Camberwell grimly. 'I want you to help me find him.'

'A stowaway, sir?' said the curly-haired boy, his eyes shining with excitement. 'Of course, sir. Do you know what he looks like, sir?'

For a moment Richard Camberwell stared at the boy, wondering how many stowaways the lad thought were likely to be on board. 'What's your name, lad?' he asked.

'John, sir. John Spencer,' said the lad.

'Well, John Spencer, the boy I think may be hiding on this ship, is only a few years older than you, is a good few inches taller, and has hair the colour of ripe corn. Does that help?'

'Yes, sir. I'll institute a search of the ship right away, sir,' said

Midshipman Spencer importantly, and trotted off to enlist the aid of the bo'sun and some of the sailors.

Richard Camberwell started his search on deck, looking amongst the piles of tarred rope and rigging. He saw sailors searching the poop deck, and others the fo'c'sle. Looking about him, he had just decided there was really nowhere else to hide on deck except for the longboats, when there came a shout from one of those very vessels.

He ran to where Midshipman Spencer was yelling his head off, provoking the bo'sun to also run towards the boy. By the time Camberwell had reached them, both were helping a very unsteady young lady out of the boat. For an instant, Richard Camberwell's heart lifted because he thought it was Megan, but on closer inspection he received an even greater shock. It was not Megan, but Sarah Harvey.

'Miss Harvey?' he said in astonishment. 'What on earth are you doing here?'

The girl stood on the deck, wan and contrite. She lifted a face, pale with sea-sickness, to him and said, 'I'm sorry, Captain,' then turned and abruptly ran to the ship's rail, leaned over it and proceeded to be very violently sick.

'You know this girl, Captain?' Someone had fetched Captain Ross, who, together with the army and other ship's officers, joined the group at the longboat. Ross did not look pleased.

'Er, yes, sir. That is, she lived at the house where Major Underwood, Captain Shaw and I had lodgings in Portsmouth, sir.'

'And have you any idea what she is doing on my ship?'

Ross was staring at him, obviously thinking that the two were romantically involved. For some inane reason, Richard Camberwell blushed. 'None, sir,' he said. 'I hardly know the girl.'

Sarah Harvey managed to compose herself, and allowed Midshipman Spencer to assist her back to the officers where Captain Ross gruffly asked her the question he had asked Camberwell.

'I'd rather not say, Captain,' she said timidly.

Ross made an explosive noise while Richard Camberwell found himself feeling sorry for the rather pathetic figure.

'I want to know what you are doing on my ship, girl!' said Captain Ross again, louder this time. The girl seemed to shrink away from his voice, and Richard Camberwell felt an almost over-

127

whelming urge to hold her close and protect her from the Captain's anger. He watched as she took a visible hold on herself and said firmly, 'I wish to go to Portugal, sir. I have nursing experience, and think I may be of some use to the army.'

This seemed to nonplus Elijah Ross, who had not been expecting such an answer.

'I'm sure there must be more conventional ways of offering such services,' he said at last.

'I dare say there are, Captain, but there was no time to go through more formal channels. It was quite a sudden decision,' said Sarah. 'Oh dear! Please excuse me!' She made another dash for the ship's rail. Richard Camberwell had to make a conscious effort not to run and comfort her, but when she returned to the group again, she caught him staring and gave him a tremulous smile that made him catch his breath. Her grey eyes stared straight into his as if willing him to know the real reason she had stowed away on the ship. And suddenly he did.

'Does your father know you're here?' he asked, suddenly feeling flustered, and not knowing what else to say.

'I left the family a note,' said Sarah with a hint of vivaciousness. 'I don't think they'll be surprised.'

Captain Ross, meanwhile, was looking resigned. 'Bloody hell!' he said. He looked towards the horizon as if wishing the ship back to port and shook his head. 'Too damn late to go back now.' He turned to the girl. 'I hope you realise that stowing away is a very serious offence, young lady. And now what am I to do with you? The lads aren't going to be too happy about having a female on board.' He frowned at the girl who met his gaze, and Richard Camberwell was struck by her beauty as her eyes flashed momentarily at the ship's commander. Captain Ross's eye for a pretty woman had been in no way destroyed by years at sea either, and this young lady would surely be very handsome when she was cleaned up a trifle. His tone was gentler as he said, 'Some say it's bad luck, you know, to have a woman on board ship, though I have never had much truck with that superstition myself, neither am I one to put a lady in the brig, though, by rights, that's what should happen to you seeing that you're a stowaway. And having a woman on board with all my jack tars gawping all the time isn't going to be easy now.' He scratched his bearded chin thoughtfully. 'But no doubt we'll make do and find somewhere to put you.' His bluff speech was rather spoiled when Sarah Harvey had to make another ignominious run for the ship's side before he had finished. 'What do you suggest we do with her, Mister Grimshaw?' Ross asked the bo'sun.

'Reckon she could sling an 'ammock in your day room, sir,' suggested the large bo'sun whose face, lined and weathered by the sun, was looking rather perplexed at this turn of events. He scratched thinning grey hair. 'We can put up a partition. Can't think of anywhere else, sir.'

'Happen you're right, Mister Grimshaw,' said Ross. 'And she can work her passage by helping the cook. Come with me, young lady,' he said to the girl who had recovered herself again. 'A tot of rum will soon fix that stomach, though I fear that as we're not even out of the Channel, and have yet to sail through the Bay of Biscay. You may feel somewhat worse before you feel better.'

Solicitously taking the girl's arm, Captain Ross led Sarah Harvey to his cabin, with Captain Shaw and Major Underwood close behind them.

'That wasn't your stowaway, Captain,' observed Midshipman Spencer, watching them go.

'No, it wasn't,' said Camberwell. 'I suggest we carry on the search, Mister Spencer.'

Going below deck and searching amongst the cannon that stood roped and ready behind the closed gunports, Richard Camberwell thought about this very startling discovery. That in all probability the girl had come on board because of him, was even more astonishing, yet that look had told him it was so. Had she, in the few fleeting moments of their transient meetings during the time he had stayed in her house, felt the same attraction for him as he did for her? It would appear that was the case. But to give up everything she knew, her family and her home, to follow him to war, that was rash in the extreme. After all she knew nothing about him. It was doubtful if she even knew his name.

He tried to put the girl out of his mind, and concentrate on his search for Will, still sure that he was somewhere on the ship.

† † †

Will and Megan had spent an uncomfortable morning. Will was weary after a nearly sleepless night, though the precariousness of their position made him alert and helped to overcome his tiredness. The galley next to the hole they had found for themselves was nearly always occupied, so they had to be quiet. They ate the food that Will had brought along and had both sneaked on deck to the heads when the night was still black, to relieve themselves, but the prospect of not being able to perform that function until night fell again was not comforting. Megan almost wished, now that they were at sea, that they would be found, although she knew her uncle's anger would be dreadful. Their cubbyhole was hot away from the sea breeze and there was no room to move. Megan castigated Will roundly in whispers for finding them such an uncomfortable hiding place, and Will promised to look for somewhere better after nightfall.

His attention was taken by footsteps coming towards the galley. At first he thought it was the cook's assistant, but then the footsteps stopped before the galley and he heard muttering. Whoever it was carried on towards them and Will instinctively dragged Megan further back into the shadow of the bulkhead, making Midshipman Spencer, for it was he, nearly miss the two, but he was being thorough in his search. He peered into the dark space.

'Ah, there you are,' he said cheerfully. 'So the army Captain was right. You'd better come out. The whole ship's being turned upside down looking for you.'

Knowing the game was up, Will crawled out of the hole, and Megan crawled after him. 'Another girl!' said John Spencer in surprise. 'That's not going to please Captain Ross. Follow me if you please.'

There was nothing Will and Megan could do but follow the boy up to the main deck. They climbed up the companionway and walked slowly, both stiff from the cramped conditions in which they had spent the last twelve hours. Captain Ross was summoned and the sailors told to stop the search.

'What the hell's going on?' Captain Ross was really angry when he surveyed the latest find. 'Do you people think this is some sort of pleasure cruise? Jesus Christ! And another girl! What...?'

His tirade was stopped by the arrival of Richard Camberwell who pushed past the ship's Captain, reached out a hand, and yanked Will nearly off his feet by the scruff of his neck then threw him across the deck where he landed heavily in a bundle of netting.

'You little thief! You devil! Why did you bloody well steal my horses?' he shouted loudly. He picked up the terrified Will who was scrambling to his feet, and punched him hard in the face. Will's nose immediately spurted blood. 'Damn it, boy! I can't believe you did this!' He shook Will hard like a rat, making his teeth rattle. Blood flecks sprayed the deck. The ship's crew, Ross, the army officers, and several soldiers drawn by the noise, stood dumbfounded at the display. Will was trying hard to open his mouth for long enough to say something but he was given no chance. In the end it was Megan who flew at her uncle and grabbed his arm that was drawn up to hit Will again.

'Uncle Richard! Stop it! It wasn't like that! Stop! I can explain!' she said.

'Megan?' In his haste to give Will what he thought were his just deserts, Richard Camberwell had completely missed his niece who had been standing behind some of the sailors. 'What the hell are you doing here?' Camberwell still held Will in a tight grip while he viewed his niece with mixed emotions. His first feeling was one of overwhelming relief that she was not in Portsmouth, his second was anger that she was not safely back at Camberwell Hall.

'Would someone like to tell me what the hell is going on here?' roared Captain Ross, trying to regain charge of the situation. 'I gather you know these stowaways, Captain. As you did the last one. Are you conducting some sort of free passage scheme here?'

'No, Captain,' said Camberwell grimly, staring hard at Will. 'I assure you their presence on board has nothing whatever to do with me. I suspect that it's this little bastard's doing.' He raised his fist and, despite Megan's pleas, hit Will again hard, sending him tumbling to the deck once more.

'Stop, Captain! That's enough!' Major Underwood came forward to intervene. 'I'm told you were undertaking a search for this lad, so you must have some idea what he's doing on board.'

'Those two horses Readman bought yesterday belong to me. I recognised them just before the ship left port. This is the boy I told you about, the thief who stole my purse. Now he's stolen my horses. And my niece too, it would seem.' Camberwell glared at Megan.

'There you are, Captain. You see I was right all along,' said Major Underwood with a smirk of satisfaction. 'You should never have employed him...'

'No! It's not like that at all! It was all my idea! Will came to protect me!' Megan shouted the words, determined to be heard, and she was. There was a sudden silence while everyone stared at her.

'What say we repair to my cabin and hear what the young lady has to say,' said Ross diplomatically. He was essentially a fair man and curious to know why he suddenly had a rash of stowaways on his ship. 'Pick up the lad, bo'sun, and put him in the brig.'

'No!' Megan shouted and ran to intervene, but the Captain stopped her.

'In case you didn't know, miss, it's a crime to stow away on a ship,' he said harshly. 'And if you weren't a girl, the brig is where you'd be too.' He jerked his head, indicating to Mister Grimshaw that he should take Will below. Will was lying on the deck, groaning and half stunned. The beefy bo'sun dragged him to his feet and hauled him away. Richard Camberwell was so angry he missed the look of distress on Megan's face as she watched Will go. His expression thunderous, he took her by the arm and marched her to the Captain's cabin.

A corner of the cabin was already being partitioned with pieces of wood and old sails to give Sarah Harvey some privacy. Megan was defiant. She had known her uncle would be angry once he discovered herself and Will, but the immensity of his anger scared her. However, his treatment of Will had brought back her courage, and not a little guilt. It was because of her that Will was in all this trouble, and she was determined to take the blame for the whole enterprise, if only her uncle was prepared to listen. She had seen him angry before, and knew he was often unwilling to accept others' points of view, but she had to make him see that Will was the innocent party.

Also aware of the young officer's anger, anger that could possibly cloud his judgement, Captain Ross was the first to speak.

'Now, lass,' he said. 'Explain yourself, if you please.'

So Megan, undeterred by her audience and Richard Camberwell's stern gaze, and fortified by her own indignation and resentment at everyone's treatment of Will, told the whole story, from the time Will had heard her taking Dinah out of her stall at home, up until they had stowed away on the frigate. The only thing she left out was the fact that Will had stolen money. It was obviously a crime and would get him into more trouble, and it occurred to her that his victim was possibly one of the other two army officers present.

As he listened to the tale, Richard Camberwell felt his anger subsiding a little, and in its place came a feeling of guilt. He realised that he had maligned Will badly, assuming all the wrong things. It appeared that Megan was entirely to blame for the whole enterprise, and Will had gone along merely to protect her. With the guilt came anger at his niece who, after the tale was told, received the length of his tongue for her foolishness.

'Well, Richard,' said James Shaw who had listened to Megan's story with interest, a lazy smile on his face. 'It seems the lad's innocent of all wrong doing. In fact, he appears to have been a model of good behaviour. I would say you should be thanking him instead of beating his brains out.'

'Perhaps you're right, James,' said Richard Camberwell ruefully. He turned to Captain Ross. 'Would you consider releasing the lad, Captain?'

'He still stowed away on my ship, Captain,' said Ross. 'A crime, as I pointed out. I think we'll give him another day in the brig to mull over his sins.' He looked at Megan. 'Maybe it'll make him think twice before being persuaded again into criminal activities by pretty young ladies.' Megan blushed. She wondered what the officers would say if they knew about Will's real crime. The heavy purse he had stolen was at the moment secreted at the bottom of her carpet bag.

Ross turned to her uncle. 'I would be obliged if you would keep both young ladies below decks as much as possible, Captain. They may take the air between second and third watch each day and that is all. I can't have the crew's minds and eyes being taken off their work.'

'Of course, sir.' Richard Camberwell reddened slightly. Elijah Ross obviously considered Sarah Harvey his responsibility, and Megan was frowning at him, wondering who the other woman was probably. Damn them both! What on earth was he to do with them once they reached Portugal?

After the officers had left the room, Richard Camberwell quizzed his niece further as to her reasons for leaving home. She explained her boredom and that she wanted to become a nurse, a suggestion that set her uncle laughing.

'A nurse, Megan? You don't have a compassionate bone in your body, girl!' The laughter continued at her look of indignation, but then his tone became more serious as he said, 'My dear, you have no idea at all what war is like, what horrific injuries men suffer, or what a hellhole a field hospital is. I can't begin to tell you either, because you'll probably think I'm exaggerating, but when you see them, you will know that you will never be a nurse.'

'Well, what can I do instead? There must be something.' Megan's tone was sullen and she tossed her head defiantly in a way her uncle knew only too well.

'I suppose you could do the men's laundry. There's always plenty of that.' Richard Camberwell's tone was teasing, and he smiled at the horrified look on Megan's face. She had never had to wash so much as a handkerchief in her life, though now she was on board ship she would have to learn how. And quickly. The thought tickled him. Megan had always been a proud girl, snobbish and disdainful of other people, especially those she considered beneath her, and the more Richard Camberwell thought of what was ahead of her, the more he considered that maybe it would not be such a bad thing for her to see how the other half lived. It would be hard. Very hard. But, despite the fact that there was a war on, not all that dangerous. The wives, mistresses and whores who followed the army were a law unto themselves, but were kept well out of the way of the fighting. If Megan insisted on going with them instead of being sent home on the next available ship as he thought she should be, she was definitely in for a big shock, but it might make a woman out of her.

Richard Camberwell spared a thought for his mother who would be out of her mind with worry. On hearing that Megan had not even left her a note, he reduced her to tears for her thoughtlessness and vowed to send a letter as soon as they docked in Lisbon, to be delivered on the next ship returning to England.

It was while he was berating her that the canvas was pushed aside from the partition, and Sarah Harvey peered around it. Her face was puffy with sleep, pale with sea-sickness, and her light hair was in a tangled halo. Having been provided with a low cot, she had quickly fallen into an exhausted slumber, but had woken to Richard Camberwell's loud voice berating his niece.

'Excuse me,' she said. 'I couldn't help overhearing, and I was curious to hear a woman's voice.'

Megan stared with tear-stained cheeks at the fair-haired girl as she walked into the room, and then stared with even more surprise at her uncle who was suddenly blushing and seemingly at a loss for words. In a flash it came to her that this girl meant something to him, and she stared with more interest. The girl was tall and slim, her face had a gamin quality, yet there was a steeliness about the set of the jaw and, although a little embarrassed, she spoke confidently.

'Won't you introduce me, Captain?'

'Oh...yes, of course. Miss Harvey, my niece, Megan Camberwell. Megan, this is Miss Sarah Harvey, also a stowaway. She is the daughter of the merchant we rented lodgings from in Portsmouth and, like you, has it in mind to go to Portugal.'

The girl gave her a friendly smile and Megan found herself smiling back, despite the fact that this girl was of the merchant class, and therefore only on a middle rung of Megan's social ladder. Richard Camberwell noticed the smile and was inwardly pleased. Maybe roughing it with Will for a week had already had a softening effect on his niece's supercilious attitude.

'It seems we are, quite literally, in the same boat,' said Sarah. 'I must say, it will be nice not to be the only female aboard. I presume we shall have to share sleeping quarters, so we will be friends.'

Megan, who had not had a female companion since leaving school, was dubious. She did not make friends easily. At school she had found that girls shied away from her because of her snobbishness and a tendency to say the wrong thing and offend people, personal characteristics she did not realise she had. The only girl who had befriended her was a pale wimp of a thing who had idolised her, and now, when she infrequently thought about Sadie Halliwell at all, it was with some shame because she knew she had played upon that idolisation and that she had certainly not returned the friendship in any way.

'I suppose we shall,' she now said in answer to Sarah Harvey's comment, though it was said with bad grace. However, this did not deter Sarah who seemed quite happy to have someone to share the voyage with.

'Can I go and see Will?' Megan asked her uncle.

'I'm not sure. You'd better ask the Captain,' said Camberwell.

'I'll help you find him. The ship is quite a maze until you know where you're going.' He turned to Sarah. 'If you'll excuse us, Miss Harvey. I think my niece is feeling somewhat guilty as her partner in crime is at present residing in the brig.'

'Of course, and as we are to be fellow passengers, please call me Sarah. Miss Harvey is so formal, and makes me feel so old!' The girl smiled a pale smile at Richard Camberwell, who was struck once more by her elfin beauty. He stammered a reply but was doubtful if she heard it because she suddenly gave a hurried apology and ran behind the screen again as the motion of the ship once more made itself felt.

While following her uncle up companion ways and along corridors to the bridge where he expected to find the ship's Captain, Megan was tempted to ask him if he and the other stowaway meant anything to each other, but for once she held her tongue. Richard Camberwell's anger at herself and Will may have abated, but it was not far beneath the surface and any further embarrassment might set him off again.

In hoping to see Will, Megan was disappointed. Captain Ross told her that the boy would have to stew for a while and visitors to the brig were not allowed.

'Makes them think about their evil-doings, girl,' he told her in between puffs of a foul-smelling pipe while staring out at grey clouds on the horizon. 'Now, if I were you, I'd get below before that storm up ahead hits us. On deck might not be the best place to be in an hour or so.'

Captain Ross's forecast was pretty accurate. The storm hit them round about the Bay of Biscay, and carried on for the best part of the night. Richard Camberwell found himself one of the few passengers not afflicted by seasickness and spent a great deal of time tending to those who were. Major Underwood cursed the foul weather and his stomach in equal measure. James Shaw seemed unaffected, but the two girls both wished with all their hearts that they had never embarked. The soldiers all wished themselves on dry land, even the war-torn Peninsula, and vowed that meeting the French could not be worse than being tossed around like a piece of flotsam on the ocean, and feeling as though their stomachs were turning inside out.

By the next morning there was just a fresh breeze and a damp, smelly ship. The sailors went about their business, hoisting sails to take advantage of the wind, and the passengers set about cleaning their living space as best they could with sea water drawn up from the side. Megan, her stomach fragile and her face still with a greenish tinge, managed to forget her own troubles for a while when she saw Will who was at last released from the brig. He had not suffered from seasickness but had been forced to endure his own torment with the rats, an aching head, and the fact that everyone had been so busy trying to keep the ship afloat that no one had remembered to feed him.

Richard Camberwell felt a huge pang of guilt when the bo'sun brought Will to his cabin as ordered by Captain Ross. Will's face was drawn and his eyes told of sleeplessness. His cheek was bruised and blood-smeared where he had wiped the blood away from his nose, and the filth that clung to him from twenty-four hours in the brig that was not cleaned at all regularly, made him stink worse than a pig.

'It appears I owe you an apology, Will,' he said. 'Megan told me what happened. I'm afraid I jumped to all the wrong conclusions.'

'Not to worry, sir,' said Will, magnanimous in his relief that the master was not annoyed with him any more. He had spent the night worrying whether he would be in for more rough treatment when he was released from the brig.

'You and I will talk later, but in the meantime I think a good wash and a meal would be welcome, would it not?' said Camberwell.

'Yes, sir,' answered Will.

'I'll find you some food, Will,' said Megan hastily. She was feeling worse than she could have imagined. Will's suffering was all her fault and the least she could do would be to go to the galley and fetch him food, even though just the thought of it at the moment made her feel queasy.

Once fed and fairly clean, dressed in trousers and a shirt that Megan had begged Midshipman Spencer to borrow from one of the sailors for him, Will felt a whole lot better, though very tired. He couldn't remember when he had last slept. Seeing how tired he was, Richard Camberwell gave up his bunk for the rest of that day and Will slept like a baby. Camberwell woke him to eat supper, and Midshipman Spencer brought him a hammock which they slung between the bulkheads of the cabin. Although these sleeping arrangements felt very strange at first, Will was soon rocked back to sleep, and awoke in the morning refreshed and looking forward to the voyage ahead.

Later that day, standing on the fo'c'sle, feeling the great ship surging ahead beneath him through the waves and watching the endless horizon, Will felt a thrill of excitement. His future was still to be decided, but he was on his way to a foreign land where he would meet new challenges, new people, a whole new way of life. He was to get his wish, and become a soldier.

And, best of all, Megan was going with him.

10

Portugal, October 1811

The sun beat down on a landscape barren of all except low hills, short grass and a zig-zag of sparkling river water that ran like a lightning strike behind banks of earth and between clumps of trees. A bare hard track wound its way ahead of the slow-moving column of men, horses and wagons, following the course of the river. Nothing else moved in a countryside that drowsed in the heat of the day, the only sounds the tramping of booted feet, the thudding of horses' hooves, the jingle of harness and rumble of wagon wheels. The dust that the boots, hooves and wheels produced, and the effort involved in walking in the heat, prevented much conversation and the forty-eight infantry recruits walked in silence while the officers on horseback kept a watchful eye for the enemy.

They had been in the Peninsula for four days, crossing Portugal to reach Wellington's army which, rumour had it, was concentrated around Sabugal, near the Spanish border. Captain Ross's frigate had not carried the soldiers to Lisbon but, at Major Underwood's request, had put in further north, at Oporto. Having studied a map, the Major had decided they would have fewer miles to walk than if they docked at Lisbon.

It was still a very long walk, especially for men more used to treading the leafy lanes of England. The country was full of hills and valleys and the ground was hard as iron after the baking summer sun. They had gone only seventy miles, following the River

Douro as much as possible, at a snail's pace according to Under-wood who was hot and irritable and who periodically urged Ser-geant Readman to make the men walk faster. However most of the forty-eight recruits had feet so blistered they were unable to go any quicker, so Robert Underwood grumbled in vain.

In front of the column, riding Dinah next to Hades, Megan Camberwell viewed the landscape with mixed feelings. She thought how different it was from that of England. To her surprise, she missed the tall trees, the lush green, and even the gentle rain of her homeland, things she had never before thought of as anything other than background to her pampered life. Now she shifted uncomfortably in the saddle. Sweat was making her stick to it, and the perspiration trickled down her neck to settle around the waist-line of her dress. Megan felt dirty. Was dirty. She couldn't remem-ber when she had last washed all over but for sure it hadn't been for weeks.

And she was tired. A good night's sleep was a thing of the past. The voyage by ship had been horrible; a torment of seasickness and hot, cramped, weary work helping out in the galley, a penance, so Captain Ross maintained, for daring to stow away on his ship. Megan had hated every minute of it and was extremely pleased to disembark at Oporto, though the journey through Portugal thus far had been little better as far as pleasure was concerned and had provided poor relief. So far they had stayed in hamlets along the way, mostly in barns, though once in a house which was a mere hovel and no more comfortable than a stable. Megan's nights had been spent in hot discomfort, fighting off the countless insects that seemed to abound in this unfamiliar country. Even as she thought of feather beds, hot water and scented soap, a persistent itch under her armpit forced her to scratch and she really hoped that she didn't have lice, though suspected it was a forlorn hope. The yearning for a soft mattress and bathing water was permanently with her, but every time the remembrance of the comforts she had left behind threatened to become overwhelming, she would pull herself together and think only of the future, determined to prove her uncle wrong. He had been persuaded with difficulty that she should not be immediately returned to England, yet still thought that she would end up begging him to send her back. However, her stubbornness and strong will would not let him be proved right

139

and, so far, she had met the discomforts of the journey without much audible complaint.

Megan turned in the saddle to see the column behind her. Sergeant Readman led the recruits who were laden down by their packs and had muskets slung over their shoulders. Most of them were walking with dull, expressionless faces, merely willing their sore feet and aching legs to keep going. A few were wincing at the pain, but quietly, knowing they would get no sympathy from either sergeant or officers. The dust that their boots kicked up swirled around them and almost hid the four wagons, drawn by oxen, that transported the supplies brought from England on the ship, and food for the journey. Megan could just make out Sarah Harvey, sitting with the driver on the seat of the first wagon. Sarah had been offered Lightfoot to ride, but said she was frightened of horses and had never ridden one in her life, so Lightfoot carried the officers' baggage and was tied by a long rope to the third wagon. Behind the wagons came a small herd of thin cattle, driven by a scrawny Portuguese who seemed to be able to walk for ever without tiring. The cows were the soldiers' meat rations for the journey.

Will marched near the front of the column, walking beside George Trim. He looked up and smiled at her and Megan wondered again at his cheerfulness. Of all the infantrymen, he was the only one who looked happy, even wearing the hated boots which she knew he detested. Despite her discomfort, she found herself returning the smile, wondering as she did so why that grin always seemed to cheer her up. She felt that Will was probably the only one of the weary soldiers really enjoying himself.

Which was true. Will was happy. He was a soldier. He was out in the fresh air, albeit dust laden at the moment. He was fed morning and evening and he could look up and see Megan whenever he wanted to. Life was good.

The days on the ship had been good too. At Captain Ross's command, and because he suffered no seasickness and had a head for heights, Will had spent the time as a sailor, quickly learning the sailor's skills. So swiftly had he become adept at climbing the rigging and setting the sails, that Captain Ross had felt obliged to request that he stay aboard and become part of the crew, but Will had other ideas. Discussion with Richard Camberwell had decided Will's immediate future. His determination to become a soldier had vied with the fact that he was still in Lord Camberwell's employ, so the two had come to a compromise. Will could join the army, but it would be as Richard Camberwell's servant. Also, Camberwell hoped that arrangement would keep him out of the way of the worst of the fighting. Having heard from his niece that Will was in no way responsible for stealing the horses or of encouraging Megan's foolhardiness, Camberwell's attitude towards him had reverted back to that of master and, if anything, their relationship had been strengthened by the whole episode. Will did not resent the beating he had received from Camberwell, knowing it had been thought justified at the time, and he was quite happy with the arrangements that had been made for him. Now he marched comfortably with the other recruits, the only one in civilian clothes as there were no spare uniforms. The uniform items that had been with the supplies had been left behind on the ship by mistake.

From Hades's broad saddle, Richard Camberwell stared at the countryside and thought it was good to be back. Once his wounds had healed at home in England, he had fallen pleasantly into his position as lord of the manor, yet there had always been a restlessness, an itch that he couldn't quite scratch, and he knew that returning to this land would cure it. He was a born soldier, a man who could envisage doing nothing else for a living because his interest in the placid responsibilities at Camberwell Hall always paled after a very short time and he would hanker for the excitement and adventure of his other life as an army Captain. Thinking on it, he supposed that was why he had spent much of his time at the Hall riding his horses. It sent him away from the dullness of home, and the feel of muscle and flesh galloping beneath him over the fields and moors reminded him of more adventurous times. It was also one reason he had been amenable to Will's wish to join the army. He could understand the youngster's need to be more than just a stable boy. There was a whole world out there, and Will wanted to see it as much as Camberwell himself had when he was a youth. Yet Lord Richard's experiences at war would not let him give in wholeheartedly to Will's request. He had seen first-hand, and many times, what the war could do to lads such as Will, hence his decision to take him on as a replacement for Jeremiah Todd. An officer's servant had a much better chance of survival than did an ordinary private, and he wondered again how Todd had died because he was unlikely to have been in the front line of a fight. It was probably the fever which, when it caught a hold, saw off as many of the soldiers as did the French.

His eyes scanned the hilly horizon, always on the look out for bands of marauding Frenchmen or deserters. The river ran below them like a diamond necklace sparkling in the sun. It was not just the French that he searched for. Partisans roamed these hills and not all were friendly towards the British. Some of the hardened fighters resented all foreigners of whatever nationality, and their ways of dealing with them were fierce in the extreme.

During the stops along the way, and on board ship, he, Captain Shaw and Sergeant Readman had drilled the soldiers for long hours in loading and firing the muskets they now had slung over their shoulders. They had learned the basics of training at Winchester but Richard Camberwell knew only too well that very often a soldier's life depended on how quickly he could load his musket, and he was determined that these men, the best of whom would belong to his own Light Company, should be able to fire at least three shots a minute by the time they engaged the enemy. He himself had one of the much admired Baker rifles which were used by the Rifle units and some of the Light Companies. The rifling inside the barrel meant that a bullet could be fired with much more accuracy over a greater distance than that of a musket. The rifle had been presented to him by a Rifles' Colonel who had been impressed by Richard Camberwell's ability and bravery on the field at the Battle of Talavera. The Rifles' Colonel had wanted him to transfer and become a Rifleman, one of the army's elite infantry troops, but Lord Richard's own Colonel, William Drew, would not release him. Richard Camberwell could load and fire four balls in sixty seconds, and sometimes even be loading a fifth before the minute was up if there was no wind. But it had taken years of war to make him an expert and he knew he could not reasonably expect these boys to fire more than twice a minute in the heat of battle, if that, because nerves, as much as the French, would stand in the way of success. Richard Camberwell kept a good eye open for any sign of life in the sleeping countryside, having no wish to engage either the French or the Partisans with this small and inexperienced company.

He glanced at Megan riding beside him. Major Underwood had

142

grudgingly agreed to return his horses, and Megan was made to give back the money she had been paid for them. Richard Camberwell was pleasantly surprised at the amount Will had haggled for. It seemed the boy had a good business head on his shoulders. So, for now, Megan had her horse back, though officially Dinah was part of her uncle's string. Camberwell studied Megan's face and chestnut curls, dulled now with dust. She was bearing up well, he thought, though he suspected that she was hiding a lot of what she felt. He smiled to himself, knowing that she was deliberately uncomplaining because of what he might do if she did. It struck him how alike they were. He too was a stubborn cuss, and she shared his wish for excitement in her life. It was a pity she hadn't been born a boy. Thinking of boys, he still wondered about her feelings for Will. They had certainly shown no romantic interest in each other that he had seen, yet he could not forget the anger she had shown when he had beaten the boy and he had been taken to the brig. That she cared for him was obvious, but how much was not.

Which sent his mind off on another tack. Sarah Harvey. There had been no romantic attachment there either, yet there was an interest. He could feel it in the looks she gave him when she thought no one was looking, the way in which she engaged him in conversation whenever possible, limited to the dinner table aboard ship. There had hardly been any chance to talk since then as he was always busy or with the other officers when they camped for the night. Sometimes, when he thought of her, he could feel himself breaking out into a sweat that added to the constant perspiration brought on by the heat, and when they did speak he often found himself stumbling over words like a shy schoolboy, a most unusual experience for a Camberwell who was always forthright and hardly ever at a loss as to what to say in a given circumstance. It was most disconcerting, but he could not rid himself of the knowledge, unspoken but certain nonetheless, that Sarah Harvey had stowed away because of him, and neither could he stop dreaming of her in his bed at night.

'Blimey! It ain't 'arf 'ot!' Nat Binns, a small, sharp-faced man of indeterminate age, with long greasy hair and legs that were so bandy he looked like he was permanently riding a ghostly horse, took off his shako and swiped a hand across his wet forehead. 'Don't it ever rain in this bleedin' country?'

'It rains,' said Sergeant Readman affably. 'And then all this dust becomes a quagmire. Be thankful yer ain't 'avin' to walk through mud, and put yer 'at on, Binns. Yer make the place look untidy. It'll get cooler the closer we get to the mountains.'

Binns replaced his shako. He winced as he trod on a stone that pressed on a particularly virulent blister. ''Ow much further, Sarge?'

Readman studied the sky. The sun was still high. 'Long way yet. We ain't covered 'alf the distance the Major wants us to go today.'

'Bloody 'ell!' was Binns's mumbled comment. Binns, like many of Britain's soldiers, was a convict. He had been caught red-handed breaking into the London house of a minor politician with intent to deprive him of any valuables he may have had lying around. However, because there had been no stolen property on him at the time, and despite the presence of a jemmy and a large sack which showed his intent, Binns had managed to escape the Newgate Morris dance of the gallows, and had been offered the king's shilling or deportation instead.

'Can't we stop for a rest, Sarge?' asked Binns's neighbour, a pale youth called Maurice Hargreaves. He was limping badly.

'Not a chance, lad,' replied the Sergeant cheerfully, knowing that if they stopped, the column of men would be hard to get moving again. 'Pick yer feet up there, Trim! This is a march, not a bloody walk in the park!'

'Me bloody feet are killin' me!' muttered George Trim to Will who was walking next to him, though he did try and step out a little more briskly to avoid the sergeant's further recriminations. 'Don't walk so fast, Will! Ain't yer feet 'urtin'?'

'Not 'specially,' answered Will, 'but then me boots are too big and don't rub. I'd much rather be walkin' barefoot. Me bloody feet'll be gettin' soft.'

'Yer mad,' said George. 'Anyway, slow down a bit, will yer?'

Will obligingly slowed his step to match that of his suffering friend. More soldiers were now complaining to Sergeant Readman who bellowed at them to shut up and march.

They carried on for another hour, then the road wound round a rocky hillside, on the other side of which was a fine view of the river, running beside a ridge of similar rocky outcrops. Nestled beside the river was a small hamlet of half a dozen houses with a bridge that crossed the water. Smoke curled up into the still air.

'Maybe we could stop here and water the horses and ourselves,' suggested Captain Shaw. Although he did not have the problem of ill-fitting boots and aching legs, he was just as hot as everyone else and would welcome a refill of his canteens.

Major Underwood halted the march, much to the recruits' relief, and studied the small village. 'A reconnaissance, Captain?' he said to Camberwell on his left.

'Yes, sir.' Every village, big or small, that they had passed through had been surveyed by Captain Camberwell and a few of the men before the main column had entered, in case it was being held by the French. Most had received only a cursory inspection because they could usually tell from a distance that all was well. If women were going about their daily chores, and animals were grazing contentedly in the fields, then nothing was amiss.

Richard Camberwell scrutinised the hamlet in the valley below. Nothing moved, but it was siesta time and the village looked peaceful enough. He could see no saddled horses or any other sign of the enemy and the smoking chimneys spoke of normal peasant occupation, yet he had a bad feeling, a sixth sense that told him something wasn't right. Experience had taught him to take heed of such feelings. They had saved his life more than once.

He turned in the saddle. 'Sergeant, six of your best shots if you please.'

'Yes, sir.' Readman called out six names and those men slid the muskets off their shoulders and loaded them.

Will was included in the six. Richard Camberwell had been extremely surprised to find out that his stable boy was very proficient with a musket. Will had offered no explanation for his skill but had earned Captain Camberwell's admiration, especially when he quickly learned to load and fire the weapon three times in a minute, something that not many of the other recruits could accomplish as yet. Unfortunately Will's remarkable skill meant that Camberwell's good intentions of keeping him away from the front line, would probably not be so easy to accomplish. So far he had been an automatic choice for reconnaissance details such as this.

Camberwell led the six soldiers on foot himself. As Captain of a Light Company he often had to lead his men in the skirmish line, to harass the enemy infantry and pick off the officers. Skirmishers

145

used rifles because they were more accurate but Richard Camberwell was the only one of the seven who possessed one, which meant that if they encountered any of the enemy, the other six would have to get really close to have a good chance of killing a Frenchman.

Skirmishers worked in pairs; one loading while the other fired, giving cover for each other. It was a system that worked well but the soldiers had to work fast and only the best marksmen made it into the skirmish line. Richard Camberwell had high hopes of several of the new recruits, including, unfortunately, Will, and George Trim, whose grandfather had been a soldier and who had taught George to shoot at an early age. Will and George had become fast friends on the voyage to Portugal, and now walked down the hillside towards the village together.

Will kept to as much cover as possible, an easy thing for a boy who was used to blending into the landscape after stealing a purse or a watch. Now he kept to the tallest grass and the stunted trees, moving quietly, George treading in his footsteps and copying his stealth.

The soldiers reached the bottom of the slope and cautiously crept towards the village, Captain Camberwell motioning them to stay close. Will and the others held their loaded muskets ready. They had also caught the feeling that something was wrong. No dogs barked, no chickens pecked for grain in the yards. The thin smoke still wafted from two chimneys in the still afternoon air but the village had an unoccupied air, and the soldiers moved forward with a sense of foreboding. And now they were closer, they could smell a sickening stench. Richard Camberwell knew what it was. It was the stench of death.

Will, on the outside of the group crouched down behind a ploughshare and stared at the river, only feet away. A willow tree leaned over into the water, its roots pulled half out of the soil by a past flood. Something was stuck in the cleft of one large root and the muddy bank, something round, red, and black. Will stared at it, trying to decide whether it was a boulder or maybe a pig's bladder that had been used by a child as a ball. There seemed to be fur on it, fur that spread into the rippling water that lapped at the mud. Will shifted a little, the better to see the object, then his stomach gave a sickening lurch and his mouth went dry. He was looking at a head, a human head. Forcing himself to his feet, unable to take his eyes off the ghastly thing, he went closer and felt the vomit rising up as he gazed at the head. What he had taken for fur was black hair, matted with blood that was spread over the contorted features and concentrated in one eye socket. What was worse, there was no body. The head had been cut from the body as cleanly as a scythe cut corn. Will turned away, knowing that if he looked any more he would be sick. He had seen dead people before in the Thames and streets of London, but never one without its body. He ran at a crouch towards the nearest house which Richard Camberwell was preparing to enter.

'Sir, over there. An 'ead,' he whispered urgently.

Camberwell glanced in the direction Will was pointing and grimaced. 'I fear that's not all we'll find,' he said grimly. Now he knew what his sense of smell and his instinct had been telling him all along, and he almost baulked at walking into the innocent looking building beside him for fear of what he would find there, but he had to do his duty.

'Cover me,' he said to the soldiers then went inside with Will close on his heels while the other five trained their muskets up and down the village street.

It was worse than either had envisaged, and both just stood and stared at the horror in the dim room. Will felt his stomach churn, and swallowed in a valiant attempt to keep the vomit down. Flies rose up in buzzing angry clouds, then settled again in black, crawling, obscene clumps.

'Oh, Lord!' Richard Camberwell felt his own gorge rise at the dreadful sight. He had seen death many times on the battlefield, all of it horrible, but he had rarely seen it in this guise. The family who had lived in the house were all lying in blood-soaked horror amongst the broken furniture. There was blood everywhere, splashed on the stone walls and puddled on the floor. An old man lay amongst the ruins of a rocking chair, with half his head missing. A man of perhaps thirty had at least three bullet holes in his chest, his hand across the face of a young woman who lay next to him, naked from the waist down, her skirts around her waist and her stomach a bloody mess. What finally made Will lose the battle against his churning stomach was the sabre slash across the back of a child of three or four years who lay in a pool of blood beside the woman.

And the fact that the woman had been pregnant.

He ran out of the house and vomited in the street.

'What is it Will?' George Trim asked the question tentatively but the only answer Will could give when he finally wiped a hand across his mouth, was a shocked face washed of all its colour, and eyes that told of unimaginable horrors.

The soldiers' hands that held the muskets trembled as they glanced at each other, frightened and shocked. Nobody had told them war would be like this. They looked up as one man when Captain Camberwell emerged slowly from the doorway. He was as pale as Will and visibly trying to get a grip on himself.

'We have to check the other houses,' he said bleakly. 'Go in pairs and be careful. We don't know if any of the enemy are still here.'

The soldiers went very cautiously into each house. The story was the same in every one. People, dogs, everything dead. Men who had lived in towns and cities where violence was rife, and strong farmer's sons who could cut a pig's throat or wring a chicken's neck without a qualm, none could stop the involuntary physical reaction to what they saw and soon the stink of vomit was added to the stench that pervaded the village.

'Bloody 'ell!' said one soldier, a hefty ex-blacksmith called Ron Parker. 'But whoever did this must be the very devil 'imself!'

Richard Camberwell also wondered at the savagery that had been inflicted on these seemingly innocent people, but in one of the houses he found the reason why this village had been massacred. On a wall were written four words in blood that had dripped down the whitewash. 'Mort a le Partisan' – Death to the Partisan. This then had been a village which had protected and helped the Partisans. Some of its occupants had probably been members of a Partisan band. The French had found out, and destroyed them all. But it was no excuse. Nothing could excuse such barbarity.

Camberwell called the small group together. There had been no sign of the French.

'Tomkins, go back and tell the Major it's safe to come down,' he said. Bob Tomkins ran, glad to get away from the village if only for a few minutes. 'We'll have to bury the bodies,' continued the Captain, 'but you lads have done enough already. Parker, Sims, go to the other end of the village and keep lookout. We don't need to be surprised by the bastards who did this. Ripley, you stay here and grab Tomkins when he comes back. Will, you and Trim go to the bridge. Keep a good lookout, lads. I want to know if anything moves but us. And all of you fill your canteens from the well.'

'Well's fouled, sir,' announced Titus Sims. 'It stinks like a midden. The buggers've pissed in it.'

'Damn!' It was a common way of preventing the British from getting fresh water. 'We'll just have to boil river water again. But go upstream where it'll be fresh.'

The Major and the rest of the soldiers came down the hillside to the village, the wagons trailing slowly behind.

'Good God, man! What the hell's happened here?' Major Underwood pressed a large handkerchief to his nose. James Shaw whitened as he saw the pools of vomit left by the forward patrol, and guessed what they had found.

For answer, Captain Camberwell took Underwood into the nearest house. Only seconds later, the Major staggered out again, his normally florid complexion whiter than a sheet. 'Fire the houses,' he said.

'Not a good idea, Major,' said Camberwell. 'The French'll see the smoke and know we're here. I've a feeling they're not too far away.'

Underwood's face paled even more. 'Of course,' he said. He pressed the handkerchief closer to his face so that his voice was muffled as he said, 'Get them buried then, Captain. And quickly. I'll keep the women away.' He mounted his horse and trotted swiftly back to where the wagons had stopped some distance from the first house. Camberwell wryly watched him go. Trust Underwood to pass the buck and get as far away as possible from the stink.

Quickly he gave orders to the men to get shovels from the wagons and advised Captain Shaw, who was looking very ill, to find a suitable place for them to dig a mass grave. Shaw looked vaguely about. There was a patch of tilled land behind one of the houses. 'Over there?' he suggested. Camberwell nodded. It was the only piece of ground that looked anywhere near soft enough to dig.

It took hours to dig the big hole. The men worked in shifts but it still took until the sun was very low on the horizon. Megan, and Sarah Harvey, watched from a distance but at Underwood's insistance turned away when the soldiers began carrying bodies from the houses, a grisly task that would have emptied more stomachs had there been anything left inside them. At last the job was done and the grave filled again. The men washed upstream in the river and stood to attention around the long heap of soil while Underwood said a few words, commending the souls of the villagers to their Maker. There was no firing of muskets for the same reason as they had not set fire to the houses.

'Where do you suggest we camp, Robert?' asked Shaw as they walked away.

'Anywhere but here,' said Underwood flatly.

'The French are in front of us,' said Camberwell. While the grave was being dug, he had investigated the road that led across the bridge. The hoof-prints of many horses overlaid others. The French had come into the village from the east, and gone back the same way. It had been a deliberate massacre. Somehow they had got wind of the fact that this village harboured Partisans and they had set out to destroy it, with devastating effect. The British had found not one French uniformed body.

'Have you any idea how far away they are?' Underwood sounded anxious.

'No, but wild animals hadn't had time to get at those people and their fires were still warm. I reckon we only missed the French by a few hours. Some of the pools of blood had barely dried.'

'Damn!'

'And it's getting too dark for the wagons and horses to travel safely,' Camberwell pointed out. 'None of us know the road. I don't wish to stay here any more than you do, Robert, but I vote we cross the bridge and camp on the other side.'

'I suppose that'll have to do,' said Underwood sourly. 'Give the orders, Richard.'

Richard Camberwell did so. The men were not happy though, and wanted to know why they couldn't travel on to more congenial surroundings. They were tired and very uneasy.

'What if they come back?' Gerald Butterworth, a pale, thin, bespectacled youth looked around him nervously, as if expecting Frenchmen to materialise out of the ground beneath his feet.

'You'll know about it if they do, son,' said Sergeant Readman dryly 'but I doubt they will. No, their work 'ere is done, and they're off lookin' for other prey. Now get yer arse over that bridge with the rest of 'em, lad, and 'elp set up camp.'

No one ate or slept much that night, despite all the hard work and emotional trauma of the day. Those that did sleep, woke up in a cold sweat, dreaming of the terrible sights they had seen. The pickets stayed in pairs and tried to curb their fanciful imaginations that made enemies out of dark shadows and a fitful wind. Richard Camberwell, too restless himself, saw a faint orange glow on the distant horizon and knew it was firelight, the French camp. The British had been ordered not to light fires, and, although some were hungry, the men had rested knowing that hunger was better than cold steel in the belly.

The next morning, the men roused themselves very early and started walking, eating any cold food that they had in their packs. Gone was the silent suffering of men only thinking about sore feet. The feet were still sore but now minds were more concerned with the knowledge that the French were not too far ahead of them. Sergeant Readman tried to restore their confidence by telling them the French were poor shots and bad swordsmen, but all knew he lied.

Riding Dinah, Megan too kept her silence. The finding of the village had shocked her. Up until now, she had looked upon her wish to go to war as something of an adventure. Even the discomfort and cramped conditions of the sea voyage had been an education, but the broken, bloody bodies that she had been unable to resist staring at in morbid fascination as they were brought from the houses in the distance, had brought home to her that war was savage, destructive, and horrible. She had turned away from the sight of the dead children and had gone over to Sarah Harvey, whose face was as pale as her own.

The older girl had taken her hand, and Megan, who might have objected to such familiarity in other circumstances, felt comforted by it.

'There is nothing we can do.' Sarah still stared at the growing pile of corpses, a world of despair in her voice.

'Yes there is.' There was determination in Megan's. She looked at the girl who had dragged her white face away from the dreadful spectacle. 'We can fight whoever did this. We can fight them, if not with guns and swords like the men, then with our hands and our hearts. I know I'm not a very caring person. The only person I've ever really cared about is myself, but I want to help, Sarah. I want

151

you to teach me what to do to be a nurse. Will you?'

'Gladly.' Sarah had smiled a faint smile and felt her courage return. She kissed Megan on the cheek. 'You and I will be part of this war, Megan. We'll show the men that women are needed.'

Now, riding slowly along in the growing heat, gazing at the seemingly endless white road in front of them, Megan mentally tried to be optimistic. She knew, as did Sarah, that the officers viewed them both as unwanted encumbrances and she had done her very best not to upset any of them, curbing her wilfulness and trying to be helpful. She had learned many things about army life already; how to wash her own clothes, and, with Will, those of her uncle; eating without complaint the sometimes very unpalatable food; sleeping in all sorts of disgusting conditions and listening to the men's often uncouth and ribald comments and conversation. The recruits had received a strong caution to watch their foul tongues in the girls' presence. However, they frequently forgot this injunction and Megan had learned more swear words in the last few weeks than she knew existed. The massacre at the village had forced her to think about things in a more serious vein, but she was determined to see this venture through.

She still wondered if her uncle and Sarah were romantically involved. She had noticed the embarrassment her uncle sometimes felt when Sarah was present, but had seen no other sign. It seemed strange to Megan that a hard, forthright man such as Richard Camberwell should feel anything other than confident in any situation. She was sure there was something between the two, yet had not liked to ask Sarah in case she was imagining things.

Richard Camberwell was also letting thoughts of Sarah Harvey slip into his mind as they followed the hoof-prints that told him the French had passed this way before them. He found the memory of that sweet face with the big grey eyes, and the slim yet shapely body kept intruding into his thoughts, and he cursed them. He cursed the girl for stowing away on board the ship and coming between him and his duty. There was danger here, and yet he could not stop thinking about her. And knowing she was but a few short yards behind him was hell. He turned to Major Underwood.

'Permission to scout ahead, sir,' he said formally.

Underwood seemed somewhat surprised by the request, but shrugged and granted it anyway. 'If you wish, Captain,' he said. 'If you wish.'

Camberwell cantered his horse away from the group towards the rocky hills. The road and the river wound its way between them. The river valley narrowed and the hillsides became higher. An ideal place for an ambush, Camberwell thought, and hoped that the French had not noticed they were being followed. He wished there was another road they could take but the wagons would not be able to negotiate the narrow rough tracks over the hills, and they did not need to be halted by a broken wagon wheel or axle.

He rounded a buttress of rock and sent Hades up one of the tracks, onto a wooded ridge. There he reined the horse and gazed at the surrounding countryside. He could see parts of the road, and behind him, to his left, the column following slowly along it. He stared off to his right, and his eyes narrowed. Was that smoke he could see, or the morning heat haze quivering the air? He looked harder. It was smoke. Thin trails of it in the still air, but definitely smoke. The French camp, and they were making a much later start to their day than the British had. He surveyed the terrain, grinned, and an outrageous idea swept into his mind.

Quickly he rode back to the column. Underwood saw him coming at a gallop and called a halt.

'What is it, man? What's the matter?'

Camberwell reined in, raising a small cloud of dust. 'The French are about a mile ahead, Major. They haven't struck camp yet.'

'Well then, we'll wait here awhile and let them move on,' said Underwood decidedly.

'I was thinking we could outflank them, Major. Pay the bastards back for what they did to that village.'

Underwood looked shocked. 'Are you mad, Captain? You wish to deliberately engage the Crapauds? No, we'll wait here until they get well ahead of us.' He raised his hand and brought the column to a halt.

Richard Camberwell frowned and seemed about to object but then he remembered the forty-eight recruits. Maybe it would not be a good idea to involve them in a fight at this early stage. He said nothing further and dismounted, then gave a curt order for pickets to stand guard, but it was plain to all that the senior officer's decision had not been well received.

For two hours, the column relaxed in the growing heat of the day until the pickets on the high ground reported that the smoke had disappeared.

'Right, we can carry on now,' said Major Underwood, leading his horse towards a rock which he could use as a mounting block to heave his not inconsiderable bulk into the saddle once more.

'Better to wait a bit longer, sir,' Camberwell suggested. 'Could be they haven't actually left yet. After all, we often put out our fires before saddling the horses and striking tents.' He turned to the sentry who had reported the disappearance of the smoke. 'Did you see a dust cloud?'

'No, sir.'

Underwood turned to his Captain, a look of head-masterly forbearance on his face. 'Richard, first you want us to attack them head on, now you want us to wait. They must have gone. We travel on.'

Richard Camberwell scowled and someone in the ranks sniggered.

'Quiet that man or I'll cut yer bloody tongue out!' growled Sergeant Readman.

The column fell into line, one or two of the recruits looking apprehensive. What if Captain Camberwell was right and the French were still there? They began to march without enthusiasm.

Richard Camberwell wanted to say something, to object to Underwood's peremptory decision, but he held his tongue. The man was insufferable and the longer he served under him, the more insufferable he became. The Major had been fairly new to command before his injury at the battle of Fuentes d'Oñoro. How he had managed to obtain permission to go home and recuperate from what was only a minor wound, no one knew, though Captain Shaw, in a quiet aside to Camberwell one day at their lodgings in Portsmouth, had indicated that Underwood was related to the Colonel of the regiment which probably accounted for it. Having been forced into his company, both at Winchester and Portsmouth, Richard Camberwell found Underwood surly, disagreeable, and boorish, whereas James Shaw, a new commission to the regiment, was an easy-going and amusing companion. Lazy as hell, of course, as a lot of young gentlemen were, but his charm and wit made up for his indolence. Though from similar backgrounds, all three officers were totally different characters, and Richard Camberwell sometimes wondered if he was the only one who realised that they were actually going to war here. Both Shaw and Underwood seemed to be viewing this march merely as a rather uncomfortable excursion.

The column wended its way slowly down the river valley and round the buttress of rock below the wooded ridge from where Camberwell had seen the smoke. The soldiers trudged along, sweating under their thick cloth uniforms and heavy packs. They had done some forced marches back in England, but there the trees spread their leafy shade across the narrow lanes. Here there was no shade at all by the road except where the track ran close by the river, and the sun beat down relentlessly.

Camberwell tried to judge just how far away the smoke had been. It was hard to tell with the rocky terrain that hid the road. He was about to suggest that he scout ahead again, when they passed the site of the French encampment. The sparse grass had been flattened by tents and many feet, there were piles of horse dung where the French horses had been picketed, and the ashes of camp-fires.

'There, you see!' said Major Underwood triumphantly, turning to Camberwell, 'I told you...'

His speech was cut off abruptly by the crack of a musket and the Major's eyes suddenly opened wide, as did his mouth. Blood started to run down his back and he slumped forward in the saddle.

11

The shocked recruits and officers stared as Major Underwood slowly tumbled out of the saddle. His horse skittered nervously, pawing up dust and pebbles. Richard Camberwell was the first man to gather his wits as more shots rang out.

'Take cover!' he shouted.

Amidst a hail of bullets, and screams as two recruits were hit, the startled infantry ran for the meagre cover of rocks and bushes.

'Megan! Get back to the wagons!' Lord Richard yelled. Not needing to be told twice, the girl yanked Dinah's head round and kicked her heels back, rousing the willing mare into a gallop. Richard Camberwell dismounted and slapped his own horse's rump, sending Hades cantering after her. As he ran for the hillside

155

himself, Camberwell cursed the fallen Major, at the same time trying to work out where the shots were coming from.

Sergeant Readman was shouting at the new boys, making sure their muskets were loaded and trying to chivvy them into responding to the barrage of gunfire that now bombarded the column. Most of the recruits had their heads down behind what cover was available, frightened to death, though one or two guns fired at the rocky hillside slightly in front and to the left of them where the French had hidden themselves to await the British. The bastards had probably spotted them hours ago, thought Camberwell. He saw that two wounded redcoats were attempting to crawl towards the sparse bushes at the roadside, leaving the still body of Robert Underwood lying in the dust.

'Get those buggers off the road!' he shouted. 'Cover them!'

Four soldiers dragged the wounded the last few yards while the rest sent sporadic covering fire in the direction of the French. Richard Camberwell looked back at the wagons and was glad to see they had stopped some way down the road and that Megan was nowhere to be seen. Dinah and Hades were tied to the first wagon and he presumed both Megan and Sarah were hiding inside.

'Sergeant!' he shouted to Readman. 'Take ten men and protect the women and the wagons!'

'Sir!'

'Fire as fast as you can to cover them!'

Camberwell watched as Readman gathered up the ten men nearest him and scrambled behind rocks and shrubbery, then made a run for it as the rest of the recruits fired raggedly at the rocks ahead. It didn't matter much that they had no targets to aim at, it was merely a matter of keeping the enemy's heads down so that Readman and his men could reach the wagons safely. Richard Camberwell knew that the wagons were the real target of the French. The supplies they carried would be as welcome to the French troops as to the British, and so had to be protected. He watched as Readman and his men took up defensive positions around the stranded wagons. Turning back to the opposite side of the road, he tried to get some idea of how many enemy there were and decided this was probably just a large patrol, and not a full Company as he had feared. Captain Shaw was about twenty paces away, crouched behind a rock. Richard Camberwell took a deep breath and scampered at a crouching run, then flung himself onto the ground beside Shaw as shots followed him across the few yards. The cattle standing with the wagons bellowed uncertainly, frightened of the musket fire.

'Pretty rum do,' said Shaw, busily loading a pair of chased silver pistols. 'Looks like we should have followed your advice and not Robert's. We should have waited.'

'Stupid bastard might still be alive if he had,' agreed Camberwell. He glanced up at the rocks behind him. Scared faces stared back, looking to the two Captains for leadership. Camberwell ducked as a bullet whinged off the rock he crouched behind while Sergeant Readman's voice came from the wagons at parade ground strength, urging the men to keep loading and firing. There was another flurry of shots from the French which was answered by British muskets. Camberwell grinned. These men, frightened though they were, would not give up without a fight.

'You are trapped Englishmen!' shouted a cultured French voice in accented English from the rocks. 'Put down your weapons. You will be our prisoners.'

There was a chorus of abusive replies from the recruits.

'Bugger off, Frogs!'

'You ain't beaten us yet you bleedin' bastards!'

'We ain't come all this way to get beat, Frenchies!'

Richard Camberwell smiled again, glad to hear that the lads, despite their fear, had plenty of fighting spirit in them.

'Damn! Missed the bastard.' Shaw had fired a shot, making an ill-advised blue-coated Frenchman duck down behind a rock.

Rifle in hands, Camberwell tried to spot an officer to aim at. 'When did you get your commission?' he asked Shaw.

'What? Oh. In July. You?'

'May. I suppose that makes me the senior officer. So get your arse back to the wagons, James, and fetch more ammunition while I think of a plan. God knows how long we're going to be pinned down here.'

'Me? Go back there?' Shaw turned a shocked face to the other man who glared at him.

'Yes. I can't send a recruit. The buggers are scared. He'll be cut to ribbons, and Readman's already there, or I'd send him. Go on now, and keep your head down.'

Shaw saw he had no choice and went. More shots followed him but he managed to reach the cover of the few trees near the wagons safely. Richard Camberwell took another look at the lie of the land.

The French had taken up a good position for the ambush. On the left of the road the rocky, tree-strewn hillside gave plenty of cover which spread around to the right, where the road disappeared around a bend. The cover on the right hand side of the track, where the British sheltered as best they could, was sparse and the men were pinned down with nowhere to go. It was possible they might have climbed to the top of the slope and escaped down the other side, but they couldn't leave the wagons, and the horses would find the going difficult as the hillside was steep. Richard Camberwell spat another bullet into his rifle and rammed it down. He saw a blue coat and the glint of gold lace for a few seconds, fired the gun, and had the satisfaction of hearing a cry of pain.

There were a few cries from his side of the road too, though these seemed to be of shock rather than pain as the French came close to finding their mark and bullets ricocheted off the rocks. He cursed the fact that he had none of his Light Company skirmishers with him. Their accuracy and rifles would make mincemeat of this enemy patrol but the muskets the recruits had were only accurate at very close range. These recruits had never fought before and few of them could fire a gun accurately in the best of circumstances, let alone crouched behind a rock with fear turning their bowels to water. His mind raced as he wondered what to do. The fate of this small contingent of raw troops lay in his hands and, at the moment, he had no answers.

Someone else did though. Will was further along the road and much higher up the slope than Richard Camberwell. He had clambered to some high rocks, his natural agility helping him to do so as soon as the order to take cover had been given. From his vantage point he could see the French clearly and he could also see that, contrary to the amount of fire which suggested otherwise, there were only about thirty of them. Already Will had used his musket to good effect, firing and loading so quickly his cheek was powder-smeared black and his shoulder ached from the recoil. The French had seen him too, recognising a better than average marksman, and several had tried to stop his lethal fire, but those close enough had met with a painful death or injury. Now Will saw that some trees standing close together at the edge of the road just around the bend, could provide cover, giving him a chance to cross the track, climb up the other side, and so outflank the French. If he could reach an outcrop of rock that stuck out of the hillside above the enemy, and make them think they were surrounded, maybe there was a chance they could get out of this more or less intact.

Bob Tomkins and George Trim were nearby. Will called to them, and pointed to the trees, then made a circular movement with his hand and pointed upwards. They grinned, nodding understanding, and prepared to move with him.

Further down the hillside, Gerald Butterworth whimpered, his glasses sliding down his nose with the sweat of fear. So far he had not fired a shot because his hands were trembling so much they seemed unable to hold the musket steady. Movement caught his eye and he watched in silent awe when three of his fellows suddenly started to creep from rock to rock down the hillside and into the trees that bordered the road on the bend. So taken by their bravery, insane though it was, it infused him with courage and he suddenly found that the musket was steady in his hands. He took careful aim at a blue coat who appeared from behind a rock within shooting distance, and fired the gun, then yelled in delight when it was followed by a scream and the coat's owner fell down.

The three boys negotiated the track without being noticed by the enemy. Clambering amongst the rocks on the French side of the road, Will wondered belatedly if he should have asked permission to do what he was doing, but he was so used to taking the initiative, that it had not occured to him to do so until now. Besides, with Major Underwood gone, he was not sure which of the Captains was in charge. Still, he thought, it was too late to bother about such things. Nimbly he scrambled around a rock. Behind him he could hear the laboured breathing of Bob and George. He stopped for a moment and crouched down, waiting for the other two to catch up with him. 'We need to get up there,' he whispered when they had fallen in beside him. He pointed to a ridge of rocks on the top of the hill, above the French. The enemy were close now, the nearest man a mere nine or ten paces away, his back to them, watching for a British target across the road. Putting his finger to his lips, Will waited for another spate of gunfire before moving away. Once out of sight, the three clambered on.

Richard Camberwell turned at a sudden flurry of dust, and James Shaw slid into the cover of the rocks and bushes he was crouched behind. Shaw was clutching a bag of ammunition.

'Take some out and pass the bag on,' said Camberwell. Shaw did so. 'Look up there, Richard,' he said laconically, and pointed to the rocks that stuck out into the bend in the road. 'Seems your young thief is taking matters into his own hands.'

Camberwell looked up in time to see Will and two others sneaking up the hill on the French side of the track before they were hidden by rocks and he lost sight of them.

'What the hell's the bloody boy doing?' he exploded in a harsh whisper. The French fire had died down as they realised that the battle was at something of a stalemate, with neither side willing to give way and no one exposing himself for long enough to be hit by an enemy bullet. French insults came again, to which the British boys replied, but Richard Camberwell didn't hear them. He was watching Will, visible for only seconds at a time, creeping up the hillside. So far the French had not noticed him and his two companions and Camberwell held his breath, expecting at any minute that the three would be spotted and fired upon. As Will climbed higher, Camberwell suddenly realised what he was trying to do, and smiled grimly.

'Good lad!' he said, half to himself. 'Good lad! James!' he turned to his fellow Captain. 'Get up amongst the lads and tell them to stop firing. Make sure they're loaded and ready to stand and fire when I give the word. They're to fix bayonets too. We're going to charge the bastards!'

'We are?' The look of shock on Shaw's face was comical.

'Yes. Now go and tell them.' Camberwell pushed Shaw towards the nearest recruits, then loaded his rifle and waited, watching and listening for a sign that Will's plan was working. He hoped the lad knew what he was doing.

Suddenly shots came from above the French position. And screams. Taken by surprise, some of the Frenchmen stood up, the better to see where the shots were coming from and Richard Camberwell took his cue.

'Stand and fire!' he roared.

Thirty-three men and two officers stood up and fired a volley at the French.

Richard Camberwell threw down the rifle and drew his sword. 'Charge!'

Amidst the smoke of their own volley, the new redcoats ran down the hillside, across the road and up the other side, yelling and screaming to give themselves courage. Will and his snipers kept up a steady stream of withering fire from above as the French suddenly found themselves faced with a shouting mob of madmen intent only on killing.

'That's for them poor buggers at the village, yer bastard!' said Nat Binns, stabbing a gabbling Frenchman in the throat, cutting off the terrified man's words in a gurgle of blood. The British boys clambered on up the slope, knowing they were winning, yelling and laughing, suddenly invincible, and the terrified French couldn't take it any more. Instead of a simple matter of an easy ambush, they were fighting for their lives and these fiends from hell just kept coming forward. Those who could, ran. Some stayed, unwilling to be cowards, and they died for their pains because the British were now in a killing frenzy. All remembered the terrible sights they had seen the day before at the partisan village, and they gave no quarter. Richard Camberwell had a brief thought that he should encourage the lads to take prisoners, but a picture of the pregnant woman and her small son flashed through his mind, and he parried a French lieutenant's sword with his own before running the man through.

In minutes it was over. Twenty-two Frenchmen lay dead, three had been taken prisoner. Four men had escaped, but Camberwell doubted they would last more than a few days in this inhospitable landscape unless they were lucky enough to come upon more of their own side.

The men cheered and slapped each other on the back. They had won their first fight. Only two men had been wounded and none had died except Major Underwood. Looting began immediately. The French bodies were swiftly and meticulously searched for anything of value, the soldiers' reward for a job well done.

'Good work, lad.' Sergeant Readman's gruff voice surprised Will as he reached ground level again. The business with the horses had annoyed the sergeant and he had been less than pleasant to Will since he had joined the recruits, his temper sharp. When they had camped for the night it was always Will who had the dirtiest jobs to do, a factor that was not lost on Will who bore the treatment stoically, realising why he was being picked on. Now, for the first time since he had sold the horses to him, there was a smile on Sergeant Readman's ruddy face. 'It was a bloody stupid thing to do, but it worked. Maybe y'are somethin' other than a damn liar and a cheat after all. Well done, lads,' he said as George Trim and Bob Tomkins slithered to the bottom of the slope.

Richard Camberwell forced his way through the looting, laughing soldiers to the sergeant's side. 'You bloody fools!' he said, his face grim. 'I should damn well have you up for insubordination.' The soldiers' noise suddenly ceased and the victorious men stared at the three who had outflanked the French. Bob and George looked scared, Will defiant, then a broad smile creased Richard Camberwell's face. 'Instead, I must thank you,' he said. 'You did a good job.' The boys grinned self-consciously and the soldiers started cheering again. Camberwell turned to Will. 'However, next time you decide to take on the enemy by yourself, lad, I'd like to know about it first, all right?'

'Yes, sir.' His eyes went beyond Richard Camberwell, to where Megan and Sarah were in earnest conversation with Captain Shaw, who was pointing at him, obviously telling the girls what had happened. Will saw Megan turn an incredulous face towards him, and she smiled that wonderful smile which melted his heart, and he grinned back, his heart lifting till he felt on top of the world.

Megan received her first nursing instruction as Sarah Harvey doctored the two wounded men. They were not badly injured. One had been grazed on the hip by a bullet, the other had been shot in the arm but the bullet had gone through flesh without breaking the bone. The rest of the soldiers spent some time burying the dead Frenchmen and Major Underwood. Nat Binns was heard to complain that, so far, his army career had been mostly spent digging holes in the ground and maybe the army would be better off employing sextons instead of soldiers, a wry comment that caused general black-humoured laughter. This time the grave-digging was being done in a much more light-hearted vein, though all had to put on solemn faces when the Major was laid to rest and the Company gathered round the newly dug earth. Captain Shaw read from a prayer book borrowed from one of the more religious recruits, and they fired a volley into the air as a mark of respect. Most of the solemnity was hypocritical. Major Underwood had not been a popular commander. When he had roused himself enough to give orders he had been short tempered and irascible, and none felt he would be sadly missed. In fact the men were pleased when they heard that Lord Richard Camberwell was now in charge because although he was known to have a short temper himself, he was essentially a fair man and gave credit where it was due. And he was a much better soldier.

Richard Camberwell addressed the men as the sun went down that evening. One of the cattle had been slaughtered and the men were eating a very welcome hot meal.

'Men, I'm proud of you. You've spilt your first blood and can now consider yourselves true and tested members of the British army.'

The men cheered and, for the first time since leaving England's shores, were glad to be soldiers.

Two days later they came upon the four Frenchmen who had escaped the British during the fight. Someone else had wreaked vengeance. The men stared at the broken, mutilated bodies beside which was a message of stones in the dust.

It read, 'Obrigado.' Thank you.

The Portuguese had had their revenge.

12

The mountains bordering Portugal and Spain, December 1811

Will huddled into his borrowed greatcoat, and shivered. The hand holding his musket was so cold his fingers were sticking to the metal. Putting the gun under his arm he blew on them, his breath coming out in clouds, but it did little good and he dared not put his hands in his pockets for fear one of the sergeants saw him. He wished Richard Camberwell wasn't away at the meeting Wellington had convened for his senior Company officers. By rights, Will should have gone with him but orders stated that the meeting was confidential and no servants could attend, so he had stayed behind and that meant doing normal soldierly duties while his master was absent.

From his vantage point as sentry atop the rocky hill, he stared out over the amazing vista of hills and valleys. The pine-forested hills rose to mountains, their peaks covered in snow. Snow drifted in the valleys and on the hillsides, but it had been several days since the last fall and the snow was packed solid, the weather too cold to start much of a thaw. The stream that ran down the hillside to pass close by the village was partially frozen so that only a thin trickle of water ran through the steep-sided gully. The wind was icy, and although Will was wearing more clothes than he had ever worn in his life before at one time, it still went through him like a knife through butter.

Far below, he saw a patrol coming back from one of the mountain passes. Wellington had quartered his troops for the winter in the hill villages between Guarda and Agueda on the Portuguese-Spanish border and a regular watch was maintained for French patrols spying on the British.

The troops were kept busy with shooting practices and drills and filled their time by making fascines and gabions. The fascines, large bundles of sticks lashed together for laying on dugout or trench parapets, and gabions, wicker baskets filled with earth, were supposed to help protect soldiers against musket and artillery fire and were piled high already. Mules and bullock carts had been assembled in large numbers, no one really knew what for but all thought that, come spring, the fighting would begin again and all these things would be needed for the purpose of war.

Usually Will was quite happy to stand sentry, though today the cold was vicious and he rather wished he had been assigned some other duty. He liked to be alone, gazing at the surrounding countryside, letting his mind wander while keeping the necessary lookout for anything extraordinary. His independence had been severely curtailed since coming into Lord Richard Camberwell's employ and privacy in the army was well nigh impossible to achieve, so he revelled in the chance to just be by himself and think about things. He thought now about the fire that would be waiting for him in the stone cottage he had called home for two weeks already, the house he shared with the officers of the Light Company; Captain Camberwell, Captain Shaw, Lieutenant Holt and a young ensign called Edward Wooliscroft. Captain Shaw had found himself a servant, a sprightly old soldier named Dodge, but Will did most of the cooking, fetching and carrying for all four officers, leaving Dodge to do the greater part of the laundry and cleaning which suited Will fine. He also had care of the horses, a duty he enjoyed. Every day was busy and he rarely had any time to himself.

He thought about their arrival at Wellington's headquarters a few weeks previously. They had not run into any more trouble after the ambush and although the march was long and tedious, had arrived in good spirits. The story of the ambush was soon common knowledge. Two days after their arrival, Will heard from George, who had overheard Captain Shaw talking with Lieutenant Holt, that Wellington had given Richard Camberwell charge of the Light Company in place of Major Underwood. This was confirmed at a parade during which the action of the newest recruits was commended. Will stood and gazed with awe at Wellington mounted on his great horse, as did most of the other soldiers there. The army's commanding officer was not lavish in his praise, it was not in his nature, but he did say that if it were not for extraordinary action by three privates, and excellent leadership, the outcome of the ambush might have been very different with important supplies being lost to the French. Will, George and Bob positively glowed, and Will imagined that Wellington glanced at them when the praise was given, though afterwards he thought he was probably mistaken because it was doubtful the British Commander-in-Chief even knew which of the men standing before him had perpetrated the flanking manoeuvre.

At last someone came to relieve him of sentry duty and Will walked thankfully down the hillside to the village outside of which three companies of the battalion, including Richard Camberwell's Light Company, were encamped. Most of the soldiers, rather than sleep in cold tents, had used their enforced leisure time to build crude huts of wood, sod, and stone. This activity had stood them in good stead as winter took a fierce grip on this desolate place but despite the inclement weather and being cold, dirty and uncomfortable, the men were happy enough. There was a great sense of camaraderie about the settlement. The villagers had accepted the soldiers' presence, glad to have them around as protection against the French. Food was short but daily patrols went hunting and brought back wild boar, ducks, deer and rabbits to swell the cooking pots that were topped up with vegetables grown and stored by the villagers, and supplies that arrived infrequently from army headquarters.

Will tramped between snow drifts towards the small house in the main street of the village where the Company's officers were billeted and looked forward to a supper he would probably have to cook himself. Lieutenant Holt had gone hunting with a couple of his fellow officers the day before and had shot two wild geese. One of these would make a good stew added to some root vegetables that the woman who owned the house, Senora Mendez, had given them in exchange for the other goose with which she would feed herself, her husband and two children. With all these people, the small house was overcrowded. The two Captains shared a room that was just about big enough for two straw mattresses, the lieutenant and ensign shared another, and the family a third. That left Will and Dodge to sleep in the stable with the horses and the Mendez's mule but, more often than not, Will slept rough with his friends in their makeshift shelters because Dodge snored fit to wake the dead. Life for Will in this high country was no worse than it had been up to now, and, in some respects, was considerably better. He whistled as he walked, calling and answering greetings to his fellow soldiers, quite happy with his lot.

Megan Camberwell, on the other hand, was far from happy. Behind another house in the village which she shared with Sarah and three families, two of whom had given over their own dwellings for army officers, Megan broke the ice on top of a water butt and dipped her bucket into the freezing cold water. Her hands were already numb, despite the rough gloves she had fashioned for herself from pieces of rabbit skin, and so cold they ached, red and raw from washing clothes, her own and Sarah's. Sarah had a hacking cough and a nose that seemed to run perpetually and although Megan sometimes felt sorry for her friend, she resented the fact that she had to do most of the housework and cooking for the two of them.

Pulling her cloak closer about her, it being the only really warm item of clothing she had brought from a temperate English autumn, she lugged the heavy bucket into the shelter of the over-hanging roof where the wind wasn't quite so keen. Taking up a skirt and blouse that were wearing very thin, she knelt on the

166

hard-packed earth and started to scrub with a block of hard soap that refused to lather, making her swear under her breath. She had found that swearing to herself made her feel better. So used to hearing the men cursing as part of their everyday speech, she found herself copying them when things became hard to cope with, but today it didn't seem to be working and she felt the tears prick her eyelids. It wasn't fair. She hadn't been born to be a scullery maid. Goodness! Even Lizzie, the scullery maid back at Camberwell Hall, had a better life than this! She stopped scrubbing for a moment and looked at her hands. Gone was the white, soft skin of a few months ago. Now, even when they were not raw with cold, her hands were rough and wrinkled and the nails were broken to the quick. Suddenly she was unable to stop the tears from spilling over and she let them run unheeded down her cheeks, hot on her cold face.

Megan knew that it wasn't just the hard work to survive that was getting her down. A lot of her misery stemmed from the attitude towards her of the other women in the camp. The soldiers were deferential, under strict orders from Captain Camberwell to be so, and most treated her and Sarah like favourite sisters or daughters. But the camp followers; wives, mistresses and whores who followed their men to war, were a different matter altogether. From a social strata she had never been this close to before, they intimidated and sometimes even frightened her. They were uncouth, loud-mouthed and had loose morals, and Megan despised them. It hadn't taken them long to find out that she was not of their kind and they avoided her. None had ever said anything about her supercilious attitude in her presence because all knew she was Captain Camberwell's niece and they liked the tall, handsome officer but she had seen the looks and knew that the dislike was returned. Yet, in a way she could not define, she was envious of the raucous, hard women who stood up to the inconveniences and deprivations of life in the camp so much better than she. They went hungry, had no privacy whatsoever, lived in appalling, overcrowded and dirty conditions, yet they were never heard to complain. They squabbled and laughed, performed their ablutions, loved their men and gave birth to their children, all in very public view of the enlisted troops, but mostly they just got on with the job of living and trying to provide a few home comforts for their husbands and lovers. Megan wished she could be more like them in their total disregard for the discomforts they had to endure. She remembered how, on the march to their present cantonment, the troops had slept in fields on occasion and one night she had heard a noise coming from nearby in the shadowy darkness lit only by a waning moon. Raising her head to see what it was, she had been horrified and disgusted to see a half-naked soldier and his equally bare woman making vigorous love right out in the open, not even under a blanket! It had made her so embarrassed she was sure her face had still been red the next morning. They were coarse, vulgar people, but they had an indomitable spirit that she longed to emulate.

Now she heaved a great sigh, wiped away the tears that had made her nose run, and picked up her skirt again, scrubbing hard on the material with the soap, suddenly angry that she had only herself to blame for her present situation. Pressing even harder with the soap there was a sudden tearing noise and she stared in horror at the gaping hole that had appeared in the material.

'Damn and bloody hell!' she said loudly and the tears came again. She rocked back on her heels, put her head in her hands, and sobbed.

Several minutes later, she was surprised to feel an arm go around her heaving shoulders. Thinking it was Sarah, she said, her voice muffled in her hands, 'Go inside. It's too cold.' Then she realised it wasn't Sarah when a kindly voice said, 'There, there, luv. It can't be as bad as all that.'

Megan looked up in alarm and blinked wet eyelashes at a large, round woman who was smiling at her. The woman's face was fat, her eyes in the chubby cheeks a faded blue, and her greying, greasy, lank hair was tied back from her face with a piece of string, but the smile was genuine and kindly. Megan recognised her as one of the camp followers but did not know her name. Mortified at being seen in such an unfortunate situation, she got hastily to her feet and wiped her tears away with a sleeve.

'Thank you, but I'm all right now,' she said with as much pride as she could muster.

'No you ain't, dearie. A body don't cry like that without there's a reason,' said the woman, folding ham-like arms and looking at her sympathetically, obviously intent on staying until Megan explained her distress. She was not even wearing a coat, Megan noticed, just

168

a worn, cotton dress, a voluminous shawl and an old pair of army boots over long woollen socks. 'Now just you tell old Ginny what's the matter.'

Megan heaved back a sob and a tear trickled down her cheek as she held out the wet skirt in her hand. 'It's this,' she said. 'My skirt. And I only have two. It tore.' It sounded so lame, so childish, that she looked down at the ground, embarrassed again. The woman took the skirt and studied it carefully.

'Nothin' that a needle an' thread won't put right,' she said cheerfully. 'You just leave it with me, luv, an' I'll 'ave it mended in no time.'

'Why would you do that for me?' asked Megan in a small voice. Her embarrassment was made worse by the remembrance of the way she had shunned and reviled women such as this one who was being so kind to her.

'We all of us as to pull together, ducks,' said the woman brightly, wringing out the skirt over the bucket. 'Our men're 'ere fightin' fer us, an' we 'as to 'elp 'em as best we can.' She gave Megan a look that made her feel uncomfortable. 'An' we 'as to 'elp each other too. This country's an 'ard place, an' it's 'ard livin'. If we don't 'elp ourselves, sure as 'ell no one else will.'

With that, the woman gave Megan a pat on the shoulder, and walked away, carrying her skirt, leaving Megan feeling like crying again, but this time not with anger, but with shame.

Just then, Will walked past, musket under his arm, on his way to the officers' lodgings. He was about to call a cheerful greeting when he saw Megan brushing damp hair from a face that was wet with tears.

'What is it? What's happened?' he asked urgently, running to her and clutching her arm. He and Megan saw a lot of each other, and Richard Camberwell kept a good eye on his niece, but Will still felt somehow responsible for her, especially now, when the Captain was away. And the feeling of attraction he had for her was as strong as ever. He stared at her in alarm.

'Has someone tried to...? Has someone touched you?' he asked. He knew that most of the rough and ready men he mixed with every day would give their eye teeth for a chance to get better acquainted with Lady Megan Camberwell.

'No. No.' Megan gave him a tremulous smile. 'I'm all right.

Really. My skirt tore.' She told him about the woman who had helped her.

Will grinned and stepped back, relieved her distress had been caused by nothing more serious. 'Oh, that'll be Ginny Makepiece. A real good sort, she is. Often brings us tommies when we're on sentry duty. Says she can't 'ave 'er soldier-boys goin' 'ungry.'

'What's a tommy?' asked Megan, wiping her eyes.

'It's a sort of fried cake made with flour and water,' answered Will. 'Not much of a thing unless it 'as salt in, but it's fillin'. Yer should try it sometime.' He grinned again. 'Ginny treats us all like we're 'er own sons, she does. I like 'er. Reckon she likes me too.'

'Will!' Megan was shocked. 'She's old enough to be your mother! Maybe even your grandmother!'

'I didn't mean like that!' Will laughed. 'She tells me I'm too thin, and often gives me extra to the others, though I tell 'er not to, 'cos it ain't fair.'

Megan smiled and looked at Will properly for the first time in weeks. Yes, he was thin, but he looked well. The merry twinkle in his eyes was still there. His hair was, if anything, bleached even lighter by the sun and stood out in stark contrast to his face which was burned brown, and the grin was just as mischievous. His youthful face made him appear like a small boy playing at soldiers but Megan knew that the musket in Will's hands had killed men and was anything but a toy. Megan had overheard comments from the soldiers, those who had travelled from England with them, and others, that Will was fast becoming one of the best marksmen in the Company and whenever she heard him being spoken of in that manner, she felt a stirring of pride that he should be so well thought of. She felt pride in him now. Soldiering became Will. He looked like a soldier despite the oversized greatcoat, yet there was still an element of the ragamuffin he used to be about him and she supposed that was why women like Ginny favoured him.

The wind blew a gust around them, and she shivered. Will put a hand on her arm again. 'Are yer all right, Meg? I mean are yer gettin' enough to eat? 'As yer uncle made yer comfortable? D'yer 'ave wood enough for the fire? If not, I can go and cut some, yer know.'

She was touched by his concern and almost let the tears come again but pride wouldn't let her. Instead she smiled. 'Yes, Will. I'm fine. Really I am.' She bent down to the bucket again. 'Now I'd better get this washing done. As it is, it'll take forever to dry, and you'd best be getting back to the house and start cooking or the lieutenant and Mister Wooliscroft will have something to say.'

Will suddenly put both his hands on her shoulders and looked into her lovely hazel eyes that sparkled with unshed tears. 'I want yer to promise ter come ter me if there's ever a problem yer can't sort out yerself,' he said and she nodded, surprised at his seriousness.

He turned away before he gave in to an almost overwhelming desire to kiss those full lips reddened by the cold. Will knew Megan was still holding onto the impulse that had made her travel here in the first place and that, despite her words and the deprivations she must be suffering, she would never admit she had made a mistake. He wished he could alleviate her suffering.

But he wished, above all, that he could tell her how much he loved her.

Three days later a new contingent of fourteen recruits marched into the camp, sent by the regiment's headquarters and led by a lieutenant and a sergeant. They had left England some weeks after Will, and comprised a motley crew of felons released from Newgate and given the choice of deportation or enlistment, together with a few men found by the recruiting sergeants. Richard Camberwell, newly returned from the officers' conference, could not be said to be overjoyed to see them. Conditions were tough enough as it was without another sixteen mouths to feed. However, he put a carefully neutral look on his face when the men were paraded in the village square for him to welcome and inspect as the only senior officer available that day. The Lieutenant-Colonel, and the other Captains and Majors who were billeted in the village, had gone fox-hunting, a sport that Camberwell despised and had never entertained even as lord of the manor. Walking along the line of men, he saw the same pinched faces and blank expressions he had seen many times before. These men had had it rough, marching through snow, rain and cold winds to get to this place. He walked on, inspecting a musket here and there, until he came to a sudden halt. The man in front of him had a face that wasn't blank but smiling, the grin sardonic and humourless. It was a face he knew.

'Right glad I am to see you again...sir,' said the man whose head leaned close to his, the voice soft and menacing. Richard Camberwell's eyes narrowed. Amos Wilkins. Last seen in an inn's stable, and the man who might have been the death of him if Will Tucker had not intervened.

'Can't say the feeling's mutual, Wilkins,' said Camberwell just as quietly, the nearest men staring straight ahead, pretending they could not hear the exchange. He leaned closer towards Wilkins, making the man take an involuntary step backwards, out of the line. 'Just remember you're in the army now. You're a private. And I'm an officer. Get out of line here and I'll have you flogged.'

'Oh, I won't forget, sir,' said Wilkins slyly. 'That I won't.'

Camberwell walked on, feeling Wilkins's gaze following his progress until the sergeant shouted at the man to stand to attention or there'd be trouble. Camberwell completed his inspection, told the sergeant where the men could erect their tents, and walked with the new lieutenant, who had introduced himself as Lord Paul Deaville, to his own lodgings where room would have to be found for him.

'You know one of the recruits, Captain?' The lieutenant was a young, lean, graceful man with fair hair and a boyish, handsome face marred only by a scar that ran across one cheek. Somehow he had managed to keep his uniform clean on the long journey from Lisbon and cut a dashing figure that made Richard Camberwell feel positively dowdy.

'Unfortunately, yes,' answered Camberwell. 'He used to be in my employ. He stole from me so I dismissed him, then he tried to kill me.'

'Good heavens!'

'I'm willing to bet he's not a volunteer.'

'You'd be right. Stole a horse, I believe. He was lucky not to dance on the gallows. Chose the army instead of Botany Bay.'

'Pity,' said Camberwell. 'I heard we were to expect twenty men. Where are the others?'

'We started out with twenty, sir, but had a spot of bother on the way. Had to shoot some of the blighters,' the lieutenant said airily.

Camberwell looked sharply at the man, wondering what the 'spot of bother' had been. 'Whose company are they?' he asked, sincerely hoping he would not have Wilkins in the Light.

'Not yours, Captain,' said the lieutenant reassuringly. 'I was told you command the Light. These men are certainly not the best of the best and will never make a Light Company or the Rifles, though I can't say the same for myself, of course. I have high hopes of commanding a crack company of my own in the not too distant future. It is to be hoped that we engage the French early in the new year. Battles have a way of creating vacancies and I intend to fill one of them.'

Richard Camberwell was struck by a thought that would have been funny if it were not potentially irritating and dangerous. It seemed that here was a man who, except for his good looks, could have been Robert Underwood all over again. This young man was already showing himself to be ambitious and over-confident. He hoped he would not prove to be as indolent and foolhardy as the Major.

'Is this our lodgings?' The new lieutenant's mouth turned down in disgust as they arrived at the house assigned to the officers. 'I have to say I was hoping for something better.'

'You could see if any officers from the other companies have room,' suggested Camberwell hopefully, 'but from what I hear, we're all pretty cramped.'

'I dare say I'll survive,' said the officer rather grumpily.

The young officer leaned closer to Camberwell as the latter reached for the door handle and said quietly, 'Tell me, Captain. What are the women like here? Any beauties to be had?'

Camberwell laughed. 'You can take your pick of the whores over there, Lieutenant,' he said, pointing to the sprawling British camp. 'I believe there are some who are reserved for officers only. Most of the village girls are already spoken for, though there are some who work from the tavern.' He smiled at the younger man. 'We've been here quite a while. It doesn't take soldiers long to find girls willing to satisfy their lust. I doubt you'll find anyone to suit you here.'

But the very next day, Lieutenant Paul Deaville found someone he thought would suit perfectly. He had spent an uncomfortable night on a straw pallet that graced the floor of the room he had to share with Holt and Wooliscroft. After eating a breakfast of hard bread and fat bacon which, although an improvement on soldiers' travelling fare, was disappointing to say the least, he decided to explore a little. He was walking along the village street when he

173

saw coming towards him, a vision of loveliness in the form of Lady Megan Camberwell.

The day was sunny, a welcome change from the lowering clouds of the past week, and Megan had decided to get away from the village for a while and take a walk after having seen that Sarah was comfortable. Sarah's health was improving and Megan felt in much better spirits today. Ginny Makepiece had brought back her skirt, dried, and mended so neatly that she could hardly see where the tear had been. Megan had been so grateful that she had invited the woman to take tea with her, a practice she kept up in a pathetic attempt to establish a little civilised living in these rough circumstances. The tea was rationed and she only had some at all because the regimental Colonel's wife had seen to it that she took some with her from army headquarters before travelling to the hills.

'A gentlewoman must never be completely without the trappings of civilisation, my dear,' she had said to Megan. 'And tea is always such a refreshing strengthener, I find.'

So Megan had shared some of her precious horde with Ginny as a way of showing her gratitude. The meeting proved a revelation. Ginny, settling her obese body comfortably, if rather precariously, on a stool by a fire that was more smoke than flame, seemed completely at home with someone whom she would probably never have met, let alone taken tea with, in normal English society. The kindly woman had chattered on about life in the camp, happenings Megan had never realised were going on just yards from her doorstep. Megan had listened, fascinated, and realised that if Ginny was typical, she had badly misjudged the women who went to war. These were resiliant, sentimental and, above all, courageous people. They, and their children, had to put up with every sort of indignity and hardship yet they stayed – because of their men. Megan, even now, did not have it as bad as these women did and listening to Ginny's uncomplaining account of life in the camp, which she somehow managed to make sound lively, jolly and inspiring, she once again felt shame and wondered if she would ever love a man enough to live as they did.

It was with pleasure and, she had to admit, some curiosity, that she had accepted an invitation to visit Ginny's 'house', a stone and sod hut that she shared with her four children and another family of three, and thought she might go that afternoon. She was thinking about it as she walked down the street towards her uncle's lodgings, so wrapped up in her own thoughts that she nearly bumped into a man coming the other way.

Megan looked up and was surprised to see a face she didn't recognise. Then she remembered the new recruits who had arrived the previous day. This officer must have come with them. She apologised for nearly running into him and prepared to move on, but he stepped in front of her.

'Pardon me,' he said, 'but I don't think we've had the pleasure of meeting.' He took off his shako. 'Lieutenant Paul Deaville at your service, ma'am.' He took her hand and kissed it, seeming not to notice the rough skin and broken nails.

Megan was entranced at being addressed in such an elegant fashion. She stared with undisguised curiosity at the new officer. His fair hair framed a young face, yet his eyes were all mature male, staring back at her with frank interest, and they had a look in them that suddenly made her blush and study her feet. In her innocence she did not recognise the look for what it was, for Paul Deaville was mentally undressing Megan Camberwell and deciding that here was a girl worth having. He had known many women and, despite the layers of worn clothing that covered her, he could tell that there was a nubile young figure underneath them and her face was that of an angel. A spirited angel too by the sudden toss of the head as Megan looked up again. He decided there and then that he would have her.

'If you will excuse me, sir, I have to go and see my uncle,' said Megan, suddenly wanting to get away, and unable to think of a better excuse.

'Of course.' Deaville stepped out of her way but before she could walk on he said, 'Your uncle is...?'

'Captain Richard Camberwell,' said Megan. 'Goodbye, Lieutenant.' The dismissal was abrupt but for some reason Megan felt uneasy under the young man's stare that seemed to rake her up and down. She resisted the urge to look back at him but could feel his eyes on her all the way to her uncle's door, and it was with relief that she found it unlocked. She almost ran inside.

So that was Camberwell's niece, thought Deaville as he carried on towards the camp where he hoped to find a sutler who would sell him some decent wine. A pretty piece and no mistake, he was

175

willing to bet that no one had had their hands on that little baggage before. But she was ripe for the picking, he could tell. It would be a challenge to get her into his bed, especially right under Camberwell's nose, and it would give him something to do in this God-forsaken place. Paul Deaville had not come to Portugal willingly. As a third son, he had been forced into military service by an autocratic father after he had made two maids and his own cousin pregnant. He fingered the scar on his cheek. His cousin's eldest brother had given him that; a sword stroke that had nearly taken his eye. The bastard had almost killed him and it had been the final straw. Lord Clarence Deaville had sent him to war in the hope that a commission in the army might make a man of his son and cure his lecherous and debauched ways.

Away from the family home, Paul Deaville intended doing everything he could to continue them. Over the next two weeks he joined in every diversionary activity the officers and men devised, from horse and mule races across the valley, to boxing contests, to theatricals, to informal balls where every woman in the camp and village who was not already attached would dance with every available man. He soon acquired a reputation as a libertine, a philanderer and a gambler of note, and it was all Lieutenant-Colonel Davenport, in overall charge of the cantonment, could do to remind him at times of his duties.

'The man's incorrigible,' he grumbled to Richard Camberwell one day. 'Seems to think this is some sort of endless party. Can't you say something to him, Richard?'

'I've already tried, sir,' said Camberwell. He had had several talks with the young lieutenant, all to no avail, and all he had succeeded in doing was alienating him. Even Will, who hardly had a bad word to say about anyone, had been heard to grumble that he now had two masters instead of one. On one occasion Will had risked official reprimand when he had been woken in the middle of a stormy night and told to go to the soldiers' camp in order to procure a cure for the lieutenant's bellyache, caused by drinking too much sour wine the previous evening. Will had refused to go, and the lieutenant had screamed and shouted so much that a frightened sentry had fired a shot from his musket, waking half the camp. The officers had come running, thinking they were being attacked by the French. Will had been reprimanded for causing the

176

furore, but so had Deaville.

'Well, it can't go on, Richard,' said the Lieutenant-Colonel now. He was a gruff, portly man with bushy mutton-chop whiskers and a propensity for fine cigars and good food. 'I can't send him back to headquarters without a good reason but he's bad for discipline.'

Richard Camberwell agreed. He had finally heard, via the army grapevine, what had happened to cause the deaths of the other six recruits who had been in Deaville's care. It seemed that two had deserted, and Deaville had been so angered by this that he had picked four men at random, had a very unwilling Sergeant Hesky line them up, and had shot them as a warning to the others. The two who had deserted had been found later, half starved and exhausted, and had been hanged. Richard Camberwell had no sympathy with deserters either, thinking them the cowards they undoubtedly were, and knew that hanging was the usual punishment for men caught committing such an offence but he found the random shooting of the other four men difficult to condone. It would seem that Lieutenant Paul Deaville had it in mind to go his own way and get as much pleasure out of being in the army that he possibly could while he was about it.

'I'll ask Browning to have a word with him, sir,' said Camberwell now to the Lieutenant-Colonel, though he thought it would do little good. Jeremy Browning was a Major, and officer in charge of B company, the one to which Deaville had been assigned together with the remaining recruits who had travelled with him, including Amos Wilkins. Browning was a tough soldier, good at his job, but Camberwell doubted anything the officer had to say would penetrate Deaville's thick skin.

It was soon after the arrival of the newest recruits that Will encountered Amos Wilkins. He had been instructed to go with Sergeant Readman, and several others of the Light Company, to help instruct the new men in musketry. Sergeant Hesky had taken his fourteen recruits to the patch of ground the camp used for shooting practice, and told them that they would each have a man at their shoulder to give advice. The partnerships were chosen at random but Will was horrified to recognise the man given to him. His heart skipped a beat and his mind rushed back to that night in the 'Jug and Bowl' stables.

'Well, well, now ain't this a surprise,' said Amos Wilkins with a

177

snide grin when he recognised his young partner. Will's grip on his own musket tightened, and he cursed the quirk of fate that had brought this man into his life again, and that of Captain Camberwell. Wilkins was thinner than Will remembered and his black beard had been cut shorter, but the eyes and voice were as menacing as ever. Wilkins lowered his voice. 'I ain't forgot that night, young 'un. Broke my damn arm, you did. Ain't forgot the Captain neither...' Anything else he might have had to say was lost in a bellow from Readman who demanded his men load and fire at the targets as quickly as possible, timing them for a minute. Will and the rest of the marksmen fired almost in unison and all were loading, or had fired, a fourth ball by the time he called a halt.

'When you can shoot like that, you can call yourself soldiers,' shouted Hesky, impressed. Someone else was impressed too. The startled look on Amos Wilkins's face made Will feel much better and he had no more threatening remarks from the man for the rest of the session, though his grudging silence and dumb insolence were intimidating enough.

One evening, a few days later, Will sat with George Trim and Bob Tomkins beside a fire that had been used to cook a communal meal. The boys were tired and glad to relax. One of Captain Shaw's horses had cast a shoe that morning, and Will had walked her the four miles to the next village where a regimental blacksmith had his portable smithy. George and Bob had gone with him to keep him company but the four mile walk had taken some time because of the terrain and the lame horse, though they had taken turns to ride the horse on the way back. As they had no saddle, and Bob and George were even less experienced on horseback than Will, this was an hilarious affair and they had taken a long time to return, which did not go down well with either Sergeant Readman or Captain Shaw. Whilst at the village, they had exchanged news and early Christmas greetings with men from other Companies. If the weather held there was to be a horse race on Christmas Eve between the officers who were billeted in the two villages, and there was much good-natured rivalry between the soldiers who had their own particular fancies as to who the winner would be.

Now the three boys huddled closer to the fire for warmth, glad they hadn't been given picket duty that night. George was sitting on a log, reading a letter that had been delivered with the last mail from headquarters. It was from a girl he said he had been seeing before joining the army. Although written very shortly after he had left England, the missive had only arrived three days before, and he treasured it as if it were gold dust, reading it over and over again. Bob was whittling a wooden soldier. He had a talent for woodwork and was making the toy for the small brother of a girl he had taken up with recently whose father was a sergeant in A company. The night was cold, the boys were wrapped in greatcoats, and the fire was doing its best to warm the cold room. Will poked the logs with a stick so that flames blazed up briefly before dying down again.

'Why ain't you got yerself a girl then, Will?' asked Bob, shaving off a sliver of wood. 'Ain't yer missin' a bit o' female company?'

Will laughed. 'I suppose so,' he admitted. Not for anything would he tell his friends about his unrequited love for Megan Camberwell.

'Did yer 'ave a girl back 'ome?' Bob was always asking questions, wanting to know everything. At times he could be a pain in the arse, but if there was something in the camp that you wanted to know about, he was the one to ask.

'Not really,' answered Will. 'There was a girl I sometimes saw, but we weren't attached or anythin'.'

'You goin' to be like George 'ere and save yerself 'til yer get back?' Bob laughed at the very thought of doing that himself. He and his Molly had had several very satisfying encounters already in the dark of the night when her family was asleep.

'Are yer, George?' asked Will, evading the question.

'I don't know. I'd like to but...yer know.' George folded his letter carefully before putting it back in his pocket.

Will did know. Sometimes, lying on a pile of hay in the stable or on a straw pallet in his friends' hut, he would think of Megan and be consumed by lust, a condition that tormented and depressed him. He had seen girls in the camp looking at him in a way he recognised very well, but he fancied none of them, and he was very afraid that the thought of Megan was spoiling him for anyone else.

His ears caught the tail end of something Bob was saying. 'That girl in the tavern's quite a beauty. 'Course, she's Spanish.' He said this as though it was something contagious. Bob was an Englishman through and through and had no desire to mix it with other races when it came to girls, though many of his fellows had no such

179

prejudices.

'Which girl's that then?' asked Will.

'Yer'll see which one I mean at the Christmas Ball,' said Bob. 'She's the prettiest there by a mile. Juanita 'er name is.'

There were to be two dances to celebrate the festive season on Christmas night. One, for the officers, was a formal affair at the village tavern, the other, much more informal, was a dance to be held in a nearby barn, the only place large enough to accommodate all those who would attend. Several of the soldiers could play musical instruments; a guitar, a flute, even paper and comb would be brought into play that night, and the Lieutenant-Colonel had arranged with the tavern keeper to have people from the village play music for the officers. The whole camp was looking forward to what promised to be a pleasant and diverting evening.

'Will yer be able to come to the dance, Will?' Bob and George sometimes envied their friend being Captain Camberwell's servant. Although he had far more work to do than they did, he often had the benefit of better food, and less harassment from the sergeants.

'Dunno,' answered Will. He would have to serve food and drink at the officers' ball and he knew it would go on until there wasn't one man left sober. 'Chances are they'll get drunk quicker'n you lot 'cause there'll be more to drink. Maybe I'll get ter go ter t'other dance later.' He stood up. 'I'd better go and see if the Captain wants me ter do anythin' afore he goes ter bed. 'Night.'

'See yer, Will,' said Bob.

''Night, Will.' George looked up from the fire dreamily. He hoped his girl would write again. God knew when he would go home, but it was nice to think there was someone there, waiting for him.

Christmas week came, and with it snow, sleet and ice, and the village became, for a time, a little outpost of England. Homesick men and women gathered any greenery and berries they could find from the pine trees on the mountain slopes and bushes in the valley, and decorated their huts and tents. Carols were sung around the campfires, and even small gifts were made for the children; wooden whistles, kites made from rags, sticks and string; garlands of greenery for little girls' hair. There had been some good hunting before the snow had penned them in. Meat was keeping well in the cold air, and all would get a reasonable meal on Christmas day.

180

The excitement started on Christmas Eve. There had been a slight fall of snow the night before, but it lay powdery in the valley and was not enough to put off the race. The officers from the nearest village rode over, followed by a straggling column of supporters. The ground in the valley near the home village stretched flat for a distance of nearly a mile, following the course of a stream, and was ideal for horse-racing because the ground was softer there than anywhere else. The whole camp, women and children included, came out to watch and cheer on the officers. Even the unpopular ones had their supporters because each man wanted his own Company to do well. Will and Richard Camberwell had spent hours training Hades for the race, knowing that the ground at the bottom of the valley would suit her because it was similar to the fields she used to gallop on in England. During the time in the village, Will had become a better rider due to Richard Camberwell's tutelage, and his liking for horses had deepened. Now Hades was as fit as he had ever been, despite the rationing of fodder and corn.

The surrounding hills seemed alive with people as the contestants lined up and Lieutenant-Colonel Davenport fired his pistol to start the race. There had been much illicit betting and everyone cheered as the riders yelled and the horses galloped away, throwing up clods of earth, snow and mud as they went. People shouted, urging on their favourites. Will, Sarah and Megan stood together, eyes alight with excitement, shouting for Richard Camberwell and Hades. One horse stumbled, tipping its rider onto the ground, fortunately on the outside of the runners so he avoided being trampled but there was a collective scream from the women and a groan from those men who had bet on the horse and rider. Another horse lost its rider who screeched as a horse behind stamped on his arm, breaking a bone. One of the rules of the race was that no spurs or goads of any kind except voices and heels could be used, so it was a contest purely of fitness, speed and skill.

The best horses drew clear and rounded the pole that denoted the halfway mark at the end of the valley. Now they were galloping back again, their breath steaming in the cold air, their hooves drumming on the ground like a cavalry charge. Will and the girls jumped up and down in breathless excitement for Hades and Richard Camberwell were gaining on the leading two horses, one ridden by Major Browning, and the other by a Captain of A company. Will cheered himself hoarse as Hades drew level. The Major's horse was slowing, Hades was past, then it was a neck and neck race for the line between Hades and the other Captain's roan. The two horses galloped furiously, their riders urging them on with shouts and heels. Will, Megan and Sarah capered about in delight when Hades put on a final spurt and galloped across the finishing line a nose ahead of his rival. Richard Camberwell brought his stallion to a slithering, steaming halt, shook hands with the loser, and held aloft the prize – a bottle of best French brandy Lieutenant-Colonel Davenport had gleaned from the last battle he had fought. It seemed as if the whole hillside nearest the village erupted as the men and women cheered the Captain, a popular winner.

Will was so excited that he grabbed hold of Megan and kissed her soundly on the lips. She was so surprised that, for a moment, she didn't know what to say.

'Early Christmas present,' said Will, grinning hugely, then he was off, scampering down the hill to add his own congratulations to that of the rest of the Light Company who seemed to be doing their best to get there before him while a bemused Megan stood and watched him go.

13

The proposed Christmas dance entertainments set the whole camp in a frenzy of excitement and unprecedented activity. With little else to occupy their minds, and wanting to celebrate the festive season in style, the men polished and scrubbed, trying to make their uniforms as smart as possible, though some of the soldiers, veterans of more than two years of warfare, had a hard job to make their rags any more presentable. The women somehow found time in the hard daily grind to make themselves suitable clothing by using material stolen from other garments and sewn together to make 'new' dresses and skirts.

On Christmas morning a religious service, conducted by Lieutenant-Colonel Davenport, was held in the village square. All the soldiers were compelled to attend. Himself a confirmed Protestant, Davenport knew that a large number of the soldiers were Irish

Catholics, but they didn't seem to mind too much that he read from the Book of Common Prayer. The service vied with that held at the same time in the small stone village church, which was undeniably Catholic. As the local priest was a hell-fire and damnation preacher, his voice carried to the soldiers. The village priest conducted his service in a mixture of Portuguese and Spanish and it is doubtful whether many of the Irish soldiers could understand a word he said, but his passionate manner of speech delivered a forceful message and many were seen crossing themselves. Several times Lieutenant-Colonel Davenport frowned in the direction of the church, and raised his voice in an attempt to speak louder, provoking amusement amongst some of the younger lads who received warning looks from the sergeants for their levity, but when it came to the hymn singing, the soldiers drowned any noise from the church as their lusty baritones and basses rang around the surrounding hills.

That afternoon Will spent hours polishing Richard Camberwell's badges, boots and buttons, scrubbing his best uniform jacket and trousers, and brushing his shako. He took pride in his work, wanting Camberwell to be the best dressed officer at the ball. He hoped Lieutenant Deaville wouldn't ask him to tart up his uniform too. Dodge had agreed to help out Lieutenant Holt and Ensign Wooliscroft with theirs but Will wanted to find time to fix his own clothes as well, such as they were. During his time at the camp he had acquired a faded red jacket and some grey flannel pants that had been patched and rendered wearable by Ginny Makepiece whose skill with a needle was undeniable. As Camberwell's servant, he would be required to serve drinks and food at the tavern ball, and he looked forward to it because Megan would be there, though he thought that the soldiers' dance would afford more pleasure for him in the way of drink and comradeship. Maybe, if he played his cards right, he could attend both functions and go to the dance once he had seen Richard Camberwell to bed. The Captain would probably drink too much, as officers tended to do on such occasions, but the rank and file entertainment would still be going strong at breakfast time.

To mark the occasion, Will even took himself to the icy stream and treated his hair to a wash, though he baulked at exposing the rest of his body to the freezing cold water. At least the cold kept most of the lice at bay, he thought as he dunked his head in the stream to get the soap off, shivering, and rubbing his hair briskly with a thin towel. He had submitted to a haircut since coming to the village but the woman who had cut it for him had left it hanging over his ears – 'to keep the cold out, luv' – so it was still fairly shaggy, but at least now it was clean.

On the night of the ball, Will helped Captain Camberwell dress in his newly cleaned uniform. Senora Mendez had allowed Dodge to use her smoothing iron to press all the officers' clothes and Will had given his own jacket and pants a quick once over before the heat went out of the iron.

Richard Camberwell buckled on his sword and placed his shako on his head.

'You look very smart, sir,' said Will, proud of his efforts. Indeed the handsome officer would turn many a lady's head that evening.

'You don't look so bad yourself, Will,' said Camberwell. The officer smiled at him, noticing that he'd obviously made great efforts with his own appearance. 'I wouldn't be at all surprised if you don't have the girls flocking round you tonight.'

Will grinned. There was only one girl he wished to impress and he would be quite content just to be in the same room as her for a whole evening. As for the Captain, Megan had only the other day told him that Sarah had finally confided her great liking for Richard Camberwell and that he was the reason for her stowing away on the ship. It was not really news to either Will or Megan for they had suspected it all along, and both decided they would try and promote a romance between the two.

However it seemed no intervention by them was necessary. From the start of the evening, Richard Camberwell had eyes for no one else. He and Sarah, Megan and Captain Shaw sat at one of the small tables dotted around the empty space in the middle of the tavern's largest room. Sarah looked lovely in a royal blue gown that was the one pretty dress she had managed to bring with her. Megan was wearing emerald green, a dress she had only had made by her dressmaker a month or so before leaving England, and that she had been determined not to leave behind. Now she was glad she had brought it with her. Cleaned and pressed, it outshone many in the room and she knew it set off her chestnut curls to advantage. For the first time since leaving home, she felt truly civilised. Megan looked around at the people in the room, officers from the three

184

Companies billeted in the village, most of them escorted by village girls, their wives, or the camp whores reserved for the officers. The headman of the village and his wife were there and several other villagers important enough to be invited, not very many people really but enough to make a good party, though 'ball' was rather a misnomer, she thought. It was certainly not as refined or decorous as the balls she had been to in England, not even country balls, and would have been laughable to gentry back home, but if this was the best the Peninsula had to offer, she resolutely decided to make the best of it and enjoy herself.

Will, other officers' servants, and girls employed by the tavern owner, served chicken, mutton, venison, pork and meat pies, fresh bread, fruit pies, cheese and wine. Plenty of wine, together with brandy, port and rum. The smoke of cigars filled the room, and the loud laughter and conversation made everyone forget for a while the cold outside and the generally miserable conditions of their day to day existence so far from home. By the time the small band of guitarists and violinists struck up their first chords, the officers and their escorts were ready for anything, but before they could release new found energies on the dance floor, one of the serving girls, attired in a red and black, frilly, wide-skirted dress, took up a stance in the middle of the floor.

The officers fell silent as the music started and the girl started clapping her hands, dancing slowly at first, her heels tapping in time to the music, then faster, her skirt whirling round, showing a pretty pair of ankles, and the men started to clap as she stamped and twirled, faster and faster, to the increasingly wild music.

Will, standing in the doorway leading to the tavern's small kitchen, stared spellbound. The girl, with her long, black hair falling over bare shoulders, was beautiful. Her slim arms lifted and fell, and Will was taken back to the night he and Megan had spent with the gypsies, and the way the young girl there had seemed to dance just for him. This, he knew from talk in the kitchen, was Juanita, the girl Bob Tomkins had told him about. One of the tavern's Spanish whores, but it was hard to think of her as such, watching her dance so exquisitely.

He looked at Megan, also staring, fascinated by the music and colourful dress. Also beautiful, but in a different way. Megan's was an English beauty; a creamy complexion, curly hair that shone like a tawny halo in the light of the candles and lamps that lit the room, and hazel eyes that he wished more than anything would look on him as Sarah Harvey was gazing at Richard Camberwell right now. The Captain, who held Sarah's hand and was staring back at her with equal admiration, appeared to be the only man in the room unaffected by the dancer. Juanita was sultry. Copper skin, dark eyes, a sinuous grace. A very different beauty, but one that took Will's breath away, and seemed to have captivated every other man in the room.

The girl's dance finished with a resounding stamp of the feet and strum of guitar strings. For a moment there was silence, then the officers were on their feet, clapping and cheering as the girl, flushed with exertion, curtsied and ran from the room.

'Now there's a woman to make your eyes water,' said Francis Anver, a lieutenant in B Company, signalling a servant to bring more wine.

'Keep your hands off her, Anver. She's mine.' Paul Deaville lounged back in his chair and poured himself another drink.

Anver laughed. 'Is there a girl in the village you haven't rogered yet, Deaville? I'm amazed you don't have the pox.' He pinched the bottom of the serving girl who brought the wine, causing her to squeal. 'That one's a rare beauty though, you lucky devil.'

'But not as beautiful as she is,' said Deaville, staring at Megan Camberwell.

'Camberwell's niece? You have to be joking.' Anver downed another glass of wine as the small band struck up a lively tune and officers took their partners onto the dance floor. 'The Lady Megan's tied up tighter than a nun's knickers, man. Her uncle practically has her under lock and key. Besides, she must be a virgin.'

'She wouldn't be a virgin for long with me,' said Deaville, still staring at Megan who was laughing at something James Shaw had said, her curls dancing, eyes sparkling. She seemed to feel his eyes on her, and briefly met his with her own, before lowering her gaze in confusion. He made a decision. 'I'm going to ask her to dance.'

'What? Are you mad?' Francis Anver watched in amazement as Deaville threaded his way between the tables to Richard Camberwell who was asking Sarah to accompany him onto the dance floor.

'Sir, may I have permission to dance with your niece?' Paul Deaville put on his best smile. He knew he looked good tonight. He

186

had been tempted to ask Camberwell's servant to spruce up his uniform but had decided against it. After the embarrassing refusal he had received when he'd tried to obtain relief from his stomach ache, he was not about to risk another. Damn it, the boy should have been punished severely for that. He had disobeyed an officer's direct order and had only received a reprimand. What was worse, so had he, for making a fuss over nothing and startling the sentries. However, it had not been difficult to find a girl in the camp willing to clean his uniform and, he had to admit, she had done a sterling job.

Surprised by Deaville's request, Richard Camberwell's first thought was to refuse it. He did not like the ambitious lieutenant. Although outwardly obsequious towards senior officers, there was an underlying hypocrisy in Deaville's manner. He was too smooth by half, and Camberwell had heard tales of the man's dalliances which appeared to be legion. Preparing to deny the request, he happened to glance at Megan's face, pleading with him to be allowed to dance, and he capitulated. After all, the girl had little enough pleasure in her life at the moment, and what harm could one dance do? Deaville would not dare try anything untoward with all the senior officers present.

Grudgingly, Camberwell gave his permission, then took Sarah onto the dance floor. Having done very little to further anything other than friendly relations between them since her arrival on the ship, he had determined to find out tonight whether his instinct as to her true feelings was correct. Certainly she seemed to have lost all her shyness with him, and was enjoying his attentive company, so, without further ado, he took her hand, and left Megan to Lieutenant Deaville.

Megan could hardly believe her good fortune. She too had heard tales of this very handsome officer with the thin scar that only added to his attraction, yet she could not believe them to be true, and passed them off as exaggerations, and maybe jealousy. That he should ask her, a girl of sixteen, to dance, was more than she could have hoped for when her best expectation as to dancing partners would have been her uncle, nice-but-too-old Captain Shaw, or maybe Ensign Wooliscroft who blushed every time he spoke to her. Smiling prettily and remembering the etiquette she had been taught at school, Megan accepted Lieutenant Deaville's hand and allowed him to lead her onto the dance floor.

Will, coming into the room with another bottle of wine for Lieutenant-Colonel Davenport, stopped and stared, astounded to see Megan dancing with the lieutenant. That Captain Camberwell could allow that scum Deaville to go anywhere near his niece was unbelievable! He must have heard the stories of Deaville's philandering. How could he let him dance with her? Probably too taken with Sarah Harvey to bother, thought Will. A feeling of acute jealousy welled from the pit of his stomach, and he stamped back into the kitchen, completely forgetting the bottle in his hand.

The night wore on and the officers became increasingly drunk, their dancing and conversation wilder, and the music louder. Lieutenant Deaville managed two more dances with Megan before Captain Shaw demanded a turn. Then Ensign Wooliscroft, emboldened by too much wine and brandy, eventually plucked up courage to ask her, but proceeded to step on her toes so much she finally had to ask him if they could sit down again. Feeling most unwell after whirling around the dance floor, Wooliscroft reeled out of the door to get some fresh air. Momentarily left alone at the table, Megan glanced around for Will, suddenly thinking she had not seen him for some time, but he was nowhere to be seen. Deaville, noticing her sitting by herself, walked across to the table and sat down beside her.

'May I get you some wine, or maybe a plate of food, my lady?' he asked.

'Er...No. No, thank you.' Megan felt momentarily tongue-tied, overwhelmed by the sheer male presence of the man.

'I expect all this is not quite what you're used to,' continued Deaville. 'No doubt you went to balls all the time in England.'

Megan did not want to admit she had been to very few. 'I expect you did too, Lieutenant,' she countered.

Deaville inclined his head. 'My brothers got invited to more than I,' he said. He grinned suddenly and put a hand on hers, an action Megan was very aware of and one which sent a delicious shiver up and down her spine. 'I'm the black sheep of the family, I'm afraid.'

Megan didn't know what to say to that, but it excited her. However, Deaville was prevented from saying anything further by the music ending and the arrival of Richard Camberwell with a flushed Sarah Harvey, whereupon the lieutenant rose from the

188

chair, gave a sloppy salute, and left.

'What was he saying to you, Megan?' her uncle demanded.

'He was only making polite conversation,' said Megan sharply. 'Why do you ask? Am I not allowed to talk to other officers now?'

Camberwell was familiar enough with his niece's wilful disposition to realise that if he expressed his misgivings about the suitability of Paul Deaville as a potential suitor, he would drive her straight into his arms, so he merely said, 'You should only do so with a chaperone, Meg.'

'Stuff and nonsense!' said Megan. 'Will and I spent days together without any chaperone.'

Yes, but Will is not Paul Deaville, thought Camberwell. Will Tucker might have been dragged up in London's filthy streets, but he had proved himself more of a gentleman than Lieutenant Deaville would ever be.

'It is not fitting for a lady to engage in conversation with a young man without a chaperone, Megan. Will is a servant. It's different.'

Megan made a noise that indicated her feelings precisely, and she might have disagreed, but then the musicians started to play again. Captain Shaw came back from talking to friends at another table and begged her to dance with him, leaving Richard Camberwell to turn his attention back to Sarah.

It was only towards the end of the night's revelries when the moon was already losing its brightness that Will appeared to do his duty and escort Captain Camberwell home. Lieutenant Deaville materialised at the table at the same time, studiously ignored Will, and asked that he might escort Megan to her lodgings. Richard Camberwell had not drunk so much that he did not divine the younger man's intentions.

'You may accompany myself, my niece and Miss Harvey to our lodgings, Lieutenant,' he said. Will saw Deaville scowl and permitted himself a small smile, knowing that was not what the lieutenant had had in mind at all, but Deaville recovered himself and agreed, helping Megan on with her cloak.

Camberwell turned to Will. 'I shall not need you further tonight, Will,' he said. 'Why don't you go to the other dance and enjoy yourself?'

'Thank you, sir,' said Will, without much enthusiasm. Lieutenant Deaville's obvious attention towards Megan had completely spoiled his evening, and made him realise even more that they were poles apart and could never be more than servant and mistress.

Most of the officers managed to stagger back to their lodgings, some slipping on the frozen snow and having to be helped by friends and colleagues. They left behind a young ensign from A Company, stretched out in slumber on the floor, and a lieutenant sleeping peacefully with his head on the table in a pool of wine. Pedro, the tavern-keeper, surveyed the scene of spilt wine, trodden food, dirty glasses and broken bottles and shook his head, muttering something in Spanish which Will took to mean that he didn't think much of British officers. Pedro decided it was too late to clear away the debris; the mess would still be there in the morning. He was blowing out the guttering candles when he saw Juanita, picking up glass from the floor where a drunken officer had dropped a bottle.

'Leave it,' he said to her in Spanish. 'It will do tomorrow. You don't have a customer tonight?' He was surprised. Juanita was never short of admirers and officers generally paid well. His other girls were all in their rooms with officers already. He would make a lot of money from them tonight which would make up for all the mess they had left.

Juanita shook her head. The new lieutenant had warned her before the evening started that she was not to take anyone but him to her bed, so she had ignored the lewd remarks, the suggestive glances, even the money that had been pressed into her hand by other men in the room, expecting Deaville to accompany her upstairs after the ball had ended, but she had seen him walk out with that pretty girl from the army camp. She felt no jealousy. She did not even like the officer. His love-making was rough, and he cared nothing for her but to gain his own pleasure. However, his money was good, and she was hoarding it carefully because she had no intention of being a whore all her life.

'Go to the dance, Juanita,' said the tavern-keeper kindly. 'Enjoy yourself.' He snuffed out another candle.

Juanita went into the kitchen and was surprised to find Will there, leaning against the open back door, gazing into the darkness, seemingly in a world of his own. She had not taken much notice of the officers' servants. There hadn't been much time, everyone had been so busy, but now she looked at this one closely for the first time. He was good looking with that bright hair that differed so much from her own, but he didn't look very happy.

'You do not want to dance?' she asked in broken English.

Will jumped at the sound of her voice and turned towards the girl Bob had told him about, the one who had danced so magnificently. She still wore the red and black dress, the neckline wide off the shoulders, allowing her breasts to peep beguilingly over the bodice.

Will shook his head. The noise of the soldiers' dance came on the cold wind yet Will did not feel he wanted to be part of it. Neither did he want to go to his lodgings. The picture of Megan taking Lieutenant Deaville's hand, and the happy look on her face as she danced with him, just wouldn't go away. He walked over to a table and took from it a half empty bottle of brandy, looked at it for a moment, then tipped a lot of the smooth liquid into his mouth. It hit his stomach like liquid fire and went straight to his head, reminding him that he had eaten nothing all evening. He looked at the girl who was watching him, her dark eyes curious yet knowing, deep pools seeming to see into his very soul. He poured some more of the brandy down his throat, not taking his eyes off her, and he knew what it was he wanted.

She knew it too. 'You want to go to bed with me.' It was not a question. Her voice was low, warm, inviting as she moved closer to him and stroked a long finger down his cheek.

'I've no money.'

'It is 'oliday. I give you present.'

The words reminded Will of the kiss he had given Megan on the day of the race. Megan, whom he loved above all others, but was destined never to be his.

Juanita took his hand and led him to the stairway. They were climbing the steps when the tavern-keeper saw them. He called something to the girl. She laughed and answered him.

'What did 'e say?' Will asked as they turned to walk along the landing to her room.

''E say I take from the cradle, that you are only a baby. I tell 'im you not such a baby. I see it in your eyes.'

Smiling, she opened the door to her room and they went inside.

† † †

Paul Deaville, jacket and sword on the floor by his side, sat on a chair in his cold lodgings, drinking from a skin of sour red wine and listening to the drunken snores of James Shaw and Edward Wooliscroft. The evening had not gone his way at all. He fumed over Captain Camberwell's decision to accompany Megan and himself to the girl's lodgings where he had been forced to kiss her hand, thank her for her company, and then leave her at the door. Yet Camberwell had gone inside with his niece and that other girl, the one he had danced with all evening, because she had offered him a warm night-cap. Warm night-cap indeed! Camberwell had probably had her dress off before the glass was filled!

He stood up and paced the room, what little he could of it, up and down the side of his mattress. He was restless, dissatisfied, and drink was doing nothing to combat his restiveness. He needed a woman. Then he stopped his idle pacing. Juanita. He had told her she should have no one else because he could not bear to think of another man enjoying that delectable body. He had paid her well for her services so far. And she had promised.

Quickly he put on his jacket and went out into the night. It was raw, with a cold wind. Sounds of merriment still came from the barn where light flooded onto the hard packed snow and figures could be seen moving across the wide open doorway or walking back to the camp, arm-in-arm. Within minutes, Deaville was back at the tavern. The door was still unlocked, though there was no light downstairs but, looking up, the lieutenant could see the flicker of a candle's flame at Juanita's window.

He walked past the sleeping ensign and up the stairs.

† † †

Will lay naked on the bed, his arms folded behind his head, and watched with delight as Juanita, equally naked, swept back her long black hair and knelt with her knees either side of his hips. He smiled at her, appreciating her beautiful, lithe body, the perfect smooth skin and her lovely face. He reached towards her and fondled a round breast, feeling the nipple harden to his touch and she leaned over to kiss him.

They had made love once already, a hurried affair, he with his shirt still on, she lifting her skirts to him readily, realising his urgency. He had come embarrassingly quickly, for which he had apologised profusely, but she had pressed a finger to his lips, telling him it didn't matter, that soldiers often did, it being a long time since they had bedded a woman. Next time would be better, she told him, and now, lying on the bed, Will forgot Megan for a little while, and just gloried in the wonderful feelings of desire her experienced fingers were arousing within him.

Suddenly the door burst open.

Juanita's head spun towards it, and she gave a cry of alarm. Will half sat up, the girl's weight still on his thighs, and stared aghast at Lieutenant Deaville who, in anticipation, was already undoing his belt, but he stopped and stared furiously at the two on the bed, as shocked as they.

'You!' he spat. 'Get the hell off that bed, boy! The girl's mine!'

Juanita scrambled off Will and grabbed her dress. She pulled it against her breasts to hide her nakedness and watched in horror as Deaville quickly divested himself of his belt.

'You little whore! Didn't I tell you not to bed anyone else? You're mine, you understand? Mine!'

The belt lashed out and caught Juanita on the hip. She screamed as the leather stung her skin, and cowered away from the angry officer who loomed over them both. Will, unheeding of his own nudity, leapt to his feet and made a grab for the belt, but Deaville whipped the leather strap hard against his side, drawing blood with the buckle and leaving a vivid red weal. Will yelped but did not move, standing on the mattress, trying to catch hold of the belt so that Deaville could not hit Juanita with it.

Deaville snarled with rage, spittle spraying from his lips as he swung the belt again and again, forcing Will to totter backwards as the strap and buckle flayed him. He slipped off the edge of the bed and tumbled onto the floor and looked around desperately for a weapon of some kind.

Juanita screamed again as the belt came down on her bare shoulder. On the floor, Will saw a chamber-pot under the bed. Quickly he dragged it out and threw it at Deaville. Unfortunately the pot was not empty, and urine splashed on the lieutenant who yelled his anger and turned his attention back to Will.

'You'll pay for that, boy,' he shouted and flung the belt hard, but this time Will nimbly avoided it.

Suddenly all of them heard voices. The noise had roused the

193

tavern's other occupants. Footsteps pounded along the corridor outside the room and the door was flung open again. Richard Camberwell, sword in hand, stood menacingly in the doorway.

'What the hell's going on here?' he asked angrily. 'Lieutenant, put that belt down!' He pointed the sword menacingly at the younger man.

Slowly, grudgingly, Deaville lowered the belt.

'Will?' Camberwell looked questioningly at him.

Deaville glowered in Will's direction, as if daring him to say anything.

'Lieutenant Deaville 'it the girl with 'is belt, sir,' he said.

'And you too, it would seem.' Camberwell stared at the naked blood-smeared figure. It was obvious what had happened. Deaville had come upon Will and the girl making love, and was jealous. Well this time he had gone too far.

'Get your clothes on, Will,' he said. 'Go to the house. You, Lieutenant, will be escorted by me to the lodgings and a guard will be placed at the door to make sure you stay there. You may expect to be summoned before Lieutenant-Colonel Davenport tomorrow morning.' He turned to Juanita. 'As will you too, ma'am, if you would be so kind. It is not the British officer's way to treat women in this manner. I apologise on the army's behalf for the intrusion, and the violence shown to you.' Juanita inclined her head slightly in acknowledgement. She looked like a frightened doe, her dark eyes large and wary.

Deaville, protesting loudly, was hustled out of the room by the Captain, and Will slowly got dressed. Juanita, still wrapped in the wrinkled dress, watched him from the bed, but when he was in his uniform again, she stood up, dropped the dress, and walked over to him.

'*Gracias.* Thank you,' she said quietly and kissed him on the mouth. He saw she had recovered her composure again. 'You must come tomorrow. We 'ave...'ow you say...unfinished business?'

Will nodded. 'If I can.' He touched her shoulder gently where the belt had caught it and had left a wide, angry red mark.

'Do not worry,' she said. 'I will see to it. Go. Your Captain will be waiting for you.'

He kissed her again, and left.

Back at Captain Camberwell's room, Will bathed his own

wounds. He remembered the salve given him by the old gypsy woman, fetched it from his pack and smeared some on himself, immediately feeling the cool, soothing effect.

Will watched as the Captain poured a glass of brandy and then handed it to him. 'Drink it, and tell me what happened,' he demanded.

So Will told him the story, from the time Camberwell had left the inn, until he had burst in on them. When he had finished, he had a question of his own.

''Ow did yer know somethin' was goin' on, sir?'

'I was walking back from Sarah and Megan's lodgings when I heard a scream,' was the reply. 'I decided to investigate.'

'I suppose I'll be discharged now, won't I, sir?' There was deep despair in Will's voice. To have come so far only to be sent home again would be too much to bear.

'Discharged? Why should you be?' Camberwell frowned, not understanding.

'I 'it an officer, sir.'

'Yes, you did, Will, and under normal circumstances that would be a serious offence, but you were protecting a lady and I'm sure that will count for something at the enquiry.' He smiled suddenly. 'I would like to have seen you throw the chamber-pot at him.'

Will grinned. Looking back, it must have been a funny sight, and one which he supposed he would remember with amusement in the future, but now he was worried that, despite the Captain's reassuring words, he would be discharged from the army because of it.

He had no need to worry. Lieutenant Deaville stood no chance at the enquiry that followed the events of Christmas night and took place in the largest house in the village which Davenport had commandeered for his own use. For one thing, the Lieutenant-Colonel was feeling somewhat under the weather, and did not wish to be conducting a disciplinary hearing at all that day. For another, his dislike of Lieutenant Deaville added weight to the evidence brought against the officer by Richard Camberwell, Juanita and Will. Deaville tried to draw attention to the part where Will had hit him with the chamber-pot, but Davenport's pertinent comment that he should be grateful it was only a chamber-pot and not a sword, did not go down well.

'You were flogging a woman, Lieutenant,' he said dourly. 'Did you expect the lad to sit by and watch you do it?' He turned to Juanita. He remembered the ball the night before. Seeing the girl dance had made him momentarily wish he were not so heavily married. 'My dear, I apologise for the action of one of my officers and assure you that you will be well protected during the rest of our stay here. As for you, sir.' He looked at Deaville again. 'I am tempted to recommend your discharge or, at the very least, to revoke your commission, but as I know your father wishes the army to make something of you and he would be extremely disappointed to hear that we were unable to do so, I will put your disgusting behaviour down to a surfeit of alcohol and jealousy and give you another chance. Your pay will be docked for the next month.' He wagged his finger at the protesting officer and raised his voice. 'But take heed, Mister Deaville. Your obnoxious and undisciplined behaviour will no longer be tolerated. Start behaving like an officer or I will ensure you are demoted to the ranks. Is that understood?'

'Yes, sir.' Deaville was angry. It showed in the set of his jaw and the malevolent glare he flashed at Will and Richard Camberwell. Both knew they had made another enemy.

'You are dismissed.' Davenport waved him away. Without another word, Deaville saluted, turned on his heel and stamped out of the room.

Davenport leaned back in his chair, belched, winced, and held his distended stomach for a moment before looking up at Camberwell. 'See the young lady home, Captain.'

'Sir.' Richard Camberwell let Juanita precede him out of the room, and Davenport turned to Will. 'Are you all right, boy?' he asked.

'Yes, sir,' Will answered, assuming the officer was referring to his lacerations.

Davenport smiled and said nothing for a moment while Will fidgeted under his gaze. 'You're a lucky lad, you know that?' said the Lieutenant-Colonel.

'Sir?'

'There's many a man would give their right arm for what you had last night, and no mistake. I observed several of my colleagues whisper sweet nothings in that girl's ear and offer her money for what I assume she gave you free of charge.' Will shifted his feet uncomfortably. Davenport well knew that the average private was always poor. 'She's a rare beauty and I can't really blame Deaville for being jealous, though of course I don't condone his way of dealing with it. Yes, you're a lucky lad.' He stared at Will again. 'Now get out of here and let me spend the rest of the day in peace.'

'Yes, sir.'

Will went, glad to escape, while Lieutenant-Colonel Davenport, forty-four years old, overweight, and prone to bouts of indigestion when he over-indulged, sat and wished himself unwed, good-looking, and twenty years younger.

† † †

Next day, the episode after the officer's party was the talk of the camp which rarely had such a juicy piece of gossip to discuss. Lieutenant Deaville went about with a face like thunder, knowing that he was being laughed at behind his back, while Will found that his friends and colleagues looked upon him with undisguised admiration and envy; the first for having dared to attack the lieutenant who was known to have the worst temper of any of the officers, and the second because he had scored with the prettiest girl in the village, whore or not. Will basked in the glory for most of the day, but was brought down to earth again late that afternoon when Megan confronted him while sitting on a tree stump outside the house, skinning two rabbits for supper.

She strode up to him and stood with hands on hips as he plied the knife deftly.

''Lo, Megan,' he said cheerfully.

'Is it true?' She almost shouted the words and Will looked up, startled at her tone.

'Is what true?'

'That you slept with a Spanish whore last night.'

'Yes.'

There was silence for a moment. Will kept on with his work, wondering at her mood, afraid to look at her. He had not liked admitting his infidelity, if it could be called that, but he couldn't lie to her. To him, his time with Juanita was merely a soldier's dalliance, a lustful encounter that relieved physical needs pent up for too long. His higher, more emotional feelings for Megan had not altered at all, and he wondered that Megan should sound so cross

197

with him. After all, she knew nothing of his true feelings for her, and it could not possibly bother her that he had bedded someone.

Megan sat down on an upturned wooden crate. 'Why, Will?'

'Why?' He almost laughed.

'Yes. Why did you go to bed with her? Because she's beautiful?'

'I suppose so.' It was all he could think of to say. How could he explain to the girl he loved that he had needed a woman last night? That the drink had worked on an empty stomach and made Juanita's allure all the more enticing to a young man devoid of sexual companionship for a long time, a young man frustrated by unrequited love.

'But...she's a whore, Will! You can catch things from whores.'

'I know that, but Juanita doesn't 'ave the pox.'

Megan almost cringed away from the word. Why was she speaking to Will about this? She didn't really know. Yet the talk that was going around the camp had shocked her to the core. Will wasn't like that. He was good, and pure, and she had never thought of him in that way before. As a man. With needs like other men. After all, he was only seventeen. He wasn't even a full-grown man yet!

'Will you go to bed with her again?'

'I might.' Will grinned at her, and suddenly she could see what Juanita, girls like her, and like Nell and Connie back home, saw in Will. Not just a willing hand with the chores, or a friend to talk to. Not even a boy, but a very handsome, sexually attractive young man. Her mind flew back to the times he had kissed her on the lips. Had they just been playful kisses – or something else entirely? She recalled her feelings then, her confusion, the tingle of desire they had awoken in her. Flustered, she realised all at once that what had brought her here this afternoon was jealousy, plain and simple.

She took refuge in anger. Glaring at him, she said, 'Well, I think you're stupid to risk disease for some trollop of a peasant girl.' She saw Will's expression change and knew she had said the wrong thing, so she carried on hurriedly and with a very superior air, 'I hope you noticed that Lieutenant Deaville paid me a lot of attention last night. Now he's a proper gentleman.'

'Like 'ell,' said Will shortly.

'I heard what he's supposed to have done but it must have been exaggerated, wasn't it?'

'No. Would yer like to see what 'e did ter me?'

198

'No.' Megan's confidence faltered. Was what she had heard about him beating Will and the tavern whore the truth? It couldn't possibly be. She knew her uncle didn't like him, but Lieutenant Deaville had been nice to her, and he was so exciting to be with. No, she refused to believe he could be so violent without a good reason. Will must have provoked him in some way.

'Well, if he asks me to keep him company again, I shall say yes,' said Megan decidedly.

'Then yer a fool,' said Will, suddenly hacking at the rabbit with unwonted viciousness.

'Don't you call me a fool, Will Tucker! I'm a Lady remember!' Megan said furiously. Except for her uncle, no one else dared to talk to her as Will did, and what made it worse, he just didn't care when she castigated him for it.

'You're not a Lady, Megan. You're just a silly girl whose 'ead's been turned by a depraved lecher,' retorted Will, angry that she couldn't see Deaville for what he was, and anxious to make her face the truth. 'Stay away from 'im. 'E's bad news.'

Tears pricked Megan's eyes and she shouted, 'Oh, I hate you, Will Tucker! I hate you!' and she turned and ran away from him.

Leaving Will feeling more alone and desolate than he had ever felt in his life.

14

January 5th 1812

The long column of men, women and children, horses, wagons, oxen and mules trudged through mud that stuck to their boots, hooves and wheels like thick brown glue. Rain ran off shakos and hats down necks and over faces set in grim determination. Snow from the hills drifted across the roads, turned to brown slush by the rain and an army on the move.

The call had come the day before. Richard Camberwell had woken Will with the news that the army was moving out. 'Napoleon's made a big mistake, Will. He thinks we won't move during winter because of the weather and because the cold's making the men sick.' Camberwell had chuckled. 'Little does he know that the army's healthier than it's been for months. The country air's worked wonders. All the summer fevers have gone. The men are fit and raring to go. And apparently we don't have to worry so much about Marshal Marmont stopping us either. The exploring officers have found out Napoleon's sent some of Marmont's soldiers away from the north. Around fifteen thousand of the buggers, it's said. They're believed to be on their way to Valencia which is miles away on the east coast. Even if he gets to hear we're on the move, he poses little danger now. So the way's clear for us to take Ciudad Rodrigo and Badajoz.'

'Why do we need to take 'em, sir?' Will had asked, shrugging on his jacket.

'They're fortified towns, Will. The gateways to Spain. They guard the only roads strong enough to take our heavy artillery. We have to take them if we want to get any further into Spain.'

That day the army had hurriedly prepared itself for war.

As Lord Camberwell said, contrary to Napoleon's belief, the British were in good health and good spirits. The soldiers had benefitted from the months of enforced relaxation in the hill villages. Now they marched confidently, if slowly, towards Ciudad Rodrigo, eager and ready to do battle.

Will walked through the muddy slush and puddles, musket slung over his shoulder, the muzzle plugged with a wad of cloth, and another tied around the pan in an attempt to keep out the pouring rain. The day before, he had waded through the freezing River Agueda, the water nearly up to his shoulders, arms linked to the men next to him to avoid being swept away. That was an experience he would not want to repeat.

His pack was heavy, though not as heavy as some. Many soldiers carried around sixty pounds on their backs, but he had no sentimental belongings, only the gypsy girl's stone which he carried around his neck. All he carried were purely functional things; a canteen, cartridge pouch, powder and spare flints, his few civilian clothes, food, and a thin blanket. Though he and the men were cold and wet, the banter was cheerful and some were even singing as they marched.

'Just like England,' commented Nat Binns, plodding along like the rest. 'Makes me feel right at 'ome this weather does.'

'Bet you wish you'd gone to Botany Bay instead, Nat,' said Titus

Simms. 'I 'ears it's 'otter there.'

'Nah. If I were there, I wouldn't 'ave the pleasure o' your spark-lin' company now, would I?' Nat replied.

'I think I'd rather 'ave the bloody snow than this,' said Bob Tomkins, trying to shrug his chin further into his greatcoat. ''Ow about you, Will?'

'I bet our Will'd rather 'e was keepin' a certain little lady warm 'n cosy,' said Binns before Will could reply. He shook his head sadly. 'I still can't believe a mere lad like you got off with the best lookin' broad in the village, young Will. What you got that I ain't, that's what I want to know?'

There was a chorus of suggestions from the nearby soldiers, most of them poking fun at Nat's gnome-like face and bandy legs. He laughed good-naturedly. 'Well, I 'ave ter admit I ain't got a face that draws the women like Will 'as, but I got me good points yer know.'

Trying to find out what they could possibly be, covered the next half mile of the march.

Will walked stolidly on and thought about Nat's comments. Christmas night was still talked and laughed about. He had kept out of Lieutenant Deaville's way since then, a task made easier by the officer's decision to quit Richard Camberwell's lodgings and join some of the officers from his own company instead. As for Juanita, Will had spent a restless early evening after the talk with Megan, in two minds whether or not he should take advantage of the tavern girl's offer to finish the business halted by Lieutenant Deaville. After Megan had revealed her revulsion that he had spent the night with a whore, Will wished he had managed to resist Juanita's allure, though he knew it was nothing more than a pass-ing attraction. The heated words, and Megan's own actions with Deaville at the ball, had made it quite plain that he would never be anything more to her than a servant, yet the feeling was still there that he wanted to be her friend, and more. And he would be there, watching over her even at a distance, for as long as he could. Thinking on this, Will felt a small pang of guilt that he had betrayed her by dallying with Juanita, though it had not been a strong enough deterent to send the girl away when Juanita herself had surprisingly sought him out in the stables while he was settling the horses later that same evening.

She had explained that Pedro at the tavern was insisting she had a paying customer that evening, so she had come to Will of her own accord, remembering her promise of the night before and wanting him to have some reward for his bravery in trying to protect her from Deaville's violence. Unable to resist the temptation, Will had given in to baser instincts and they had spent a very pleasant hour rolling in the hay.

Now, listening to his friends' banter as they trudged after the men in front, he wondered if he would have any more encounters with Juanita, for since that night James Shaw had taken over his role as her protector. Consequently, Juanita was with the camp followers as the Captain's lover, a role she enjoyed because James Shaw was a pleasant, personable and rich young man who was madly in love with her, promising her that when the war was over they would be wed and she would live the life of a lady, a promise she hoped he would live to keep.

Megan had hardly spoken to Will since the afternoon of their argument. Will was sad about that and still smiled at her whenever he saw her, but she would turn away and ignore him as she had done when they had first met. It upset him more than he would admit, and he wondered if she had somehow found out about Juanita's visit to the stable, though he was as sure as he could be that no one had seen them. However, his optimistic nature shrugged off Megan's bad mood and he had plenty of other things to occupy him. There were still the horses to be taken care of, food to find and cook, and nightly shelter to be found for Captain Camberwell, Megan and Sarah.

'Pick yer feet up there, you idle sod! D'yer want ter get there tonight, or don't yer?' The shout came from a sergeant somewhere down the line. Not knowing to whom the NCO was referring, or even where 'there' was, several slouchers nevertheless put a little more effort into their stride. The rain continued to teem down and the men slogged on.

The day was darkening towards nightfall when a staff officer cantered down the line, his horse's hooves flinging up clods of mud to stick to that already on the soldier's trousers and boots.

'Colonel's compliments, sir. There's a village half a mile ahead and you're to turn into fields when you come to a gate on the right,' he said to Lieutenant-Colonel Davenport, riding at the head of the battalion. 'Arrangements have been made to accomodate you and your officers in two of the houses. Your men can camp beside the stream.'

'Thank you,' said Davenport sourly. 'More lice-infested hovels, I expect, Richard, and I doubt the men need a stream for water with this damnable weather,' he grumbled to Camberwell mounted beside him. 'Still, it'll be good to get out of the rain.'

The men thought so too, but there were never enough tents to accomodate all the soldiers, their women, and children, so, once they arrived at the village, which was little more than a hamlet, the next hour was a flurry of wet activity as the men chopped branches off trees and made themselves rough shelters. It was to be an uncomfortable night with no fires and only as much cold food as the soldiers carried in their packs.

The officers fared better. The villagers were paid to cook for them and, although the food was plain, at least it was hot and there was rough wine with which to wash it down. Will was given a heaped plate of food which he shared with George and Bob. The rum ration was doubled in an attempt by the officers to make up for the lack of food, an action that brought laughter when Nat Binns wryly commented that the officers obviously thought that if they were all drunk, they wouldn't mind empty bellies.

By the next morning the rain had turned to sleet, and the cold, tired soldiers walked on towards Ciudad Rodrigo in numb silence. It was reported that three men of the 3rd Division had died from the cold during the night. Another regiment had joined the 4th in the hours of darkness, making the column even longer. Bob Tomkins told those marching nearest to him that an Irishwoman had given birth by the road-side in the wet and cold, had picked up her new born infant afterwards, and carried on walking as though nothing special had happened. This news lifted the soldiers' spirits, and although they did not personally know the father, the men in the battalion gave three cheers for the baby and took heart from the mother's fortitude.

They camped that night in more fields but this time they were lucky enough to be given the use of two barns and, best of all, dry wood with which to make spluttering fires for long enough to cook some ration beef. The men ate hungrily, made tea, and drank their rum. Later that night, wrapped in damp blankets, Will and his colleagues lay like sardines on piles of hay. Though the smell of damp, sweaty, dirty men and clothing was somewhat overpowering, they were glad at least to be out of the persistent drizzle and with stomachs not cramping with hunger.

'Yer a daft 'un, Will,' said Bob, quietly. 'I bet yer what yer like Camberwell ain't managin' on vittels like what we 'ad.'

'I'd rather be with you lot,' said Will. 'Once the horses was seen to, 'e said I could go. Anyway, 'e's dinin' with the Colonel and Davenport tonight.'

'There y'are then. If yer'd 'ung about, reckon yer'd've bin able to get us some good grub.'

Will shrugged.

'We'll be there day after tomorrow,' said Nat Binns. 'At Ciudad Rodrigo. I 'eard Shaw tellin' the Sarge.'

There was an indrawn breath from Gerald Butterworth, lying nearby. His timidity and glasses were the butt of a great number of jokes in the battalion, yet the men who had been with him since recruitment had seen him find courage when it mattered most at the ambush, and treated him with fond concern.

'You scared, Butters?' asked Bob.

'Of course not.' Gerald Butterworth lied. He had slept hardly at all since they had left the mountain village. Not that any of them had had more than a few hours disturbed sleep a night due to the terrible weather, but Gerald was scared stiff, though he would never admit it to these companions who seemed to be actually looking forward to meeting the French.

All knew he was lying. 'You'll be all right, lads,' said a voice from the dark. Matthew Davis was a corporal and had been at the battle of Talavera, and several lesser ones since. 'So long as you keep your 'eads and spit those bullets down your muskets, we'll beat the buggers. The French don't like our volleys. And they always come at us in columns so's not many of 'em're able to fire at one time while we stand in line so everyone can fire at the bastards.'

'Yes, but we're attackin' a fortified town, not a column,' Bob pointed out.

'That we are, lad, that we are. And I won't tell you it'll be easy, 'cos it won't. There'll be a lot of bloody noise and artillery fire and men'll get killed, but the officers won't send you lot in the front line. Not unless the front line gets massacred of course.'

'Proper little ray of sunshine, ain't yer?' someone grumbled. The whole of Will's end of the barn where the newer recruits were, listened now to the corporal. They wanted to know what lay ahead, something they had been trying not to think about, but the time was fast approaching when there would be nothing else to occupy their minds.

'What's it like in a battle?' asked Butterworth nervously. 'I mean really like?'

There was a moment's silence, then another voice, a harsh, deep, Scottish brogue said, 'It's bloody noisy, laddie, an' the air's sae full o' smoke yer canna see a bloody thing beyond yer own musket. It's like yer in yer own soddin', noisy, smoke-filled world, but some-where out there the enemy are waitin' fer yer. Then yer'll hear 'em, laddies. The French'll beat their drums and shout their war cry, 'Vive l'Empereur!' and it sounds like thunder on yer ears. They dae it tae scare the shit out o' us.'

'What do you do?' Butterworth's voice was small and quiet in the silence.

'Dae, laddie? Yer pray. Yer pray that death when it comes'll be quick and that yer don't get wounded bad enough tae go tae the surgeons, 'cos they'll still kill yer, but more slowly. And yer let the noise and the smoke and the killin' wash o'er yer because if yer dinna, yer'll gae mad at what yer seein' an' hearin' and yer'll be a-wonderin' how God can let a man dae such terrible things tae another.'

There was utter silence as the veteran soldier's words sank in. Gerald Butterworth was glad it was dark because tears of terror were trickling down his cheeks. Bob Tomkins, George Trim, Will and all those who had volunteered, lay on the straw and wondered what on earth had possessed them to join the army, and those who were pressed men from the prisons or running away from the law thought it sounded a helluva lot worse than a hanging.

Then another voice rang out. 'Stop scarin' the men, Jim McKinley. These are good lads. They'll do a bloody sight better than you did in yer first battle. I could smell yer a mile away when them Frenchies started their drums. Messed yer britches, didn't yer? Well my lads are brave and they've already fought their first battle. Look what they did to that French patrol what killed them Partisans. Nothin' bothered 'em then, did it? Followed orders to a man and won the fight, and none of 'em so much as pissed in their pants doin' it neither!'

Sergeant Readman's voice was calm and assured, trying to put confidence back into the men. He could feel their terror like a physical presence and he vowed to bawl McKinley out the next morning and put him in the front line of any attack for trying to scare them, though he knew that what the man had said was the truth. He also knew well enough that every man was afraid before a battle. It was only natural to be so, and it was said that if a man didn't feel fear before a fight, then he wasn't a good soldier, but what these boys needed most at this point was hope and confidence, reassurance that they were going to come out in one piece, and that they could win.

'We'll be all right, boys,' he said. 'A siege ain't like a proper battle. Once our cannon start batterin' their walls down, we'll get in easy, see if we don't.' He neglected to tell them of the Forlorn Hope, the volunteers who would go into the breach first. If by any marvellous good fortune the leader of a Forlorn Hope, usually a lieutenant, managed to live to tell the tale, he was sure of promotion, but ninety-nine times out of a hundred he, and the rest of the men with him, would be killed. Readman also did not tell his inexperienced soldiers of the weapons usually employed by the people under siege; the bombs beneath the ground near the fortifications, the hidden emplacements protecting cannon that could fire across a breach, the sustained musket fire from the walls, and the barricades of sword blades that stuck up waist high, guaranteed to cut and pierce any man unfortunate enough to encounter them. It was a rare town or fort that surrendered without a fight. Most had to be battered into submission, and did not give in easily, meaning huge loss of life on the attacking side if the defenders were given time to prepare.

'Anyway, lads,' he said, 'just you settle down now and get some sleep. One thing's for sure, once we start attackin' the town yer won't get much.'

The soldiers lay on the dirty hay and tried to sleep, each man thinking his own thoughts about what was to come. All knew that Sergeant Readman's words were meant to reassure them, but all suspected that it was Jim McKinley who had spoken the truth. Gerald Butterworth thought about his family; his father who had

206

forced him to join the army because he had been an officer once himself, and his sisters who had thought him so handsome in his uniform and who had kissed him goodbye when he had marched away from Winchester. Bob Tomkins thought of Molly, and wished her ma had not caught him giving the girl the Christmas present of her life on Christmas night after the dance. Molly's ma had chased him, butt naked, out of their hovel and into the snow, brandishing a skillet that she vowed would hit him where it hurt most, and then had forbidden him to see Molly any more. Maybe if he distinguished himself in the coming battle she would think differently about him. George Trim put a hand over his heart, on his pocket where he kept the special letter, and thought of his girl back home, wondering whether he would ever see her again. And Will thought of Megan and wished himself back in England with her, travelling the country roads. A time that seemed long ago and idyllic in comparison to their lives at the moment.

No one slept much that night. And two days later they came to Ciudad Rodrigo.

On the morning of January 8th, Will got his first look at Ciudad Rodrigo. The 4th Kent Infantry was one of the first regiments to reach the fortified town. The French sentries, muffled against the cold, jeered from its ramparts at such a small force, still under the impression that there could be no serious attack at this time of year. Wellington ignored them, knowing that once he heard the news of their arrival, Marshall Marmont could bring his depleted French army to the town's aid if he so wished and that the British, fresh from their winter's rest, must work, and work hard, so that the French would see that they meant business, and get the job done as quickly as possible.

Ciudad Rodrigo was a formidable sight. The rain and sleet had given way to snow the day before, lending the place a deceptively fairy-tale aspect. The town, with its huge gates, was encased in solid walls several feet thick that had been standing for centuries. The church spires and snow covered roofs of the buildings were the only things visible above the impressive stone ramparts. French and Spanish flags flew defiantly.

The French had built a redoubt, a first line of defence, on an

207

outlying hill, surrounded by a snow-laden glacis and a deep ditch.

'We'll have to get rid of those buggers first.' Richard Camberwell, seated on Hades, pointed to the smaller fort. 'Once we're past that, we can start digging parallels towards the town. Ditches.' he said smiling down at Will who stood beside him looking puzzled. 'We dig ditches so that we can get close to the walls without being seen. That's where all those gabbions and fascines you lads made come in. They help to soak up the artillery fire.'

To Will it sounded scary. It seemed impossible to imagine ever getting through or over those massive walls. He could see Frenchmen standing on the ramparts watching them, and townsfolk too now, come to see the British who were marching in ever increasing numbers onto the frost-hardened ground, though still far enough away not to be within range of the cannon that faced them from emplacements in the walls. Allied Portuguese troops had joined them and the ground was filling up with men, followers, and equipment, the air filled with shouts and curses as the sergeants tried to organise them all.

A staff officer came cantering through the snow, his horse blowing clouds of breath into the cold air.

'General's compliments, sir,' he said to Camberwell. 'You're to meet with him at headquarters, sir, on the double.'

'Thank you, Lieutenant,' said Camberwell. 'And where may headquarters be?' He looked around at the mass of people, horses, tents and wagons. Children ran, shrieking at play, getting under foot. A baggage handler was chasing a mule that had escaped its tether and was running amok, sergeants were shouting orders, women were arguing over which patch of rock-hard ground was going to be theirs for the duration. It was like a town gone mad, and nowhere was there any sign of order or military discipline that might have indicated where the senior officers had made their headquarters.

'Half a mile back, sir,' said the lieutenant, pointing away from Ciudad Rodrigo. 'Near the bottom of that hill. Lord Wellington has his tent there.'

'Ah, thank you, Lieutenant. I'll be there directly.' Camberwell turned to Will. 'Find a good spot to pitch the tent, Will, and be so good as to see to Hades and Dragoon for me.'

'Yes, sir.'

It was late afternoon before Will saw Richard Camberwell again. The intervening hours had been hectic. Camberwell's, Shaw's and Megan's horses had been picketed, rubbed down, fed and watered, the officers' tent had been erected and their baggage found, and Will had gone to one of the sutlers and managed to buy a scrawny chicken for the evening meal. In between times he had cleaned his musket, paraded with the battalion, and finally he was sent by James Shaw with a message for Juanita.

When at last he found her, she was in close conversation with Lieutenant Deaville, which Will thought rather odd, given the events of Christmas night. Seeing them together behind a wagon in the baggage park, Will instinctively hid and watched, not wanting to interrupt. He saw a note change hands, from the girl to the officer, and was even more surprised when Deaville planted a kiss on Juanita's mouth, though she pushed him roughly away. Will waited until Deaville walked off, then strolled across to Juanita who greeted him with her ready smile, though she glanced briefly in the direction Deaville had taken, as though afraid that Will had seen them together, and her eyes took on a hunted expression. Will opened his mouth to say something about the meeting he had just witnessed, but some instinct told him to say nothing. Instead he explained his presence and gave Juanita the written message from Shaw. Juanita asked him what it said, not being able to read English. Neither could Will, but he guessed it was a love letter, so he told her so. She smiled. ''E loves me,' she said to Will.

'I know 'e does.' She was all James Shaw talked about.

'I like 'im. 'E is a good man. You must tell 'im I love 'im too.' She folded the paper and put it in a pocket of her skirt, then gently kissed Will on the mouth. 'You I like too,' she said softly, and playfully teased a finger down his cheek.

'I 'ave ter go,' Will said hurriedly. He backed away. 'Take care, Juanita.' He ran, her tinkling laughter following him.

Richard Camberwell arrived while Will was cooking supper. Some of the army's herd of cattle had been slaughtered, the meat distributed, and the air was full of campfire smoke. The great army had more or less settled down to camp life again already, and Will marvelled at the speed with which order had been made from chaos.

'Have you seen Megan, Will?' asked Camberwell, sitting down on a log Will had found to use as a seat. 'I've been looking, but for the life of me I can't find her.'

'She's over there, sir,' said Will, pointing with a spoon he was using to stir the stew. 'She and Sarah are sharin' a tent with another two girls, Ginny Makepiece's daughters. Old Ginny's got 'em tearin' up petticoats to make bandages.'

'Good,' said Camberwell and added grimly, 'I expect we'll need them in the next few days.' He smiled suddenly. 'I must say Megan's bearing up rather well, don't you think?'

'Yes, sir.'

'Much better than I thought she would. Do you think she's enjoying herself at all?'

'I doubt enjoyin' is the right word, sir.'

Camberwell chuckled. 'You're probably right, Will, though she'll never admit she made a mistake in coming here. Stubborn as hell our Megan. It's a Camberwell failing.' He peered into the cooking pot. 'Give me a plateful of that stew, lad. It smells good. What's in it?'

'Rabbit, sir. George and Bob shot a couple this afternoon. And there's turnips, potatoes and carrots Senora Mendez gave me. I've bin keepin' the vegetables, sir. Thought we should celebrate getting 'ere.'

Camberwell laughed. 'You carried them all this way! Good for you, lad, but the time to celebrate is when we get past the wall. Then you and I will get drunk, eh?'

'Yes, sir.' Will fetched the Captain's plate and a spoon and ladled out some of the stew. Camberwell ate hungrily.

'This is very good Will. It's even got salt in.'

'Yes, sir. Senora Mendez gave me some of that too.'

There was silence for a while. Will spooned some of the stew onto his own plate and ate it. Camberwell finished his and wiped his mouth with the back of his hand.

'Well, that'll give me plenty of energy for tonight,' he said.

'Tonight, sir?'

Richard Camberwell leaned his dark head towards him and lowered his voice. 'We're attacking the redoubt.'

Will's eyes lit up with anticipation. 'We are, sir?'

'Not you, Will. Not you. Colonel Colborne of the 52nd's taking three hundred of the Light Division. We're not going to give the French any time to get used to us being here and once that's taken,

210

we can dig towards the walls.'

'I'd like to go too, sir. Can't I volunteer?'

Camberwell shook his head. 'It's night work, Will. Bloody difficult. He's only taking veterans who've done this sort of thing before.'

'I'm used to night work, sir.'

Camberwell regarded him with a canny look. 'I know your previous employment gave you cat's eyes but the answer's still no, lad. Besides,' he smiled, 'you only just got here. There'll be plenty of time to get a shot at a Frenchman.'

Will was disappointed but reflected that the Colonel was probably right in not taking new recruits. After supper he gave Camberwell's rifle a good clean, went to the armourer who put an edge on the captain's sword blade and was there much later when Camberwell and the veterans of the 4th Light Company, together with others, assembled under a cloudless starry sky. Some of the men carried scaling ladders, hastily constructed that afternoon. The men were cheerful, relaxed, and ready for action after the long winter break. Will still wished he was going with them.

'Take care, sir,' said Will as the men made ready to join Colonel Colborne and the rest of the Light Division.

'I will,' answered Camberwell. 'If you climb that hill back there you'll be able to watch, but keep your head down. No one else is supposed to know about this.'

'Yes, sir.'

The men moved off. The redoubt was half a mile away, a darker bulk in the surrounding gloom. Will walked up the slope of a hill behind the tents and crouched in the shadow of some bushes. It was freezing cold and he was glad he had on the greatcoat Camberwell had managed to scrounge for him, but still he shivered. The campfires, dying down now as the men settled for the night, looked comforting, melting patches of hardened snow around them. Those men without tents huddled together as close to the fires as they could get for warmth and the sentries stamped their feet and paced back and forth. At least the rain and snow had stopped and the night was clear, thought Will. It would help the attackers. It could also mean they might be spotted, but that depended on how vigilant the French sentries were. He caught only glimpses of the British creeping towards the redoubt, and heard the occasional clink of an officer's sword as it bumped against something, hope-

211

fully unnoticed, though sounding unnaturally loud in the stillness of the night.

While he was watching the Light Division's progress, Will suddenly became aware that he wasn't alone. He could hear breathing and the soft scrape of shoes against the hard ground. Instinctively he shrank back into the bushes, thinking it might be an officer who would disapprove of him wandering about outside the camp. The footsteps came closer, two people walking down the hillside. They stopped near Will's hiding place.

For a moment there was silence. Will tried to peer through the foliage, but it was too thick to see anything. However, his sharp ears picked up snippets of conversation. He heard the loudly whispered words, 'Did you deliver the message to the French?' and 'tonight's attack', then a chuckle and, 'The British won't know what's hit 'em!' The other, even softer voice answered, but Will couldn't catch the words, then both sets of footsteps went away, past his hiding place. He waited until he could hear them no more before coming out from behind the bush.

The figures were soon lost in the darkness but something white was on the ground a few steps away, where before there had been nothing but hard earth and a patch of frozen grass. Will picked it up and saw it was a piece of paper with some writing on it. He squinted at it, but as he couldn't read, it meant nothing to him and despite the light from the rising moon, the night was too dark to make out the words anyway. He stuffed the paper in his pocket and stared back at the redoubt, trying to make out the Light Division, thinking hard.

Will stared into the night, then took the paper out of his pocket again, his imagination playing over what he had seen and heard. What if this paper was important? What he'd overheard could mean a betrayal, couldn't it? Maybe someone had let the town's garrison know that the British were attacking the redoubt tonight. Was the person who dropped the paper the message writer or the messenger?

Excitement bubbled in him, sure now that there was a traitor in the camp. Two traitors, because someone had written this message, if message it was, and someone else had delivered it. He glanced across at the dark ground between the camp and the hill on which the redoubt stood like a squat, black bulldog, guarding the town, and he knew what he had to do. He ran, swiftly and silently down the slope, away from the camp towards the fortification on the far hilltop.

15

As he ran in the direction taken by the Light Division, thoughts whirled around in Will's head like leaves in a storm. The first thing he had to do was get to the British before they reached the redoubt and a possible trap. The second, and probably the more difficult, was to persuade the officers that the expedition might be in extreme danger. He moved quickly, remembering the lie of the land as he had seen it during the day, and using the moonlight to advantage. While skirting the camp, taking care not to be seen by the sentries, part of his mind was wondering who the traitors were and what would make someone turn against their country and their fellow soldiers.

He had little time to ponder on it. He caught up with the Light Companies a bare two hundred yards from the redoubt. Moving slowly and as quietly as they could because of the darkness and the danger of being heard by French sentries, the soldiers' minds were primarily on where they were putting their feet. So it was that Will scared the life out of Corporal Billy White, walking carefully at the rear of the group, when he suddenly materialised close enough to slit the man's throat.

'Jesus Christ!' White took a step backwards in alarm, instinct and training already making him unsling his rifle, though it was unloaded. Colonel Colborne had insisted on the men not carrying loaded weapons to avoid an accidental shot being fired and alerting the French. 'Who the hell are you?' White whispered loudly, recognising the British greatcoat. 'You nearly got yourself killed you bloody fool!' Will thought it could well have been White who was the dead man, but said urgently, 'Captain Camberwell. Where is he?'

'God knows. Up yonder somewhere, I suppose,' whispered White indicating vaguely in the direction of the other men ahead of him. 'Why? What do you...?' but Will was already gone, running and creeping through and around the ranks, past the blundering soldiers, his agility and good memory helping him to move a great deal faster than most of them. The men were trying to move quietly but they were going uphill now and their booted feet sounded shockingly loud and he heard muttered curses and muffled oaths as they slipped and slid over the rocky, frost-hardened ground. At last he saw the familiar outline of Camberwell's tall figure ahead of him.

Richard Camberwell got a huge shock when Will suddenly tapped him on the shoulder. He turned round so quickly he almost fell.

'Will! Good God, boy! What the devil are you doing here? I thought I told you not to come! Go back!' he hissed angrily.

'Sir! It's important I speak to Colonel Colborne. I think it's a trap! I 'eard people talkin' and I found this paper after they'd gone! Maybe it's somethin' to do with it!'

'What? Show me!' Camberwell's lean face was a pale blob in the gloom as he stared at Will.

Will showed him the paper. It was so dark that Camberwell couldn't make out the words.

'What does it say?'

'I dunno know, sir.'

'Why not?'

'Can't read, sir.'

'You'd better not be having me on, boy,' said Camberwell suspiciously.

'No, sir. 'Course not, sir. I 'eard 'em, I swear.'

'Come on then.' Camberwell hauled Will bodily through the men, packed more solidly here, until he was suddenly beside Colonel Colborne. The Colonel was young, only thirty three, a vigorous, enthusiastic man and a good leader who kept on moving up the dark hillside while Camberwell spoke quickly to him, then stopped suddenly and looked at Will sharply. The men closest to him stood still, and whispers went down the line until the scuffle of boots died away and all they could hear were the sounds of the camp and the night. From somewhere in the town came music, incongruously gay and lively, seeming from a different world to these cold, hard men who were about to kill or be killed in a very short while.

Colborne looked at Will sceptically. 'Are you sure of this, lad?'

'Yes, sir.' The more he thought about it, the more sure Will was that the British had been betrayed tonight. He gave the Colonel the paper, hoping as he did so that it did have some bearing on the matter and that it wasn't just someone's laundry list.

'Damn!' Colborne swore. It was still too dark to read what was written on the paper and he did not dare strike a light for fear the French would see.

'If you're lying to me, lad, you'll swing for it.' Colborne's low voice was deadly earnest. He stood silently for a moment while the men waited quietly and patiently for the order to move on. Colborne's mouth set in a grim line.

'Tell me what you heard,' he said.

Will repeated the few overheard words again. Colborne listened. He had to admit it certainly sounded like a betrayal. He looked towards the dark, forbidding bulk of the redoubt on the top of the hill, so close now that they, and the first of the British soldiers, were crouched almost in its shadow. There was nearly complete silence for a few moments while he wondered what to do, the only sounds some nearby heavy breathing, and the faint noises on the air that told of thousands of people not too far away. Will waited, then the Colonel seemed to reach a decision.

'I need a scout,' he said. 'We have to know if the French are waiting for us.' He turned to Camberwell. 'Find me a good man, Captain.'

'I'll go myself, sir,' said Camberwell.

'No sir. Let me go.' Will was eager. He wanted to be part of this adventure, and excitement welled up in him like a spring. 'I'm smaller 'n you, sir.' He grinned and his teeth showed a flash of white in the gloom. ''Sides, sir, I'll be quieter.'

'You've not had the experience, lad,' said Colborne not unkindly. 'No, it'll have to be someone else.'

'This rogue was a pick-pocket, sir,' said Camberwell wryly. He thought for a moment. 'Could be he'd do the job, sir.'

Will felt, rather than saw, Colborne's eyes on him. 'Can you do it, son?'

'Aye, sir.'

There was another silence. Colborne stared at Will. He could almost feel the tension in the boy, the eagerness. Time was getting on and he needed to make a decision fast. 'All right then,' he said, though there was still an edge of doubt in his voice. 'You can go. I want you to get as close as you can. Tell me how many French you

215

see and where they are. Look for anywhere we can get to the walls without being spotted. And artillery. Tell me if they have manned artillery.'

'Yes, sir.' Will sat down and to everyone's surprise, started to take off his boots.

'What the hell are you doing?' Amazement was in the Colonel's low tone.

'Takin' my boots off, sir.'

'I can see that, lad. But why?'

'Won't make so much noise, sir.'

'But your feet'll freeze, boy!'

'Won't be still long enough, sir. 'Sides, I've bin barefoot in weather worse 'n this.'

During the winter months, Will had often gone without the hated boots so that his feet wouldn't get soft, thinking that if he ever had to go back to his previous employment he would need to be silent-footed again. In doing so he had endured strange looks and amused comments, but was glad now that he had done so.

He tied the boots by the laces to the string that held his trousers up and was ready to go, but before he could do so, Colborne put his hands on Will's shoulders. 'If you're spotted and fired upon, all will be lost, lad,' he said grimly.

'Yes, sir'

'Take care, and be as quick as you can. It's bloody perishing, and the lads'll catch their deaths if they don't get moving soon.'

'Yes, sir.'

Colborne turned his head to say something to Camberwell and when he looked back, Will had gone.

'I hope your faith in the boy is justified, Captain,' he said, moving into the shadow of a tree.

So do I, thought Richard Camberwell. So do I.

† † †

It took Will only a few minutes to reach the glacis, the wall of earth that sloped up towards the deep ditch he knew would be on the other side. Keeping in the black shadow he looked at the walls of the redoubt perched like an ugly great bird on top of the hill, and saw sentries there. As he watched, an officer strode along the wall towards one of the sentries and spoke to him. Nothing seemed any different from what one would normally expect and Will's stomach took a dive. Had he somehow misunderstood the mysterious voice in the dark?

He looked further along the wall, and a faint glow caught his eye, then it disappeared, and reappeared again. Keeping it in sight, he moved along a line of thorny bushes until the small light was opposite him. He crouched down. There was a gun emplacement set in the wall. The light had disappeared once more, then he caught sight of it again. Suddenly Will realised what it was. Behind the cannon was a lit brazier, and men kept walking across in front of it, momentarily hiding the glow. What was more important was that one of the men had a linstock in his hand; the long-staffed match with which to light the fuse that fired the cannon. The brazier was not just to keep the sentries warm on a cold night, but was to provide the flame to light the linstock. He looked along the wall, and could see there was another embrasure, and another, and all the guns had been run out and were ready for the order to fire. There were also French gunners, quietly crouched behind the cannon and staring out in the direction of the British who must surely be seen if they advanced any further. He looked more closely, surely there were a lot more men on the walls than there should be if they were just on sentry duty?

Will crept back into the darker shadow of the glacis and went on around the redoubt. It was the same all round; a lot of very wide awake Frenchmen, and cannons ready to fire at a moment's notice.

It was only when he came to the back of the redoubt, on the side facing Ciudad Rodrigo that Will saw a place where the British might have a chance to scale the walls. Here the glacis was higher, the shadows deeper, the towers and ramparts of the redoubt hiding the moon, the only light that of another brazier and two torches that lit the gun platforms on this side. There were cannon and sentries, but fewer than elsewhere. It seemed the French thought this side was the least likely to be attacked because of the steeper glacis. Will looked about him and saw that a piece of the redoubt's wall jutted out near the corner, sloping down towards the ditch before becoming part of the main wall again. The part that stuck out formed a V with the corner and Will took a chance and scrambled in the shadows over the part of the glacis opposite the V and into the ditch, then up the other side, thanking his lucky stars that here the ditch had not been well-maintained and was full of grassy tussocks to help him climb. When he reached the redoubt itself, he found he was hidden from any eyes above. He saw there was room for maybe fifty men in the V and, looking up the sheer wall, he could see there was ample room for scaling ladders.

Quickly he went down into the ditch and back over the glacis, then ran as swiftly as he could to the British troops, waiting near the base of the hill.

'Well?' Colborne's quiet voice was hard and impatient as Will suddenly scared a sentry into a hissed, 'Who goes there?', and appeared beside him.

'The French are all over the ramparts, sir, and they've got cannon ready to fire...'

'Damn!'

'But there's a place where I think yer can get up the wall, sir, but only with a few men, sir, to start with.'

'How many?'

'Forty. Maybe fifty, sir.'

'Camberwell! Take half your company and two scaling ladders. The rest of us will follow you.'

'Yes, sir.'

Colborne prepared to move, but Will stopped him. 'Sir, the French are watchin' in this direction, and if yer go any further this way, they'll see us for sure.'

Colborne cursed under his breath. 'Which way then?'

'There, sir.' Will pointed away from the redoubt towards trees and rocky ground. 'I'll take yer, sir.'

'All right, lad. Lieutenant Holt, tell the men to prepare to move out and to be silent.'

'Sir!'

Camberwell passed whispered messages to his officers and sergeants who soon had half his men assembled. 'Lead the way, Will, but when we get there you must go back to camp,' he said.

Will said nothing. He had no intention of going back now and pretended he hadn't heard the order. Boots swinging from his waist, he led the men into the darkness.

† † †

Wellington was on the hillside with his generals and one of his aides, near to where Will had found the paper. He was staring through his telescope at the distant redoubt. He did not expect to see much of his men until they were very close, at least he hoped he would not see them, because if he could, then so could the French. But the complete lack of movement where he thought the Light Companies should be, puzzled him. They should have reached their goal by now. All sorts of possibilities for the delay crossed his mind, but he was thankful that, as yet, the task force had not been spotted. There was no sign of alarm at the redoubt.

'What the devil's the hold-up?' he said impatiently, more to himself than to the men with him.

'I saw a shadow move, sir!' The excited voice of his aide, who also had a telescope, broke in on the question. 'Over there! They're going behind the redoubt.'

Wellington moved his telescope a little. 'So they are, but what the devil for? The glacis's not so steep on this side, and it's away from the town. Colborne told me he was going to attack from this side. What the devil's caused the change of plan?'

No one could answer him, and soon the one or two dimly seen soldiers were lost from view completely. Wellington fretted and fumed, while he wondered what was happening to his best companies.

Richard Camberwell panted, his breath forming small clouds in front of his face as he scrambled up the steep inside slope of the ditch towards the wedge of wall that Will had pointed out to him. It was hard going. His sword scabbard kept catching on the slippery ground and he could do nothing about it because he needed both hands to help him climb. His men were following him, the only sound their heavy breathing and the occasional thud of a boot. It was imperative that they move quickly, before the French realised what was happening. Once the scaling ladders were placed against the side of the ditch, climbing was made easier but Camberwell found he was holding his breath every time one bumped against the wall of earth, sure that they must be heard and seen by the sentries above. It appeared that those sentries were not paying much attention. Voices floated down on the night air, and Camberwell's knowledge of the French language told him they were bored. One

219

Frenchman was even of the opinion that they were wasting their time because the Goddamns, as they called the British, were sleeping and would not venture out on such a cold night.

Richard Camberwell reached the top of the ditch and hauled himself over the edge, then turned and pulled a man over, and another, then men climbing the ladder joined him. More soldiers scrambled over the side and they propped the ladder against the stone wall. Camberwell was the first one on it, clambering up the rungs that bent ominously under his weight. It had been hastily constructed of unseasoned wood and he thought it would be just his luck for it to break. Soldiers put another beside it and men started to climb. Camberwell was halfway up when he heard a shout and knew the French had spotted them. There was a rattle of musket fire from above and bullets hit the wall and whined away into the darkness. Expecting at any minute to feel one drilling into him, Camberwell nevertheless carried on climbing.

He had nearly reached the top when he heard Colborne shout the order to fire and a hundred rifles and muskets spat bullets and smoke from the edge of the glacis at the unwary sentries. Camberwell clambered over the parapet and heard shouts, and saw Frenchmen running towards him from inside the redoubt but the wall nearest him was empty except for half a dozen dead or wounded men. British infantry and riflemen were pouring over the walls from the ladders. Camberwell shouted, 'Charge!' and ran down stone steps into the fort.

In the heady excitement of the moment, Will conveniently forgot Camberwell's injunction to return to camp and scrambled up the ladder, following soldiers who eagerly climbed ahead of him. He could hear shouts and screams from inside the redoubt now as the British fought their way forward. There was a cry, and a man fell from the top of the ladder. Holding his breath, Will pressed himself hard against the rungs to avoid falling as well, and the soldier tumbled past him. Then he was moving again. He reached the top and climbed over the ramparts. Inside the fort was a large area bare of grass, filled with redcoats and green-jackets running towards startled Frenchmen who were hastily trying to rouse themselves into defending the fort. Torch-light glinted off a sword that a French Colonel brandished as he shouted, urging his men into action.

Will stood back against the wall, letting British soldiers run past him. A musket flashed and he heard a bullet whine, then ricochet off the wall near his hip, making him flinch. It occurred to Will that he had no musket, and he looked frantically about him for something to use as a weapon. Suddenly the night was rocked by a huge noise as a cannon roared, swiftly followed by an explosion of soil as the ball landed over the glacis, and over the heads of the waiting British. Glancing to his left, Will saw Frenchmen in an embrasure reloading the gun but the French had not been expecting an attack from this side and the men were slow. The cannon roared again but the ball once more sailed over the heads of Colborne's men crouching and firing from the slope of the glacis. Will heard a cheer and knew that Colborne was bringing the rest of his men through the ditch to scale the ladders.

More men thumped past him and he was shoved, none too gently, from behind. 'Get movin' son,' snarled a sergeant, pushing him towards some stone steps. Will stumbled towards them. The inside of the redoubt was a mass of men, sword blades and bayonets flashing in the glare of flame torches and the screams of the wounded vied with the shouts of friend and foe alike. A musket banged close to him and Will automatically ducked but the ball was not aimed at him. Suddenly a sword flashed out of the darkness and he swerved to avoid it. The man behind the blade growled a French curse and swung again but Will ran down the steps and was gone before the sword made contact. He needed a weapon.

On the ground he was nearly bowled over by two soldiers fighting each other furiously. A bayonet skimmed past his side and he jerked out of the way. The flaming torches gave the mass of fighting men a devilish, hellish look; faces grimacing in pain and savagery. Swords and bayonets flashed and Will caught a glimpse of stocky Sergeant Readman swinging his empty musket, lifting a Frenchman almost off his feet when the butt cracked against his ribcage.

A green-jacketed rifleman went down near the wall. Will ran over to him and snatched up the man's rifle, swiftly rummaged in the soldier's pouch for cartridges, then crouched in the lee of a doorway to load it.

There was a lot more noise now as more Frenchmen ran from the redoubt's walls and the French Colonel was still shouting, trying to rally them into some sort of defence, then his cries were cut off when a musket ball took him in the throat. Despite the enemy's fore-knowledge of the attack, the British had caught the French by surprise and were pouring over the ramparts, a seemingly endless stream of shadowy, battle-ready, eager figures, lit only by the torches and braziers like demons from hell. A bayonet scythed past Will's side again and he brought the rifle up at point blank range, punching a hole through the blue coat and into the Frenchman who wore it. The man fell against him, and Will pushed him down, then quickly loaded the rifle again.

Suddenly Richard Camberwell was there beside him. 'Damn it, Will!' he growled. 'I thought I told you to go back!'

'Not possible, sir,' said Will, aiming the rifle and firing it, then smiling happily as another enemy went down.

'Bloody liar,' said Camberwell grimly, then he grinned. 'But it's nearly over. The fight's gone out of 'em, Will. Look! The bastards are surrendering.'

It was true. Seeing themselves leaderless, and unable to cope with the ferocity of the British, the Frenchmen who were still alive were putting up their hands in defeat and Colonel Colborne was shouting at his men to cease firing. A man was already raising the British flag. The redoubt had been taken in less than twenty minutes.

† † †

On the hill, Wellington saw the Tricolour come down and the British flag hoisted. He put down his telescope, smiling slowly in satisfaction. 'They've done it!' he said. He turned to one of his engineers. 'Commence the first parallel.'

'Yes, sir.'

The engineer ran down the hill to arrange for the digging of the first ditch that would take the soldiers closer to Ciudad Rodrigo. Wellington knew that not a moment must be wasted and now that the redoubt was in British hands, there would be no danger from that quarter. The only opposition they could expect would come from the big guns in the town itself and he wanted the first ditches dug before the French in Ciudad Rodrigo noticed what they were doing. He put the telescope to his eye again. The Light troops were cheering, standing on the ramparts, waving muskets and rifles towards the British camp and shouting derisive comments in the direction of Ciudad Rodrigo. Wellington overcame an almost over- whelming urge to wave back. 'Well done, lads. Well done!' he murmured instead.

Will did not sleep that night. By the time the wounded had been taken to the surgeons, the prisoners locked into stone-walled rooms in the redoubt, and the dead carried outside for burial, the sun was already shining. With the adrenalin of victory still running high, he and the rest of the Light Division marched back to the camp where they were greeted with cheers and slaps on the back. Colborne was particularly pleased at the light losses the British had taken; only six men killed and twenty injured. Will was still bare- foot. The French bayonet that had nearly taken a strip off his side, had slashed through one of the boots so that it was half cut through. Richard Camberwell had advised him to take a pair off a dead man, but Will said no, he would mend the leather, this pair that had now moulded to his feet being preferable to any other.

Even back at camp, the weary soldiers were still allowed no rest. Lord Wellington insisted on thanking them personally so they had to parade as they were, with no attention paid to dirty, bloody uniforms, blackened muskets, and powder stained, grimy faces. Wellington sat astride his horse and commended Colonel Colborne and the men for the swift execution and victorious outcome of the attack. After the men had been dismissed and told to eat and get some well earned rest, Wellington dismounted and gave the reins of his horse to an aide. His long face took on a grim expression and he said to Colborne, 'Now that is done, let us get to this business of treachery. You mentioned a letter?'

'Yes, sir, I have it here.' Colborne took the paper from his pocket and handed it over. As soon as he could, he had read what was on the paper, as Wellington did now. It proved to be a message to the French, informing them of the attack, but provided no clue as to either the sender or recipient.

'It was not a joke?'

'Definitely not, sir. The French were waiting for us.'

'So. We have a traitor in our midst.' Wellington stared thought- fully towards the redoubt. 'How did you come by this letter?'

'One of the lads found it, sir. Captain Camberwell's servant.'

'A soldier?'

'Yes, sir. Will Tucker. He's in Camberwell's Light Company but he's a new recruit, sir, so wasn't in the picked men at the start.' He smiled. 'But I'm willing to bet he will be next time, sir.'

'How so?'

'Distinguished himself, sir. Scouted the redoubt and led us to the only place where we could get to the walls without being seen. I believe he picked up a rifle and did for a few Frenchmen too, sir.'

Wellington raised his eyebrows. 'Did he now? I'd like to meet the fellow. Bring him to my tent, Colborne.'

'Yes, sir.'

'And Colborne...'

'Sir?'

'I'll inform the exploring officers about this, but if you see or hear anything untoward, let me know immediately. Keep it quiet though. Maybe the traitorous bastard who wrote this will make a mistake. I don't want him to know we found the note. Rather let him think that maybe it wasn't delivered and the trap wasn't set after all.'

'Yes, sir.' Colborne saluted and went off to find Will who had fallen onto a blanket in Richard Camberwell's tent and was sound asleep. He was still groggy when he found himself some ten minutes later, standing in front of the army's commander, a situation he might have found awe-inspiring if he hadn't been so tired. Colonel Colborne, Richard Camberwell and two Light Division Majors stood or sat beside their chief.

'Will Tucker, your Lordship,' an aide announced, disdain very apparent in his tone. His eyes scoured Will from head to toe with a withering look.

Wellington looked up from some papers on the table he was sitting at. He frowned at the aide's arrogance.

'That will be all, Lieutenant,' he said frostily.

'Sir,' said the aide blushing at the implied rebuke.

Wellington turned his aristocratic face towards Will, surprised to see one so young. He had been expecting an older man. 'You are Will Tucker?' he asked.

'Yes, your honour...er...your Lordship.' Will had no idea how to address the army's commander.

Wellington leaned back on his chair and stared at the dishevelled youngster who absentmindedly scratched a stray louse that suddenly made its presence felt in his hair, hair that was tousled and dirty.

'You are the one who found this letter?' Wellington pointed to the paper on the table.

'Yes, sir.'

'Tell me about it.'

Will repeated what he had told the other officers, while Wellington listened intently. 'You saw no one?' he asked afterwards.

'No, sir. I 'eard 'em but it was dark, sir.' Will did not mention that he had been hiding in case the mysterious speaker was an officer who would disapprove of him being away from the camp.

Wellington was silent for a moment, then seemed to dismiss the letter. 'Colonel Colborne tells me you were of great assistance to him last night.'

Will blushed to the roots of his hair. 'I did what I could, sir,' he said.

Wellington's conversation seemed very odd to Will, careering off at tangents because the next thing he said was, 'What did you do before you joined the army, lad?'

Will reddened again and glanced at Camberwell who was trying hard not to smile. He decided the truth would do. 'I was a pickpocket, sir.'

'Ah. I suppose you're here because it's slightly better than a hanging, eh?'

'No, sir.'

'No?' Wellington looked surprised. 'Don't tell me you volunteered?'

'It's a long story, sir.'

Wellington's face cracked into a rare smile. 'One day I think I'd like to hear it.' The smile went and he turned to Captain Camberwell. 'I seem to remember hearing the name Tucker before. Could you enlighten me, Captain?'

'The ambush when I was bringing the recruits from Oporto, your Lordship,' replied Camberwell. 'Will and two other lads outflanked the French, sir.'

'Ah, yes.' Another pause while Will shifted his feet embarrassingly under the piercing gaze.

'I understand from my subordinates that some reward should be your due for your efforts in subverting a plot that could have decimated my best companies. I have decided you may keep the rifle I'm told you used to advantage in the attack.'

'Thank you, your Lordship.' The thanks was heartfelt. To the uninitiated, a rifle might sound a poor reward, but for Will it was glory indeed. Only the best marksmen had the Baker rifle, and they belonged to the Rifle Companies; the green-jackets – the best of the best. To be the owner of a rifle was to be acknowledged as one of the best marksmen in the army and respect was shown accordingly. It was an honour that Will appreciated.

'Before you go, Mister Tucker, I was wondering why you have no boots on. Have you lost them?'

'No, sir. One needs mendin', sir. 'Sides, I don't like wearin' 'em much, sir.'

'Mmm.' Wellington picked up his pen. 'All right. You may go.'

'Thank you, sir.'

Will left the tent and in a few minutes was fast asleep again.

'A scoundrel if ever I saw one,' said Wellington to no one in particular after he'd gone. 'But an interesting scoundrel. Look after that one, Captain Camberwell. I've a feeling I'll be meeting him again.'

16

The next six days and nights were filled with hard work, endless crashing noise, and sights too awful to contemplate. Men worked in shifts, digging trenches. The work never stopped, not even when the French sent deadly grape shot and howitzer shells to pound the workers to bloody ribbons. The fascines and gabions soaked up some of the storm of metal but it was a common sight to see soldiers being sprayed with earth and ducking down against trench walls, while the trenches filled again with the soil they had just removed. The long ditches filled with bodies as well. Once the enemy gunners had the range, many of the missiles were plumb on target, and British casualties were high.

Will, like the rest, took his turn to dig. The only saving grace was that the weather held. Although still freezing, especially at night, the days were fine. The ground was hard with frost under its layer of packed snow and was difficult to dig, but at least the digging was a means of keeping warm. Will took to wearing his mended boots, and was very touched when Megan presented him with a pair of woollen socks she had knitted herself, badly to be sure, but no less acceptable for all that. She seemed to have forgiven him his indiscretion with Juanita and said nothing more about it, so Will gladly accepted her overture of friendship and was pleased she was talking to him again.

Despite the barrage of cannon fire from the town, the digging went ahead and by the fifth night, when Will's company took another turn at digging, the British trenches were well forward and very close to the walls.

The work, as well as being hard and dangerous, was made more difficult at night by poor light, though this was abetted by the flashes of gunfire from the walls of Ciudad Rodrigo. Howitzer shells screamed overhead as Will banged his spade down into the frosty ground. The men didn't talk, no one could hear anything below a shout anyway. Batteries had been dug out; gun emplacements ready for the assault on the town's walls. One of them, empty as yet, was near Will and the half dozen men inching their way along the hard, rocky soil. The French guns seemed to have targeted the battery for special attention tonight. Shells crashed into the surrounding ground one after the other, showering the soldiers with earth and splinters of rock and providing an endless background of ear-splitting noise.

They had been digging for only a little while when suddenly a man yelled 'Down!' and the soldiers flattened themselves in the bottom of the trench, arms over their heads, as a shell whined overhead and landed just feet away. The resulting explosion rocked the trench, sending piled soil cascading down on the men beneath and metal shards falling all around. A man screamed, and Will lifted his head to see a spike of jagged metal sticking out of the eye of Peter Tenet, a pleasant boy who wore glasses. Tenet was known to be quite a scholar and he kept a detailed diary, saying that one day he would write a book of his experiences. Now Tenet was screaming and clawing at his face, his left eye a mess of bloody jelly and splinters of glass from his broken spectacles. Will, fighting back nausea, lurched to his feet and took two steps towards him then another explosion shook the trench, sending him flying so that he sprawled across the wounded soldier. Briefly the trench was filled with light and rocks, earth, and bits of metal rained into it. Will felt a rock land on his back with a thump.

When he finally thought it safe enough to lift his head again he saw that none of the men near him had escaped unhurt. Three were not moving at all. The others were moaning or screaming. Will slowly pushed himself to his feet, stones, and soil running off him. He felt wetness running down his leg inside his trousers and thought at first that he had done what every soldier dreaded and wet himself in fear, but he saw that the material was torn and that something sharp had cut him just below the knee. The blood was dripping into his boot and a dark stain was spreading rapidly over his trousers. It occured to him that Tenet had stopped screaming. A glance confirmed that the man was dead, his one eye staring, unseeing, at the stars. Will scrambled to a crouch, stepped over him and limped three paces to George Trim, his heart in his mouth because George lay like a dead man.

'George! George!' His voice could hardly be heard as the shelling continued and another gout of earth sprayed him, but he ignored it, reached his friend and collapsed beside him. 'George!' he shouted in the boy's ear and was relieved when there was a moan and George opened his eyes.

'Where are yer 'urt?' Will shouted.

'What?'

'Where are yer 'urt?' Will yelled louder.

George sat up and felt himself all over. 'I don't think I am,' he said in a slow, wondering voice.

'Yer bloody well scared me 'alf ter death!' shouted Will. He crawled back to Tenet and fumbled inside the boy's coat, pulling and tugging at his shirt until a piece of the material tore off. He tied the strip tightly round his leg above the wound, hoping it would slow the bleeding, then staggered upright and limped over to see if any of the other men were alive. Suddenly he was roughly pushed down again.

'Bloody 'ell, lad! You tryin' to get your bloody 'ead blown off? Stay down, you bugger!' Sergeant Abe Chalmers practically sat on Will as he dived down with him just before a cannon ball crashed into the far side of the trench further along. The explosion sent tremors along the trench and they received yet another shower of earth. Chalmers wiped his face with his sleeve, mixing the dirt with

228

sweat. ''Ell, but the buggers're lively tonight. Lieutenant says we're to take the wounded and leave 'em to it. Lost 'alf the bloody men at this end of the trench already. You 'urt, lad?'

'Cut on the leg, Sarge, that's all.'

'D'you think you can 'elp Jessup over there?' Another shell landed nearby and earth sprayed over them again. 'Jesus Christ!' The sergeant swore. 'If we stay 'ere we'll be buried alive afore mornin'!' Will looked towards Ben Jessup, a slight, dark-haired youth who was holding a desperate hand on a wound in his side that was pouring blood.

'I'll 'elp 'im, Sarge.'

Will started to crawl towards the injured soldier. Chalmers risked a peep over the edge of the trench. The straw baskets of earth that were supposed to soak up the shelling had long since been blown away. 'Wait for the next one and then make a run for it,' he said. 'It takes 'em about a minute to reload, I reckon. Take Trim too. Looks like 'e's lost 'is senses.'

'Blast knocked 'im for six, Sarge.'

The sergeant's reply was lost in another explosion, then Will was up, pushing and pulling George, his other arm around Ben Jessup, helping them both along the trench, then down another. Explosions ripped through the air, but now Will and the others were going away from them. They went slowly, too slowly Will thought as he stumbled in the dark through loose earth and slid on frosty ground, expecting at any moment to become another victim of the endless barrage. They passed a group of soldiers digging more successfully, glad they were not the ones being targeted tonight. Jessup was almost a dead weight, and George, still dazed, no help at all, so that Will, his leg throbbing and making him limp more and more, was almost at the end of his strength when suddenly willing hands were hauling them out of the trench and all three collapsed on the ground.

'You all right, son?' The inquiring voice was that of another sergeant.

'Yes,' said Will, then fainted clean away.

† † †

He awoke some time later in one of the tents that were being used to accommodate the wounded. A bandsman, doubling as a medical

229

orderly, was washing his hands in a bowl of bloody water that stood on a wooden crate. He glanced at Will, then shouted out of the open tent flap. Will saw it was still dark outside and that the other cot in the small tent was occupied by a bearded man who had a bandage around his head and appeared to be asleep.

'The lad's awake, sir!'

A few minutes later a man came into the tent; solid, bushy-bearded and barrel-chested. His white apron was bloodstained and his hands raw from washing and the cold. Will knew him to be the battalion's surgeon, John Barker.

'Ah, you're back with us, then, lad. How're you feeling?' he said in a loud voice.

'All right, sir.' His right leg throbbed, and he felt a bit weak, but otherwise Will felt fine. He tried to sit up but the surgeon pushed him back firmly.

'Oh no you don't, son. You lost more than a drop o' blood and it won't hurt you to rest there for a while. The army'll manage without you for a few hours.'

Will sank back onto the cot. ''Ow're the others, sir?'

'The ones who were with you?' Will nodded. 'The lad who got knocked out is fine. A bit groggy but he's up and about already. The other one'll mend in time but he won't be killing any Frenchies for a while.' He grimaced. 'They're the lucky ones. I've had to take off two legs, an arm, and seen four men die under my hands already tonight. Rest until I need your bed for someone else.'

Some ten minutes later, Will was delighted when Megan walked into the tent carrying a mug. Having been roused from sleep to tend the wounded caused by the French bombardment, she had been run off her feet and had not even known Will was there. Having done what she could to help with the walking wounded, thanking God she had not been asked to assist the surgeon like Sarah, she had then been put to scrounging the camp for tea, brewing it and adding rum, then taking it round to the injured.

'Oh, God! Will!' she said, nearly dropping the mug in horror seeing him lying on the cot. 'I didn't know it was you in here! What happened? Are you badly hurt?' Her face, already drawn with fatigue, drained of its colour.

'I'm fine,' said Will. 'Just a cut on the leg. Must've gone a bit deeper than I thought, is all. I s'pose I'm only 'ere 'cos I went an' passed out.' He pulled a face in self-disgust. Megan sat on the cot and handed him the tea with a hand that shook, making the liquid spill onto the blood-stained sheet.

'Damn!' she said, and tears sprang to her eyes. She put the cup down and ineffectually mopped at the stain with a dirty cloth that the bandsman had left. He put a hand on her arm.

'Please don't cry,' he said gently. It hurt to see her upset.

Unfortunately his words only loosened the dam that had been holding back the tears for so long and Megan found herself quite unable to stop. Clumsily, Will hauled himself into a more upright sitting position and put his arms around her.

Sobbing into his shoulder, Megan wondered at herself. Usually so full of confidence, she wondered why she had become so much more emotional in the last few months. Many times she had felt like crying but her pride, or the company she was with, had kept the tears at bay. Now Will, dear Will, had been hurt and she cried for him. But not only for him. She cried for herself. For the difficulties and hardships she had to face every day. For the life she had left behind. For her girlhood. Now she was no better than the rest of the women who followed the army. A Lady she might still be in name, but in reality a Lady no longer. The tears of self-pity vied with those of concern for her friend and she despised herself because she knew not for whom she cried more.

Gradually the weeping slowed then stopped. Megan pulled away from Will's arms, sniffed, and looked into his blue eyes that were watching her with an expression she couldn't quite identify. If she had been more experienced in the ways of men she might have recognised it for what it was. Will, more than anything in the world, wanted to kiss her, to hold her close again, to tell her he loved her, but he held off his racing libido and brushed away the teardrops on her cheeks instead with a gentle finger. Megan stared at him through wet eyelashes and something quickened inside her, the same feeling she had experienced when Will had kissed her in the wood at Camberwell Hall. Time ground to a halt while they continued to stare at each other.

Suddenly the bandsman burst through the tent flap and the spell was broken.

'The doc says you're to come, Miss!' he said urgently. 'There's another lot of wounded comin' in!'

231

'What?' Megan dreamily turned her head towards him, then seemed to realise what he had said. Flustered, she jumped to her feet. 'Oh! Yes! Of course! I'm coming!'

The orderly left and Megan wiped her face with the hem of her skirt. 'Now go to sleep,' she said in a voice that was meant to be brisk and efficient but shook a little. 'The doctor says everyone who's injured needs to rest.'

'Yes, ma'am,' said Will with a grin and obediently lay down and closed his eyes. All was quiet, and he thought she had gone but then he felt lips gently brush against his. When he opened his eyes the tent was empty except for the sleeping soldier.

He smiled, and despite the noise of the guns, fell peacefully asleep.

† † †

Paul Deaville was a worried man. He lay on his cot watching the flickering shadows made by the only candle and listened to the noise going on outside. He wondered how on earth the two officers who were sharing his tent could possibly sleep. It sounded as though the French were trying to rid themselves of all their artillery ammunition in one night, and the tent shook on more than one occasion when a shell overshot the trenches and dug another crater in the ground between the British camp and the parallels. However, Deaville had more to worry about than whether some of his countrymen were being pulverised, and it was his thoughts more than the noise that kept him awake.

The attack on the redoubt. From his point of view, it had been a disaster. What on earth could have gone wrong? He had given the note to Juanita and told her to deliver it, yet the attack had gone off without a hitch. Surely if she had followed his orders the British would have been blown apart before they had got half way to the redoubt and the attack would have failed. Damn the girl!

She had appeared to be really keen on him when he had first slept with her. Before Christmas it was. He remembered how her eyes had lit up at the amount of money he had promised her and she told him of some impossible dream she had of going to Madrid and becoming something better than a whore. As though she ever could! But after the night of the ball, when Camberwell's damn servant brat had got into her bed and he had been so angry and hit her, she had taken up with James Shaw and since then had been reluctant to even see him. It had taken all his powers of persuasion and a promise of more money which he hadn't any intention, or even any hope, of paying, to make her take the letter into Ciudad Rodrigo.

The day after the successful attack on the redoubt, he had cornered her behind the British lines. Hell! He'd felt like killing the bitch! Yet his strong-arm tactics had been in vain, though he could tell she was scared. The whore had kept insisting that the message had been delivered as planned. If that were the case, why had the French not blasted the Light Companies to pieces? No, the bitch was a damn liar. She obviously hadn't given the note to Colonel Jean Reynard at all. Reynard, the French Voltigeur officer, one of the men he had played cards with that night in Lisbon all those weeks ago when they had first landed in Portugal, and to whom he had lost a great deal of money. So much money in fact that the Frenchman, who was a hot-tempered bastard, had offered to cut his throat if he didn't settle his debt quickly. Having no immediate funds available, and after much sweet-talking, the man had reluctantly taken a promissory note, but Deaville could tell at the time that the Frenchman was not happy about it, not knowing whether their paths would ever cross again.

Now, because of Reynard, Deaville was involved in treachery and betrayal of the British cause, not that guilt weighed heavily on his conscience in that regard. He couldn't give a damn who won the war, so long as he benefited from it in some way, so whether he became a senior officer for the British, or was lauded by the French as a British spy if the enemy won, it was all the same to him. To this end he had recruited Juanita as a messenger and at the time had thought it a good idea. Being a native, the girl was able to go into Ciudad Rodrigo without causing any suspicion, at least until the town's gates had been closed to prevent anyone entering or leaving.

He had been surprised when Wellington had proposed an attack on the redoubt so soon after their arrival, but even more surprised when Juanita had brought him a letter that very same day from Colonel Reynard who was part of the town's French garrison. It didn't take long for whores to make a conquest, he mused. She must have gone into the town almost as soon as they arrived in its vicinity. And to have met Reynard of all people was a horrible coincidence. He balled his fists at the thought of her indiscretion in mentioning his own name. The French Colonel might never have known he was here otherwise. Now Reynard wanted him to betray his country. Temporarily more frightened of the Frenchman's revenge if his debt was not paid, than of Wellington, he had scrawled a quick note in return, told Juanita what to do, and sent her off with a basket so that she could, at the same time, buy fresh fruit and vegetables to lend a legitimacy to her excursion. The bitch hadn't wanted to go. He remembered the argument when they had met secretly in the baggage park the afternoon before the attack. He had been so angry then he could have struck her, instead her anger provoked other urges in him and he had kissed her hard on the mouth. By God, the bitch was beautiful when she was angry, but she had fought with him, pushed him away. He would have taken her anyway but for fear of discovery in such a public place.

Events suggested that she had never delivered the message, and, if not, then what had happened to the letter? What if she had lost it? He had heard nothing to suggest that anyone had found the treacherous piece of paper. Did she still have it, he wondered? If so, there was every chance she would tell someone about it, and of his complicity with Reynard, who would undoubtedly be angry because the British had been the victors of the attack on the redoubt. Suddenly Juanita's reluctance, and the fact that the French had seemingly not been aware of the British attack beforehand, pointed strongly to Juanita having decided not to be his accomplice after all. Yet no one had questioned him. It was all very baffling, but one thing stood out like a signal beacon. He had been stupid to have ever trusted Juanita and he would have to do something about her before she gave him away. A thought that had been lurking at the back of his mind since he had first realised the plan had misfired, pushed its way to the forefront.

He would have to get rid of her. For good. And that meant a murder.

Usually having no scruples when it came to killing, he did have misgivings about doing this particular murder himself, and almost wished it didn't have to be done. Juanita was, after all, a stunningly beautiful woman. Good in bed too, and it was a shame that all that would now be lost to him, but for his own peace of mind he would be prepared to lose her. There were other women equally as lovely.

234

Take Lady Megan Camberwell for instance. Young she might be, but the very thought of her aroused his passion. He had spoken no more than two words to the girl since Christmas night, but he had watched her, and had seen the looks she gave him; coy, shy looks that he took to mean she was interested. Very interested. And he would have her. Sometime soon, he would have her. In the meantime, he would find someone to get rid of Juanita for him. But who?

A huge explosion rocked the tent and sent Deaville diving under the bedclothes, though he knew the British camp was well out of range of the French guns. When it was relatively quiet again, and feeling rather stupid, he peered over the blankets at his companions. Disturbed by the noise, they opened bleary eyes, saw everything was as it should be, turned over and went back to sleep. Deaville, his hand shaking, picked up a nearly empty wine bottle that had fallen over beside his cot, drank from it, then lay down again, pondering once more on the problem of Juanita.

He thought back to the journey from Lisbon with the ex-convicts. Surely there must be a man amongst them who would do the job for him? One name immediately sprang to mind. Amos Wilkins. Now there was a bad lot if ever there was one. He had a feeling that Wilkins would kill his own mother if there was some profit in it. But the man would want paying, and he had no money other than that needed for basic food and other necessities. That bastard Tucker had seen to that, making Davenport dock him a month's pay for that business with Juanita back in the hill village. Now he was up to his neck in debt with the sutlers, for he could not survive this goddamn army without wine, brandy, good food, and whores. He reached for the wine bottle again and, as he did so, guttering light from the candle glinted off the ring his father had given him for his twenty-first birthday. It was gold, ornately engraved, and nearly half an inch wide, a family heirloom and, more to the point, valuable. He thought back to the card game with Reynard. Even the ring had not been enough to pay what he owed, and the man had refused it, saying he would never wear it, nor would anyone buy such an ugly thing. But, if he knew his man, and he was sure he did, it was something that Amos Wilkins would be pleased to have, if only to sell, and he wouldn't take much persuading because Wilkins was a thief and had the acquisitiveness of a magpie for bright things, especially if they were worth money. Yes, tomorrow

235

he would seek out the bastard and put the proposition to him.

Feeling much happier, Paul Deaville finished off the wine, blew out the candle, and finally fell asleep.

† † †

Will awoke to a hand shaking his arm. Daylight flooded the tent and Megan was there with a piece of hard bread and a mug of water for him. She looked immensely tired. The noise of the French artillery fire was still there in the background, a never-ending noise like distant thunder.

'You 'aven't slept,' he said as she sat on the bed.

'No.'

Will took the water and drank it, looking over the rim of the mug at her. She seemed more composed this morning, but quiet. There was a tender look in the eyes that watched him drink.

'Was it awful?' she asked, then, 'That was a silly question, wasn't it?'

'Yes, and yes.' Will thought back to the horror of the trenches. The barrage of noise, the fear of being buried alive by the gouts of earth, lying on top of Tenet, a dead man; the mangled bodies. He shuddered and Megan put a tentative hand on his. She still felt shock at seeing him here and she could see he was thinking about the horrors he'd experienced. He looked at her, at the dishevelled curls and the weary eyes that looked so concerned and his heart gave a leap of desire. It was all he could do to stop himself taking her in his arms and kissing her.

'Doctor Barker says you can get up,' she said.

'Good.' Will, for the first time, looked under the thin blanket at his legs. There was a piece of bloodstained material, some woman's petticoat, strapped around the wound. His trouser leg had been cut with shears to the knee. 'Damn! My one good pair of trousers,' he said, gloomily.

Megan smiled, thankful he could worry about something so trivial, though her eyes took in the large blood stain and she swallowed hard. However she made her voice sound light as she said, 'Stuck to you, I expect. I'll wash them and give them to Ginny. She'll fix them in no time. Wait here.' She went out of the tent and reappeared some minutes later carrying a grubby pair of trousers. 'Here, these should fit well enough,' she said, holding them out to

236

Will. She grimaced. 'The soldier who wore them won't be needing them any more, I'm afraid.'

She had to help him put them on. During the past night she had seen many naked men, and she had had no time to be embarrassed about it, but strangely the sight of Will's nakedness made her blush. Once dressed, he stood up and tried to walk. His leg was sore and made him limp a little but it was workable.

'There, good as new,' he said with a grin.

'I'm to change the dressing tomorrow.' Megan sighed, 'I'm getting quite good at it.'

'Yer must've 'ad a rough night.' It was a sympathetic comment. Will could tell that Megan had seen and done awful things during the hours of darkness.

'Yes,' she said and gave a big sigh. 'I don't think I'm cut out to be a nurse, Will. Not like Sarah. She's really good at it. I get all queasy when I see...' She grimaced, remembering. 'But I have to do something here, something useful, otherwise Uncle Richard'll send me home.' She looked at him. 'I wish I could fight like you.'

Will laughed. 'Yer don't, yer know.'

'Yes, I do. Did you know I've been practising shooting again?'

Will stared at her. 'No. Who's been teachin' yer?'

'Ensign Wooliscroft. But don't tell Uncle Richard.' She reddened suddenly. 'Edward likes me and I suppose I took advantage of him by persuading him to coach me. Not that I like him, of course,' she said hurriedly. 'Not in that way.'

'Why didn't yer ask me to teach yer again?' Will felt a sudden surge of jealousy that someone had taken over the task he considered his.

'You're always too busy, Will.'

It was a fact. When he wasn't seeing to Captain Camberwell's needs and those of his horses, Will was given soldierly duties and he rarely had time to himself, but he vowed now to make time. Teaching Megan to shoot was his job. He wanted to ask her if she was seeing anything of Lieutenant Deaville but was afraid that the answer would be one he didn't want to hear, so he said nothing.

Just then Richard Camberwell strode into the tent. 'Will! Are you all right? I came last night when I heard, but you were asleep. Can you walk?'

'Yes, sir.'

237

'Good, because I have a job for you.'

'Sir?'

Camberwell turned to the tent flap. 'Come to my tent and I'll tell you all about it. You, my young friend, are about to become a spy.'

17

Will followed Captain Camberwell to his tent. It was empty, James Shaw being officer of the day and on duty elsewhere. The walk had made Will's leg ache and he was grateful to take a seat on Captain Shaw's cot while Camberwell sat on his own.

'You remember the letter you found?' The Captain too looked tired, as if he hadn't slept at all the night before.

'Yes, sir'

'Our intelligence officers have been trying to find out where it came from but have had no luck so far. However, they think it could be an officer who's the traitor.' Will's eyes widened. 'We attacked on the day we arrived and only the officers knew of it until the men were informed late that afternoon. The intelligence officers have also had some thoughts on how the letter was probably delivered to the French, though why it was not then destroyed is another mystery. The only people who managed to get in and out of the town that day before the gates were closed, were some of the women. They suspect it was one of the camp followers who delivered the message. One who has a liason with a British officer.'

Will's eyes opened wider. He immediately thought of Juanita, then just as quickly dismissed the thought again.

'No, sir! It can't be...!'

'Juanita? I'm sorry to say that it could well be her, Will. The women who went into town were Portuguese and Spanish. Women who can speak the language and could pretend they live locally. But Juanita's not the only suspect. There are other peasant girls who've hooked up with officers and I, for one, doubt that James Shaw is a spy. He neither has the energy nor the motivation. His family has enough money to pay his debts and he's so damn lazy it would never occur to him to become a traitor. No. If Juanita's a spy, then someone else has her on a lead and I've a pretty good idea who it might be.'

So did Will. Paul Deaville. He might have his doubts about Juanita, but he could believe the lieutenant capable of anything subversive.

Richard Camberwell saw from his face that Will had also thought of Deaville. 'Yes, Deaville, though I've kept my thoughts to myself as yet. If the intelligence officers have it right, it could be any one of the women who went into the town that day. Juanita may be entirely innocent and I hope for James's sake that she is, because the man's in love with her. But all the local women are under suspicion and Wellington wants them watched. When Lieutenant-Colonel Davenport was told about this, he suggested I put you onto the job of watching Juanita, given your...er...relationship with her.'

I 'aven't got a relationship with 'er anymore.' Will wanted nothing to do with this. He liked Juanita and couldn't believe she was a spy and he didn't want to spy on her himself.

Camberwell heard the sulkiness in his voice. 'Don't be difficult, Will. These are orders. Look, I know it won't be easy for you. Juanita's a nice girl and she gave you a good time, but it's vitally important we find the traitor. If all our plans are given to the French, we won't win this war. We were damn lucky the other day. If you hadn't found that letter and overheard the conversation, we could have lost a lot of our best soldiers. As it is now, the guns in that redoubt will help protect our men when we storm the town. Besides,' he smiled suddenly, 'maybe you'll be able to prove that Juanita's not involved at all, and that would be a good thing, wouldn't it?'

Will nodded. He still didn't like the idea, but that last remark had the desired effect. He could, perhaps, prove Juanita's innocence.

'What about Captain Shaw, sir?'

'What about him?'

'Well, if I start 'angin' around Juanita again, 'e might wonder what's goin' on, sir. 'E might think I'm after 'er.'

'You'll just have to be a bit circumspect then, won't you?' said Camberwell. 'Only the senior officers and divisional commanders know about this because we suspect junior officer involvement. James knows nothing, as yet. All I want you to do is see who she meets, who she talks to. You don't have to get too close to her if you don't want to.' He smiled slowly again. 'Did you know that you came under suspicion for a while?'

Will was horrified. 'Bloody 'ell!' then mumbled, 'Sorry, sir.'

'Someone told the officer in charge of the investigation that you were close to one of the peasant girls and that you are also my servant and so had opportunity to learn vital information. Luckily someone else pointed out that you would hardly have brought the letter to the attention of the attacking force if you'd written it yourself.'

Will was silent for a moment. They had suspected him of treachery, if only briefly! Still somewhat shocked, he listened as Camberwell stood up and said, 'So find out if Juanita's up to something, Will. I'm willing to bet you know some more of the local lasses with the camp followers too, so keep your eyes peeled and let me know if you find out anything.' He put on his jacket. 'If you think about it, you may be the ideal person for this job. You have a foot in both camps, so to speak, and people like you. They'll talk in front of you, whereas if an officer starts to ask questions, they won't say a damn word.'

Will stood up awkwardly. 'I'll do my best, sir,' he said, though he still wished he hadn't been asked to do it.

'Good lad.' Camberwell jammed his shako on his head. 'And now I have to join all the other commanders of the Light Companies at headquarters. I've a feeling something's in the wind. Maybe the attack's going to start in earnest soon. And look after that leg, you hear?'

'Yes, sir.'

Camberwell reached the tent flap and then turned back. 'It appears my niece is making herself useful to the surgeons.'

'Yes, sir.'

'Good. I will write to mother and tell her.' With that he was gone, leaving Will to ponder on his new task.

† † †

By January 14th, the British had taken all the outlying suburbs of Ciudad Rodrigo, including the convent which the surgeons were now using as a hospital. Not wanting Marshall Marmont's small army to get close enough to pose a threat, Wellington waited no longer to lay siege to the fortress and ordered his guns to start firing at the walls. Much of the heaviest artillery was still making its way from Almeida but he had plenty of fire power. For five days the noise of the guns was overwhelming until at last a breach was made, closely followed by a second. Excitement took a hold of the British soldiers. They knew an assault was imminent and were ready for it. For too long they had been taking punishment from the French guns, and the casualties were high. They wanted revenge, and the only way they were going to get it was by storming the town.

On January 19th, Wellington gave his orders: 'Ciudad Rodrigo must be stormed this evening.' The army received the news with enthusiasm and the utmost confidence. The town's garrison boasted less than three thousand men. There was no doubt in anyone's mind but that they would win.

'Picton and the 3rd are to attack the larger breach while Craufordʼs Light goes for the smaller one. Some of the Portuguese are to make a feint attack further along the wall to draw some of the fire. The rest of the army will support,' Richard Camberwell informed Will late that afternoon when he was helping him take off the trappings of uniform that marked him as an officer. It was a well known fact that the officers were the first targets of the enemy so Camberwell was wearing the uniform jacket he had worn as a private, plain, and unadorned with badge or braid. Except for a red sash and his sword, he would look like any other soldier. 'Napier's commanding the storming party of the Light. He's asked for three hundred volunteers.'

'I know, sir. I already volunteered.' Will handed the Captain his belt.

Camberwell gave him a hard stare, then shrugged. 'I suppose I can't stop you,' he said. 'Have you got ammunition for that rifle of yours?'

'Yes, sir. Scrounged some from the 95th.' The Rifle Companies were the only ones to have the coveted Baker rifle like the one Will now owned, thanks to Wellington's generosity.

'You probably won't even get to fire it,' said Camberwell. 'Climbing a breach is damned hard work, and you'll need to use both your hands, then if you get to the top of the wall, all you'll want is the bayonet.' He handed his sword to Will. 'Take this to the Dragoons, Will, and ask their man to put an edge on it and get him to sharpen your bayonet at the same time.' He tossed him two shillings. Will caught them. 'By the way. How's the leg?'

''Ealin' well, sir.'

'Good. Be off with you, then.'

When Will had gone, Camberwell picked up a piece of bread and cold meat and ate it pensively. He felt the usual anticipation mixed with a certain element of fear that he always felt before a fight, like a spring that was wound too tightly, a feeling he knew would only be released when the battle began. He wondered how Will and the other new recruits in his company would be feeling. Damn scared probably, though they would be doing their best not to show it. Being a good shot was not enough in a fight like this, where the defenders had all the advantages until the moment the attackers were over the walls. Finishing the food, he put his shako on his head and strode out of the tent. He would go and talk to the men; reassure them and give them what little advice he had to offer. There would be no time once the attack started.

† † †

Amos Wilkins skulked in the baggage park, leaning on a wagon wheel, hidden by several carts and wagons from the baggage master and his minions who were handing out boxes of ammunition and loading cannon balls and case shot onto carts for the big guns. Half an hour ago a drummer boy had delivered a message saying that Lieutenant Deaville wanted to meet him here, and Wilkins was wondering why. Although in the same Company, he had had hardly anything to do with the officer since their arrival at the winter camp. Indeed it was obvious that Deaville wanted nothing whatever to do with him because the man generally ignored him. Why the sudden interest was a mystery.

The baggage park, usually so quiet, was a hive of activity at present. Wilkins watched as subalterns hurried to and from the park, some to pack away labelled precious belongings in case the owners were killed, in which case their effects would be sent to their families. Others carried boxes of ammunition or came with instructions from officers. Some gave orders for carts to be made ready to carry back the wounded once the attack started. Thinking of his own mortality, Wilkins fingered the dirty skin inside his stock and wondered if his neck would have been stretched by now if he'd stayed in prison. Probably. Although he had no desire to

242

fight for his country, while there was life there was hope, so they said. Always on the lookout for opportunities, he knew he was better off here with an army he cared nothing for, than languishing in jail or being deported to a penal colony where he'd always be an ex-convict. In the army it didn't matter what you'd done, so long as you could carry a gun. Not that he had any intention of getting involved in the battle. Keep to the rear and look busy, that was his motto. Hold back until the breaches were taken and let the fool-hardy lads at the front be the ones to get themselves killed.

He pulled away from the wheel he was leaning against and his face creased into a crafty grin when Paul Deaville, looking right and left as furtively as any thief, came round the end of the wagon. Deaville looked worried, and, as he came closer, Wilkins could smell the wine on his breath. He gave a sloppy salute.

'Ah, Wilkins,' said Deaville as though surprised to find him there.

'Sir.'

There was a pause while Wilkins looked expectant and Deaville anxious, almost as if he didn't know how to begin whatever it was he wanted to say. Eventually he said, 'I...er...I was wondering, Wilkins, if you would do me a small favour.'

'Sir?'

'Do you know a woman by the name of Juanita? She's a whore with the camp followers. Spanish. Captain Shaw's woman.'

'That I do, sir. That I do.' Who didn't know Juanita? She was the prettiest of the local girls by far.

'She's done me wrong, Wilkins. A grave wrong.'

'Sir?' Wilkins wondered if the lieutenant was referring to the incident on Christmas night. Like the other soldiers in his Company, he had heard, and laughed, about it.

Deaville leaned back on the side of the wagon and stared without seeing at the cart next to them, piled high with officers' baggage. On hearing that the assault was imminent, he had toyed with the idea of using Juanita and sending another message of information to Reynard. The matter of the debt still insinuated itself into his thoughts despite all efforts to forget it. Two things had stopped him. For one, he wasn't sure Juanita could be trusted any more, for another he was sure the bitch wouldn't want to do it. Nothing had been heard concerning the letter, but she could still betray him. Therefore he'd decided to stick with his original plan of getting rid of her, downed a bottle of wine, and arranged this meeting. Repaying his debt to Reynard would have to wait.

'I want you to do something for me,' he said to Wilkins who fidgeted impatiently, waiting for the officer to continue. 'I want you to kill Juanita.'

Amos Wilkins was not easily surprised by anything bad that his fellow man could do, having done many of the worst things himself, but his eyebrows lifted now.

'Kill 'er, sir?'

Suddenly Deaville turned towards him and the piercing blue eyes flashed. 'Yes. Kill her. You can do that, can't you?'

Wilkins shrugged. It wouldn't be the first time he had murdered someone. 'I can, sir, but I was wonderin' why yer would want me ter kill the girl. She's a beauty, sir, sure she is.'

'I know.' For a moment Deaville's voice was wistful, then the hard look was back. 'But I need her dead. Why, is not your concern.'

A sly expression crossed Wilkins's face and he stroked his rough black beard. 'Now what would yer be payin' me ter do this small thing for you, sir?' he asked.

'I have no money to pay you,' said Deaville coldly.

Wilkins gave him a look that plainly showed his disbelief, and made as if to go. 'Well in that case, sir, reckon as 'ow you'll 'ave ter find someone else ter do yer dirty work,' he said.

'Wait!' Deaville was desperate. He had burned his bridges now. Wilkins could blackmail him. The scum had to be made to carry the plan through. 'I have this.' He held up his hand and the ring glittered in the afternoon sunlight.

Wilkins's eyes glittered too, and Deaville gave an inward sigh of relief. He hadn't missed his man after all.

'It's pure gold,' he said. 'Very valuable. You could sell it easily in Lisbon or any big town.'

Wilkins stared. Gold. He was very partial to gold. You could do a lot with gold.

Deaville wrenched the ring off his finger and held it out. Wilkins snatched it greedily and bit it, just to make sure it was the real thing, then secreted it somewhere about his filthy person. 'What does I 'ave to do?'

Deaville smiled. 'Everyone's confident we're going to win this battle. If we do, all hell'll be let loose inside those walls. One more dead body won't be noticed and if she's found they'll think the French killed her. I'll send her a message once the Light Division's gone and pretend it's from Captain Shaw, saying he'll meet her beside the first church inside the gates.' Deaville had no idea of street names so had made this landmark a possible meeting place. 'You can see the spire above the ramparts. As soon as you get inside, wait there and kill the bitch when she comes.'

'And then?'

'And then do what the hell you want. Find yourself a woman and get drunk. Everyone else will.'

Wilkins pondered on the plan. 'And if we lose?'

'Then I'll have to think of something else, won't I?'

Wilkins said, 'Seems ter me, sir, it might be 'ard ter find the girl in the town. I mightn't get to 'er before someone else finds 'er.' He grinned, showing blackened stumps of teeth. 'Girl like 'er'll be fair game for anyone. Maybe I should do 'er in before, like. It'd be easy enough ter get 'er away from 'ere. Make it look like a French patrol done 'er in.'

'No. You won't be able to get close enough to her before the attack. That damn servant of Camberwell's has been hanging around her like a flea on a bitch for days.'

Wilkins's expression changed to one of murderous hatred. 'I could do 'im in for yer as well, sir. Got a score to settle with that young bugger.'

Deaville frowned. 'What do you mean?'

Wilkins told him the story of his attempt to seek revenge on Richard Camberwell and how Will had helped frustrate it.

'So you don't like our brave Captain either?' said Deaville thoughtfully.

'Like 'im? I 'ates him! And the boy!'

'It seems we share similar sentiments then. Maybe if you see off Juanita right, and the French don't get them first, I'll have another little job for you in the future.' Deaville was sure he could use this piece of information to advantage. 'Now, tell me again what you have to do.'

'Aye, sir. I gets into the town when the brave lads've stormed the breaches, then find the nearest church and wait until I see 'er, then...' he moved his finger from side to side across his throat.

Deaville swallowed. Put like that it seemed so final, but it had to

245

be done. 'Right. That's it then. I'd better go.' He suddenly got up close to the other man until their faces were nearly touching. 'And not a word of this to anyone, you hear?'

'No, sir. 'Course not, sir. Mum's the word.'

Wilkins watched Deaville walk away. The man was a fool. He'd got himself into some sort of bad trouble with this girl and he wanted out. Amos Wilkins wasn't stupid. He figured that Deaville was an officer so he must be a gentleman and in his experience all gentlemen were rich. He didn't take Deaville's professed penury seriously. The man was lying. There must be money there and he would do well to stick close to the young officer to get his hands on some of it. He took the ring out of his pocket and looked at it, then tossed it into the air and caught it again. Money for old rope. Smiling, he walked away from the baggage park.

✝ ✝ ✝

The attack began just before seven that night. Will, crouched in a ditch, waiting with the storming party volunteers of the Light Division, heard the first crash of musketry and the responding explosions of heavy artillery from the River Agueda on the other side of Ciudad Rodrigo. The town's ramparts were lit with French fireballs, then from his right, Will heard shouts and the 3rd Division were running for the glacis in front of the main breach, clambering up it, dropping into the eleven-foot ditch on the other side and swarming over the hill of rubble that had been blown out of the ancient thick walls by the British guns. The whole place became thick with noise and smoke as the French poured musket fire onto the tide of men clambering up the stones. Most of the Forlorn Hope was blasted to smithereens, their flesh and blood splattering the men behind who slipped and slid over them, screaming, shouting and falling.

Will heard and saw the horror of the attack on the main breach, lit by flames from straw bales the French threw down at the impudent enemy and felt his bowels churn, together with an almost overwhelming urge to pee. He glanced at George beside him. George's normally ruddy complexion was chalk white and he stared straight ahead as if not daring to move. His hands that grasped the unloaded musket were as white as his face. He felt Will's glance and turned to face him.

'If I die, send my things to my mother,' he said in a shaky voice. 'The address is in my pocket.'

'You're not going to die,' said Will firmly, forcing jocularity into his voice. 'In a couple of hours we'll be drinking French brandy and have a girl on each knee, you see if we don't!'

George gave him a faint smile, then winced at a particularly loud explosion from the main breach. A magazine had exploded, killing friend and foe alike and piling more bodies onto the breach. The survivors' horrors weren't over yet either. The first men to reach the top of the breach discovered that a sixteen-foot ditch had been dug on the other side. Under constant fire, and with officers shouting for ladders, they bravely started to try and cross it.

Will shifted his grip on his rifle. The soldiers had been told that they must not go in with loaded weapons, that if they couldn't do the job with bayonets, then it wouldn't be done at all, but Will wished he had a bullet in the breach of his gun. He thought back to the fight at the French ambush, and the attack on the redoubt. Then he had had no time to think of the consequences. Now it was different. Now there was time to think and he wished there wasn't.

The soldiers at the main breach continued to suffer heavy losses but still they pressed forward, then Will had no more time to consider their fortunes, or his own, because there was a shout from ahead, and he was being pushed to his feet from behind, as was George, and they were running towards the smaller breach with the rest of them.

It was like some horrible dream. The worst nightmare. Clambering up the side of the glacis, across the ditch, up the other side and onto level ground, running towards that heap of rubble that marked passage into Ciudad Rodrigo, his heart thudding wildly, George keeping pace with him, Bob Tomkins and Gerald Butterworth just behind, no one speaking, breathing hard. Then the noise, the whine of musket balls, the explosion of a big gun and the awful sound of canister spinning past him and the patter of iron balls thumping into the ground and flesh; screams as men were hit and fell to the ground. Grape-shot and canister whining all around the soldiers again and again, a never-ending torment of deadly hail thudding into men already dead, sending others tumbling. He stared amazed at the body of General Crauford, an early victim, then was forced to carry on when pushed from behind again. A

247

roundshot passing overhead, and the shock of the explosion as it hit the earth, rocked the running soldiers.

Still Will was running on, stumbling in the dark, suddenly blinded by the flash of fireballs that lit the sky. The men were scrabbling at the stones of the breach. His rifle looped over his shoulder and using both hands, Will started to climb, overtaking others, then falling when the soldier in front fell backwards with a cry on top of him. Breathlessly he scrambled to his feet again, then whimpered in holy terror when the man to his left caught a flaming straw bale right in the face and fell screaming, dragging two men down with him. Will brushed frantically at burning straw that was making his sleeve smoulder, singeing his fingers. Looking up, he could see men on the ramparts, their white cross-belts standing out against dark blue. French soldiers waiting like vultures, aiming their muskets at him and his fellows. One fired and the man ahead of him fell on his side, his brains flying onto Will's face. Horrified, Will spat and brushed his arm across his eyes and mouth to rid himself of the awful mess. Vomit rose in his throat.

Men stopped in front of him and he smacked into the back of one, not seeing. He heard a shout, 'Napier's down!', then the General himself, shot in the elbow, was urging the soldiers on, and the British moved upward again, wanting to do their duty for a brave officer. A musket bullet spun off one of the stones and a man grunted as the ricochet hit him. It was a scene from hell, firelight lighting faces grim with determination or frozen in terror, bodies sprawled, soldiers slipping on blood and pieces of flesh that had once been men, musket balls whining through the air. Will felt that all his senses were being assailed at once; the stink of blood, smoke, and burning flesh in his nostrils, all-pervading smells that he could taste in the air; the noise of the guns and men's screams that hurt his ears; the sight of the bodies he crawled over that assaulted his eyes; the feel of the sharp stones, slippery with blood, grazing his fingers; and all the time trying to refrain from crying out, to shout to the world that he wanted it all to stop.

Still Will stumbled on until, finally, there was a great cheer and a mass of men ahead of him swarmed over the stones at the top of the breach.

Will hauled himself up the last few feet and was thumped on the shoulder by a rifle that was shoved past him, the bayonet plunging into the stomach of a Frenchman reaching a blade down towards him from the top of the wall.

'Watch yourself, Will!'

The breathless voice was that of Richard Camberwell, already running along the parapet towards a gun embrasure from where several of the enemy were firing down at the men still climbing the rocky slope. Men were pouring through the breach now, some clambering down to the ground below to open the gates for the rest of the army, others following Camberwell's shouted orders and going to the parapet right and left to scour the French from the walls. Will went with them. Two lightly wounded Frenchmen still inside the gun embrasure where Camberwell and others had left a small heap of bodies, lunged out at Will as he ran past. Ducking nimbly out of the way, he stabbed one with his bayonet, then swung the blade around to face the other, a lieutenant, catching the man's coat and ripping off a button. The Frenchman's sword clanged on the bayonet and for a few seconds there was a tussle as each fought to stab the other, then Will suddenly pulled away, wrong-footing the officer who stumbled. Will kicked him on the legs and the man fell, screeching, to the ground below. Will ducked involuntarily when a huge explosion at the main breach sent a tower of sparks and flames high into the air, lighting up the night sky and plunging the rest of the wall into deep shadow. Later he was to learn that the French had planted a mine under the breach. Smoke billowed up, hiding the wall to Will's right, and the screams of the wounded were terrible to hear.

No more Frenchmen were near, so Will turned his head this way and that, searching for steps down from the walkway. His injured leg was aching and he leaned momentarily on the wall. The nearest steps had a knot of attacking soldiers fighting their way past a group of defenders, some on the walkway, some on the steps. Will saw George and Bob there, together with Ron Parker and Gerald Butterworth and they were having a hard time of it, outnumbered at least two to one with French reinforcements gathering at the bottom of the steps. Levering himself off the wall, Will ran towards them, lucky to avoid a musket ball that flew past his face, so close he felt the wind of it. Another took a chip out of the wall close to his shoulder. Will saw Gerald Butterworth go down, then a Frenchman's bayonet stabbed Bob in the leg and he too fell.

Stamping on the yelling boy's leg with his foot, the Frenchman raised the bayonet for the killing blow but before he could deliver it, Will was there, roaring like an enraged bull, slashing and hacking at the enemy. Bob's assailant went down in a welter of blood and Will felt a madness rise within him, a primal rage, a huge anger that could only be assuaged by killing these beasts who dared to hurt his friends. His blade stabbed again and again and he barely saw the weapons of the enemy, so great was his fury. He did not realise he was screaming, a fearful, feral sound as he rampaged through the Frenchmen on the steps. Given courage by Will's wild disregard for his own safety, the surviving soldiers fought back too until the few Frenchmen who still lived turned tail and ran. The British cheered wild whoops of joy, then followed Will who ran down the nearest steps and into the town.

With Will at their head, the victorious soldiers cavorted in the streets, shouting, madly excited, searching for the enemy, all filled with the same frenzied bloodlust and wanting revenge for the deaths of their comrades, for the dangers they had survived when digging the trenches, for restless nights when the heavy French artillery had driven sleep away, and for being forced to see and do things that no man should ever have to. They ran through streets lit now by more than torches and the moon, joining others as the allied soldiers ran riot; looting, burning, yelling and shouting, waving bloody bayonets and hastily loaded muskets, all discipline gone. What they wanted now was plunder, women and liquor, and they were determined to find all three as soon as possible.

Will and his followers ran round a corner. A woman and a small child cowered away from the mob. One of the soldiers grabbed the woman and tried to drag her into a doorway. The child, a girl in a drab green dress, wailed for her mother. Will turned at the sound of her cry, and stopped in his tracks, letting the rest of the men flow around him and continue their way down the street. The running footsteps died away, and with them went Will's madness. The sight of the soldier already yanking with one hand at the string that held up his trousers, and the little girl vainly tugging at the big man's leg, trying to pull him off her mother who was screaming in Spanish, tore the final shreds of madness from his brain and replaced it with raw anger.

He ran to the man and dragged him away from the woman, then

250

swung him round and cracked him hard on the jaw with the muzzle of the rifle. The man crumpled at his feet. 'Run!' said Will to the woman. 'Go! Go!' He flapped his hands at them. The woman gave him a brief look of frightened thanks, grabbed the child's hand, and ran swiftly away. The soldier on the ground looked at Will, holding his broken jaw. He started to get up, murder in his eyes, reaching for his musket that had fallen on the ground, but Will was running again, his leg aching so much it was making him limp now. He ran down an alley, listening to the screams and yells of the people of Ciudad Rodrigo who were finding out what their defiance had cost them. He heard shots and breaking glass, then came into a small plaza, an open area surrounded by buildings and dark alleyways. People were running and soldiers fired their muskets into the air, making the plaza thick with acrid smoke. Dogs were barking, frightened horses whinnied, tugged at their tethers and stamped their hooves. A shop was on fire, and two mules pulling an empty cart careened across in front of Will as he stared at the chaos. Dark figures carried bundles away from the burning building while others were looting a wine shop, pouring wine and brandy down their own, and each others', throats. The pall of smoke was growing, hanging over everything, blotting out the moon and the stars.

Moving under a covered esplanade, Will stumbled, and almost fell over the body of a French soldier who had blood dripping from a smashed face, lying beside another who was holding his broken leg and moaning. Will remembered belatedly that his rifle was unloaded so he quickly rammed in a bullet, thankful that he had done so when he heard an ear-splitting scream from an open doorway nearby. He ran to the door and peered round it. In a small room a half-naked bearded soldier was on his knees across a young woman who was screaming Spanish curses at the top of her lungs and hitting the man with her fists. As Will stepped over the threshold, the man slapped the woman hard on the cheek and growled at her to shut the hell up. She quietened a little but continued to struggle.

'Get off 'er!' Will shouted above the uproar outside.

Startled, the man looked up, then smiled, his casual glance seeing only a tow-headed private he imagined was scared stiff of all that was going on, and more than likely held an unloaded weapon. 'Now there's no need for that, lad,' he said. 'You can 'ave 'er after

251

me, if you like.'

For answer, Will cocked the rifle. 'Get off 'er, or I'll damn well shoot yer,' he said again and then the man noticed that the gun pointing at him was a rifle and that the hands holding it were rock steady. Maybe it was loaded after all. The woman was quiet now, watching them both.

His smile disappeared. 'Look, you snot-nosed bugger, I'm a-goin' to 'ave this woman whether you like it or not and a striplin' like you ain't a-goin' to stop me.'

Will moved the rifle a little and pulled the trigger, the shot sounding horribly loud in the confined space. The man stared disbelievingly at a smoking hole that had appeared in the thin rug not two inches from his bare knee.

'Jesus!' he exclaimed and backed off the woman, hurriedly pulling up his trousers. 'All right, lad, you want 'er that much, you can 'ave 'er. I'll find meself another. Jesus!' Not taking his frightened eyes off Will, he carefully backed out of the room.

The young woman slowly got to her feet and adjusted her clothing.

'I'm sorry,' said Will. She stared at him like a frightened doe. 'I'm sorry,' he said again, feeling somehow that he should apologize for the behaviour of the whole army to this woman.

'*Gracias*,' she whispered.

'Lock the door,' said Will, miming turning a key with his hands. She nodded, but as he reloaded the rifle then stepped warily out of the house, watchful in case the would be rapist was lying in wait for him, Will wondered how long it would be before someone else kicked the door in and the woman was raped anyway. The whole world seemed to have gone mad, himself included for a time.

Out in the plaza again he looked around for someone he knew, but his friends and comrades were long gone. He stared at the rooftops, half hidden in smoke. Poking up above them and lit by blazing buildings was a grey church spire. For almost the first time in his life, Will felt a need for the peace and comfort of religion. He looked again at the chaos around him. Across the plaza was a narrow street which seemed to lead to the church. He started to walk towards it.

It was then that he saw Juanita.

18

Was it Juanita? Will couldn't be sure. In the flickering light of a pitch torch he had caught sight of long black hair, but half the peasant girls in Spain and Portugal had long black hair. He stared again, hoping for another glimpse. Yes, there she was. Now he was sure it was her. He knew her walk. Will shouted her name, but the noise in the plaza was too great and she didn't hear, so he started across the square in pursuit, watching her disappear down the street that he presumed led to the church. What was Juanita doing here? No one in their right mind would come into Ciudad Rodrigo from the British camp on a night like this, with the army turned to devils or drunkards and the threat of danger around every corner. For sure even laconic Captain Shaw would rouse himself to a fury if he knew his lover was walking the streets. A girl like her would rouse any man's passion on a calm night, let alone when the soldiers were drunk on wine and victory. Even now Will saw a soldier move towards her and he hurried to catch up, afraid for her.

† † †

Will had spent quite a lot of time with Juanita over the past few days, contriving to talk to her while doing his chores, mostly fetching water or wood. She had spoken to him quite easily, seeming pleased to accept his company. If she was surprised by it, she gave no sign. Neither did she give any indication by speech or action that she was the spy the intelligence officers were looking for. Their conversations followed normal patterns and only on one occasion did she give him food for thought.

The day before the assault he had accepted a lift on a sutler's cart as far as a thick wood some distance from the British encampment. Wood for fires was getting scarce about the camp and he had with him some rope with which to tie the logs and sticks into a bundle and drag it back to camp if necessary. He had been glad of the lift and hoped he could find a carter or someone to give him a ride back because his leg was still painful. Megan had changed the bandage on the wound but dressings were in short supply and he had not had a clean one on for three days. However, he had applied some of the salve the gypsy had given him and the gash appeared to be healing.

He had come upon Juanita in the wood, sitting on a fallen log. She was wearing a thick woollen dress and a cloak, for the day was cold. And she was crying.

At first she was unaware that he was there. Her sobs wracked her, making her shoulders heave. Concerned, Will stood still, wondering what to do, then he said her name.

'Juanita?'

She looked up, startled, cheeks wet with tears.

'Oh, Will! It is you,' she said.

Will limped over and sat down on the log beside her. 'What's wrong? 'As somethin' 'appened? Is there anythin' I can do?' he asked.

She shook her head. '*Nada*. Nothing,' she said, and her voice was that of a woman who had lost all hope. For a long time, she sat looking at her hands clasped in her lap and said nothing while the tears dripped onto her fingers. Will put his arm around her shoulders, wanting to comfort her, and she leaned her head against him. They sat, saying nothing, staring at the dead leaves under the trees, some covered in fuzzy coats of frost where the sun hadn't reached them. It was quiet except for Juanita's frequent sniffs, and peaceful. The noise of the guns at Ciudad Rodrigo was muted, and seemed very far away.

Eventually, Juanita dried her eyes with the hem of her dress, looked up at Will and gave him a wan smile. 'You are a good person, Will Tucker,' she said. 'I could fall in love with you.'

'Captain Shaw might 'ave somethin' to say about that,' said Will wryly to cover his embarrassment.

She smiled a little wider and sat up straighter. ' 'E is also a good man, but not like you. 'E thinks only of 'imself. To 'im I am a plaything, something pretty to show off. But 'e is good to me and buys me things.'

' 'E loves yer.'

'*Si*, but I do not love 'im. Maybe I did at first, but now...?' She shrugged her shoulders expressively. 'It is not good to fall in love with a soldier.'

She was quiet again, then she said, 'Do you love your country, Will?'

Did he love England? He didn't much love London's streets, but

254

they had been his home for sixteen years and sometimes he missed them. 'I suppose I don't want old Boney to 'ave England for 'imself,' he said after some thought. 'For a start, 'e'll be 'avin' us eatin' frogs legs an' snails!'

She smiled at his answer, at the same time winding a loose thread from her cloak around her finger, not looking at him. 'Do you think everyone in your army fights for 'is country?'

'No.'

Juanita lifted her eyes from the thread and stared into the trees. 'I love my country.' She turned her head and looked at Will. 'Is it wrong to want things for yourself as well as for your country?' she asked.

Will shook his head. 'I don't think so. Everyone wants things for themselves. It's 'ow they go about gettin' 'em that's the problem.'

'What do you mean?'

'Well now, take me for instance. Before I came 'ere, I was livin' alone on the streets. I 'ad no money and needed ter eat, so I stole food, or jewellery, or money so I could buy some. A lot of people would think that was wrong, but if yer don't eat yer die, and I didn't want ter die, so I stole.'

'I think I understand. If you are rich, stealing is wrong. If you are poor, it is not.' Juanita made it all seem so simple.

Will laughed. 'Somethin' like that, yes. Like Robin Hood.'

Juanita frowned, not understanding, so he explained. 'Robin Hood was a man who lived a long time ago. 'E robbed the king and 'is lords then gave the money ter the poor people.'

''E must have been a good man.'

'The king didn't think so.'

Wistfully she said, 'I dream of rich things, Will. Nice dresses and lots of food. A big 'ouse and servants. Sometimes I think I will never 'ave. My...'ow you call it? That in your 'ead that tells what is right?'

'Conscience.'

'*Si*, that is it. Conscience. I 'ave conscience and when I do something bad I feel bad too.' She was quiet again for a few minutes, lost in her own thoughts. Thoughts, Will would have been shocked to learn, that involved Lieutenant Paul Deaville, a message that she had delivered verbally to a Frenchman, and a letter she had wanted to keep to prove Deaville's treachery if she got found out.

A letter she had lost somewhere. Will wondered what the girl was getting at. Something was obviously troubling her, but it was equally apparent that she wasn't going to tell him what it was. He shivered. It was cold, sitting here.

Finally Juanita heaved a great sigh, then reached out a hand and stroked his hair. '*Gracias*, Will,' she said.

'What for? I ain't done nothin'.'

'You 'ave done more than you know. Sometimes I dream of a man with yellow hair and a face like yours. One who looks after me as a woman likes. You are a boy in years, Will, but you are a man up 'ere.' She pointed to her head. 'I want to be with someone like you.' Will blushed. She leaned forward and kissed him full on the lips and he felt desire rush in, but then she gently drew away from him again and stood up.

'Come. Let us find wood, or we will freeze tonight.' She pulled him to his feet and philosophical thoughts were forgotten in the need to gather sticks and logs.

† † †

Will thought back to that strange conversation now as he followed Juanita and the soldier down the narrow street. A baby cried in a house as he went past, but then he heard a mother hushing it, so he carried on.

The street led into another, dominated by the church that stood grey and silent almost halfway along, its spire highlighted behind by flames, where a building burned in the next street. It was quieter here. There were no shops or taverns, merely a few poor houses, so the street had, so far, escaped the depredations of the soldiers. Will stayed hidden, peering round the corner of a house. He watched Juanita hurry up the steps towards the church door. The soldier Will had seen following her seemed to have vanished.

Juanita was nearly at the top of the steps when a figure materialised from the shadows of the building. A tongue of flame suddenly flared up from behind the church and a tall man was outlined against the light; a tall man with a dark beard. For a moment Will thought he was staring at Amos Wilkins, but then the flame died down and there was only a dark shadow again.

But the shadow was very close to Juanita.

'No!'

Too late, Will realised what was about to happen. He shouted, and started to run. The girl gave a muffled cry, struggled with the dark figure for a moment, then slumped to the ground. Will put the rifle to his shoulder and fired, but the street was black and Juanita's assailant had melted back into the shadows. As he reached her, Will heard the sound of booted feet running away.

Kneeling beside her, Will lifted the girl's head onto his lap, his eyes wet with tears. Hers were open but there was a great hole in her throat from which the blood ran, wetting his groin, and he knew there was nothing he could do.

'Will.' The word was so faint he had to bend his head to hear it. Her mouth formed another word and he strained to hear. It sounded like 'evil', then she breathed, 'kiss me.'

With his lips on hers, she died.

Will could do nothing but kneel there in shock with Juanita's head in his lap, the tears falling onto her cold face like warm rain.

He never heard the gun being cocked, or saw the figure in the shadows behind him lift a pistol that flashed briefly in the glare of flames that suddenly leapt up from the burning building behind the church. He never knew someone was trying to kill him until he heard the gun go off and a bullet thudded into his back, breaking a rib and ricocheting off another before embedding itself in muscle.

The force of the bullet knocked Will forward so that he ended up sprawled on the ground and across Juanita's head. Shocked and bleeding he stayed where he was, then the pain hit him like a second blow. He tried to get to his knees, to crawl, but the pain was too bad and he fell forward again. He whimpered, the tears that had so soon before been for Juanita, now for himself. What seemed a long time later, two feet and the bottom of a long robe swam across his vision. Slowly lifting his head, he saw a gentle concerned face gazing down at him. It must be God, I'm in heaven, he thought, before he sank into unconsciousness.

Trying to round up his men, Richard Camberwell had finally found half a dozen of them carrying illicit bottles of liquor away from a wine shop. The soldiers were at first reluctant to hand them over and he had been forced to show who was in charge by knocking a few heads together before they had relinquished their prize. By the time he reached the plaza where Will had first spotted Juanita, he had found nearly thirty of the Company, including two sergeants and George Trim. He asked George if he had seen Will anywhere. George said he hadn't seen his friend since the fight on the steps.

'He went at the bloody French like a mad thing, sir. I ain't never seen 'im like that afore. Last I saw, 'e was runnin' into town.'

This was bad news. Richard Camberwell hoped that Will had not fallen prey to the lunacy that seemed to have taken hold of most of the army in their thirst for revenge. He would have to go and look for the boy before he went and got himself arrested, or worse, but first he would despatch these men with the sergeants to look for more of their own Company, try and stop the looting, and protect the town's citizens. Ciudad Rodrigo had already officially surrendered. Lieutenant Gurwood, who had led, and miraculously survived, the Light Division's Forlorn Hope, had accepted the Governor's sword, and now the French were showing no more resistance. Those who lived were giving themselves up as prisoners.

Camberwell had just finished giving the sergeants their orders when he saw a priest hurrying towards them, carrying a pitch torch.

'*Por favor!* Please! You must come! Quickly!' The priest was portly and out of breath.

'What is it?'

'A soldier shot and a girl killed with a knife. Here.' He pointed to his neck. 'I hear shots, I go to look.'

'Where?'

'Outside my church. There.' He pointed back the way he had come.

'You five come with me,' Camberwell said to George and four others. 'The rest of you go with the sergeants.'

At a run, the six ran in the direction pointed out by the priest, the fat man waddling along behind. Coming out of the narrow street, with the church opposite, Camberwell stopped.

'Spread out,' he said, 'and keep your eyes skinned.' The street was quiet but the whole town was in an uproar and it could become a hotbed of violence here at any moment.

He could see a shadowy lump at the top of the church steps and ran towards it; two people, one lying flat, the other slumped over. It was only when he knelt down and the priest caught up with him, wheezing and gasping like a stranded fish, and the torch light fell onto the figures, that he recognised Will.

'Oh God! No!' he breathed. The back of Will's jacket was wet with blood. Gently Camberwell turned him over. There was a big stain on his lap, and at first Richard Camberwell thought the injury was to his groin but then he realised it wasn't his blood because Will was losing his life through the hole in his back. He put a hand in front of the boy's mouth and nose to see if he still breathed. There was a faint puff of air.

'Trim! Parker! Binns! Get over here! It's Will and he's hurt bad. Oh, Jesus!' he had just discovered that the dead girl was Juanita. 'And Juanita's dead.'

The soldiers gathered round, appalled.

'Will!' George knelt down beside him, horrified. 'What d'you think 'appened, sir?'

'I have no idea, but what I do know is that Will needs help quickly,' answered Camberwell grimly. He looked up at the priest. 'My men are going to put this girl in the church and I want you to look after her body until someone comes for her. Do you understand?'

'*Si, senor, si.*' The priest bobbed up and down. Two of the soldiers carefully picked up Juanita and followed the priest into the church.

'Help me, George.' Between them George and Camberwell lifted Will until he was lying across the Captain's shoulders, arms and legs dangling. 'Pick up his rifle, Binns.' Nat Binns did so. 'Right,' said Camberwell grimly. 'We're going to the convent. If anyone gets in our way, shoot them.'

The small procession made their way through the streets, ignoring itinerant soldiers Richard Camberwell would have put on a charge less than half an hour before. With Will's full weight on his shoulders, Camberwell nevertheless strode purposefully towards the convent that had been commandeered for use as a hospital, his face set in grim lines.

Nat Binns, clutching his musket and with Will's rifle slung over his shoulder, stayed by Will's head and talked to the unconscious boy whose light hair hung down near his shako. George, on Camberwell's other side, heard snatches of the one-sided conversation.

'Ah, Will, lad, what the bloody 'ell were yer doin'? Did yer try ter save the little lady? Is that what 'appened? 'Appen yer were, lad, 'cos yer a good 'un, our Will.' And later, 'Don't yer worry none, now, Will. Yer gonna be all right or me name's not Nathanial Ezra Binns.'

''E can't 'ear yer,' said one of the soldiers.

'Shut yer bloody gob!' Binns rounded on the man. 'I'll talk ter 'im if I wants ter!' and he continued the one-sided conversation as they hurried along.

When they had gone down several streets, George asked Camberwell if he didn't need some help carrying Will, but the answer was a curt negative. They came at last to the convent. Camberwell pushed his way through crowds of people in the cloisters; bandsmen and soldiers bringing in the wounded, officers, doctor's assistants, women acting as nurses. The other soldiers who had accompanied them stayed outside but Binns and George kept as close as they could to the Captain, using their muskets more than once to force a way through. The noise was terrible. Screams and moans, shouts and wails. They passed a man lying on the floor with a shattered arm, calling for his mother. Another was calling Jesus's name, over and over. Many asked for water.

'Where's a surgeon?' Camberwell shouted at an orderly who ran past them.

'Upstairs. To the left.' The orderly ran on.

Up the stairs they went, bumping into people hurrying to and fro, Camberwell ploughing ahead as though the staircase was empty. George glanced at him and thought he had never seen the Captain so angry, not even when he had caught Will and Megan stowing away on the ship. Stretcher-bearers shouted for them to make way but Richard Camberwell carried stolidly onward, along a corridor, demanding to know the way of anyone who went past, until at last they came to a room that seemed to George like a scene from a bad nightmare.

There were men in the room. Everywhere. All over the floor. Packed like fish in a basket, they lay in rows, with just a narrow aisle down the middle. The smell was enough to make a strong man gag. Blood, sweat, faeces, urine, putrefaction, all combined to produce the most foul odour George had ever smelled. He swallowed hard, determined not to vomit.

Two surgeons, assisted by orderlies, were busy at two tables running with blood in the centre of the room. Richard Camberwell went straight to one of them.

'Put him with the others, Camberwell,' said Surgeon John Barker without looking up. 'I'll get around to him.' There was a strong smell of rum on his breath.

Richard Camberwell did not move. The surgeon was deftly folding a flap of skin over part of a stump while the poor soldier on the table screamed through a piece of leather in his mouth. George saw with horror that the other part of the man's leg was on the floor under the table. He staggered, sure he was going to faint. Nat grabbed his arm.

"Old up there, lad,' he said quietly to George. 'Yer don't want ter disgrace yerself now do yer?' George forced himself to stay upright, closed his eyes, and opened them in time to hear Richard Camberwell say, 'In my pocket is a purse containing sixteen guineas. If you put this lad on the table next, the money's yours.' The surgeon paused in what he was doing and looked up. He saw a man whose dark angry eyes bored fiercely into his. A man who looked to have had a long day and a very hard night. A man he knew to have a quick temper and a short fuse. And sixteen guineas was sixteen guineas. He nodded briefly.

The patient on the table had his stump cauterised with pitch and fortunately fainted. He was removed and Richard Camberwell was at last able to put Will down with the soldiers' help. He flexed his shoulders and felt the adrenalin that had enabled him to carry Will so far drain out of him so that he was suddenly incredibly weary. He looked down the length of that dreadful room, at the men unconscious or in pain, and felt guilty that he had inflicted similar suffering on the enemy. Then his heart lifted because Sarah was picking her way between the wounded towards them. She had on a simple light grey dress and an apron that was blood-spattered. Her hair was up in a bun. Her pretty elfin face, though drawn with strain and weariness, was a sight for tired eyes and he smiled, very glad to see her. And there, following on her heels, was his niece.

'Richard!' Sarah's eyes were full of worry. 'What is it? Who...?' Her eyes travelled to the table. 'Oh God! Will!'

Megan screamed and put her hand to her mouth. The surgeon frowned at her.

'If you can't stand to watch, girl, then go elsewhere,' he said curtly, mistaking her horror for disgust. Her uncle put his hand on her shoulder.

'What happened? asked Sarah.

'Miss Harvey! Are you going to chatter all night or are you going to assist me here? You boys stand back now.' The surgeon broke sharply into her words while George and Nat shuffled backwards and then were shoved even further to one side by two stretcher bearers.

'Yes, of course,' said Sarah, gathering her scattered wits.

'Now where are the damn shears?'

Sarah found them on the filthy floor. Barker dragged off Will's jacket, then cut his shirt that was now stuck to his back with blood, and exposed the wound. He felt around it. Will moaned and jerked under his touch.

'Now don't you wake up just yet, young feller,' said the surgeon brusquely. 'It'll serve you much better to sleep a little longer.'

Eventually his prodding fingers located the bullet below Will's right shoulder blade. 'Hmm,' he said. 'Bounced around a bit. A couple of broken ribs by the feel of things. A lot of tissue and muscle damage, but I don't think it hit anything vital. Damn lucky.' He cut deeply into the skin and Will jerked again as blood welled from the wound.

'Mop it up, girl, mop it up,' Barker said sharply to Sarah, who dabbed with an already bloody cloth. 'You'd best hold him down, Captain. We don't want him jumping off the table now, do we?'

Richard Camberwell took his hand off Megan's trembling shoulder and held Will's legs firmly. Sarah wiped sweat off the surgeon's brow with the same grubby cloth. It was dripping off him, into the wound. The soldiers were silent while the surgeon did his work. The noise went on around them but none heard it. All were watching Barker and Will.

Will dreamed something was jabbing at his back. He squirmed, trying to escape it but there was a weight on his legs and he couldn't move. The pain got worse, stabbing, twisting inside him and he moaned and cried out but still the fog that held his brain wouldn't lift enough for him to open his eyes and see what was happening. The pain stabbed again and again and he shied away from it and heard voices but what they said would not penetrate the fog. A final stab, something warm flowing over him, and a scream. Was it him screaming? Then peace.

'That was close.' Barker, his face red with sweat and exertion, held up the battered iron ball in his forceps. 'I thought he was going to wake up there for a minute. I do so hate it when they do that. Causes no end of trouble. They struggle like rats in a trap and do yell so. D'you think he'll want to keep it? A lot do.' He wiped the ball on his blood-smeared apron.

'I don't know. Maybe. I'll take it anyway.' The surgeon dropped the mis-shapen lead ball into Camberwell's outstretched hand, then picked up a long stick from the bucket of hot pitch that stood next to the table. 'Hold him tight now,' he said.

There was a horrible smell of burning flesh as Barker cauterised the wound. Camberwell winced and George went even whiter than he was already, thinking that if Will wasn't deeply unconscious before, he certainly was now.

'Will he be all right?' Camberwell asked.

'Right as any of 'em provided it don't go bad. Now, I believe a sum of money was mentioned?' The surgeon held out his hand.

Camberwell dug into his pocket and pulled out his purse, then handed it to the surgeon who pocketed it quickly.

'Friend of yours is he?' asked Barker, thinking that it was the first time he had ever been paid by an officer to operate on a private.

'Yes,' said Camberwell, realising for the first time that it was so. Will was more than just a servant or a private in his Company. Somehow he had found Lord Richard Camberwell's tiny soft spot, and had become his friend too.

'Get him off here, then.' The surgeon was terse now. 'There's plenty more needs seeing to.'

Camberwell and George lifted Will off the table and immediately two men slung another soldier onto it, bleeding from a shattered leg. Wide awake, the poor man looked terrified.

'Where shall we put him?'

'You appear to be a rich man, Captain. He'd stand a better chance if you were to find a house and pay someone to nurse him. More soldiers die on the floor here than ever do on my table.' Barker was cutting a swathe up the man's trouser leg as he spoke. The soldier moaned loudly. 'Shut up, man!' said the surgeon unsympathetically. 'I haven't even started yet!'

Sarah put a fond hand on Richard Camberwell's cheek and whispered that she would see him later. They wrapped Will in his jacket, and George's as well, commandeered a stretcher, then left the room and carried him downstairs. Megan followed. She had spent the hours since the start of the attack in the convent doing whatever the people in charge there asked of her and her mind was a whirl for she had never been so busy in all her life. She had held bowls that were filled with blood, vomit, or urine, she had bandaged bloody wounds, she had held the hands of dying men, fetched and carried all night long, and now here was Will, who might die of the sepsis if he stayed here. She felt stunned, as though her body was doing what was expected of it, but her mind was somewhere else, trying to block out all the horrible things she had seen, done and heard. She wondered if she would ever feel normal again.

'Where are we goin', sir?' George asked the question as they reached the cloisters.

'Anywhere we can away from here,' said Camberwell grimly. 'The trouble is I just gave my last few guineas to that greedy bastard. I can't afford to get lodgings but he'll be better off at the camp than here, so that's where we'll take him.'

'I've got money, uncle.'

'Put him down for a minute. Near the fire.' Camberwell gave the order and George and Nat laid the stretcher gently on the ground quite close to a pile of burning wood. It was a lot warmer here outside than in the convent. There were fires all over the place, some caused by rampaging soldiers, others deliberately made to keep the men warm.

'Now where did you get money from?' Lord Richard asked his niece. 'Did you bring it with you from home?'

'No.' There was a slight hesitation as Megan wondered whether to tell the truth, then, 'Will stole it. In Portsmouth.'

'Good God! Why? No, don't tell me now. How much?'

'Twenty five pounds and six shillings.'

Stolen money. Richard Camberwell fought briefly with his conscience. And lost. They needed money now. Tonight. Will needed a proper bed and proper care. The decision made itself.

'All right,' he said. 'Nat, you go and find a decent house and a woman willing to nurse him. Tell her we'll pay her well. George, you stay with Will and keep him warm. I'll accompany Megan back to the camp and fetch the money.'

'If he wakes up, lad, give him some of this.' Nat took a bottle of

French brandy out of his pocket and gave it to George. Richard Camberwell gave him a look. 'Found it, sir,' said Binns, eyes widely innocent. 'Fell off a cart, I expect.'

'I expect so, Binns,' said Camberwell, knowing the man was lying but unwilling to castigate him for it now. 'Come on Megan. Let's go and get your ill-gotten gains. I left Hades in the care of Ginny Makepiece's lad, just in case he was needed. We'll get to the camp quicker on horseback. I don't expect there'll ever be any chance of Will's victim getting his money back so we might as well do something useful with it, though really, Megan, I do wish you wouldn't conspire with Will in these matters...'

He was still mildly chastising her when they reached Megan's tent. Quickly she rummaged in the bottom of the carpet bag where Major Underwood's money purse had lain since the day Will had stolen it.

The purse wasn't there.

The money was gone.

19

'It was here! I know it was!'

Megan stared at her uncle, then rummaged through the bag again, flinging clothes out, but the purse was not there. Richard Camberwell frowned in frustration.

'When did you last see it?

'This afternoon. While everyone was getting ready to go. I hadn't spent a penny of it but then I wanted to do something to cheer myself up so I thought that maybe tomorrow I would wash my hair with some proper soap. Betsy Makepiece told me that one of the sutler's has some but that it's very expensive.' She lowered her voice and her head. 'I know it was stolen money but I really wanted that soap, uncle. I hate having to use the hard stuff every-one here uses. I wanted to smell nice again. Was that so wrong?'

Richard Camberwell felt an unfamiliar pang of sympathy for her. Life had been very hard for a well brought up girl whose most difficult problem in life until a few months ago had been to decide which particular dress to wear. He put a paternal finger under her chin and lifted her head.

'No, that wasn't so wrong, Meg, but unfortunately it would appear that the money's now been stolen again. Who else knew it was there?'

'Only Will.'

'Do you think he might have it?'

She shook her head. 'No. He's never mentioned it since we were on the ship. Anyway, why would he want it just before going into battle?'

Camberwell had no answer. He helped her to her feet. 'Well there's no use worrying about it now. Our first concern is Will. He needs a decent bed, so we're just going to have to act like the victors we are and commandeer one.'

Megan crammed everything back into her bag, then they hurried outside the tent and mounted Hades again. Despite the lateness of the hour, the camp was wide awake with fires lit, some people talking and laughing, celebrating the victory. Many more waited anxiously to hear if their men were coming back to them. Camberwell wondered where Wellington was. Sitting on Hades's back he could see the flag flying high over the staff headquarters, but of the man himself there was no sign.

'Hey, Captain? You seen my Fred?' shouted Ginny Makepiece from a nearby fire. She and some of the older women had been doctoring the slightly wounded who had managed to make their way back to camp, and were looking after the children who had been unable to sleep with the noise and excitement while the younger women helped out at the makeshift hospitals.

'I did, Ginny. He was one of the first through and nary a scratch on him. He's probably drunk as a lord by now.'

'That's my man,' said Ginny proudly. 'I'm glad you came through all right yourself, sir.' She looked about. 'Where's young Will?' She was surprised not to see him with his master.

'I'm afraid he's hurt,' said Camberwell grimly.

'Oh Lordy, sir! Not badly I 'ope?' Ginny heaved herself to her feet and walked as quickly as she could over to them, her fat chins wobbling in her hurry to hear more.

'Bad enough. Went through the breach like a dose of salts, then got himself shot in the town. We're going to try and fix him up with a bed there. The hospital's so full you can barely walk between the men.'

'Seems to me yer might need some 'elp there, Captain,' Ginny said determinedly. She shouted to Betsy, one of her daughters. Her older daughters were helping at the hospital. 'You see to the young'uns our Bets. I'm goin' with Captain Camberwell.'

'You be careful, our Mam,' shouted back Betsy Makepiece who was sitting beside the fire with someone else's baby in her arms, and her young brother by her side.

'I will, lass. I'll take me brolly.' Ginny Makepiece's large black umbrella was her pride and joy, used to protect her from the rain in bad weather, and as a parasol in fine. To her mind, it was as good as any more conventional weapon, and had been used as such more than once in the rough and tumble of camp life. 'Now, sir. There ain't much room for me on that there 'orse, so 'ows about yer finds me another.'

Somewhat astonished, but not knowing what to say to prevent her accompanying them, Richard Camberwell told Megan to dismount and then cantered to where the horses were picketed at the rear of the British lines. There he found Lightfoot and a saddle. Wondering if Ginny had ever ridden a horse before, he brought the Welsh cob back to Megan and between them they hoisted Ginny and her umbrella onto Lightfoot's broad back. It became apparent very quickly that Ginny had never been on a horse in her life but as there was no room for anyone else to ride with her, she had to manage as best she could, though Megan kept hold of the pony's tethering rope so that all Ginny had to worry about was clinging to Lightfoot's long mane and the saddle.

In this fashion they rode through the guarded open gates of Ciudad Rodrigo and came to where George was sitting on the ground beside Will and several more soldiers, all there for the warmth the fire afforded and drinking from bottles or wineskins. On seeing Captain Camberwell ride up, the men melted away into the alleys, but he took no notice of them. The air was full of smoke, bright with flames, and noisy with shouts and shots from the streets. Now that the full surviving complement of the Light and 3rd Divisions were running loose in the town, the rioting was at its height. Nat had also returned and was warming his hands by the fire. George's mouth opened in a round of astonishment when he saw Ginny but she gave him no time to say anything.

267

'Don't stand there gawpin' like a fish out o' water, George Trim. 'Elp me down off this walkin' bog-trotter. I've 'ad better rides in ox-carts across ploughed fields!'

George helped Ginny to the ground, not an easy task, and one that involved much billowing of skirts and clutching of ample flesh. Finally able to put one foot on the ground, Ginny trod heavily on his toes and George only just managed to avoid uttering a very coarse swear word by clamping his mouth tight shut, though he did hop about a bit afterwards, much to Nat Binns's delight.

Ginny bent down at Will's side. 'Ah, me poor lad!' she exclaimed. She lifted the jackets covering him and saw the livid black marks where the cauterising pitch had been applied. 'And the bugger of a surgeon never even put a bandage on yer!'

'Did you find a house, Nat?' asked Camberwell urgently.

'Yes, sir. Just down the road aways. Woman can't speak a word of English but I told 'er as 'ow you'd pay 'er, sir. Me Spanish is comin' on a treat, sir,' he added proudly.

'Well done, man. Unfortunately though, the money I was going to use has been stolen.'

'What? Whoever stole it's a right thievin' bastard!' Nat had a thief's sanctimonious hypocrisy towards others of his trade.

Camberwell gave him a look. 'As I have no desire to evict her, I will have to appeal to this woman's good nature and hope she'll let us lodge Will with her until he's well enough to be moved back to camp.'

'Don't you worry none, sir. I'll see she don't kick up a fuss,' said Ginny confidently. 'You just pick up the lad, now, and let's be goin'. The sooner 'e's bein' properly looked after, the better.'

So it was that they proceeded down the street, Nat leading the way followed by Camberwell and George carrying Will. Ginny hurried along behind, with Megan riding Hades and leading Lightfoot.

The house Nat had found was only two streets away and seemed to be the largest and the least damaged of all the buildings there. Most of the others had had their doors kicked in, all had windows smashed and one was on fire, but a lieutenant had found some fairly sober soldiers and was attempting to put it out by means of a bucket chain from a well. A squad of British soldiers were marching a group of Frenchmen towards the town square where they would be held prisoner in the buildings previously used as the French garrison's headquarters.

Nat knocked on the door of the house and it was opened by a small, middle-aged woman holding a lamp that sent quick shadows into a narrow hallway and showed a staircase leading to a second storey. Rather gaudily dressed, her long greying hair done up with combs, she smiled when she saw Nat, and at Richard Camberwell behind him. She beckoned them in, but the smile went when the little entourage made to follow.

Tying the horses to the broken window frame, Megan thought she heard a giggle and a man's voice. Looking up, she saw a window lit by flickering lamplight above her head. There was more laughter, then her attention was taken away by rising voices nearer at hand. The others had scarcely manoeuvred Will's stretcher through the doorway, and the woman who owned the house was spouting a flood of Spanish, pointing at Ginny, Megan and Will. Nat frowned, trying to understand her, but the speech was too quick for his limited knowledge of the language, though it was obvious she was angry about something. Talking, waving her arms and gesticulating, the woman stamped her foot and pointed upstairs, then at Captain Camberwell. Nat caught one or two important words, and light dawned. His face went a bright red.

'There's bin a bit of a misunderstandin' 'ere, sir,' he said to Camberwell sheepishly. 'Seems this is an 'ouse of ill-repute, so to speak.'

'What? A brothel?'

'Yes, sir. When I told 'er we'd give 'er money, she thought I were a-bringin' you to sample the delights of the...er...ladies, sir.'

That explained why the house was more or less intact, thought Camberwell. The soldiers hadn't wanted to destroy a place where they might find some pleasure. Just then they heard footsteps on the narrow wooden stairs. All except Will looked up to see Lieutenant Paul Deaville coming down the stairs two at a time, pulling on his gloves, his smile one of deep satisfaction.

The smile disappeared quickly when he saw the faces staring up at him from the bottom of the staircase. Shock took its place, then embarrassment when he saw that Megan was with the party. She was staring at him with a look of dismay.

'Captain, sir,' he said, recovering himself with difficulty. He walked down the last two steps and saluted. 'My Lady.' He nodded at Megan but avoided her eyes.

'Deaville,' said Camberwell coldly.

There was an embarrassed silence, then the woman started shouting again, and tried to push Ginny whose bulk was blocking the doorway.

It was a pointless exercise which in other circumstances would have been amusing. The Spanish woman was not much more than half her size, and Ginny stood as immovable as a rock until finally she lost her temper and swatted the whore-house madam on the behind with her umbrella, an action that only caused the woman to shriek louder, so Ginny batted her again, a bit harder.

'Now, listen 'ere!' she said to the woman in a voice that George was sure could be heard all over Ciudad Rodrigo. 'We won this bloody fight so we gets some say in what goes on afterwards, see? We've got a sick boy 'ere who needs a bed and I'm a-bettin' you've got some dandy feather mattresses up there.' She pointed the umbrella upwards. 'You just lets us 'ave one of 'em, lady, with clean sheets mind, an' don't expect no money for it neither. We's supposed to be on the same side 'ere and we've rescued your town from the bloody Frogs. Our men'll treat any wounded 'ere with respect, so you do the same for ours!'

Most of the people in the small hallway stared at her, the Spanish woman included. Although she understood none of the words, she was realising that here was an opponent more formidable than all the four soldiers present put together. Will moaned, starting to come round. Only Megan noticed Paul Deaville glance down at the stretcher to see who the wounded man was, and she saw his face blanch when he recognised him.

Their eyes met and she was puzzled by the sudden look of fear in his. Without another word, he scurried out of the house but she had no time to think about him because now Ginny was organising things her way. Within ten minutes Will was lying in clean sheets on a goose-down mattress and his wound was being dressed by Ginny who had commandeered one of the woman's cotton petticoats by the simple expedient of rummaging through a chest of drawers until she found something suitable to tear up for a bandage.

When she had finished, she declared that she would nurse Will herself, that her youngsters would be fine in Betsy's care. Megan asked if she could stay too.

'Of course yer can, dearie. I knows 'ow much the lad means ter you. Yer'll be a great 'elp, I'm sure.' Ginny said, then shooed the male members of the party out of the door and down the stairs. 'If I needs anythin', I'll send Megan to find yer, Captain,' she said, 'so be so good as ter leave that there flat-footed beast behind. And don't worry, I'll not let 'er go alone. I'll find 'er an escort.'

So it was arranged that Lightfoot would be stabled in the small yard behind the house and that Ginny and Megan would look after Will.

'You stay too, George,' Camberwell decided. 'There's no knowing who might come in here, and the women could do with some protection. Do you have ammunition?'

'Yes, sir.' George patted his cartridge pouch.

Before he left, Richard Camberwell kissed Ginny on her fat cheek, making her go pink with pleasure.

'Thank you, Ginny,' he said with heart-felt relief that Will was in the best of hands. 'You're a marvel.'

'Oh, go on with yer, Captain,' she said. 'Will's a good lad. There was many a time 'e caught a rabbit or shot a duck for us an' the kids when we was up in them 'ills. An' when our Sammy were poorly, 'e gave me some medicine 'e said came from a gypsy woman and it made 'im right as ninepence in no time. 'An I'm not the only one 'e's 'elped neither. 'E's got a good 'eart, 'as Will. I'd like ter give all our lads a comfortable bed instead of leavin' 'em lyin' on the floor in that there convent, but if I can't do that, then at least I can give one o' the best more of a chance. Now just you go an' do whatever it is yer 'ave to do, lad, an' leave young Will to me.'

Camberwell left, feeling a whole lot better about the situation and, with Nat, went to find the rest of his Company.

† † †

Paul Deaville, meanwhile, was hurrying through the streets and trying to avoid all senior officers who might make him do anything that remotely resembled soldiering. He was scared, and needed time to think.

Will Tucker wasn't dead. The sight of him, if not actually alive and kicking, but certainly alive, had come as a shock because the bastard should be dead. He had aimed for the lungs, and with the

271

boy's back to him, how could he have missed? It was the bloody poor light, he supposed. Spying on Wilkins to make sure he didn't weasel out of the deal, he'd been horrified when Will had seen Wilkins shoot Juanita and then run to her aid. Too late to save her, to be sure, but he was almost positive she had said something to him before she died. Had she told Tucker about his involvement in the attack on the redoubt? People often confessed their sins before they died, didn't they? He couldn't take the chance. The bullet should have killed him on the spot, and no one would have suspected a thing in the chaos that was going on all over Ciudad Rodrigo tonight, except that he'd messed up again, and the boy wasn't dead.

Suddenly seeing a line of prisoners being marched unwillingly to the garrison headquarters, made him think of Reynard. God! What if he saw him? He fingered the pistol in his belt. Was he prepared to kill him too? It would certainly be the answer to that problem. He skulked in a dark doorway until the prisoners slunk past, then nearly jumped out of his skin when a voice said in his ear, 'Got any more work for me, guv?'

Amos Wilkins was hidden in the shadows by the wall. He had a bottle in his hand which he tucked under his arm while he loosened his breeches and relieved himself prodigiously against the stone-work, making Deaville move quickly out of the way.

'Did the girl good an' proper, I did,' said Wilkins above the noise.

'Yes.' Deaville recoiled from the combined stink of urine and brandy. He did not want to reveal that he had watched the murder, but bumping into Wilkins had given him an idea.

Good man,' he said, thinking quickly 'and, yes, I do have some-thing else for you to do.'

Wilkins fastened his breeches and sidled closer to him. 'You ain't got any money, remember, Lieutenant.' He was wondering what other valuables Deaville had hidden away that might be his before the night was over.

'It so happens that I do have money.' Deaville thought of the heavy purse secreted at the bottom of his baggage pack, the purse he had seen Megan Camberwell with. He had been on his way back from his meeting with Wilkins in the baggage park when he had passed Megan's tent, glanced through the open tent flap hoping to catch a glimpse of her, and seen her counting a lot of money. Unnoticed, he had watched her tip the coins back into the purse and hide it in her carpet bag. He'd gone away, only to return later when she and Camberwell's wench had gone to the convent. It had been the work of a moment to remove the purse to his own safe keeping, telling himself that he needed the money far more than Megan did, and with an army made up of thieves and vagabonds, there were thousands who would be suspected above him when it was missed.

Wilkins looked sceptical at Deaville's sudden admission of wealth, but then he smiled slyly. He'd known all along the man had been lying to him about having no money.

'How come you had no money this afternoon and now you have?' he sneered.

'That is no concern of yours,' Deaville said coldly. 'Suffice to say that I have money to pay you. Do you want the job or not?'

'Depends what it is, guv'nor.'

'Something you'll enjoy. That servant brat of Camberwell's is lying wounded in a house not far from here and I'm willing to bet he only has women protecting him.'

'So?'

'So it's a brothel and it'll be easy enough to get in and finish the job, but you're to be careful. One of the women is Megan Camberwell.'

Wilkins's face twisted in hatred. 'I'd like to do that bitch in too. Treated me like dirt when I worked for them Camberwells, she did.'

Deaville's hand suddenly caught hold of Wilkins's throat and squeezed hard. His face was so close that when he spoke spittle flew into the other man's eyes. 'You do anything to that girl, and I'll kill you,' he said angrily. 'You leave her alone. Understand?'

Wilkins nodded. Suddenly he did understand. So Deaville had a thing for Lady High-and-Mighty Camberwell did he? Pity. He would have liked to have rogered her before slitting the rich bitch's throat.

Deaville let go, and Wilkins coughed and choked for a while, getting his breath back. 'I'll just get the boy,' he said when he had recovered.

'Fine.'

'How much to do 'im?'

'Five pounds.'

Not much, thought Wilkins, but it would buy him a good few

273

bottles and women, and if it would get rid of the bugger who had prevented him doing for Richard Camberwell, it was worth it.

'When? Tonight?' he asked.

'How much have you had to drink?' Deaville looked hard at him.

'I ain't drunk if that's what yer mean,' said Wilkins, offended. 'I can 'old me liquor. It takes a lot to make Amos Wilkins not know what 'e's about.'

'All right. I'll show you the house, but then I'm going.' Deaville wanted to find himself an alibi so that no one would suspect him of being involved.

Together, they walked back towards the brothel.

† † †

Will fought back the fog of unconsciousness and groaned. He hurt. Even breathing was painful. Lamplight came from a corner of the room, making shadows on the walls. He realised that he was lying on his stomach, his head turned to one side facing away from the light, and that someone was talking. He recognised the voice.

'Megan?' His voice sounded funny, far away. He coughed to clear his throat, and gasped as pain seared through his side and back.

'Yes. Oh, Will! Are you all right? Do you feel well enough to drink some of this brandy? Ginny says it'll help with the pain.'

'Ginny?' Will turned his head the other way so that he could see Megan. She was sitting on a chair beside the bed he was lying on, holding a mug.

'She's here too, but she's downstairs at the moment, badgering the woman whose house this is to make some broth for you.'

'What 'appened?' Will blinked his eyes, trying to clear the last remnants of fogginess from his brain.

'Don't you remember?'

'No. Yes.' Some of it was coming back. Juanita and a loud bang, awful pain, then nothing. 'Juanita. I saw someone kill her.'

'You saw it?'

'Yes.' Will was quiet for a moment while he dredged his memory, then, 'I saw 'er in the plaza. She was 'eadin' for the church. I was worried she would get molested so I followed 'er. A man was followin' 'er as well but 'e disappeared, then I saw 'im. With a knife.' A pause, then he whispered, 'I didn't get to 'er in time.'

Tears pricked Megan's eyes, but she didn't know whether they were for Juanita, whom she had rather despised for leading Will astray, or for Will who was obviously upset and blaming himself.

'It wasn't your fault. You didn't know.'

No. He hadn't known that someone wanted to kill Juanita, but he couldn't help thinking that if he had fired more shots when he saw her assailant, he might have saved her life. Scared the assassin away.

'Can you remember what happened to you?'

Will thought about it. There had been the loud bang, then the pain, and he had a vague memory of seeing God's feet. 'A bang, that's all,' he said. He lifted himself enough to drink some of the brandy Megan offered him, gasping at the pain. Sinking back to the pillow, he asked her what damage the bullet had done.

'The surgeon thinks two broken ribs and muscle damage. You lost a lot of blood.'

'I should've seen 'im.' Will was angry with himself for not being more vigilant. To have gone through the breach and fought the French on the wall without getting hurt made his wound seem all the more stupid. He looked beyond Megan to the room itself. 'Where is this place?'

Megan told him what had happened after he was found.

'I'm in a brothel?'

'Yes. Nat found it.'

''E would.' Will laughed, then groaned when it hurt. He felt weak and helpless, not a good feeling. He swore under his breath just as Ginny and George came into the room. Ginny was carrying a bowl of fragrant broth.

'Ah, good. Yer awake.' said Ginny cheerfully. 'That bitch downstairs finally saw sense an' found me some chicken an' a few vegetables.' Megan glanced at George who grinned. Ginny had, by miming and flinging open every cupboard in the small kitchen, found what she wanted and forced the Spanish woman to cook the soup, standing over her while she did it.

'Now then, Will. Don't you go movin' around there,' said Ginny. 'You want those broken ribs to heal and you ain't up to much yet, lad.'

'I ain't movin', Ginny,' Will replied. 'I can't.'

'Good. You want anythin', we'll get it for yer. Now drink this broth and then get some sleep. You too, miss,' she glared at Megan.

'If I know anythin', it was 'ard work in that there 'ospital and yer look right pasty, girl, that yer do.'

Megan nodded. She was tired. Working in the hospital had been horrible, and what with all this business with Will, she felt exhausted, emotionally and physically.

Ginny started to spoon the broth into Will's mouth. Lying on his stomach didn't make it easy, but he dutifully raised his head enough to drink it. Between mouthfuls he said, 'George, I saw Bob and Butters go down on the wall? Are they all right?' Will remembered seeing them fall and then the madness had overtaken him during the fight and he had run off with a lot of others. Now he thought he should have stayed to help them.

'Bob lost a lot of blood but 'e'll be okay. They've managed to save 'is leg. So far.' Everyone knew that often limbs that seemed to have a chance of healing had to be removed later when the sepsis and the gangrene set in. George lowered his voice. 'Gerald died. Sword in the neck. It was quick.'

There was silence, then Will muttered, 'Poor bugger.' He remembered how scared Gerald Butterworth had been during the French ambush on the way from Oporto and how courageously he had fought anyway. He had never been cut out to be a soldier. But were any of them?

He tuned in to what else George was telling them. 'Crauford's dead.'

'Yes. I saw 'im.'

'Napier's wounded. Captain Shaw got hit by the canister in the shoulder but they say he'll live, though he may be left with a stiff arm.' George then reeled off the names of several soldiers, men and boys in their Company, who had died.

'Jesus!'

Will finished the broth and thankfully put his head back on the pillow. Even that small activity had tired him.

'Go to sleep now, all of you,' said Ginny. I'm goin' ter 'ave a talk with that there madam about breakfast. It's not far off dawn.'

Soon the room was quiet, all its occupants in exhausted sleep, careless of the continuing noise outside, while the women in the house plied their trade to victorious soldiers, and Cuidad Rodrigo suffered.

Will slept for an hour, then the pain woke him up. Megan was asleep in a chair across the room, and he watched her by the light of the lamp, dimmer now that dawn was approaching, loving the way her face was so free from care in sleep, her long lashes fanned on her cheeks. George had curled himself up on the rug and was dead to the world. He had no idea where Ginny was. For a long time, Will stayed awake with his thoughts. Who had shot him? Had it been a random accident or had someone intended his death? A Frenchman or an Englishman? It could have been the same person who had killed Juanita, but he had heard that person running away, hadn't he? Anyway, why would anyone want to kill him in Cuidad Rodrigo? He didn't know anyone there except the British troops. Had someone mistaken him for a Frenchman? Surely not. And what had Juanita been trying to tell him before she died? It had sounded like 'evil'. What was evil? Was she referring to the way the British were taking their revenge on her countrymen or was she speaking about the man who had knifed her? It was all very perplexing. He gave up thinking about it. His brain wasn't up to it at the moment.

George woke up and expressed a need for the privy so he went downstairs, leaving the door ajar. He had only been gone a few minutes when Will heard footsteps on the landing. Thinking it was George back already, he barely glanced at the door, which he could see well, the bed being right opposite, but then he had a shock and stared harder because the figure standing in the doorway was not George, but Amos Wilkins. And he was carrying a knife.

'Well now, ain't this a sight for sore eyes,' said Wilkins quietly. He cackled and his eyes glittered in the dim lamplight. He turned his eyes from Will to Megan who had heard his voice and was waking up. 'Little Lady Camberwell too. Better an' better. Now don't you make a sound, missy,' Wilkins said quickly as it became apparent Megan was about to scream. He walked towards her, eyes fixed on her shocked face that was staring at him as if she thought she was still dreaming. Now was his chance, he thought. He'd just enjoyed the services of one of the whores along the landing, but the sight of the girl was exciting him again. Bugger Deaville. He would roger her before he killed them both. The boy was no threat, all bandaged up the way he was, and he had all the time in the world to have his way with the arrogant little bitch. It would serve the bugger right to have to watch him do it. Then he'd have to kill her

277

because she'd seen him and would give him away. Leave no witnesses, that was his motto. He would tell Deaville that it couldn't be helped.

Will stared at Wilkins in horror, and realised his intent. The man was going to rape or kill Megan and there was no way he could stand by and let it happen. He saw that his rifle was leaning against the wall by the side of the bed.

Rage conquered pain and he reached out his hand for the rifle, levering himself upward as he did so, screaming with pain and anger. Cocking and aiming the gun, he pulled the trigger. There was a flash but no bullet came crashing out of the gun and Will realised, too late, that the rifle was empty.

Wilkins moved towards him, the knife glinting in the lamplight.

'Forgot to load it, didn't yer?' he said, an ugly smirk on his face, though truth to tell, Will's effort to kill him had come as a shock. 'I doesn't know who put yer in that bed, lad, but I do know who's goin' ter keep yer there.'

Will put out his hands to ward off the blow he knew was coming. The rifle fell onto the bed and he gripped Wilkins's arm, using all his strength to push the knife hand away from him, but he was weak, and what little strength he had was ebbing quickly. The knife came closer to his neck and he knew he was going to die.

George was shouting in the doorway, but as reached for his musket, Wilkins spun round and the knife went flying across the room. George yelped as it stuck in his arm, and he stared at it in disbelief while blood dripped to the floor. He slumped against the wall. Wilkins laughed and started to walk towards him, while Megan seemed frozen, watching him, eyes wide with fear and horror. Somehow Will struggled to his feet. His ears sang and he held his breath, not daring to inhale because it hurt so much. He picked up the rifle, staggered two paces and brought the muzzle round in a swinging arc that made him scream with pain. He felt bone grate against bone in his side. The metal connected with Wilkins's body then Will's legs refused to hold him upright any longer, and he fell.

Wilkins yelled, his hand clutching his shoulder where the rifle had hit it and he turned on Will, his face murderous. 'Bastard!' he shouted. 'Bastard!' He took another few steps and yanked the knife out of George's arm provoking a scream of pain, then he lunged towards Will, lying on the floor, unable to move. Through a haze, Will saw the man coming towards him and knew he didn't have the strength to stop him.

There was a sudden loud bang that hurt everyone's ears, and the expression on Wilkins's face turned to one of surprise. He staggered, tried to say something, and fell forward, his blood splashing Will as he landed on the floor beside him with a thud. Will stared past him at Megan who was holding a smoking pistol and looking aghast at what she had done, then everything slowly faded away.

When Ginny came into the room, carrying her umbrella like a cudgel, alerted by the screams and sound of the gunshot, she found Megan shaking, the pistol on the floor at her feet where she had dropped it. She seemed stunned.

'Lawks, girl! What 'appened?' Ginny said, pushing her gently back onto the chair. She turned to the curious men and women now crowded in the doorway. 'Don't just stand there, you lot. Come and 'elp me 'ere!'

The British soldiers enjoying the womens' favours in the house that night helped Ginny pick up the semi-conscious Will and lay him on the bed. One gave George a slug of rum from his canteen and then helped another remove Wilkins's body.

'Put 'im in the street for the burial parties,' said Ginny grimly. 'It's all 'e deserves.'

The Spanish madam came in, screeching at the top of her voice, her gestures plainly saying that they must go, she wanted no violence in her house, but Ginny picked up her umbrella and advanced on her, telling her to get out of the room. The woman got the message and went hurriedly away. Ginny shut the door on the rest. While Megan dressed George's wound with another strip of petticoat, she told Ginny what had happened, then she had to explain to her and George why Wilkins had a grudge against Will and herself.

'How did he know we were here? That's what I'd like to know,' she said.

'Maybe 'e saw us bringin' Will in,' said George. He turned to where Ginny was washing Will's back. ' 'Ow is 'e, Ginny?'

'Not so good. 'E's bleedin' again,' she said worriedly. 'I don't know as 'ow 'e managed to get off the bed and swing that gun. 'E's all in, poor lad.' She paused, listening to shots and the sound of running feet outside in the street where the darkness of night was fading slowly away. 'I've a fancy it's goin' to be a long day, missy. A very long day.'

20

The morning of the 20th January 1812 found Ciudad Rodrigo quieter, but still reeling under the force of the attack and its riotous aftermath. In the hours before dawn, the officers and the provost marshals gained control of the army, and the Light Division and the 3rd marched out of the fortified town in great spirits, weighed down with plunder, some wearing French greatcoats, most bringing food, drink, clothing and gifts for their women and children who had worried about them all night, many men with heads as thick as fog, but all basking in the glory that was victory.

Ciudad Rodrigo had fallen. Nat Binns, marching out of the town with several bottles of good French wine and brandy secreted about his person, a nearly new multi-coloured jacket over his own faded red one, and a sack full of dead chickens over his shoulder, told anyone who cared to listen that he'd heard the French prisoners numbered one General, nearly eighty officers 'and a lot o' bloody Frogs.' It was not until later that the men learned that the British had lost over five hundred in the trenches and nearly that number in the breaches, which dampened their enthusiasm somewhat, but they took heart from the fact that the army had captured some seventeen hundred French soldiers, a siege train of supplies and a hundred and fifty heavy guns. All in all, Wellington was well pleased, and congratulated his generals, who passed on his thanks to the officers, who then passed it on to the men. The army celebrated a great victory. The northern pathway into Spain was now open.

† † †

Richard Camberwell came to see Will soon after the sun was up, and was shocked to hear of the night's happenings. George, the gash in his arm sewn up by Ginny, and with said arm in a sling, was in pain, morose, and not at all his normal cheerful self, saying it was his fault, that if he hadn't been taken short the whole episode would never have happened, but Camberwell was quick to take the blame away from him.

'You weren't to know Wilkins would come here, George,' he said. 'And it wasn't your fault that he could throw a knife quicker than you could get to your musket.' He frowned. 'I suppose he wanted to take revenge on Will and Megan for slights in the past, but I wonder how he knew you were here?' He looked puzzled for a moment, then shrugged and glanced at Megan who was wan and gloomy this morning. 'I have to say I'm amazed, Meg. Who gave you a gun, and where did you learn to shoot?'

Megan knew she would have to risk her uncle's wrath and tell the truth. 'Will taught me. I borrowed your pistol at home when you were away. Then Ensign Wooliscroft has been helping me too. He gave me the gun. It's a spare one he had.' She looked pleadingly at him. 'Please don't be angry, uncle.'

'Angry? How could I be angry? You saved Will's life, and probably your own and George's too. The man was scum and I should have handed him over to the constables months ago. You did the world a favour, girl, and I'm proud of you.'

Megan gave a faint smile, happy to have pleased her short-tempered uncle for once, but his praise did little to dispel her gloom. She looked now at the cause of it. Will was lying face down on the bed, his eyes closed, beaded with sweat and tossing in restless sleep. Thinking to make him more comfortable, she had tried to take off the stone that was threaded on a thong around his neck, the stone the gypsy girl had given him for luck, but even in the throes of a fever, Will had fought against her, so she had left it. Despite all their care, the wounds were already starting to fester. It would have been a miracle had they not. The bullet had forced dirty material into the flesh, and the surgeon had undoubtedly used unhygienic knife and forceps to remove what little he could. Red lines of poison were already beginning to thread their way across Will's pale skin from the wound.

Camberwell saw this and his troubled eyes met Ginny's over Meg's head. Ginny saw the concern in his and forced herself to sound cheerful.

'Still reckon 'e's better off 'ere than in that there 'ospital, Captain. At least 'e 'as us to care for 'im. The poor boys over there just lie in their own mess 'til they die.' Her expression changed to

281

one of determination. 'And our Will ain't goin' ter die, I'll make sure o' that.'

Just then Will's eyes opened and recognition flared in them.

'Megan,' he whispered.

'Will?' In seconds she was kneeling at his side.

He whispered something else then sank into semi-consciousness again. Megan stood up, a bemused look on her face, and Richard Camberwell could have sworn his niece was blushing. 'What did he say?' he asked.

Megan looked at him for a moment then shook her head. 'It didn't make sense,' she said, though Camberwell thought she was not being entirely truthful. However, he put it from his mind and concentrated on Will instead.

'What do you need?' he asked Ginny.

'Chicken,' said Ginny promptly. 'Chicken broth is what this lad needs. That bird the madam found for us last night weren't no bigger 'n a pigeon.'

'I betcha Nat could find one,' said George, his face showing a smile for the first time since Wilkins had made his appearance. The British, starved of good food for so long, had commandeered most of the town's livestock and poultry in one way or another, but George was sure that Nat Binns could put his thieving skills to good use and procure a chicken somehow. He was not to know that Nat had already done so, and had 'found' a dozen that he was selling off to the highest bidders.

'Right,' said Camberwell, unusually unperturbed at the idea of one of his men stealing. Sometimes circumstances called for strong measures. 'Anything else?'

''E needs medicine,' said Ginny, 'but I doubt there'll be any to spare up at the 'ospitals. Maybe one o' the lads could find an apothecary. Yer can make a list.'

This Richard Camberwell did, for Ginny could neither read nor write, and then he went away to try and find the things she asked for. Ginny's mother had been something of a herbalist and had made many of her own medicines, and Ginny remembered some of her cures, but whether the right herbs could be found in this God-forsaken country, she did not know. However, she was hopeful that maybe a good apothecary would be able to help.

The few whispered words to Megan were the last Will said to

any of them for days. The fever worsened despite the medicine Richard Camberwell managed to find, and the chicken soup Ginny force fed him. The wounds suppurated and he tried to escape the pain by moving but that only made it worse. He was light-headed and, by the second night, delirious.

'I don't know what to do!' Megan wept when her uncle entered the house on the evening of the fourth day they had been at the brothel. It was the sixth time that day he had come to see Will.

'The doctor said we should get him out of the hospital so he would get better. He's not getting better. He's getting worse!' Megan looked at Will, the tears rolling down her cheeks. The sheet had been abandoned and the sweat glistened on his back and buttocks. He tossed this way and that, moaning, his bright hair dark with perspiration. She picked up a cloth that was in a bowl of water, and wrung it out, then gently wiped his face and body.

'He hasn't eaten anything. He hardly drinks. He's going to die! And I can't bear it!'

Unused though he was to weeping women, it upset Richard Camberwell greatly to see his niece crying so hard. He took her in his arms and let her cry onto his chest. After a while he pulled gently away.

'I asked Barker to come and see him. Has he been?'

'No,' Megan sniffed. 'I don't suppose he has the time.'

'Don't need 'im,' scoffed Ginny. 'Ain't nothin' 'e can do that we ain't doin' already.' Even she, usually so optimistic, was looking worried.

They all looked at Will who appeared to be awake, but his eyes were bright with fever and there was no recognition in them. He mumbled something that sounded like 'water'. Gently Ginny lifted his head while Megan tried to pour a little down his throat. He managed to swallow some then laid his head back on the pillow and closed his eyes, falling into a restless doze again.

They were quiet for a moment, then Ginny remembered something. 'When my Sammy were ill, Will gave 'im that stuff 'e said came from the gypsies,' she said. 'Maybe we should try it. D'yer know where 'e keeps it, lass?'

'It's probably in his pack,' said Megan, her eyes gleaming with sudden hope. 'I'll ride back with you, uncle, and look for it.'

'Good idea,' said Camberwell, glad to be doing something.

On the way to the British camp, he said, 'That business with Wilkins got me thinking that maybe Will's getting shot was no accident.'

'It wasn't Wilkins who shot him. He said so himself.'

'It wasn't?'

'No.'

'It doesn't let out our side completely though.'

'What do you mean, uncle?'

Camberwell sighed. 'There's something you don't know, Megan. Will was spying for me. Trying to find out who sent that message.'

'What message?'

Camberwell told her about the plot to foil the attack on the redoubt. 'Keep it quiet, Meg. Don't tell anyone, not even Ginny.'

The girl nodded. 'Do you think Will was getting too close to the spy and that's why he was shot?'

'It's a possibility.'

Megan thought about it for a while. 'Do you think that maybe Juanita was killed for the same reason?'

'I don't know. It's possible she was involved. Will was trying to find out if she was. If he did get shot because of me...' Camberwell let the sentence tail off and it occurred to Megan that he was just as upset about Will as she was.

The gypsy medicine was found in Will's pack and administered as soon as Megan returned to the house. They also smeared a lot of the salve on his wounds. With hope and trepidation, Megan and Ginny watched Will, and waited.

† † †

Will awoke in the small hours of the following morning. Megan was sleeping in a chair next to the cot. The pain was still there but he felt better. He was uncomfortable, the bedclothes wrinkled as though they had been wet and had started to dry again, but, for the first time in days, he was alert. Memory came back with a rush and he wondered how long he had been lying on the bed. He felt totally drained of all energy, as though he had been fighting a long battle, but his mind was active, a good sign, he thought. He stared at Megan's lovely face. Her curls were uncombed, her clothing crumpled. Her face was composed in sleep but there were dark rings under her eyes. He wondered how many hours she had stayed with him and his heart went out to her.

He was still staring at her when she stirred and opened her eyes. At first drugged with sleep, she stared back, then her eyes widened when she realised he was wide awake himself. A great smile brightened her face.

'Will! You're better!' she said, and, acting on impulse, she kissed him on the cheek.

Will's broad grin matched her own. 'If I wasn't, I am now,' he said, and she laughed.

Ginny and George were just as pleased to see the fever gone and their friend on the mend. From that morning, Will's progress was rapid, and two days later he went back to the camp, thinner, weak, but much improved. The brothel madam whose house they had commandeered was mollified with a promise of money Richard Camberwell determined to procure from the army's coffers, and was glad to see them go.

With his torso swathed in bandages, Will was able to move cautiously about the camp. People greeted him kindly and he was amazed at how many people seemed to care about his welfare. He mentioned this to Megan as they sat outside Richard Camberwell's tent some two weeks after the attack. Megan wasn't surprised at all. She had known for a long time that the camp followers thought a lot of Will. When they were at the winter cantonment, she had watched the girls and women give him small gifts, usually mittens and scarves to keep out the cold, and they still did. Peeling a couple of onions to add to the stew that was bubbling on the fire, her eyes watered, yet she was not unhappy. For Megan hugged a secret to herself, a secret that she could hardly believe might be true. The three words Will had whispered to her while gripped with fever were never far from her mind, and she basked in the knowledge that though Will spread his natural charm and willingness to help around in large doses, she was the one he loved. She wondered sometimes whether or not he had really meant those three little words, 'I love you', or whether it had just been the fever talking. However, she chose to believe that he loved her because the thought of him dying had filled her with such a fearful despair, she was beginning to think she might love him too. The thought was a little scary because a part of her still balked at the idea of being in love with someone of his lowly station, yet she was finding more and more lately that she was able to forget Will's background and just take him for what he was; a caring, brave, charming and very handsome young man.

However there was the attraction she felt for Lieutenant Deaville, although that had been dimmed a little by their meeting in the brothel. At first she had been shocked that he should have felt the need for such a place so soon after their victory, but then she thought of other officers she knew. They all did it, did they not? Probably even her uncle had after other battles, before he had met Sarah, though she sheered away from that thought. Paul Deaville's sheer masculinity was overpowering. When he turned on the charm, she did not have the experience to deal with it and his persistence was flattering. It was very easy to be captivated by his smooth tongue, and the fact that this undeniably handsome officer wanted to spend time with her, a mere girl, was very pleasing.

Little did she know, but while Paul Deaville was flooding her with insincere flattery every time they happened to meet, at the same time keeping a weather eye open for her uncle who would undoubtedly disapprove of such meetings, he was catching up on all the latest gossip that Megan unwittingly recounted for his anxious ears. So it was that he heard what had happened on the night of the attack and hence what fate had befallen Amos Wilkins, whose absence he had noticed. That his henchman was dead did not disturb Deaville unduly, indeed he was glad that there was no chance of his being betrayed by the man and he would not now have to release some of the money he had stolen from Megan Camberwell's bag into Wilkins's grubby hands. But he was disappointed that Wilkins had not managed to kill Will Tucker before he had succumbed himself, and he looked at Megan with new respect when she revealed herself to be the one who had done the deed. Wilkins's demise put a stop to his plans for the present, but he was determined that he would get his revenge in due course for Will's relationship with Juanita. He hoped that her death had put paid to any chance of his clandestine activities being reported. This last, though, was causing him less concern as the days went by. He was beginning to think that maybe he was wrong in thinking that Juanita had given him away before she died. Surely if she had, Will Tucker would have told someone by now?

Something else was causing him much more anxiety at the

moment. A message had come by means of servants and tradesmen, a message from someone he had hoped never to hear from again; Colonel Jean Reynard. It seemed that fate had decreed the Colonel to be one of the officers imprisoned in the town by the British forces, and Reynard wanted out. To achieve this end, he was calling in the debt Deaville owed him, saying that if the lieutenant could find a way to release him, then nothing more would be said about the money he still had to pay. On receiving the unwelcome message, Deaville wished he had not spent so prolifically since the windfall of Megan's money came into his hands because that would have gone some way to paying off the debt, though, on consideration, he supposed that it would not have been enough to pacify Reynard for long. What was he to do? If he ignored the message altogether, then should the French Colonel somehow obtain release, he would be in mortal danger not only for owing him money, but for disregarding his request as well, yet he had no notion of how he was to help the man.

Then something happened to make his task easier. He, along with several others from his Company, were assigned guard duty at the garrison headquarters where the French officers were being held prisoner. Deaville viewed the assignment with mixed feelings. On the one hand he was excited at the possibility of being able to discharge his debt to Reynard, on the other he was scared stiff of the consequences should he be found out.

Thus it was that he was soon able to ascertain the precise whereabouts of the French Colonel while supposedly in charge of a contingent of NCOs whose job it was to supervise the guards. The task he had been given was boring in the extreme and seemed to involve interminable paper work whilst making half-hearted attempts, at Wellington's insistence, to deal with complaints from the imprisoned officers. He wished he had some female company with which to pass the long night hours as he was not allowed to leave the garrison whilst on duty. Now he had no choice but to try and help Reynard who knew he was close at hand. The Colonel was imprisoned in a small room at the back of the building, alone as befitted his rank, a fact that Deaville thought he should be able to use to his advantage, though he could not for the life of him think how. The French officers, although treated well, were heavily guarded until such time as arrangements could be made for their transportation to England and the prison hulks, hopefully to be exchanged for British officers captured previously by the French.

Paul Deaville was not an imaginative man and it took him several days to come up with a plan that he hoped would work. To this end he summoned Colonel Reynard to his small office one day, dismissed the guard who accompanied him, and, making sure they were not overheard, discussed the matter.

Colonel Jean Reynard looked lined and drawn. Older than Deaville, he was a greatly experienced officer who had served his Emperor faithfully in many campaigns, and this was the first time it had been his misfortune to be captured. He had a head of thick, greying hair and was of stocky build, a vigorous, vital man who was finding the enforced inactivity of his imprisonment extremely irksome and he looked at the British lieutenant with hope and expectation.

'I trust you are being treated well, Colonel?' said Deaville insincerely. He was finding that now the shoe was on the other foot, he was quite enjoying the feeling of power he had over this man who had caused him such trouble over a few measly guineas.

'I am, sir,' answered Reynard in almost perfect English. 'Though I would rather be with my companions in the field of course.'

'Of course,' said Deaville. 'But to the victor goes the spoils, as they say.'

Reynard inclined his head in acknowledgement. He stared at the man sitting at the desk with cold dislike, knowing from the first moment they met at the gaming house in Lisbon that he was a foppish Englishman with no backbone, and a gentleman in name only. However, his future might well depend on him, so, for now, he would put his distaste to one side and listen to what he had to say.

Deaville's voice dropped to barely above a whisper as he said, 'I received your message asking for assistance in escaping the garrison and I have a plan, but I want your assurance, in writing, that it will be in full and final payment of my debt to you and that you will bother me no further.'

The Frenchman smiled. 'I will bother you no further provided you do not lose to me at cards again, *m'sieur*,' he said dryly. Paul Deaville was an extremely bad card player and Reynard had enjoyed seeing the Englishman lose.

288

Deaville did not return the smile. Instead he proceeded to out-line his plan. Reynard would pretend to be ill, so ill that he would have to be removed from the garrison to the convent hospital. Once in that still overcrowded place it should be an easy matter to 'disappear', perhaps making out that the Frenchman had died overnight and his body removed for burial by loyalists. It was a simple plan but, should it go wrong, Deaville made it quite clear to Jean Reynard that his name was to be kept out of any enquiries. Reynard agreed, but asked that Deaville provide a horse, so that once free of the town, he could make his escape. Deaville grudging-ly agreed to this request though wondered where he was to obtain such an animal. He had rather hoped Reynard would be able to escape the town without his assistance. When putting forward the scheme, he had only intended to help free Reynard from this prison, but it seemed as though the Frenchman expected his aid in escap-ing the town as well.

Unwilling to carry on the conversation further in case Reynard thought of something else he could assist with, Deaville called for the guard and the Frenchman was taken back to his room. Deaville then lit a cigar and stood in front of the window that overlooked the plaza and the buildings of Ciudad Rodrigo. Some form of normality had returned to the town now under British occupation, the citi-zens going about their daily business, glad at least that the shelling had stopped and resigned to the fact that they had been occupied by another army, one that treated them better than the French did once the excesses of the victory night were over.

Deaville thought over his plan, but it suddenly seemed full of holes and difficulties so he put it temporarily out of his mind and turned his attention to other worrying problems that he had almost forgotten about whilst considering Reynard's escape. Will Tucker was one problem and he felt his ire rise, remembering Wilkins's failure to carry out his orders. He had seen the youngster around camp, his health improving rapidly, and the sight irked him deeply. Rumours had reached his ears that Will had been involved in the attack on the redoubt in some way other than merely taking part, but despite tentative enquiries, he had been unable to ascertain any facts. It was worrying. Had he, because of his relationship with Juanita, found out his, Deaville's, involvement? Surely not. If that were the case, he himself would have been hauled over the coals long since, yet there was the disturbing fact that the raid had gone off without a hitch and Juanita had always insisted she had kept her part of the bargain by informing the French. Reynard had confirmed that he had passed on her information to the Colonel in charge of the redoubt but somehow the British had won that battle. It still puzzled Deaville as to how they had actually done it.

At least he had never had to pay Juanita the money he'd promised, nor Amos Wilkins neither, and now both were dead, there was no possibility of his deviousness coming to light.

Was there?

21

Though eager to forge ahead to Badajoz, the much larger fortified town that barred the way into Spain further south, Wellington knew that his army needed time to recover from the battering it had received at the hands of the French in Ciudad Rodrigo, so, for a few weeks, he rested his troops. Richard Camberwell, privy to the goings on higher up in the army's echelons, told Will that for the time being they were in little danger from the French army. Marshal Marmont was not a threat any more with half his troops on the far east coast of Spain helping to capture Valencia, and the rest were scattered in the north, the nearest being some twenty miles away. Once he heard that the British had been victorious at Ciudad Rodrigo, Marmont had given up going any further towards them. 'Napoleon's got no idea what's going on here,' said Camberwell. 'My guess is Marmont's awaiting orders and wondering what to do next. Old Bony has no real concept of the problems his army's facing. He seems to move them around like pieces on a chess board, regardless of the weather, distances, and the difficult terrain. Put him here for a month, he might do things differently, but at the moment he's playing right into our hands.'

With no army to fight, the British relaxed and also awaited orders. One day Megan plonked her basket of dirty washing down on the ground beside the River Agueda and pushed her damp curls back from her face. Despite the cold weather, she was sweating. The basket wasn't that heavy but this was the second load of washing she had done that morning. There had been rain and snow for several days and so nothing could be dried. Now, at last, there was a fitful sun, and a cool breeze to blow away the clouds. Staring over the water, she wondered at herself, worrying about whether washing would dry. Before last September, it had never occured to her to even consider things like that. The care of her clothes had been left to Nel and Martha and she had never so much as thought about them except to decide what to wear on a particular day, or in choosing which to buy on her regular visits to London's shops. She sat down next to the basket and stared at the rooftops of the town beyond the wall. Smoke from cooking fires lay like a haze over them and she remembered the awful night of the attack and the following day when the smoke had come, not from cooking fires, but from the atrocities caused by the army she followed. Why did she not feel disgust that the soldiers had behaved so? Because she knew the hardships and the dangers the men faced every day. Death followed hard on their heels; death from the French guns and swords, disease, sickness and hardship. It was no wonder the soldiers sought revenge and took pleasure where and when they could find it.

Megan looked at the scudding clouds and thought today she might be lucky and the washing would dry. It would be good to wear clean clothes again. She and Sarah had not changed their clothing for days and she knew they smelled bad. But then so did everyone else in the camp. She looked at her hands, hands that she used to bathe in milk to keep the skin soft. Now they were calloused from carrying heavy buckets of water and baskets of washing, rough and red from the harsh, cold weather. Chilblains hurt, though she covered her hands with goose grease to try and soften them. Her hair was a mess, tangled and dirty, her clothes patched, and worn not because she wanted to look nice, but because she couldn't go around naked.

She sometimes yearned for the life she had left behind, for England's quiet, placid pace, for the sheer pleasure of being able to please herself what she did, and to have no menial work to do, but lately she had come to accept her lot. This was mainly due to her continued association with Ginny Makepiece and the other camp followers. If she wanted to fit in, and she did, desperately, then she had to be like them, and not forever wish she were somewhere else. Her prickly, snobbish manner had almost disappeared. Instead she had learned tolerance and compassion. The women accepted her now as one of them and she was glad of their friendship. They had helped her to see things differently, that what mattered here was not pretty dresses, material belongings, or wealth. What mattered most was finding enough food to eat, encouragement, loyalty, sharing and helping each other. It had been a hard lesson, but Megan felt she had learned it, and learned it well.

She thought back to some of the sights seen at the convent hospital where she had worked on the night of the attack, sights that had made her physically ill or turn away in horror. Tempted to run away from that dreadful place, it was Sarah who had kept her there, not by speech but by the things that she did. For Sarah was a born nurse. Nothing seemed to harass or disgust her. Compassion was in her very nature and, watching her, Megan's own conscience had been pricked and her sympathy aroused until she had found herself doing things she had never imagined herself doing if she lived to be a hundred. Afterwards, sitting in the brothel's darkened room with Ginny while Will wrestled with his demons, the kindly woman had told her she would eventually become used, if not hardened, to the sight of a man having his leg amputated, or another with his chest caved in so you could see the ribs, or a corpse lying in the dirt with his head, and the cannonball that had lifted it from his shoulders, mangled in some bushes nearby. It was difficult to imagine that anyone could be inured to such things. Yet the women, hard and dispassionate though they might be, were in some ways still warm-hearted, generous beings. Ginny had told her she should always remember that these soldiers were, first and foremost, men, with the same desires and feelings as their counterparts on the side of the enemy, and neither they, nor the French, deserved to be flung at each other like cannonballs, though she suspected it was a fact that the generals often forgot. Ginny told Megan they should be treated right, and she and the other women tried their best to do so. So Megan did too.

With a sigh that was heartfelt, Megan started to wash the dirty clothing. Some of it was Will's. His wound was healing well, but he couldn't lift anything heavy, so Dodge was cleaning the officers' clothing, and she was doing his. Scrubbing with the hard soap at a particularly stubborn stain, she was startled when a voice said close to her ear, 'What a pity those tender hands have to do such menial work.'

Megan looked up into the sardonically smiling face of Paul Deaville standing nonchalantly beside her. She had seen little of him in the last two weeks, since he was based at the garrison in the town. Wondering why she blushed, Megan wiped her wet hands on her skirt and took the lieutenant's hand as he helped her to her feet.

'You should leave that to others,' said Deaville. He was thinking that even in such a dishevelled state, Lady Megan Camberwell looked ravishing. What would she look like clean, and wearing a pretty dress and dainty shoes? His mind filled with lust at the very thought.

'Who would you suggest does the work, Lieutenant?' asked Megan spiritedly in answer to his statement. 'All the other women have enough of their own to do.'

Deaville noticed a wet pair of men's breeches laid out on the grass to dry. 'What about your uncle's servant? He should be doing the washing, not you.'

'Will is not well enough yet, and besides...' Megan blushed again. 'Besides, I couldn't be giving him my own clothes to wash, now could I?'

Deaville grinned the devilish grin that sent those peculiar feelings that she often wondered about, coursing through her veins. Then his expression suddenly changed to a scowl and he looked away over the river. 'That boy was damn lucky,' he said, almost to himself. 'Lucky his damn lungs weren't blown apart with a bullet in the back like that.' Megan, surprised at the scowl, suddenly remembered the look of fear that had crossed the lieutenant's face when he had seen Will at the brothel, and now she stared at him strangely. Seeing the look, he shrugged off his hatred, smiled again and said, 'I was wondering, my lady, if you would do me the honour of accompanying me to a dinner tonight. Lieutenant Colonel Davenport is hosting Wellington and has invited all his officers, even the most junior, to dine with him. That being so, I have been released from garrison duty for the evening, and it would give me great pleasure if you would say yes.'

Megan's thoughts were in turmoil. Nothing would please her more than to be able to dress up and spend a few hours in civilised company again, but she knew her uncle would not approve. However, if all officers were invited, then he would be there to act as

293

chaperone wouldn't he? She smiled, delighted to accept.

'I'd love to,' she said, and was rewarded by Paul Deaville's handsome face breaking out into a grin of pleasure.

'I will collect you at eight, my lady,' he said and bent over her hand to kiss it. 'Your servant.' Then he was gone.

Megan watched him stride away towards a group of officers who were exercising their horses on the softer ground by the riverbank, and smiled to herself. It was so comforting sometimes to be thought of as a lady and addressed as such. She was so used to the company of the women, and of Will who had never shown her any deference even in England, that it was very pleasant to hear the words 'my lady' again.

A thrill of excitement, and not a little apprehension, coursed through her at the prospect of an evening spent in the lieutenant's company. Although Paul Deaville was a heady companion, he also frightened her a little. He was so suave and so obviously more experienced in the ways of the world. And her uncle had, more than once, warned her against him. But that made him all the more exciting to a provincial girl. She would accompany him tonight and enjoy herself, whatever her uncle said. She deserved some enjoyment, just like the soldiers did, didn't she?

Unfortunately Richard Camberwell did not agree when she told him of the invitation late that afternoon. The two had a blazing row before Megan stubbornly flounced out of the lodgings that he now shared with Captain Shaw at the other's insistence, a small house near the town wall. She went to the tent she stayed in, refusing to share Shaw's lodgings because the tent was closer to her friends, there to examine her good green dress and heat up the smoothing iron on the nearest campfire. Meanwhile, Richard Camberwell swore under his breath and looked across at Will who sat in a chair, sewing a button on the Captain's dress uniform jacket.

'What am I to do with her, Will?' said Camberwell, for once lost for something to do that would help the situation. 'I keep telling her Deaville's no good and Megan's not a stupid girl, yet he only has to flash a smile at her and she takes leave of her senses altogether.' He shook his head in exasperation.

Will smiled faintly and said nothing, knowing a response was not really expected. Megan had been very kind to him since he was wounded, so kind that he had even begun to think that maybe she was caring for him just a little. But, like the Captain said, Paul Deaville seemed to send her silly, and it was apparent that she still had feelings for him. He frowned at the thought of them being together that night and determined to be there as well, though he would only be hurting himself as he had done at the Christmas Ball. But he had to make sure Deaville did not take advantage of Megan who surely did not realise what the lieutenant's intentions were. That they were not good was obvious to both himself and Lord Camberwell.

So it was that Will managed to wangle a position as wine-server for the dinner that night, but only by promising the regular boy who acted in that capacity for Lieutenant-Colonel Davenport that he would secrete half a bottle of port away and pass it along to him later. Davenport had taken up residence in one of the better houses of Ciudad Rodrigo, ejecting the eminent citizen who lived there. The house was thronged with people that night, brightly lit, and there was a festive air about the place while delicious cooking smells emanated from the kitchen.

Will watched as the officers took their seats at the table, a few accompanied by their ladies. He frowned when Megan was seated beside Deaville, but Captain Shaw sat on her other side. Will thought that although James Shaw was not his usual self, still suffering from the loss of Juanita, he was enough of a gentleman to make sure that the lieutenant behaved himself in Megan's presence.

The evening wore on, with Will bringing in bottle after bottle of wine; white, red and, finally, the after dinner port and brandy. His back felt the strain. It was the most energetic he had been since getting wounded and his ribs ached. So it was that while the officers, now quite drunk and rowdy after the meal, were drinking the port and smoking cigars, he went outside for a breath of fresh air and sat down on a seat under a bougainvillaea vine that grew near the steps leading to the front door.

As he sat there, appreciating the crisp night air after the stuffy, suffocating atmosphere of the dining room, he thought of Megan. That she had thoroughly enjoyed the evening had been obvious, and he had to admit it was good to see her pretty face full of laughter again. She hadn't had much to laugh about recently, that was for sure. And she looked so beautiful in the green dress that set off her chestnut curls to such advantage. Seeing the looks she gave

Paul Deaville, he wondered if she would ever look at him in the same way, and sighed. It was disappointing to realise that his faint hopes of the last couple of weeks were to be dashed once more. It seemed her feelings were for that blasted lieutenant after all.

It was while he sat contemplating her, that Megan herself suddenly appeared on the arm of Paul Deaville. Will shrank back into the dark shadows and watched as the two took a turn about the extensive gardens that surrounded the house, walking, he noticed, towards the thick shrubs and bushes that gave onto an orange grove near the boundary wall. Wondering how Richard Camberwell could let the two out of his sight for a minute, he prepared to follow them, but then he heard shouts from the front of the house, and Will recognised Richard Camberwell's irate voice calling for him with some urgency. Swearing under his breath at having to leave Megan alone with the lieutenant, he ran round to the driveway where light spilled from the open front door.

'Ah, there you are Will!' said Camberwell as soon as he appeared. 'I have to leave. Some fuss at the garrison with the French prisoners. Damn it! if I weren't officer of the day, some other poor bugger would be ending the evening in this uncivilised manner. Still, I suppose I was lucky to be invited at all tonight, being on duty as I am.' He belched loudly. 'Suppose I could walk there but, what the hell. Get Hades for me, Will. I'll ride over. I've eaten far too much to walk comfortably.'

'Isn't Lieutenant Deaville on duty there, sir?' asked Will, wondering why the Captain had been told to go.

'He is, but Davenport's indulged in too much port and saw what a good time Megan appears to be having and said to leave the bugger be. So he sent me instead. Damn and blast it!' He scowled angrily. 'Well, get a move on, lad! Fetch Hades!'

Will went to where the horses were stabled and brought Hades back to the Captain whose mood had not improved whilst waiting. Camberwell mounted and brought the horse's head round to face Will. 'Watch Megan for me, Will,' he said, 'And that bastard Deaville. Hell! I wish Megan had never come. If there's any trouble, call James.'

'Right, sir.' Will watched as Richard Camberwell touched his spurs to the stallion's side and trotted out of the gateway. The sound of Hades's galloping hooves faded down the street outside.

Watch Megan, the Captain had said. Well he would right enough. With those words in mind, Will walked quietly back towards the bank of bushes that hid the orange grove. The thought came to him that he'd done a lot of spying on people since joining the army, but then had he not spent a great deal of his life in London doing just that? Not spying exactly, but watching and waiting for a good opportunity to snatch something. This wasn't so different. Stealthily he followed the narrow pathway through the shrubbery and paused by the first orange tree. Underneath another, some twenty paces away, was a bench, and the two he looked for were sitting on it. Although the sky was clear for once, the moonlit night was chilly and Will watched Paul Deaville take off his jacket and put it around Megan's shoulders. Then the lieutenant left one arm around the girl so that she leaned against him. A flash of jealousy sparked Will into moving closer, knowing instinctively what was going to happen next. He was right. The two talked a little, though Will could not hear their conversation, then Deaville turned Megan's face to his, and kissed her on the lips.

That was enough for Will. Without further thought, he ran from his hiding place towards the two. Before a startled Deaville could stop him, he pulled the man backwards so that he tumbled off the bench, then leapt on top of him, hitting and punching, all thought of his sore back forgotten in the heat of the moment. Megan screamed, then seeing it was Will, shouted at him to stop and ineffectually plucked at his clothing, trying to pull him off the officer who, once over his surprise at the suddenness of the attack, was now hitting back and swearing blue murder.

The fight was stopped by Captain Shaw and other officers, alerted by Megan's screams and Deaville's shouts. Will was yanked to his feet and his arms pinioned by a Major while Deaville stood up and brushed at his uniform in disgust. The fracas brought Lieutenant-Colonel Davenport who was not pleased to have his after dinner pleasures of conversation, port and cigars interrupted.

'Would someone mind telling me what is going on here?' he said angrily.

'This...this...brat attacked me!' shouted Deaville, pointing at Will. 'It was entirely unprovoked!'

'Bullshit! You kissed 'er!' Will struggled in the Major's grip, still angry and roaring with jealousy and hatred.

Some of the officers, having imbibed freely of the Lieutenant-Colonel's wine and port, chuckled, both at Will's vehemence for what they saw as a very trivial offence on Deaville's part, and at Deaville himself who was milking the situation for all it was worth, demanding that Will be court-martialled.

'Methinks the lad's in love,' muttered one wag to his neighbour. Realising that he was the cause of mirth only made Deaville more annoyed, and he lashed out angrily at Will who, unable to defend himself, felt the full force of a hefty punch on the cheek that sent his senses reeling. He slumped in the grip of the man who held him and was lucky to escape another punch but men pulled Deaville back and Lieutenant-Colonel Davenport snapped, 'That is quite enough, Lieutenant!' He looked at both Deaville and Will. 'Consider yourselves lucky that Wellington had to leave early. That two men under my command should act so, is reprehensible! Lieutenant, you are confined to your quarters for the remainder of the night.'

'But sir...'

'Enough Lieutenant!' Davenport turned a veined purple face to Will. 'And you, my lad, will be incarcerated in the garrison headquarters with the French until the morrow when you will be brought to my quarters and given a hearing. And that's more than you deserve! See to it, Major!' So saying, the Lieutenant-Colonel turned on his heel and marched back inside the house while Will's captor chivvied him off to the large building which housed the French prisoners.

† † †

Richard Camberwell had gone to the garrison headquarters earlier expecting to have to sort out some minor problem and it turned out he was right in his guesswork. One of the French officers, a Colonel, had thrown his underdone chicken at one of the British privates who had brought his supper and complained in no uncertain terms as to its disgusting taste and consistency. Voluble though he was, the private understood very little of the officer's rapid speech, although he did catch the word *vin*, which he knew meant wine, so guessed the man wanted some wine with his meal instead of the customary water. Grumbling under his breath, he found a half bottle of red wine and brought it to the officer who proceeded to smash the bottle on the floor to join the chicken, pointing and gesticulating until the man got the message that the wine would have been better employed making the chicken tasty. The Colonel ranted and raved so much that the private called his superior, who looked for Lieutenant Deaville, only to be told he was having dinner with the officers at Lieutenant-Colonel Davenport's lodgings. A boy was dispatched with a message that brought Captain Camberwell, grumpy at being summoned, and in no mood to deal with an irate prisoner, Colonel or no. Thus it was that he blasted the man from head to toe, told him he should be glad he was fed at all, and ordered him to clean up the mess himself under the supervision of the private who grinned like a Cheshire cat at the enemy's discomfiture.

Richard Camberwell was even more annoyed, not to mention surprised, when, on his way out of the prisoner's room, he came across a struggling Will being pushed into a small, bare, windowless room hardly bigger than a cupboard, containing only a chair, bucket and narrow cot.

'Quit lad, or it'll be the worse for you,' growled the gaoler, a short but stocky sergeant. He cuffed Will across the head.

'Calm down, Will,' said Camberwell, moving to intervene. Will noticed him for the first time and opened his mouth to speak, but Camberwell shook his head and glanced at the sergeant. Will got the message and sat on the bed. Camberwell summarily dismissed the sergeant and then demanded to hear his servant's story.

'I told you to keep an eye on Megan. Where is she?' he said coldly.

'Still at the Lieutenant-Colonel's 'ouse, I expect,' said Will dolefully. He told the Captain the whole sad tale. 'I'm sorry, sir,' he finished. I shouldn't've gone for the lieutenant like that...'

Camberwell sat heavily in the chair and the sigh he gave was deep and heartfelt. He glanced at Will with a more sympathetic eye. 'Will, I personally wouldn't care if you killed the man, especially if he was making free with Megan's affections,' he said. 'But you hit an officer and, as you know, that's a serious offence. Davenport let you off at Christmas, but then you were defending a lady from being beaten. Deaville was not beating Megan, he was only kissing her....the bastard! This time it's a lot more serious. Men have been hanged for less.'

Will paled. He knew it. And Paul Deaville would just love that.

299

Will had his own opinion as to who had put Amos Wilkins up to coming into his room at the brothel that night because he doubted Wilkins had the gumption to do it himself. Besides, how had he known that he and Megan were there? Deaville did, and could have told Wilkins. He had seen them whispering together in the baggage park, hadn't he? He knew they were acquainted. Deaville had been the officer who brought Wilkins to the army. But Will had no proof of any wrong doing and kept his suspicions to himself. Paul Deaville didn't like him and would be very pleased to see him hang.

'Isn't there anythin' I can do, sir?' he asked. For the first time since the incident he felt more scared than angry as the implications of his rash action were made clear.

'In civilised society, Deaville was taking liberties by kissing Megan,' conceded Camberwell, 'But that's not enough to warrant any punishment for him. Did he do anything else? If he did, I'll kill him myself.'

'No, sir. Not that I saw.' Will stared at the floor bleakly.

Camberwell spoke quietly and there was nearly as much desolation in his voice as in Will's expression. 'Will, did Megan appear to be enjoying his attentions?'

Will looked up and nodded. That was the worst part of all. Until Will had rushed in so dramatically, Megan had indeed been enjoying Lieutenant Deaville's kiss.

Richard Camberwell sighed, then something occurred to him that maybe should have been apparent for some time, if only he had taken the time and trouble to notice it. He took a long, hard look at his servant. 'You love her, don't you?' he said quietly.

Will nodded again, glumly.

'Do you think she loves you?'

'No, sir. I don't think she considers me good enough for 'er.'

Camberwell said nothing for a few moments. How should he react to Will's astonishing revelation? He supposed he should feel indignant, disapproving, even angry, that an urchin from the teeming streets of London should find his niece, a high-born Lady, so desirable. But to his own surprise all he felt was pleasure, tinged with very real sympathy for him. He was put in mind of his own misspent youth and the feelings he'd had for a certain little lady called Becky Forsythe, a local land-owner's daughter, and how he had sulked for weeks when she had shown a marked preference for

Jeremy Porter, a bounder of the worst order and a senior at his school. That had led to a fight too, he remembered, and he had been suspended from school for two weeks, and soundly beaten by his father. Now here was Will, unable to control his rage when he had seen the girl he loved being kissed by Deaville, who was undoubtedly as much of a cad as Jeremy Porter had been all those years ago.

He liked Will. The lad had taken to army life like a duck to water, was a wonder with the horses, and put up with his own temperamental moods and ill-graces without complaint. He wondered if Will was wrong in thinking that Megan didn't care for him too. He remembered how upset she had been when Will was wounded, how she had stayed by his side for days when he was in the throes of fever. But maybe that was just compassion for a friend. He supposed that Will would be attractive to women. His good looks were still youthful and would harden into rugged handsomeness as he got older, yet it had never occurred to him that Megan might think of him as a potential lover. She was far too fastidious and class conscious. But it was something to consider. In the meantime he had to think of a way to get Will out of the mess he had got himself into because for sure he did not want that bastard Deaville to be the means of getting the boy hanged. He set his mind to answer Will's earlier question as to what he should do.

'Davenport was not in a good mood tonight, Will. Food and congenial company are important to him and he hates to be disturbed at meal times. However, he is essentially a fair man, and maybe I can talk to him. Persuade him to see the incident for what it was; an impulsive act on your part. It really depends on how far Deaville wants to take it.'

'Oh, 'e'll take it all the way, sir,' said Will gloomily. ''E doesn't like me. Not after that set-to with Juanita back in the 'ills.'

Camberwell nodded ruefully. 'I fear you're right, lad.' He stood up. 'But try not to worry. I'll see what I can do. By the way. I suppose you've had no luck with finding out who our spy is? Not heard anything in the camp?'

'No, sir. Not a thing.'

'Hmm. Oh, well. It's probably not important now. Maybe the bastard who did it was killed in the attack on the walls. There are no immediate plans to give to the other side, and all the French officers are well tied up in here.' Lord Camberwell ruffled Will's

301

hair affectionately and smiled. 'Cheer up, lad, and behave yourself. I'll speak to Davenport in the morning. In the meantime, I'll see you have food and water.'

'Thank y' sir.'

'Until tomorrow then.'

'G'night, sir.'

Camberwell went, and the guard locked the door, leaving Will to his thoughts which were dismal in the extreme. His anger gone, all he could do was reflect ruefully on his actions and wonder if the next view he had of his friends and Megan was to be at his hanging.

† † †

The next morning Will was hauled before a hastily convened court that consisted of Lieutenant-Colonel Davenport, two majors, two captains including Richard Camberwell, Lieutenant Deaville and a sergeant who was to act as scribe. Megan waited outside the room in the local courthouse, taken over by the British for their own use for the duration, and agitatedly paced the hallway. Guilt was overwhelming the anger she had felt when Will had attacked Paul Deaville; anger because she knew Will must have been spying on her, and because he had spoilt what was undoubtedly a very pleasant evening. Since then she had learned from her uncle that Will had been there at his insistence which had, at first, made her even more annoyed, but then when she heard that Will had been imprisoned for his actions, remorse set in. Besides, she thought she knew exactly why Will had behaved in such a fashion. He loved her and was jealous. Now she wanted to tell the court that it was all her uncle's fault because he did not like Lieutenant Deaville, but Camberwell assured her he would do that himself.

He did so, but the telling only made matters worse because Deaville who, Will was pleased to note, sported a black eye and bruised cheek, was outraged that the captain should interfere in his private affairs, though not surprised as he knew Camberwell did not like his attentiveness towards Megan. He blustered and shouted and said he had had no intention of compromising Lady Megan in any way. Hands tied, Will sat to one side of the room and was not called upon to say anything at all until right at the end of the hearing, which in a way was just as well because he might have had to admit his love for Megan, something he would rather not do in public. Davenport, grumbling that he always seemed to have to convene these hearings after a particularly uncomfortable and nearly sleepless night due to his digestive troubles, asked short questions, merely grunted at the replies, and gave the impression that he wanted done with the whole business as soon as possible.

Having heard from several witnesses, officers who attested to the fact that they had seen Will brawling on the ground with Deaville and giving him 'a right good thumping, sir' as one man put it, and with Richard Camberwell putting in his bit about him getting carried away in the heat of the moment, Davenport asked Will to stand.

'Private Tucker,' he said. 'Let us not forget that even in this God-forsaken country we must uphold British justice. That being so, have you anything to say in your defence?'

'No, sir.'

'Your reasons for attacking Lieutenant Deaville still seem a little unclear,' said Davenport. 'Why did you attack him so vehemently?'

'I thought he was goin' to go further than kissin' Lady Camberwell, sir.'

Davenport's purple-veined face almost broke into a smile. 'Might it not have been better to have waited to see what transpired, young man, before charging in like St George?' he said to chuckles from the watching officers.

Will reddened. 'P'r'aps, sir,' he said.

Will knew his real reason for attacking Deaville, but he was not about to admit it here. Let them think what they liked. He didn't care. Megan was safe. That's all that mattered.

Davenport sighed. He remembered this lad. He was the one who, with Camberwell, had repelled an ambush on the way from Oporto, and since then had acquitted himself well in the attack on the redoubt. By all accounts a good soldier. There had also been that business back in December, again concerning Lieutenant Deaville if he remembered rightly. Maybe there was some long-term animosity here. Still, the army needed more like this lad and it was a pity, a great pity, that he had to sentence him. But sentence him he must.

'Do you, or do you not, admit to hitting Lieutenant Deaville?' he said gravely, stifling a loud burp that eased his acute indigestion for

303

a few minutes at least.

'Yes, sir,' said Will.

'Then I have no choice but to imprison you, and recommend your discharge from His Majesty's forces,' said Davenport rather sadly. 'You will remain here until you can be sent back to Lisbon, and thence to England where you will be incarcerated in a prison hulk off Portsmouth with others of your ilk.' There was an explosive noise from Deaville who looked as though he was about to object and ask for a hanging, until he received a black look from Davenport and said nothing.

'But sir...' Will turned an anguished face towards Captain Camberwell who returned the look with one that was much the same.

'That will do, lad,' said Davenport, not unkindly. 'You were given your chance to speak. Just be thankful I have not involved Wellington who might well have demanded your neck, and that I am not in favour of flogging or you might have come out of this much worse. I tend to think it was a matter of over-exuberance on your part in trying to follow your master's orders, but it does not excuse your actions.' He turned towards Richard Camberwell. 'And Captain, may I say that although your concern for your niece's welfare does you credit, I feel that the person you should take that up with is the man involved, and not to put spies on the poor bastard's trail!' The officers chuckled again while Captain Camberwell scowled. Davenport turned to one of the majors. 'See that he's taken back to the garrison barracks, Major.'

'Yes, sir.'

On leaving the room, Will encountered Megan who ran after him shouting, 'Oh, Will! I'm so sorry,' before collapsing, sobbing, in Richard Camberwell's arms. Even more surprising was the reaction of a large crowd that had gathered outside the building. Ginny was there, with, it seemed, half the women from the camp, and a good many off-duty soldiers including George and Nat Binns. Ginny led a chant of 'Free him! Free him!' and, with her umbrella, threatened to attack the senior officers who left the court-house after Will, until she and the rest of the crowd were moved off, still shouting, by other officers.

'Amazing!' said Davenport to his aide-de-camp as they mounted their horses. 'Who would have thought so many people would care?'

'He's a popular lad, sir,' said Sergeant Readman who had

watched the proceedings from the back of the room and was standing nearby, angry at the outcome. 'Good soldier too. Promisin' lad and a good example to the men.'

'Not when he fights officers, Sergeant,' said Davenport sourly, grimacing at the pain that wracked his stomach again. He pulled on the reins, wheeling the horse to the right. 'Damn it! If I don't get something for this bloody indigestion of mine soon, I'll not be fit to eat dinner tonight!' So saying he touched his spurs to the bay's flanks and rode off while Will, on his way back to his tiny room at the garrison headquarters, had never felt so desolate, or so alone.

22

Will spent a sleepless night on the thin hard mattress in the small room, listening to moans and groans from the prisoner in the room next door and worrying about his situation while very much regretting his impulsiveness. He had not missed the smirk on Paul Deaville's face before he had once more been dragged off to the garrison barracks, nor the explosive noise the lieutenant had made when he was sentenced that told him Deaville had been hoping for a hanging. He had Richard Camberwell to thank for saving his neck, he supposed. The Captain had done his best to mitigate the circumstances and lay the blame on his own shoulders, only to become a laughing stock himself, but it seemed that Lieutenant-Colonel Davenport had listened to him, and taken note. Little did he know that it was Davenport's own opinion of him, as well as Camberwell's input, that had saved his life, if not his career.

For another day and a night Will suffered the indignity of imprisonment. Somehow Megan gained permission to visit him, though it was a tortuous experience for both of them as she spent most of the time crying, and her evident need to blame herself only made Will more miserable.

Richard Camberwell came to see him, and said he was going to see Wellington to try and obtain a pardon, but Will knew as well as the Captain that such a thing would be almost impossible to achieve as Wellington was a stickler for discipline, and hitting an officer was high on the commander-in-chief's list of deadly sins.

The private in charge of bringing food to the prisoners was an amiable soul by the name of Barney Crabbit. Seeing that Will was not eating much of the poor food, which was not the same as that eaten by the French officers incarcerated in the building, he tried to encourage him, saying that he would do well to keep his strength up. Whilst bringing him a late breakfast on the second day, he told Will of the night a French Colonel had thrown a plate of chicken at him, the same night Will was arrested, and the reason Richard Camberwell had been called away from Davenport's dinner.

'There was nothin' wrong with the bloody chicken,' complained Crabbit. 'Hell, the Frogs get better food than their gaolers, so they do!' He grinned suddenly, showing a wide gap where his front teeth should have been. 'Yon Captain Camberwell made the bugger clean it up 'imself while I watched. But all the bastard did all night was complain of stomach ache. He still is.' He leaned close to Will, sending a wave of halitosis into his face that made Will draw back from him. 'Cleaned off some of the bird and ate it meself,' he admitted. 'Didn't do anythin' bad to me, an' it 'ad been on the floor. Reckon the Frenchie's got summat else wrong with 'im. They're bringin' the doctor to look at 'im today. 'E's in the room next door.' That explained the moans he had frequently heard, thought Will.

'Tell you what,' said Crabbit, who, for all his faults which included stealing food meant for the officers, was a kindly man. 'I'll see if there's any of the beef left over from the Frenchies' dinner. Don't worry. It won't be from their plates, though I reckon you've 'ad worse afore now, ain't yer?' Will admitted that he had. 'I allus keeps a bit back for me own supper. Won't be long.' So saying, the man scuttled out of the room while Will sank despondently onto the bed. He sighed deeply, then saw something that made him perk up. Crabbit had carelessly left the door ajar. Hope surged for the first time in two days. He went to it and cautiously peered out, then pulled back quickly because Paul Deaville was striding up the staircase a few yards away on the opposite side of the hallway.

Will stayed behind the door and heard Deaville stop beside the next door along, the room in which the French Colonel was imprisoned. He unlocked it and there followed a hushed conversation. Something about Deaville's furtiveness put Will's senses on full alert and peering round the door once more, he saw that the hallway and staircase were empty, so he sidled along the wall towards the next doorway and listened carefully. Though he couldn't catch all the words, what he did overhear made his heart race with excitement. The two were plotting an escape.

In that instant, Will determined to take full advantage of the fact that Crabbit had left his cell unlocked. He would escape too and find out what Paul Deaville was up to.

He crept to the staircase. There was no one in sight so he sped silently down it, and found himself in another hallway. Voices drifted towards him. Quickly he searched for somewhere to hide. A very large pot containing some exotic plant stood in the corner so he ducked behind it. Two officers strode down the hall, laughing and talking. They walked right past Will's hiding place. Waiting until they had gone, he was about to emerge when he saw Crabbit coming from the same direction, a plate in his hand. Damn! His escape would be discovered any minute! Nerves jangling, Will waited for the soldier to go round the bend in the staircase on his way upstairs, then he scampered along the hall until he came to an open window. Within seconds he was through it and away into the street.

By the time Barney Crabbit started a hue and cry a few minutes later, Will was safely inside a fire-rotted tenement two streets away, reflecting that his escape had been surprisingly easy. He sat on the floor against a smoke-blackened wall and tried to think what to do next. That he had made his case worse was obvious. Even if by some miracle Richard Camberwell obtained his pardon for hitting Paul Deaville, he had compounded his felony by escaping from custody and would be hung if caught. His thoughts turned to what he had overheard, then an idea suddenly occurred to him. What if the officer next door was faking illness to facilitate his escape? He might, especially after what Crabbit had said about there being nothing wrong with the supposedly-bad chicken. All thought of his own problems disappeared in the face of this exciting possibility. It was clear what he should do. He would stay under cover for a while then go back and watch for the doctor's arrival and see what happened. All he had to do was to take great care not to be captured again, and with his background as a petty thief in the streets of London, that should not be too difficult. Blending into the background had been second nature then, though he had to admit he'd not been the subject of a serious hue and cry before. Anyway, he thought, there probably wouldn't be too much fuss made about his escape.

In this he was wrong. When Crabbit informed the proper authorities, Davenport ordered that several patrols be set up to hunt him down. Thus it was that, despite his skills, Will had the devil of a job evading them while making his way back to the garrison headquarters, and had to take long detours before reaching it that afternoon. He waited inside a nearby deserted shop for an hour before a horse-drawn carriage pulled up at the gates, driven by a man with a large bag whom he supposed was the doctor. Will had spent his hours of freedom wisely by stealing trousers and a shirt from a washing line, bundling his uniform into a sheet, and hiding it in a culvert. Smearing his face with dirt, he looked like any of the peasant boys roaming the streets, except for his hair. He knew the brightness of it would give him away, so he had smeared that with dirt too, then had been lucky enough to find an old discarded woollen cap near the culvert, and that hid his dirty blond locks nicely. Unless someone looked closely enough to see his blue eyes, he would never be taken for an Englishman. Now, filthy, barefoot and unkempt, he crept out of the wrecked shop and boldly held the horse of an off-duty officer who was upstairs in the tavern that boasted the best whores in Ciudad Rodrigo. It was right opposite the garrison headquarters and allowed Will a better view. Soldiers passed him by without a second glance. Besides, he thought as he stood with the horse, who would think an escaped prisoner would be stupid enough to return to the scene of his imprisonment?

He had only been there a short while when the doctor walked out of the gates again, closely followed by two soldiers helping a man who Will guessed was the French Colonel. The carriage, now with the doctor and prisoner aboard, rattled off towards the convent hospital. Will looped the horse's reins around a convenient tree, and followed, careful not to get too close. This was something he was good at and he had no trouble, though he kept a wary eye open for anyone who might know him. He saw a lot of soldiers, but they took absolutely no notice of him at all, taking him for a peasant boy, one of the many urchins who annoyed the troops and were best ignored.

Dusk was approaching by the time the carriage pulled up outside the hospital. The doctor called for assistance, and the French Colonel was helped inside. From his place in the shadows of a darkened doorway across the road, Will wondered what to do next. He still had the gut feeling that the Frenchman was faking his illness, but how to prove it? There was no way he could get inside the hospital without arousing suspicion. His stomach rumbled and reminded him that he'd had no food since the bowl of gruel Crabbit had brought him that morning. Well, first he would find himself something to eat, then tomorrow he would find Paul Deaville because he was as sure as he could be that the lieutenant was scheming something. Following him would maybe lead to the truth.

Keeping to the shadows, Will moved silently away to search for some supper.

Richard Camberwell was an angry man. He had been roused from a late breakfast with the message that had come from the army's temporary headquarters telling him that his ex-servant had escaped the prison barracks. He had searched the streets himself all day, hoping to come across Will before the provosts found him, but to no avail.

'Damn the boy! What the hell does he think he's playing at?! He's just making everything worse!' he raged at Megan. She was still so upset at Will's incarceration, that he had managed to persuade her to dine with himself and James Shaw that evening, in order to discuss the matter.

Megan, who adversely felt a leap of hope at the news, said, 'Will can't stand being cooped up, uncle. He's used to being free.'

'We all are, Meg, but he's done himself a great disservice by escaping because when he's found, as he must be eventually, he'll hang for sure this time, and nothing I can say or do will get him out of it.'

Megan thought she knew Will better than her uncle did, and wasn't so sure that Will would be found, despite being in a town full of soldiers who would be looking for him. He would probably have been up and away before they had even set up patrols. Then her heart fell at the thought that she might never see him again, and tears blurred her eyes.

Camberwell saw them and his anger evaporated a little, thinking that it was his harsh words as to Will's fate that had brought them to the surface. 'Don't cry, Meg, dear,' he said. 'Will was a hard worker and a good soldier, but he's done this to himself...'

'Don't say 'was'!' Megan rounded on him, her damp eyes now blazing with fury. 'He still is! Will's the best person I know and I wish I had never set eyes on Paul Deaville because it was me who got him into trouble in the first place! I'm glad he's escaped and he will get away, I know it!' So saying she turned on her heel and walked out, leaving her supper untouched and her uncle looking bemused.

'So that's how it is,' he said to himself. 'Will's feelings are returned, I think, though my capricious niece may not realise it.' He smiled suddenly, remembering his first encounter with Will, when he had not even realised the boy was there at all and relieving him of a purse full of money. 'And I think she may be right. I have a feeling Will is going to be a difficult lad to catch, and there are at least two of us who hope he won't be!'

† † †

Will spent the night in the culvert where he had hidden his clothes, snatching fitful sleep. He put on his uniform over the stolen items to keep out the cold, but still shivered. He had stolen food from the bins behind a baker's shop; half a stale loaf and a squashed pastry. At least the cold kept the bugs away, he thought as he ate them, together with an apple he had found in the gutter, dropped from a fruit seller's basket. He drank water from a butt behind a house, but it tasted foul and he toyed with the idea of going to the tavern to see if he could steal some wine, but was too tired to walk back there. Keeping out of sight of the British soldiers had taken its toll mentally and physically, and he needed to rest. Tomorrow he would seek out Paul Deaville and follow him, find out what he was up to. And he would also try to ascertain the condition of the French Colonel, though that would prove more difficult.

He was up and about before dawn, stealing like a wraith through the misty streets, on the lookout for anything to eat that might still his grumbling stomach. Since joining the army, Will had got used to being fed at more-or-less regular intervals and he thought that now he would have to get used to semi-starvation again but he was lucky that morning. In an alleyway behind a tavern he came upon dogs scavenging in the bins. Shooing them away and rummaging himself, he found an almost uneaten piece of beef on a leg bone that was probably what the curs had smelled and had drawn them to the place. Thanking his lucky stars that he had found it before they did, Will gnawed on it hungrily. It was tough, which was almost certainly the reason for it not being eaten for someone's supper, but for Will it was pure gold.

On hearing noises in the tavern's back rooms that indicated someone was awake, he slipped out of the alley and made his way to the garrison prison where he hid behind the stables, watching for Paul Deaville to come and collect his horse. He was startled by a thin stick of a man who appeared to be in charge of the stables and demanded to know what he was doing there, but Will by dint of mime and guttural sounds, made out he was dumb and was a new stable lad. None the wiser, the groom handed him a pitchfork and told him to muck out the stalls. Thus Will was there when Paul Deaville strode into the stables to demand his horse sometime later that morning.

Less than ten feet away from the lieutenant, Will covertly watched him while keeping his head down and sweeping dirty straw from the stable yard. Deaville looked as though he had spent a rough night. His eyes were bloodshot, his complexion sallow, and he was impatient, shouting at the thin man, and tapping his booted foot on the cobbles, finally hauling himself into the saddle and riding off without so much as a thank you. Will waited until the groom's back was turned then scampered off after him, catching sight of the lieutenant as he turned the corner at the end of the plaza.

Deaville was not travelling fast. Early morning pedestrians, donkey carts, and peasants delivering fruit and vegetables got in his way, and he laid about him vigorously with a cane. In fact, Will thought as he hurried along behind him, he would have done better to walk, because it became obvious that Deaville's destination was the convent which was not that far away. When he reached it, he flipped an urchin a coin to hold the horse's reins while he went inside. Will was wondering how to find out what he was doing in there when he was elbowed aside by two men carrying an unconscious boy bleeding from the head. The boy's mother and, it seemed, the rest of his large family, followed closely behind, the woman and girls wailing in Spanish. Will took his chance, and added himself to the throng.

311

Once inside the convent he followed the family along a corridor. The hospital was not the same mad place it was on the night of the attack but was still busy, and British soldiers guarded it, what against, Will wasn't sure. Coming to a cross-roads of corridors, he left the wailing group and went the other way, wondering how he was to find Deaville, or the French Colonel.

Rounding another corner, he was suddenly grabbed by the arm and pulled into a small room filled with furniture removed from other parts of the convent to make room for the wounded. 'Will! What are you doing here? Everyone's looking for you!'

Trying to still his thudding heart that the surprise attack had given him, Will stared into the face of Sarah Harvey, wide-eyed and shocked. 'God, Sarah!... Yer didn't 'arf give me a bloody fright!' he stammered. ''Ow did yer know it was me?'

'I've seen you without your uniform, remember, on the ship, and you were almost as dirty then,' she answered with a smile. 'Besides, you can disguise your looks, but you can't hide your walk or mannerisms so easily.' She looked serious again as she said, 'I can understand you wanting to escape, Will, but what are you doing here?'

'I'm watchin' someone,' said Will, unwilling to reveal his actions and suspicions even to Sarah.

Sarah's small face was serious as she said, 'There are patrols everywhere. Why are you still in town? You must get out at once.'

'I can't, Sarah. There's somethin' I 'ave ter do.'

'What?'

Will wondered what to say. He had no proof that Paul Deaville was helping a French prisoner escape. 'I can't tell yer,' he said at last.

Sarah looked at him quizzically. 'Don't give me away, Sarah. Please,' he said.

'Of course not,' she replied. 'Are you hungry?'

'No. I found food.'

'What are you going to do next?'

Will's mind was racing. Maybe Sarah discovering him was the best thing that could have happened. He decided to tell her why he was there. 'I 'ave ter find someone in the 'ospital,' he said. 'A Frenchman.'

Sarah's eyebrows flew up. 'A Frenchman? What for?'

Oh, why did girls have to ask so many questions? 'I just do, Sarah. Will yer 'elp me?'

'Yes.' Sarah caught the urgency in his voice and her eyes lit up with excitement. Whatever Will's agenda was, he was a friend, and she would do all she could. 'Who is it?'

'I don't know 'is name. I only know 'e was brought 'ere last night from the prison barracks with a bad stomach ache.'

'Oh, I know the one you mean! He's a Colonel. His name's Reynard. Jean Reynard, I think.'

'Is 'e sick? I mean really sick?'

'Well he certainly seems to be. He eats nothing and seems to be in pain. The doctor's going to examine him this morning. Why do you want to see him?' she asked again.

'Please, Sarah. The less yer know the better,' he answered. 'Where is 'e?'

'In one of the wards upstairs. He wanted a separate room but of course, there are none.'

Will thought for a moment. 'I need ter be able ter move around. Any ideas?'

'Well we have plenty of people helping out, townsfolk as well as army,' said Sarah. She studied him carefully. 'You do look like a peasant dressed like that and with that hat on. Maybe you could pretend to be one of the orderlies, but you'd have to be careful if you see anyone you know. They might recognise you like I did.'

Will nodded. 'Come on.' Sarah took his hand and peered out of the door. Two soldiers were helping a bandaged comrade down the hallway, and a woman bustled past carrying a bowl which wafted a horrible stink at them. After they had gone, Sarah and Will left the room. Nearby stood a dirty mop. She thrust it into his hands.

'There's a tap outside at the back with buckets next to it,' she said. 'Go and get one, then you can go around mopping the floors.' Her face screwed up. 'It's not a nice job. Do you think you can handle it without throwing up?'

'Yes.' Will had not lived in the filthy tenements of London town without seeing some awful sights, and his experiences since then had hardened him further. He bussed Sarah on the cheek, and grinned. 'Thanks, Sarah,' he said, then he was gone, whistling cheerfully down the corridor towards an outside door. Sarah watched him go, and hoped with all her heart, that the last sight she had of him would not be at the end of a hangman's rope.

For most of the morning Will wandered around the convent hospital with a bucket of water, mopping floors. He frequently had to empty the bucket of dirty, bloody water and soon knew his way around well. As Sarah had warned him, it was a horrible job. There was more than blood on the floor, but he did it dispassionately, keeping eyes and ears open all the time for someone who knew him. To be caught now would be the end.

It was nearly noon before he found the Frenchman he was looking for. Sarah's information as to his whereabouts had not meant he would have easy access to him. Because he was a French prisoner, he was under guard by a British soldier and to make matters worse, Will knew him to be a soldier from his own Company, and a man who might well recognise him. Will kept his distance, mopping the floor at the other end of the big, square room, looking earnestly at the floor if the soldier at the door happened to look his way. He had only got past the man by sneaking in with some nuns come to give the sufferers spiritual succour.

He was lucky enough to be in the room when the harassed British doctor came to examine the Frenchman. Poking and prodding to loud groans from the prisoner, he pronounced himself baffled and left the man with orders for the women acting as nurses to give him castor oil and watch his bowel movements closely. Will smiled to himself, and was about to take his chance and leave with the doctor, when Paul Deaville came into the room, holding a scented handkerchief to his nose against the all pervading stink.

Will sidled into the furthest corner of the room, next to the bed of a soldier who appeared to be asleep and who had his left leg encased in plaster and a bandage round his head. He watched as Deaville bent his head to talk quietly to Reynard who, eyes closed, acted as though unaware of the lieutenant's presence, but Will guessed he was listening carefully. Will glanced at the door to see that the soldier on duty there had disappeared. He moved slowly towards it himself, getting ever closer to Deaville, carrying the bucket. As close as he dared, he put it down in the narrow corridor between the rows of beds and tried to overhear the conversation which was going on in very low tones.

All he could hear were the words 'tonight' and 'dead', but then Will's sharp eyes caught Deaville surreptitiously pushing a small

bag under the blankets before moving away, still with the handkerchief held to his face, leaving the Frenchman with eyes closed and
as still as before. Will desultorily swished the mop around and
wondered what the words could mean. Did Reynard think he was
going to die? He certainly didn't look very ill. His face was as ruddy
as Sergeant Readman's. And what had Deaville hidden under the
blankets?

A sidelong glance at the apparently sleeping Frenchman gave
no clue to the frustrating puzzle and Will was wondering whether
or not to follow Deaville again in the hope of getting some insight
into the matter, when another glance at the Colonel stopped him
dead. Still lying on his back, the Frenchman's eyes were open, and
he was looking about him furtively. Will kept his eyes averted and
pushed the mop further towards the other side of the room. No
orderlies or any of the medical staff were at this end of the room
except for himself. Sneaking another look from under the greasy
wool of his cap, Will was amazed to see that the Frenchman was
now hiding his face under the bed clothes. Will stared until there
was movement and the Frenchman's head appeared again. Will
turned away, but a mere glance had shown him that the Frenchman's face was now considerably paler than it had been before.

Pushing the mop and carrying the bucket, Will moved towards
the doorway, wondering what it was he had just seen. The prisoner's face had just changed from that of a man in rude health to one
approaching death. Then light dawned, and he realised what had
happened. He grinned. Taking care to avoid the bored stare of the
soldier now back on guard duty at the door, and who, fortunately,
appeared to have other things on his mind than a peasant cleaner,
Will almost skipped out of the room. He knew now that his guesswork had been right. Deaville and Reynard were planning something.

Dragging the bucket and sloshing filthy water along the corridor in his haste to get towards the staircase that led to the lower
floor and outside, Will's mind raced, his imagination working
overtime, but his gut told him that what he was thinking was right.

It had been flour, plain ordinary flour, that Paul Deaville had
passed to the French prisoner, and Reynard had rubbed some into
his skin to give it a deathly pallor and make himself appear more ill.
Maybe as the day wore on, he would make his face even paler until,

315

by tonight he could be taken for dead, or nearly so. If Paul Deaville came to take him away, and the doctors, being too busy to care if the man were alive or dead, were unaware, then Deaville could devise some means of helping the man escape. Afraid of cholera or typhoid, any unexplained stomach problem was bound to worry the doctors and they would probably be relieved to see the back of the Frenchman.

Will left the bucket and mop against an outside wall and melted into the streets again, wondering what to do next. It occurred to him to tell someone of his suspicions, maybe Captain Camberwell, but the story sounded so far-fetched that even he had trouble believing it. No, he must find Deaville and follow him. Keep an eye on him all day, then when he was more sure that freeing Reynard was the Englishman's intention, he could maybe tell someone in charge.

Following Deaville's movements proved difficult because he was in the company of fellow officers and Will only caught up with him later in the afternoon. Although supposedly one of the officers in charge at the garrison barracks where the prisoners were held, Deaville contrived not to be there at all, but spent a large part of the day in a tavern playing whist, eating, and drinking heavily. Will could not hang around, either inside or out, for fear of being recognised by off-duty soldiers who frequented the place, or told to move on by the tavern owner, but managed to pass by several times to ascertain that the lieutenant was still inside. Once during the afternoon he saw George and Nat leading horses carrying net bags of fodder towards the British lines and was very tempted to call out to them. The sight of his friends brought home to Will the very real state of loneliness he found himself in. He could rely on no one in the army for if they did not report him, then they could easily make difficulties for themselves and he did not wish to get his friends into trouble.

However, as the day wore on, Will wondered what he could do by himself. That there was nothing wrong with the Frenchman appeared obvious to him, and should Deaville manage to somehow get the man outside the gates, then it would be himself against the two of them. They would be armed whereas he had nothing, not even a knife. No, once he was sure, he would have to tell someone. But who?

Strolling past the tavern for perhaps the fifth time that day, glancing in at the doorway to see Paul Deaville still lounging drunkenly at the same table, Will pondered the problem and the only person to come to mind was Megan, yet his mind shied away from involving her in something so dangerous. And there was no surety that she would believe him, or even take his side. He remembered the kisses the girl had shared with Deaville. She obviously liked the man, and might not want to believe ill of him. Will didn't think she would turn him in to the authorities, but would she believe him?

His thinking was disrupted by Paul Deaville suddenly appearing in the tavern's doorway, supported by other officers equally as drunk as he, though they all tried to comport themselves with some sort of dignity in case a senior officer should come by. Being drunk on duty was severely frowned upon by army officialdom. The cold air helped them achieve a reasonable level of sobriety and they pulled themselves together enough to stagger the short distance to the garrison headquarters.

Will followed at a distance but was careful not to get too close to the building itself. The last thing he needed was to be taken prisoner again. Deaville and his cronies went inside and Will, standing in a doorway to be out of the cold wind, had nothing to do but wait.

It was well over an hour before Paul Deaville made another appearance. By that time Will was thoroughly bored, and so cold that no amount of foot stamping made any difference to the numbness in his limbs. He nearly didn't see the officer because, when he appeared, Deaville was dressed in civilian clothes, and not too clean ones at that. The guard at the gate stared at him strangely as he walked past. It appeared that Deaville was not completely sober for he swayed slightly, but managed to walk with an air of nonchalant indifference that changed to one of furtive secrecy once he left the plaza. Will followed, glad of something to do at last.

Deaville walked down several streets and alleyways, none of which went anywhere near the hospital or the houses where the British officers stayed, and Will was curious as to his destination, hoping that he was not being taken on a fool's errand. However, Deaville finally stopped at a decrepit building which proved to be an ostler's, and haggled with the owner for the use of a horse and cart. Will watched from the shadows, excitement mounting. What on earth would Paul Deaville want with such a thing, if not for some clandestine activity? They could be had for the asking from the army baggage train.

His transaction done, Deaville climbed onto the driver's seat and drove the cart out of the yard and down the street. Will had to walk quickly to keep up but was glad to note that the officer was making for the convent hospital. On arrival, Deaville ordered an urchin to hold the horse and went inside.

It was some time later that he appeared again and this time he was not alone. Two men carried a third. Will instinctively knew the third man was Reynard, though he could not see his face, so bundled up in blankets was he. So, Deaville had obviously given the doctors some story in order to release Reynard to his charge, Will thought as he watched them load the Colonel onto the cart. They were probably glad to see the back of a man with some unidentifiable disease. He would have liked to have seen how pale the Frenchman had made his face now, but the blankets hid any sign.

Will was in a quandary and cursed the afternoon's inactivity. He should have told someone his suspicions – anyone. Now there was no one to tell who might possibly believe him. Yet... Suddenly he remembered Sarah. She was in this very building. Surely she would pass a message on.

Hurriedly he ran into the hospital, scampering between walking wounded, orderlies and nurses, some of whom shouted after him. Drawing attention to himself was not what he'd wanted, but he had to find Sarah. He ran to the room where he had seen her the previous day, but she was not there. Looking up and down the corridor he saw a man coming towards him, an army surgeon, and ran towards him. 'Sir! Sir. Could you please tell me where Miss Sarah 'Arvey is?' Too late Will recognised the surgeon who had operated on him.

The man with the rheumy, bloodshot eyes stared at him, but Will gave him no time to do anything but answer the question. 'Miss 'Arvey, sir. D'you know where she is?'

'Aye, lad. She's upstairs in the ward with the amputees...hey, wait! Don't I know...?'

Will ignored him and pelted up the nearest staircase, running into rooms until he came to a ward where a man with only one arm was sitting on a chair near the doorway. He stepped inside, swallowed at the sight of so many one-legged or one-armed soldiers, and looked around for Sarah. There she was at the other end of the room, feeding a man with no arms. The room stank of putrefaction and other unmentionable odours, but Will was so inured to the stink of illness and death that he hardly noticed any more. What he did notice though was that another girl stood beside Sarah. It was Megan.

Both girls turned amazed eyes on Will when he appeared at their side and said urgently in a low voice, 'I 'ave to talk to you! Please! It's an emergency!'

'Will! What are you doing here? You must get away! The army's still looking for you!' Megan looked aghast, but her heart was pounding and two red spots on her cheeks betrayed her pleasure at seeing him, dirty, bedraggled, but alive.

'Please! It's important!' Will was hopping from foot to foot in his eagerness to be gone. He had to follow Deaville otherwise he might let Reynard get away and now he would have to trust Megan with the tale.

Sarah, seeing his agitation, told a nearby orderly to continue feeding the wounded soldier while she and Megan hustled Will into a more secluded alcove, away from any listening ears.

'What is it, Will?' she said.

In whispers he told them briefly what he thought Deaville was up to. At first Megan looked sceptical, but Will seemed so sincere, and she knew he would not put his own life on the line by coming for their help if he did not think it true.

'What can we do?' she asked.

'Tell your uncle. Tell 'im what I saw and 'eard in the barracks and 'ere at the 'ospital. I think Deaville'll 'ave everyone think Reynard is dead and will 'elp 'im escape tonight.'

'But how will Uncle Richard know where to find you?'

Will thought about this, then Megan said, 'I'll come with you, Will. Sarah can tell Uncle Richard what's going on, then if we find out more, I can go and tell him.'

'No. It's too dangerous. Apart from the fact that yer mustn't be on the streets at night, I'm an escaped prisoner. If I'm caught, they'll arrest yer too.'

Megan's eyes looked more alive than they had done for weeks.

319

The prospect of adventure was heady. 'I'm coming with you, Will,' she said in a low but firm voice that brooked no argument. 'You'll go and find my uncle, won't you, Sarah?' Megan was determined that now Will was with her again, she was not going to let him go. All the trauma of his wound and his imprisonment had left her depressed and anxious, and had made her realise, at last, just how much she really cared for him.

'Yes, of course, but Will is right, Megan. You can't go!' Sarah was shocked at the very thought.

'I can and I will.' The mutinous expression on Megan's face reminded Will of a stable in England and a girl who insisted on going to war. It would seem that life with the army had not completely cured her of being stubborn. He gave in because there was no time to argue.

'All right then. Please 'urry, Sarah, but get an escort. It's gettin' late. 'Ave the Captain secure all the gates with extra men and tell 'em to search all carts leavin' the town. And thanks.' He turned to go, but Megan put a hand on Sarah's arm.

'Please tell my uncle alone, Sarah. I don't think he'll give away Will's whereabouts, but others might.'

Sarah nodded and gave her friend a hug, telling her to take care, then Will and Megan hurried down the ward to the stairs. Soldiers were coming up them, presumably to visit a friend, laughing and talking together. Will turned round and walked the other way but Megan carried on as though nothing had happened, greeting the one or two that she knew, receiving admiring looks from the others, for Megan, even in a plain dress and cloak with no fripperies, was a girl who turned heads.

When the men had disappeared into the ward, Will turned round again and made for the staircase, eventually joining Megan outside the front door.

'Where to?' she asked.

There were several gates in the town walls, but Will knew they were all heavily guarded by British soldiers. Privates had to have a reason for entering and leaving the town. Most, unless on duty there, were meant to be in the British camp outside. Will, however, knew that, at present, he looked nothing like a British soldier and wondered if he could pass himself off to the guards as a peasant. That posed another problem though because the town's inhabitants weren't allowed out either without a pass, and then only in the day time. And which exit would Paul Deaville use?

Then his wits and imagination came to the fore again. Of course! Having Colonel Reynard all bundled up in blankets in the back of the cart, Deaville could pretend that the man was a corpse for burial. He would use the gate nearest the burial grounds. Without a word he pulled Megan by the arm and began to run through the streets.

'Where are we going?' Megan panted as she ran, trying to keep up with him. Will did not answer her. The streets and alleys were black with shadows now that the sun was fading. Who knew what dangers lurked there? She began to feel afraid, and ran faster to keep up with Will, though her side was already hurting with the stitch.

At last Will slowed and pulled Megan into an alley. She opened her mouth to ask why they had stopped, but Will put a filthy hand over her face and she stared round-eyed as an army patrol marched past the entrance. Movement behind them told her they were not alone and her eyes darted to the darkness but she could see nothing. Something brushed past her skirt and if Will's hand had not been over her mouth she would have screamed, but it was only a rat.

Will dropped his hand and they were running again. Megan held Will's hand, afraid to let go. She had never been to this part of the town before. It was a maze of narrow streets with houses squashed together, their roofs nearly meeting over the fetid alleys. Babies wailed, men's voices raised in anger, women's shouts and laughter came and went as they darted between the buildings, Will's sharp eyes forever on the lookout for soldiers. Smells of food mingled with the stink of confined humanity.

At last they came within sight of the gate that led out to the flat pastures the British were using as a burial ground. They could already smell it, the stench of death.

Guards were on the gate, not, fortunately, from Will's own Company but there was a detachment of soldiers with a sergeant in charge. There was no sign of Paul Deaville. Of course, Will thought, he may have misread the man's intentions, and he could have made for another gate altogether, but some strong instinct told him that he was right, and that this was the one.

Somehow they would have to get past the guards, and he still

321

needed a weapon of sorts. Deaville was not likely to give up without a fight. There would be no guilt involved on Will's side if he had to pit himself against the lieutenant. He looked around for a clue as to what to do next but, to his surprise, Megan pulled him into the shadows of a doorway and took something from the folds of her cloak.

'If you're looking for a weapon, Will, I have this.' She produced a wicked looking knife.

Will stared at it, and then at her. 'Uncle Richard makes me carry it all the time. Just in case,' she said. She handed it to him and he stuffed it inside his shirt. It was cold against his skin, but the knowledge it was there did a lot for his courage and confidence. 'Thanks,' he said.

He peered round the stone wall of the house they crouched against and watched the guards on the gate. They did not seem very alert. Even the sergeant was chatting amiably to one of the men, and smoking a pipe. Obviously they expected no real trouble at this gate, which only led out to fields and the river. Sentries were on the town wall but they were meandering along, talking to each other, knowing that the British had control of the town and that Marshal Marmont's troops were far away, and unlikely to mount a counter attack now.

'Do you really think that Lieutenant Deaville is helping an enemy to escape?' Megan was staring at the men around the gate. Certainly there was no sign of trouble there or anxiety of any sort. She was beginning to doubt again that Will was right, and wondered if he was just trying to get his own back on the officer who had wronged him.

Will grabbed her shoulders and turned her to face him. 'I told yer. I over'eard 'em plottin', Megan,' he said, his eyes burning into hers.

'But you only heard a few words, Will. They could have meant anything.' She didn't know what Will had in mind to do, but she was suddenly frightened for him. What if he was wrong, and Deaville or others caught him? He would hang for sure.

Will let go of her. 'I know, but everythin' fits,' he said fiercely. 'I'm sure there was nothing wrong with that Frenchman, and why should Deaville be takin' such an interest in 'im?' He stared at the gate again, so agonisingly close, yet seemingly impassable. How was he to get through?

An idea flashed through his head, but it would rely on Megan's co-operation, and she seemed to be faltering in her desire to help him. So, if that were the case he would manage without her. He turned to her again. 'Go back ter the 'ospital or the camp if yer want to. I never wanted ter involve you. If I'm caught and yer seen with me, yer'll be in trouble too.'

Megan knew it. She was disinclined to believe that Paul Deaville, that exciting, handsome, devil-may-care man who made her feel so much a woman, was the traitor Will was branding him, but she couldn't leave Will now. When he had been arrested, Megan had been amazed at the feeling of helplessness and despair that had come over her, and her delight at hearing of his escape, and seeing him again now, was overcoming all her misgivings about Lieutenant Deaville's guilt. She would stay with him.

This she told to Will who rewarded her with his mischievous smile. In whispers he told her his plan. At first she demurred. It was risky and, should she be recognised, her good name would be compromised forever, but Will pointed out that with a little dirt on her face, and her curls hidden beneath the scarf she wore round her neck, there was little chance of recognition.

'What's 'appened to that girl who stole 'er uncle's gun so she could learn to shoot, and was prepared to ride off alone in the middle of the night?' he asked somewhat scathingly, hoping to goad her into agreeing.

It worked. Megan lifted her chin and spiritedly said that of course she would do as he asked. So it was that Will took her round to the back of the stone hovel they were hiding beside, and found the midden. A woman was busy emptying something onto it, so they waited behind the wall until she went inside her house. When Will stooped to pick up a handful of the filth, Megan pushed him away. 'No, Will! You can't mean to put that on me?' she protested in urgent whispers.

'It's the only way,' said Will, smearing some on himself with one hand.

'Well, only on my clothes then,' said Megan, thankful that she had on only her oldest dress, worn because she had been fearful of getting blood on herself at the hospital.

Will spattered her with some of the odorous dirt, while she tied her hair up under the scarf. She heard the drip of water nearby and on investigation it proved to be a slimy out-fall from the roof. She rubbed some on her sun-browned face, knowing that it would contain dirt as well.

'Dear God! We smell divine!' she said sarcastically when Will had finished. His teeth flashed in another smile and he grabbed her hand with the relatively clean one. 'You know what to do?' he whispered.

She nodded. 'Yes.' Excitement fluttered in her stomach as they made their way back to the street only to find that the guard detachment had been joined by two provosts.

'Shit!' Will pulled Megan quickly back into the shadows. The guards they might be able to fool, but not the provosts. The army's police were suspicious of everything and everybody.

'What is it, Will?' hissed Megan by his side.

'The provosts. They're askin' questions. Maybe they're still lookin' for me.' said Will. These particular ones may not be search-ing specifically for him, but they would have been told of his escape and every lad with no good reason to be out near dark would be a suspect. There was nothing they could do but wait.

Unfortunately, the provosts seemed to have settled in for the evening. They gathered round the brazier that was keeping the guards warm and heating a black pot of water for a drink to keep out the cold. The two army policemen laughed and joked with the sergeant in charge of the detachment. This in itself was rather unusual. The regular soldiers had little time for the provosts but this sergeant was chatting away with them like old friends. He was probably glad of some different company, Will thought, watching from his hiding place, though it was noticeable that the rest of the guards went about their own business and steered clear of the two visitors.

Should he risk his plan with the provosts there? He looked at Megan whose eyes were glittering with excitement. In the time spent in and around Ciudad Rodrigo Will had picked up a little Portuguese and Spanish, and so, he knew, had Megan. Could they pass themselves off as peasants? Certainly they looked nothing like anyone belonging to the army, and while he sat here deliberating, Paul Deaville and Colonel Reynard were probably carrying out their own plan and the latter was getting away.

He would have to chance it.

Giving Megan an encouraging smile, he whispered, 'Come on!' into her ear, and pulled her out from behind the wall.

Together they walked towards the soldiers.

23

Will, his heart pounding and wanting more than anything to run, but knowing he must not draw undue attention to himself, sauntered slowly up to the gate, his arm slung carelessly over Megan's shoulders. He bent his head down every so often to supposedly whisper sweet nothings into her ear while she giggled and playfully cuddled up to him. They were ignored until close to the soldiers and provosts, then the sergeant himself suddenly interposed his large bulk between them and the gate.

'Now then, me beauties, where be you off to?' he asked in a broad Dorset accent. He wrinkled his nose as a sudden gust of wind blew a noxious odour towards him and took a step backwards. 'Jesus wept! Where've you two bin, then? The midden?'

Will kept his head down, not wanting to show his give-away blue eyes. 'Sorry, *senor*,' he mumbled. 'We want to leave, si?'

His Spanish was crude and probably would not have passed muster with a real Spaniard but it merely annoyed the sergeant who had not bothered to learn the language. He caught hold of Will's shoulder and squeezed it hard.

'Speak English, you little tyke! What're you doin' here?'

'Looks like they want a bit of privacy, sarge,' said one of the soldiers lazily. The sergeant lifted Megan's chin with a finger. Her hazel eyes blazed back at him. 'This one's all fire and brimstone.' he said, and looked at Will. 'Yer've got yerself a fine piece of Spanish arse 'ere, boy?' He sniffed, then grinned a mouthful of rotten teeth. 'She stinks like a cow byre but she's a fair bit for all that. Mind if I 'ave 'er first?'

Forcing the man's hand away, Megan let off a stream of Spanish mixed with English, telling everyone within hearing what she thought of him and his suggestion, the sergeant's leer telling her what he had said, even though she was pretending not to understand much English. Will suppressed a smile at her reaction,

325

though his fists were balled by his sides, aching to hit the man for his lewd speech.

The sergeant laughed, and reached for Megan, and Will tensed to spring, ready to defend her at whatever the cost, but the provost intervened. 'We don't want no trouble,' he said. 'Wellington's orders are that the populace be left alone. If you want a bit of Spanish arse, Sergeant, there are plenty of whores to be had.'

The sergeant had forgotten he was talking to one of Wellington's policemen, and he subsided readily enough, though the glances he gave Megan told her what he was thinking, as did those of the soldiers nearby who were watching the proceedings with interest. Inside, Megan was seething, but she kept her temper. Will needed her to play out this role, so help him she would. She leaned closer to Will who bussed her on the lips.

'*Por favor, senor?*' We wish to go,' said Will in broken English, pointing to the gates to emphasise his point. Still keeping his eyes averted humbly, he grinned as though embarrassed. 'To make love, *si?*'

'And what's wrong with a doorway?' asked the sergeant, grumblingly, still annoyed that the provost happened to be around and had spoiled his fun.

Will shrugged and looked at Megan as though he didn't understand. The sergeant pointed to a doorway and made a lewd gesture. Will nodded in understanding, then shook his lowered head. 'Her father,' he said. 'He find us.'

This was understood by all the soldiers. At some time or another they had all run the gauntlet of irate fathers. 'Let them out, sarge,' shouted one of the soldiers cheerfully. 'Can't you remember when you were a kid and were itchin' for a girl?'

Will was getting agitated. The longer they hung around in the open here, the more likelihood there was of someone he knew passing by, someone who might recognise him. He put on his most pleading voice and said, '*Por favor, senor?*'

'They seem harmless enough,' said the provost. It was not yet quite dark and legitimate people were still coming in and out of the gates; woodcutters, patrols, people with carts containing men from the hospitals who had died from their festering wounds and fever. What were two more?

'Let them out,' he said to the sergeant, then turned to Will. 'But don't you be long, now, lad. No one's allowed in or out after curfew.' Still muttering, the sergeant stepped aside and motioned for a soldier to open one side of the gate. With thudding, thankful hearts, Will and Megan walked through.

Once on the other side, they strolled hand in hand for some distance from the walls in case the guards were watching, then Will turned Megan towards him and kissed her soundly on the lips.

'Thanks,' he said. 'Yer were great but I'm sorry they were rude.'

She shrugged and grinned, a little taken aback at the kiss which had given her that strange feeling again, but pleased their plan had worked.

'Where do you think Lieutenant Deaville might be?' she asked, to take her mind off the tingling in her toes. She still held his hand.

'They bury the dead over there,' said Will, pointing beyond some flat ground. It was getting darker now, the sun had almost disappeared behind the trees, casting a red glow and deep shadows that were spreading across the countryside. He hoped he was right in thinking that Deaville had come this way, otherwise this was all a waste of time, the French Colonel would escape, and he would be on the run again. There was a strange smell in the air, not so bad here because the wind was blowing away from them, but noticeable for all that. Will knew what it was. The stench of rotting bodies in an open grave. He wondered if he should warn Megan of what she might see.

He didn't get the chance, for at that moment he spotted a cart that had suddenly emerged from a patch of deeper shade. It was heading for the trenches. He recognised it.

'There!' he said, pointing. 'I think that's him. Deaville!'

Running and stumbling over the uneven ground, Will ran towards the moving cart, Megan keeping as close to him as she could. Will knew that despite what Megan had said about returning for help, he was now stuck with her. She could not risk going back through the town gate without him because she would be considered fair game by that sergeant, especially if the provosts had gone. He wished she had not been so determined to come.

Keeping the cart in sight was difficult as the darkness deepened, but they could hear the horse's hooves and kept a fair distance behind the sound so as not to be seen. It was not far to the burial grounds and their noses told them when they were getting close.

Will stopped, and told Megan to take the scarf she wore from round her head and cover her nose and mouth with it. He had nothing to put over his face and would just have to put up with the stench.

The cart had stopped. Will and Megan crept behind a large boulder and stared at the scene ahead of them. Cutting a deep swathe in the ground was a long, wide trench with, beside it, a huge heap of earth, and another, smaller one, of lime. Will knew the lime was for putting in the trench to help the bodies decompose more quickly. The landscape was empty of the living for the men detailed to work here had gone home for the night, back to Ciudad Rodrigo. Deaville had parked his cart some distance away, nearer to a track that led off to the river and Will thought he saw the sun's rays glint on harness amongst the trees. Earlier in the day, Deaville must have put a horse there for the Frenchman to escape on. He watched as Deaville went round to the back of the cart and did something to the bundle in the back. Will wondered what to do. Somehow he had to stop the French Colonel from escaping, for he was sure the bundle was he. He wished he had a rifle.

'Stay here,' he ordered Megan.

'But Will...' She put her hand on his arm to stop him, but he shrugged it off. He pulled out the knife she had given him and stealthily made his way towards the cart.

A very healthy looking Colonel Reynard was divesting himself of the wrapping blanket by the time Will was close enough to Deaville to spring. The lieutenant, his attention taken wholly by the Frenchman, yelped with surprise when he suddenly felt a wiry arm go around his neck and a knife blade cold at his throat.

His frightened eyes stared at Reynard in mute questioning despair, but to his surprise the Frenchman merely laughed.

'Get back into that cart, *m'sieur*,' said Will, 'or the lieutenant dies.'

There was an explosion of wrath mixed with indignation as Deaville recognised Will's voice. 'God damn it, boy! Let me go!' he ground out.

For answer the knife point bit deeper, and Deaville squeaked in alarm as a thin trickle of blood meandered down his neck, but the Frenchman seemed unperturbed. Looking up, Will saw why. He was holding a pistol which, Will presumed, had also been hidden in the blankets at the back of the cart.

328

'You may kill him if you like,' Reynard said blandly, aiming the pistol at Will and Deaville. 'He has served his purpose and is nothing to me.' Deaville let out a string of curses. Will wondered what to do. This was a difficult situation to resolve by himself and he wished he'd had the time to bring along someone like George, or even Captain Camberwell. It was also possible that Deaville had a pistol somewhere on his person but he had no spare hands with which to search.

There was no knowing how that particular situation might have turned out because just then Megan, seeing Will on the wrong end of a pistol, decided to take action herself. Without a thought for her own safety, she ran out from the trees, throwing stones that she had picked up. Most fell harmlessly to the ground but a lucky one hit Reynard on the arm making him yelp and drop the gun. Will, his attention taken by Megan, shouted at her to get back, but his inattention proved his undoing for his hold on Deaville loosened and the lieutenant leapt forward to pick up the gun the Frenchman had dropped.

'That's better.' The smile on Deaville's face was white in the falling darkness but Will could see full well the gun's muzzle was pointing right at his gut. He was momentarily distracted by the Frenchman making a move towards the trees, then jumped when a gunshot sounded loudly on the evening air. Wondering why he did not straight away feel the agony of a wound, Will stared back at the smoking pistol, but it was Reynard who cried out and fell to the ground, clutching his chest. 'English bastard!' he ground out, groaned once, then lay still.

'Come here, Lady Camberwell.' The order was terse and the gun once again swung towards Will. Her heart thudding, Megan glanced at him while he stared back at her helplessly. She walked slowly to Deaville's side and he grabbed her round the waist, still with his eyes on Will who held the knife. Will shifted it in his hand, itching to throw it, but he was too afraid of hitting Megan.

'Throw the knife on the ground over there, boy,' said Deaville, indicating with his head. A smile twitched the lieutenant's face. He was pleased with how things were going. By forcing him to kill the Frog bastard, the boy had actually done him a favour. The man had been going to kill him. That much was obvious. Now the damn Frenchman had no further hold on him. He watched Will throw the knife away. Megan was struggling in his grip. 'Be quiet now, you minx!' he said, and tapped her quite lightly on the temple with the gun, just enough to stun her so that she sagged in his arms. Will growled in anger. Helpless to do anything, he cursed himself for not seeking help while still in the town.

Deaville chuckled, his laughter loud in the stillness of the evening. 'It bothers you doesn't it, boy?' he said. His eyes were shining with a maniacal glee. 'You've got designs on her too, haven't you?' Will was surprised. He had thought he'd managed to keep his feelings for Megan well hidden and wondered how many others knew of them. 'Well she's mine, boy. And she's coming with me.' Deaville sounded horribly confident.

Will said nothing, knowing there was nothing he could say that would not further antagonise this man who was surely deranged, but his thoughts were racing, trying to hook onto an idea that would get Megan away from the lieutenant. Then his sharp ears caught the sound of horses' hooves and he smiled.

'People are coming, Lieutenant,' he said.

'What? Don't talk bullshit, boy...' but then Deaville stopped. He had heard the far away hooves too. He swore. He wanted to kill the youngster standing in front of him, a thorn in his side since he had joined the regiment in Portugal, but he didn't dare fire the gun again and draw attention to himself if there were soldiers about. His face a mask of tense anger, he backed towards the cart, dragging Megan with him. Still keeping the gun on Will he pushed her roughly onto the back of the cart and climbed onto the seat. Coming round, Megan dazedly stood up, ready to jump off, but Deaville whipped the reins and the cart jolted forward, throwing her down onto the wooden bed again. By the time she recovered herself, it was moving quickly down the track.

Now in no danger from the gun, Will ran to the trees where he thought he had seen a horse. Sure enough, there it was. Deaville had obviously forgotten about it in the tenseness of the drama. It was saddled and ready for the Frenchman who lay dead on the grass. Will waited a few seconds, listening for the hooves he had heard a few minutes before, hoping he could maybe summon help, but now there was nothing. The riders had seemingly gone the other way, through the gates of Ciudad Rodrigo. Muttering under his breath, he mounted awkwardly and set off at a trot, following.

✝ ✝ ✝

Richard Camberwell was somewhat surprised to be accosted by Sarah in the middle of his supper which he was eating with bad grace, wishing that Will had prepared it for him as the boy seemed to do magic things with a bit of tough meat and a few vegetables. Since Will's arrest, he and James Shaw had unwillingly put up with Dodge's ministrations. The older man was a good servant but a terrible cook. Camberwell was in the middle of telling Shaw that they would really have to get someone else to cook for them when Sarah burst in, red-faced and windswept, surprising both men, and rapidly announcing that Will and Megan were following Lieutenant Deaville who was helping a French Colonel to escape.

At first unable to take in the news because of Sarah's rather incoherent recounting, Camberwell made her sit down, pressed a snifter of brandy into her hand, and made her start again.

'Dear God! Are you sure?' he said when the story was told again and made more sense.

'Yes, Richard! Quickly, you have to go after them!'

'Of course.' Camberwell was already reaching for his jacket and sword, then he helped James Shaw with his. Shaw whose shoulder had been wounded by a canister during the battle, was mending well if painfully, and insisted on coming too. 'It's my left arm, Richard,' he said. 'I can still wield a sword.'

'Damn the boy!' said Camberwell, fastening Shaw's sword belt for him. 'Why did he have to drag Megan into this?'

'She insisted,' said Sarah. 'You know what's she's like, Richard!'

Camberwell did indeed. He turned to Dodge who had heard Sarah's noisy arrival and had listened to her tale as avidly as the two officers. 'Hurry to Lieutenant-Colonel Davenport, Dodge, and tell him to send armed patrols to all the town gates and give the guards there a description of Will and Megan,' he said, fixing on his scabbard. 'And light a torch. It's going to be dark by the time we get there. 'We'll try the two gates nearest the river. I wouldn't mind betting Deaville will go for the ones furthest away from the camp.'

'Yes, sir! Right away, sir!' said Dodge and he hurried away.

Camberwell gave Sarah a quick kiss. 'Stay here, my dear,' he said. 'And pray we're in time to prevent a tragedy.'

331

Wan-faced, Sarah stared after her beau and his friend as they left the room and ran to the stables.

Then she began to pray.

† † †

Paul Deaville flicked the reins over the horse's head, and the cart rumbled along the track a little faster. Now that the immediate danger was over, he wondered what to do. His brain worked feverishly, making up stories to tell if he was stopped by anyone who mattered. Without his uniform he looked like a civilian, though his fair hair proclaimed him English. The presence of Megan, although pleasing in a way, was a problem, for he could not keep her quiet for ever without killing her, and he lusted after her far too much to do that.

That he had managed to kill Colonel Reynard in cold blood surprised him. As he had felt with the problem of Juanita, killing in battle was one thing, murdering someone quite another, but he was glad the man was dead. He knew he could concoct a plausible story about that; he had merely shot an escaping prisoner, but there was still the problem of young Will Tucker. Damn it! He should have shot the boy too when he had the chance, but he was afraid that the first shot had already been heard by the riders who had obviously been close by. However, although Will's witnessing Reynard's death was a niggling worry at the back of his mind, now he thought about it, maybe it wasn't such a problem. The lad was on the run too, and would be arrested on sight if he sought the help of any army personnel, and who would believe him? Of course Megan Camberwell's disappearance would be noted, but he would make his way back towards the hills with her. It would be easy to hide there. In the meantime, where was he to go now to avoid the hue and cry that would immediately follow once Lady Megan was missed? He knew little of the area and it was getting darker which meant good cover in one way, but handling a horse and cart in the dark could easily mean an accident.

He heard the faint sound of running water and it gave him an idea. Following the river might be the best thing to do. It would at least give him some bearings, so he moved towards it. He swung his head to look back into the cart bed, and saw that Megan was sitting up, hanging onto the side of the cart as she was jolted about. She

332

screamed invective at him and he slowed the horses to a halt.
'You bastard!' she shouted. Deaville picked up the blankets in
which Reynard had been hiding. Guessing his intention, Megan
jumped off the cart and started to run, stumbling over the lumpy
ground, but Deaville had a longer stride and soon caught up with
her, bringing her to the ground. 'Easy, my lady,' he growled, sitting
astride and catching her flailing fists which beat his chest. 'Ow!
Bitch!' he yelped as she bit his hand. He struck her hard across the
side of the face. Tears of anger and hurt sprang to her eyes.
Deaville felt stirrings of lust and was very tempted to take her there
and then, but he remembered the horses he had heard, and knew
he was not yet far enough away from the town to avoid discovery.
There would be time for that later. He stood up and dragged Megan
to her feet. Clasping her round her middle he dragged her to where
he had dropped the blankets. A length of rope lay on the cart bed.
With great difficulty, because she struggled like a slippery eel, he
wrapped her in the blankets and trussed her like a bundle of
washing. Only her face was free and she let him know in no uncertain terms what she thought of his treatment of her, so he took her
scarf and tied it around her mouth to muffle curses which would
have done justice to any common soldier.

'That's better!' he said and pushed her onto the back of the cart
before climbing onto the seat and urging the patient horse on again.

Will was having a hard time on his own mount. This was not an
ambling old cob like Lightfoot whom he could ride easily now, nor
Hades who knew him. This was a fast officer's horse obviously used
to only one rider. Paul Deaville had been obliged to give up one of
his own string for Colonel Reynard, not daring to steal a mount
from another, and it was a frisky, sensitive stallion who did not like
the fact that the rider on its back was inexperienced and clumsy.
Several times Will was nearly thrown when the horse side-stepped
a rut or broke into an unexpected canter and he wished he'd
learned to ride well something other than Megan's first pony. His
back and ribs were hurting too. The walking and running he had
done with Megan had given him twinges and now the motion of the
horse conspired with his lack of ability to move with it, and was
making the pain even worse. Still, he gritted his teeth and carried

on, his desire to save Megan paramount. Guilt weighed heavily on his mind. He should never have allowed Megan to accompany him, and he urged the horse to move faster, imagining what Deaville was doing to her. However, his difficulties with the horse meant that at first he could not keep up with the cart. Even when Deaville stopped, he was still too far away for them to hear the stallion's hoof beats, or for himself to see the lieutenant, but he kept doggedly walking the horse along the track and hoped he would eventually catch up.

† † †

Will was helped on his way by a mistake Deaville made in his haste to escape possible pursuit. Hurtling round a bend too quickly, the cart went off the track and into a ditch. Clutching the reins tightly, Deaville cursed when he heard the crack of the breaking axle.

Eyes wide with terror, Megan rolled hard into the side of the cart bed, bounced back again as the cart began to tip, then fell right out. She watched, unable to do anything because she was tied in the blankets, while in seeming slow motion the cart hovered above her on two wheels, about to crash down and crush her underneath. Then she breathed a thankful sigh when a wheel sank into the mud and the cart stopped moving. Canted at an angle, with the horse screaming, its back legs in the ditch too, the cart was well and truly stuck.

Swearing roundly, bruised from being flung around the seat while desperately trying to keep the cart on the track, Paul Deaville stepped down onto the grass. Remembering Megan, he walked round to the back of the cart to assess the damage and saw the broken axle. Angrily he kicked the cart which rocked ominously. Megan was making muffled cries and trying in vain to escape the stifling blankets. He went to help her and dragged her out of the ditch and onto the grass. Ignoring her angry cries and blazing eyes, he cursed the horse, wondering what to do. Firstly, he decided, he'd better get the animal out of the traces so he went around to the front again. The task of freeing the horse was accomplished with difficulty and much slipping on the half-frozen mud, and when he had pulled it up to the top of the ditch he saw it was limping.

'Damn it to hell!' Deaville swore again and sat down on the grass. What was he going to do now with no means of transport?

And what to do with Megan Camberwell? He could not carry her, neither could he permanently loosen her bonds for then she would surely try to run away. Then he had an idea. He unwrapped the blankets and the rope, much to Megan's relief. He considered removing the scarf from her mouth but the thought of her whining or cursing deterred him. Once unbound, Megan fought and scratched like a demon until Deaville was forced to show her the gun again.

'Behave yourself or I'll use it,' he warned her. Megan wondered whether he would, but she had watched him kill Reynard in cold blood and could not take the chance. She stood still, eyes narrowed over the scarf, wondering what he would do next. It was strange how all the attraction she had once felt for this man had suddenly disappeared. How could she have been so blind as to what he was really like? Her uncle and Will had been right and she was just a stupid, immature girl who knew nothing of the ways of men but had been taken in by a charming manner and a handsome face. Tears pricked her eyes, not because of the danger she was in, but because she had been so foolish.

Deaville took the length of rope, told Megan to put her hands in front of her and then tied the rope tightly around them, leaving a long end free. This he kept in his hand and, leaving the horse to its own devices and the cart stuck in the ditch, he started to walk. Megan stubbornly stood still until she was in danger of being pulled off her feet, then was compelled to walk behind him.

Walking through the darkened countryside, still following the river, her heart plummeted as deep as the mud into which her shoes were sinking as she stumbled and slipped close to the riverbank, and she wondered what was to become of her.

She also wondered if Will loved her enough to follow her.

The thought of not doing so never crossed Will's mind as he struggled to control the stallion and keep him heading in what he hoped was the right direction. It seemed that Deaville was following the course of the river, which made things a lot easier. He wondered about the horses they had heard back at the burial grounds. At first he had hoped it was help rounded up by Sarah, but then he had realised it could not have been. There hadn't been time for her to go and find Richard Camberwell, and for him to get men together. There was no sound from behind him and now the sun had gone entirely, he was having to go very slowly, alone in the darkness of the night.

He came across the broken cart and the horse that was standing with its head down, looking very sorry for itself, and realised at once what had happened. At first wondering if there had been any injuries, or worse, in the accident, he searched around for Megan and Paul Deaville but there was no sign of either of them. In a way he was relieved for it meant that Megan was probably all right, and now the two were on foot, he would catch up with them all the quicker. This buoyed his spirits, even though the wind began to blow harder, bringing an icy rain that stung his face. He shivered in the ragged clothes, wishing he had a coat or could take shelter, but then mentally chastised himself for Megan must be feeling just as uncomfortable, if not more so. Doggedly he carried on.

† † †

The rain depressed Paul Deaville's spirits even further as he walked stolidly on, and he began to realise that they needed somewhere to stay the night. Although the river guided them, he thought that any pursuers might realise he was following it, and catch up with him. With this thought in mind, he veered away from it, but was soon lost in the inky blackness of the night. Stumbling behind him, tripping over ruts in the hard ground, Megan wished he would stop, but was afraid of what he would do to her if he did. That he wanted to rape her had been made very plain, and she hung back as much as possible in the hope that Will had been able to get help and was following her. Whilst following the river she had been hopeful, but now they were travelling across country, she wondered if she would ever be found. Her mind whirled, trying to think of a way in which she could leave a clue, then she thought of something. Pretending to trip again, she kicked off a shoe, knowing as she did so that it would make walking more difficult for her, but that might be a good thing because it would slow them down. Within seconds her foot was icy cold and soaking wet and she could feel every rut and knobble of hard soil through her flimsy stocking.

At last Deaville saw a light in the distance and he headed towards it, pulling Megan along viciously, growling at her to keep

336

up, though by now she was limping and her stocking was in shreds. The light proved to be a lantern hung from the corner of a stone building, the largest amongst a huddle of smaller ones that made up a farm. Not in the mood for diplomacy, Deaville kicked open the rickety, wooden door of the house, surprising and frightening the two people in the room beyond, an elderly man and woman.

Reacting quickly to the unexpected intrusion, the farmer, a stocky, thick-set individual, reached for an old blunderbuss that hung over the fire place but was stopped by Deaville's harsh voice and the pistol that appeared in his spare hand. The farmer went and stood by his quaking wife, a plump woman with grey hair coiled tightly in a bun. She was staring at Megan, so obviously a prisoner of this wild-eyed man who had broken into their home, while Megan stared back in mute appeal.

'Who are you?' The man spoke in his own language. Deaville, not understanding, ignored the question, but the sharp-eyed farmer had already noted the British-made pistol and he frowned. Was this man an army deserter? He wasn't wearing a uniform. The farmer looked at Megan. The girl was obviously not a friend, tied up like that, and the man looked dangerous, on edge, as though it wouldn't take much to make him fire the gun. For his wife's sake, he decided not to play the hero. He noticed that the intruder was staring at the cooking pot that hung over the fire.

'You eat?' he said in English, indicating his mouth, hoping to distract this violent stranger and defuse an ugly situation.

'Yes.' Deaville motioned for the woman to sit down. He still did not let go of the rope that was tied around Megan's hands. He looked around for something to fasten it to, and saw hooks beside the big fireplace that took up almost one side of the room. Deaville tied the end of the rope he was holding to a hook. Meanwhile the man told his wife to dish up some stew from the pot. He indicated Megan and mimed taking the scarf off so that she could eat. Deaville looked at her and reluctantly removed it, expecting a flood of invective, or a plea for help, but Megan remained strangely silent.

Megan was thinking hard. Surely here was a means of escape if she could only think of one. Noting the sympathetic looks the farmer and his wife were giving her, she was positive they would help her if they could. But Deaville's pistol was a problem and she knew he would not hesitate to use it. What was one more murder

337

on top of that he had already committed? The army would now consider him a deserter and a kidnapper, as well as a murderer, and he would be hung. More killings would make no difference to the outcome if he was caught. She watched him as he gulped the food down. The farmer's wife fed her, spoonful by spoonful and she was glad of the warm food, and the heat from the fire. Her wet clothes steamed as they dried.

Deaville said nothing while he hungrily ate the stew but his mind was working steadily. Still with the pistol in one hand he wiped the dregs of food away from his mouth, and said, 'Turn down that lantern.' The man did not understand. Deaville growled angrily and went and turned it down himself, leaving the room with just enough light to see by, then he sat himself in the only comfortable looking chair. 'Sit,' he waved the gun about and indicated the floor. The farmer's wife perched on the other chair while her husband sat heavily on the floor beside her. Megan wondered again if Will had followed them. Would he find her shoe? She pessimistically thought it unlikely in the dark and was grateful that Deaville had not realised she had on only one, but how long would that last? She sat down on the floor, the better to hide her feet under her long skirt, though that meant her hands were uncomfortably high, still tied to the rope, and she knew they would soon cramp.

It was going to be a long night.

† † †

Richard Camberwell rounded up several of Will's fellow soldiers who were only too willing to help. George Trim's arm, the one that had been knifed by Amos Wilkins, was nearly as good as new again. Nat Binns and Ron Parker professed their eagerness to see, in the words of Binns, 'that bloody bastard Deaville hang by his ruddy neck!'

They were just about to leave the camp when Sergeant Readman came hurrying up to them, putting on his jacket as he did so. 'Permission to come along, Captain,' he said, panting.

'Of course, Readman,' said Camberwell. He and Shaw were the only ones on horseback, but he knew the privates, fit men all, would be able to walk for as long as was necessary. However, the sergeant was a portly man, and already out of breath. 'Though, if you'll pardon my saying so, Sergeant,' he said. 'Will you be able to keep up with us?'

'Got meself a little 'elp here, sir,' said Readman, grinning, and he pulled Lightfoot out of the darkness. 'Took a liberty and borrowed your cob, sir, beggin' your pardon.'

Camberwell gave a faint smile. 'Heave him aboard then, lads, and let's get moving,' he said, the smile broadening as Parker and Binns shoved Readman awkwardly into the saddle.

Time was wasted as, first of all, the small group went to the wrong gate where no one had seen anyone who looked like Megan or Will. The second gate yielded no luck either but when they went to the gate closest to the burial grounds the sergeant there remembered Megan, though he was sure the lad with her had not had blond hair.

'Was a local lad, Cap'n,' he said confidently. 'Couldn't speak much English. Girl was a nice piece though.'

'The boy was probably disguised and the girl, Sergeant, was my niece,' growled Camberwell, his voice as hard as his face.

The sergeant stared appalled, as he remembered his attitude towards the girl he had thought was a peasant. 'Beggin' your pardon, Captain, I'm sure,' he said. 'I 'ad no idea...'

Camberwell ignored his blustering and ordered the gate to be opened. By the time Will was bouncing along beside the river on Deaville's stallion, they were on their way to the burial grounds. Then they were held up again by finding Colonel Reynard's body. This they did accidentally because it was now very dark, the only light coming from torches in the town not far away, and the one they had brought with them that George carried, but Camberwell decided that they had better look around as much as possible. Fearful of finding the bodies of Will and Megan, Camberwell was shocked but relieved when he nearly tripped over Reynard and, by feeling the uniform, realised it was the Frenchman.

He crouched down beside the dead man. George, who had been searching a short distance away, came running with the torch. They all stared at Colonel Reynard's body, the blood on his chest shining stickily in the flickering light.

'Who is he, Cap'n?' asked Binns.

'One of the French prisoners. He was taken ill and moved to the hospital yesterday. Miss Harvey told me Will thinks he was faking it and it was all part of a plan to escape.'

'D'you think Will killed him, sir?' asked George.

Camberwell shook his head. 'No. I don't think he has a pistol and this fellow died from a gunshot wound. My guess is Deaville turned traitor on him as well as the army. Look around, lads. See if you can see any sign of what happened to Will and Megan. Or Deaville, for that matter.'

While the soldiers searched by the waning light of the pitch torch, Camberwell searched the man's body. In a breast pocket he felt a small leather bag. He pulled it out and took it to George so that he could see what it was by the torch-light. It revealed a surprise, for the bag bore a noble crest. Inside was white with some kind of powder. Tasting a little on the tip of his finger Camberwell realised it was flour. He stared again at the crest. It was one he recognised – and his mind swept back to Major Robert Underwood in Portsmouth. Could this be the purse that Will had stolen, and that had been stolen again from Megan's carpet bag? He stood and stared at it, puzzled. Surely Reynard would have had no chance to steal it, so who...? And why had it contained flour?

It was a mystery. Stuffing the bag into his own pocket, he went back to the body and rooted through Reynard's other pockets but found nothing of interest. He had obviously been searched for valuables before being arrested. Eventually, Parker found wheel tracks in the mud by the river and Camberwell forgot the pouch, his attention taken by the more important task of finding Will and Megan.

There were hoof prints in the mud as well, overlaid by others. 'Two horses,' he said, 'and a wagon of some description.' He thought for a moment. 'I suppose one must assume that Deaville had the wagon. He must have smuggled the Frenchman out of Ciudad Rodrigo somehow, but whose is the other horse?' Camberwell knew Will and Megan had followed Deaville out of town on foot. But where the hell were they now?

They were questions he couldn't answer, but no good would come of staying here pondering. He stared into the sky, hoping to see a moon, however there was nothing but blackness, and he could smell rain on the air. It would be impossible to track Deaville and the youngsters down in the dark. He cursed, but consoled himself with the fact that they would not get far either, and would have to rest up somewhere. Decisively he strode over to Hades and mounted again while the three soldiers boosted Sergeant Readman into Lightfoot's saddle once more.

'We need more light,' he said. 'Trim, you and Parker go back and get some more pitch torches and lanterns. We'll carry on slowly following the river. You should be able to catch us up quickly enough.'

'D'you think young Will and Lady Camberwell are all right, sir?' asked Binns, carrying the torch as he walked along beside Hades, while he and Richard Camberwell searched the ground diligently for tracks to follow.

'Well, I suppose we can assume they were at this point, Binns,' replied the Captain. 'And I really hope they still are. But we must find them as soon as possible because Deaville seems to have lost all reason and I wouldn't give much hope for their chances should they confront him.'

So saying, the soldiers carried on in silence, while the night, and the rain, closed in.

24

The rain was penetrating and Will was soon soaking wet. He began to wonder if Deaville had left the river. It was now completely dark and he knew it was foolish to carry on. The horse could easily fall into a rut or ditch and break a leg. He would have to take shelter until either the rain stopped and the moon appeared, or the sun's rising allowed him to see where he was going.

He almost bumped into a tree, and stopped. It seemed quite a large one and, although there was no foliage at this time of year, was somewhere to sit if he could find a suitable fork. So, after tethering the horse to the same tree, he climbed it and perched himself in a wide fork not too far from the ground.

Despite his uncomfortable circumstances he must have dozed because he awoke later, cold and wet, to find that the rain had eased to a thin drizzle. He wondered what had woken him and heard the distant sound of hoofbeats. Peering into the darkness, he saw lantern lights wavering in the rain. Someone was following the river path as he had.

Knowing the sight of the horse would give his presence away, he was torn between clambering down and riding away as quickly as possible, or staying put. Who would be out riding at this time of night? A patrol from the town? Or maybe they were Partisans. Perhaps they wouldn't see the horse in the gloom. He decided to wait it out, but held the knife in his hand, just in case. If the lights belonged to anyone wishing him harm, then he would take out one of them first.

The flickering lights came nearer, and despite the drizzle, he could plainly hear the hoofbeats thudding on the muddy grass. The riders were followed by men on foot. He could make out their dark shapes running to keep up. Too many men. He wished he had a gun.

The three riders had capes, and hats pulled down over their faces to keep off the rain. Everything was etched in deep shadow and the lanterns shed little light in the dismal conditions. There was no sound of voices. The men seemed intent on keeping the horses following the track.

Will tensed himself to jump. He would go for the leading rider and hope that the threat of a cut throat would be enough to keep the others at bay.

The leading horseman had his eyes on the ground and nearly missed the horse tethered behind the tree, but one of his men spotted it. The leader put up a hand to halt the group, but before he could dismount and investigate, he was bowled from the saddle by a dark shape that sprang from the tree.

Within seconds Richard Camberwell was held in a stranglehold round his neck and a knife was tickling the skin by his right ear. After the initial shouts of surprise from his colleagues, there was silence, except for the sound of the falling rain.

Ron Parker made for a pistol that was in the rope belt of his trousers. 'Keep yer 'ands still,' Will ground out.

'Will? Is that you?' A shocked George Trim recognised the voice of his friend. It had not taken long to get back with more light and catch up with Camberwell's group. The first pitch torch had gone out so Camberwell and the others had been forced to stop and wait for George and Ron to return.

Will took a better look at the faces around him; George, Ron, Ned, Captain Shaw, and Sergeant Readman. Jesus Christ! That meant he had probably jumped...

342

Yes. He was putting a knife to the throat of Lord Richard Camberwell. Immediately he let go. Camberwell coughed and glanced at him wryly.

'It's good to see you, Will,' he said, wheezing a little. 'But I'd rather you hadn't done that.'

'Sorry, sir.' Will looked embarrassed, but then he too grinned, glad to see his friends. 'I didn't recognise yer. Thought yer might be Partisans.'

'Partisans don't usually advertise themselves so readily, Will,' said Camberwell. He took his first good look at his servant. 'Good Lord, lad! I would never have recognised you either!'

Certainly Will, barefoot, dressed in ragged, dirty, civilian clothes and with the woollen cap pulled over his bright hair, looked very unlike the soldier he had been just a few days before. George, Ned and Ron all clustered round Will, asking him questions and pleased to be with him again, but Camberwell looked around, then his voice took on a more serious tone. 'Where's Megan?' he demanded.

'Deaville's got 'er, sir,' said Will. 'I tried ter stop 'im, but 'e got away. I've been followin' 'em, but it got too dark.'

'Damn!' Camberwell started pacing, the rain dripping from his hat. 'You've no idea where he's taken her?'

'No, sir. 'E 'ad a 'orse and cart and 'e knocked 'er out after killin' the French Colonel.'

'So it was him,' said Camberwell, remembering the body they had found. He stared at the sky. 'We passed the horse and cart. So we must assume they are now on foot. Damn this weather, and damn Deaville! If he kills Megan, I'll...'

'I don't think 'e will, sir. But 'e might...you know...' Will's voice trailed off. The thought was unthinkable. He would kill Deaville himself if he raped Megan, or even tried to.

'He's a dead man anyway,' said Camberwell harshly, 'but if he does anything like that, he'll wish he'd never been born.' He stared at the horse. 'Where did that come from?'

'Found it in some bushes near the burial ground, sir. 'Spect it was meant for the Frenchman.'

Camberwell nodded. He looked around but there was nothing to see in the darkness, the only sounds those of the rain, and the river running by not far away. 'The path is still here,' he said, pointing to the ground, 'but I think we should spread out in case Deaville's left it somewhere ahead. George, light your torch. This bit of rain shouldn't put it out. Then go thirty paces abreast of us to your left. Ron, you take yours and go fifteen paces. See if you can spot anything.'

Ned held a lantern and stayed with the others. Will wished he and Readman could swap mounts, but it was clear that the sergeant was as uncomfortable on Lightfoot as he was on the stallion. They carried on, but the weather and following the trail forced them to travel very slowly.

It was George who found Megan's shoe. He hailed the others who joined him.

'It's Megan's all right,' said Camberwell, examining it by the light of the torch. 'And look! The grass is all flattened where they've walked. They must have left the river but God knows where they are now.' He looked ahead but it was just blackness. He tried to put himself in Deaville's place. Surely, this far from Ciudad Rodrigo he would think himself safe enough, and would look for shelter from the rain. Thoughts as to what might be happening to Megan if he had found any, passed through his head and he grimaced.

Will had been having the same thoughts and had gone ahead on the horse, climbing to the top of a small rise. What he saw there excited him. 'Sir!' he shouted. 'I can see a light!'

Camberwell joined him and stared at the faint prick of light, the lantern that hung on the corner of the farmhouse, the light Paul Deaville had forgotten about when he'd ordered the farmer to turn down the lamp in the room.

Will was already sending the horse down the slope on the other side of the hill, but Camberwell called him back.

'Wait, lad!' he said. 'It's too dark. The horse needs to see where it's going. Besides, that light could be anything, and if Deaville is there we have to make some sort of plan. If he hears us coming he may harm Megan. We first have to find out what it is. It may be nothing to do with them. They may have gone another way entirely.'

''E's there, sir. I feel it in my bones,' said Will, anxious to go. 'But I'll go and check if yer like.'

'All right. But let's get a bit closer first so that we can cover you, and the horse doesn't break a leg.'

'I'll go without the 'orse,' said Will, not wanting to put the animal at risk and eager to see if Deaville was indeed nearby.

Camberwell gave a wry smile. 'Look, lad. I know you can get there without being seen, but even if Deaville's not there, any farmer or peasant around these parts is likely to shoot first and ask questions later at this time of night. And if Deaville is around, don't forget he's a wanted man. He must be nervous, edgy, listening for any sound that might mean pursuit, and he won't hesitate to kill you. I'm surprised he didn't do it back at the burial grounds.'

''E was about to, sir, but we 'eard 'orses and 'e was afraid a gunshot would attract attention.'

'You were lucky then,' Camberwell observed. 'Right. Come on lads, let's go, but I think we'd better douse the torches. Someone might be looking out of a window and we don't want them to see us coming, or hear us for that matter. And I think we should leave the horses here. Tie them to those trees.' He pointed to two that were close by.

So saying, the horses were tied, torches were doused, as were the lanterns, and the black night settled in around them. They waited a few minutes to get some sort of night vision, then set off across the tussocky, slippery ground towards the distant light.

Paul Deaville was not looking out of a window. In fact he was having the devil of a job staying awake. The room was warm, the night had been fraught with difficulties and danger, and he was tired, yet determined not to fall asleep. The farmer was not a young man, but the life he led meant he was hard and fit and his eyes rarely strayed from Deaville's, a fact that was not lost on the lieutenant. The farmer's wife kept flashing pitying looks at Megan who, dishevelled and uncomfortable, had shuffled backwards so that she could lean against the small patch of wall beside the fireplace, but her arms and hands were numb from being tied.

Megan was far from sleep, too uncomfortable and tense even to doze. Her mind was working furiously and she returned the woman's gaze with a tremulous smile, then glanced at Deaville before smiling at the woman again. She knew that Deaville was not far from sleep and thought that if he did doze, the farmer could maybe grab his gun and the woman untie her. This she tried to convey to the woman with her eyes, but there was no answering understanding in the woman's, just that pitying look.

She glanced at Deaville and watched his eyelids droop before he shook himself awake again. She kept as still and quiet as possible, as did the farmer and his wife, knowing that the peace and stillness might encourage Deaville to fall asleep properly. She watched his eyelids droop again.

The farmer was also watching Deaville who jerked awake again and blinked. The other three occupants of the room stayed still – and waited.

At last Deaville's eyes closed, and this time did not re-open. The pistol sat loosely in his hand. The farmer stood up, and not taking his eyes from the man in the chair, he sidled across to the fireplace and took a knife from behind the candlestick on the stone mantlepiece. Quietly he sawed through the rope holding Megan's hands together. Gratefully, Megan thanked him with her eyes and rubbed her numb, sore hands and wrists, then, very quietly, stood up.

She tip-toed to the door, not knowing where she was to go, but just wanting to get away, anywhere, from Paul Deaville. The farmer crept to the chair, his eyes on Deaville's pistol, while his wife looked on silently, her hand to her mouth.

Megan was just lifting the latch on the door when a shot rang out and she jumped, her shaking hand making the latch rattle. The shot was quickly followed by a scream and wailing. Megan took a quick glance backwards and saw the farmer bleeding on the floor from a grazed arm, shot by Deaville who woke up when the old man bent over him, reaching for the gun. Terrified of the look of hate that Deaville flashed her way, she lifted the latch, and ran.

Running over the dark, wet ground, realising that the rain had stopped but with the wind cold against her skin after the warmth of the farm-house fire, Megan whimpered and heard the curses behind her as Deaville stormed out of the house and followed her. She stumbled, and nearly fell into a drainage ditch that ran alongside a pen that held goats bleating in alarm. She turned and ran along beside it, heedless of the pain in her bare foot that seemed to find every stone, trying not to cry out loud, just hoping to lose herself in the darkness but Deaville pursued her relentlessly, listening for sounds of her panting breath. She thought she was making for the river and hoped that Deaville would slip and hurt himself, for surely he could see as little in the night as she. But it seemed that Paul Deaville had the luck of the devil, for he was catching up.

He caught her when she missed her footing on the slippery grass and tumbled into the ditch. She felt his big hands grab her roughly by the arm and drag her out, screaming loudly. Suddenly the clouds parted letting the moon shine down on them, lighting the scene with an eerie, pale glow. Megan, terrified and struggling, glanced at Deaville's face and wished the clouds were back, for there was no mistaking the look of lust and hate she saw engraved on it.

'The time has come, my lady,' he growled and with one strong hand he forcefully pushed her down onto the wet, muddy grass, funbling at his belt with the other. Within seconds he was on top of her, shoving her skirt up round her waist, and ripping her underwear. Megan couldn't take her eyes off him. She screamed again, knowing there was little the old couple could do to help her now the farmer was injured, but hoping, hoping, that her noise would stop Deaville. In vain. It just seemed to excite him further, he didn't even try and stop her yells. Tears streaming down her face, she panicked and wriggled but he had her arms pinned down by her sides with his knees. She gave a great heave and tried to push him off, but he was much too heavy. She felt him forcing her legs apart, then, suddenly, the weight was removed and someone was giving a great growl of anger. Breathing heavily between sobs, she sat up, pulled down her skirt, and saw Paul Deaville grappling with someone. There was the glint of a knife in the moonlight, and then another shout. Greatly relieved, but hardly able to believe it possible, she recognised her uncle and several soldiers of his Company as they ran to the pair who were fighting.

'Will! Stop! Let him go!'

'No! Let the lad beat the shit out of 'im, sir. The bastard deserves it!'

Richard Camberwell's shouts, followed by those of Sergeant Readman, fell on deaf ears. Will was angrier than ever. He had heard Megan's screams and rushed to her defence, flinging Deaville off her as though he were a child. Paul Deaville had been about to rape the love of his life, and he was enraged. But Deaville, just as angry, was fighting back. The knife in Will's hand went for Deaville's chest and he flung an arm out to stop it, so that the blade dug

347

into his forearm instead. The sleeve darkened as blood welled, and Deaville grimaced but he still had to fight because Will was like a tiger worrying its prey and sent the heel of his hand crunching into his face, breaking his nose. Deaville crawled backwards as blood poured down the front of his coat. He fumbled in his pocket for the pistol and managed to get it out, but Will's kick came flying out of nowhere to send the weapon spinning away into the darkness. Deaville was downed by another kick and his hands went out to save himself. As they did so, his fingers touched metal. The pistol. Feverishly he grabbed it and stood up. As Will stepped towards him, he fired at close range.

The impact knocked Will off his feet. He heard screams and shouts and, for a moment, he couldn't breathe, a huge pain in his chest. I'm dying, he thought, shocked. Then he wheezed a great breath and realised that he was going to live. But how was that possible? The pistol had been aimed at his chest, and for sure, Deaville had not missed. Megan was kneeling beside him, crying and talking desperately, but it took him a few moments of painful, ragged breathing to gather enough breath and recover his mental faculties sufficiently to respond to her questions. He heard a thud followed by a squelch as Deaville toppled backwards into the muddy ditch like a felled oak, knocked out by Ron Parker, the blacksmith who had a punch no one could withstand.

The other soldiers, including Richard Camberwell, gathered anxiously around Will as he carefully sat up, then stood with a helping hand from George. He felt around on his chest, and brought out the thong on which he had threaded the lucky stone the gypsy girl had given him. The stone was flattened and chipped. He gazed at it in awe, realising it had saved his life.

'Oh, Will!' Heedless of the mud and water that splattered them both, Megan rushed into his arms and was rewarded with a hug that almost drove her breath away. Then their lips met and time became meaningless. Eventually Richard Camberwell's insistent voice and Sergeant Readman's loud guffaws penetrated their blissful reunion and they parted, still holding hands and looking somewhat embarrassed. Will wondered what Richard Camberwell would say to this joint display of emotion, but, to his surprise, the Captain said nothing about it. He was worried about something far worse.

'Will! Are you all right? And you Megan? Did that bastard...?'
Richard Camberwell stopped and held his breath, dreading the
reply.

'No, uncle. You arrived just in time.' Megan gave a tremulous
smile and wiped her tear streaked face, then shivered, partly from
the cold, but mostly she was thinking of what might have been
happening if her rescuers had not appeared when they did. Will
hugged her closer.

'Thank God!'

Nat Binns picked up Deaville's empty pistol and examined it.
'Damp,' he said. 'Probably not enough dry powder ter send the ball
as 'ard as it should. Must've got wet in the rain.'

Camberwell took hold of the flattened stone that hung around
Will's neck, the imprint of the fern now nearly invisible due to the
embedded bullet. 'You're a lucky lad,' he said. 'It'll give you the
devil of a bruise though.' Will had already worked that out for
himself. His chest felt as though a bull had stood on it, but he was
alive, and so was Megan. For that he would be forever thankful.

Suddenly there was a shout and they all turned to see Paul
Deaville running across the ground towards the farmhouse, in a
vain attempt to get to the soldier's horse. Richard Camberwell
sprinted after him but he was not as quick as either Nat Binns or
George Trim who reached Deaville first and sent him down with a
flying tackle. By the time Camberwell reached them, they had him
standing firmly in their grip. Richard Camberwell drew his sword
and touched Deaville's chest with the tip.

'Try that again, Lieutenant, and you will find you go no further,'
he said grimly. Deaville glared at him and spat in his face, but said
nothing. Camberwell, his patience ended, was tempted there and
then to run the man through. His eyes narrowed and the sword arm
moved forward, but then a hand went around his wrist and a lazy
voice said, 'Don't do it, Richard. It's too easy. He deserves to die
hard.'

There was a moment of silence, then Camberwell drew a deep
breath and stepped back a pace, knowing that James Shaw was
right. To die at the point of his sword was to give Paul Deaville an
easy death. He put the sword in its scabbard and released his anger
by delivering a very forceful punch to the man's chin instead,
sending him tumbling to the ground. 'This is the end of you,

Deaville,' he said. 'I'll be glad to see you hang!'

Deaville shook his head to rid himself of the mist that clung to his eyes and scowled at the Captain. 'That little bugger cut me!' he sneered. 'And he's a wanted man. If I hang, he'll hang with me!'

'Like hell he will!' said Camberwell.

Sergeant Readman dragged Deaville to his feet, and, like Richard Camberwell, unable to resist the temptation, cuffed the lieutenant round the head. 'Be quiet, you lyin' bastard!' he growled. 'You've no right to say anythin' against Will! He's twice the man you are!'

Knocked half senseless again, Deaville said nothing further.

† † †

But he had plenty to say two days later when he was hauled before a court martial in the large room at the court house. Once the charges were read out, he was asked to plead his case, but he seemed to have forgotten the fact that he had helped an enemy prisoner to escape, and kidnapped and tried to rape Lady Megan Camberwell. All he was worried about was the fact that Will had struck him again and inflicted a wound which, though not life threatening, was causing him much pain. He held his bandaged arm out for all to see like a prize offering, but Wellington who, because of the severity of the case was presiding over the proceedings himself, ignored it.

Deaville having had his say, Will, clean, and dressed once again in his private's uniform, gave evidence, telling the court everything that had happened since his escape. His chest was plastered with the last of the gypsy's salve for, as predicted, he had a great bruise that was painful, but he was in high spirits, glad to be able to recount his suspicions and knowledge of Deaville's bad deeds at last. The lieutenant listened quietly until Will came to the part where he had seen Colonel Reynard spreading something on his face, and indicated that he thought it was flour to make his face paler, then Deaville sneered in derision and proclaimed him delusional.

'Be quiet, sir! You have had your chance to speak!' demanded Wellington severely. He turned to Will. 'Do you have proof of this?' he asked.

'No, my Lord,' said Will, regretting the fact.

Flour. Richard Camberwell sitting at a side table remembered the purse he had found on the dead Frenchman's body. It was still in his pocket, and must be the pouch Will was talking about. Since rescuing Megan he had forgotten all about it, though he had meant to ask his niece if indeed Will had stolen it from Robert Underwood in Portsmouth. Now he brought it out of his pocket and presented it to the court.

'My Lord,' he said to Wellington. 'I believe this is the pouch that contained the flour. I found it on Reynard's body'.

Will grinned, while Deaville's face went as white as the flour, though he vehemently denied ever having seen the pouch before. He was quickly quietened, and restrained by the burly sergeants standing either side of him. The court having ascertained that the residue of the contents was indeed flour, Richard Camberwell also proclaimed the pouch to be the property of his niece, giving a sidelong glance at Will who guessed that the Captain knew who its original owner had been. Camberwell also wondered aloud how Deaville had come to have it in his possession. There followed accusations of theft, and more vehement denials from Deaville. The proceedings were delayed while Megan was summoned and called upon to verify ownership and to tell the tale of the night Will was wounded when she had first missed the purse. She was asked to leave the room again afterwards. Because it was a known fact that Deaville was notoriously short of money, and despite his protestations to the contrary, the court eventually believed that he had stolen the purse together with its contents.

Wellington pronounced Deaville guilty of helping an enemy prisoner to escape and murdering that prisoner, theft, kidnapping and attempting to rape Lady Megan Camberwell, as well as attempted murder. He was stripped of his rank and ordered to be sent back to England immediately, to languish in the prison hulks off Portsmouth harbour until he could be brought before a military tribunal who would undoubtedly sentence him to death. Then the proceedings were surprisingly interrupted when a lieutenant burst into the room, apologised, and asked to speak with the army's commander.

After a hurried, whispered conversation with Lieutenant-Colonel Davenport, a piece of paper was handed to Wellington who perused it quickly. Will, who had been watching Deaville, saw his expression which had been one of dismay, turn to terror as he obviously recognised the paper.

Wellington stared at Deaville and his face was harder than Will had ever seen it.

'It seems that not only are you a fool, a murderer, a thief and a rapist, Deaville, but you are also a traitor,' he said and there was a collective gasp from the officers in the room. Deaville staggered slightly as though suddenly too weak to stand.

'This paper proves that it was you who informed the French of our impending attack on the redoubt,' Wellington continued. 'It is a letter, dated the 8th of January, in which Colonel Reynard seeks information in return for the settlement of a debt you incurred when gambling with him. In fact...' His steely gaze pierced Paul Deaville, '...he is asking you to turn traitor. How did you come by this letter?'

For a moment Deaville said nothing, then said shakily, 'It proves nothing, my Lord. Even if I did receive such a letter, there is no proof that I did anything about it. And I might ask how the lieutenant came by it.'

Wellington frowned and Lieutenant-Colonel Davenport, sitting beside Richard Camberwell, gave a loud snort and said, 'If you must know, Deaville, your belongings were being moved from your present room in the garrison, and it fell out of your bag. The lieutenant picked it up and happened to see the French Colonel's name at the bottom, recognised it's significance in these proceedings, and read the letter which, given the circumstances, I think he had every right to do. As for you not responding, it seems strange, don't you think, that the redoubt's garrison were expecting us to attack that night? Unless we have a rash of traitors in our midst, I would say that this puts you in the front line, and that you are the one who gave the enemy the details.'

Wellington looked very stern as he said, 'I ask you again, sir. How came you by this letter?'

Will thought Deaville was going to deny all knowledge and brazen it out, then he seemed to deflate before their eyes and his voice was low as he said, 'A girl brought it to me.'

Will's mind suddenly swept back to when he had seen Juanita and Deaville together in the baggage park and Juanita had passed Deaville a piece of paper. Had that been this letter? Had Juanita been a spy after all?

Deaville's next words in answer to Wellington's request for a name, confirmed his suspicion.

'The whore's name was Juanita. She came with us from the winter camp. Being Spanish she had free access to Ciudad Rodrigo while the gates were still open and she met Reynard the first day here. Reynard took the damn woman to bed that very day and she talked more than was good for her. She let slip my name. I gambled with him in Lisbon and lost. I didn't have money to pay him. Reynard came up with a plan to get his debt paid and said he'd forget it if I gave him information.' Deaville cast Will an angry look. 'When the British took the redoubt so convincingly I at first thought that Juanita had not given him the information I told her to pass on, but afterwards I heard rumours. Something, or someone, upset my plans and the French lost the battle. Because of that Reynard was angry and refused to keep his end of the deal so when he was captured, he asked me to help him escape.'

'May I ask the prisoner a question, my Lord?' This from Richard Camberwell.

Wellington nodded briefly.

The Captain turned to Deaville. 'Did you kill Juanita?'

'No.'

'Who did?'

'How the hell should I know?'

Will's mind whirled with the suspicions he had been turning over in his head since the night he was shot. Should he speak? He was almost sure it was Amos Wilkins he had seen on the night of Juanita's death, but if he was wrong about other things...

'Permission to speak, my Lord?' he asked. All eyes turned to him and he blushed.

'You may.' Wellington's voice was cold.

'I don't think Lieutenant Deaville killed Juanita, sir, but he may have been involved. I think it was a soldier called Amos Wilkins.'

'And what makes you think that, lad?'

'I followed a man who was stalkin' Juanita just before she was killed but I was too late to stop it. The man looked like Wilkins, but it was 'ard to see for sure because there was only firelight. I saw Wilkins and Deaville talkin' together before, secretive like. Wilkins tried to kill me when I was wounded, and the only person who knew

353

where I was, apart from the people who took me there, was Deaville. George...Private Trim...told me Deaville was comin' out of the house (it was a brothel, sir) when they took me in. Wilkins was a killer, my Lord. Captain Camberwell and I'd met 'im before, in England. 'E tried to kill the Captain there once. I wouldn't mind bettin' Lieutenant Deaville paid 'im to kill Juanita. And I bet it was 'im or Deaville shot me, too, sir. There were no Frenchies around that part of town just then, sir. It was all quiet by the church when I found Juanita dyin'.'

The room erupted, the shocked officers talking amongst themselves, and Deaville, loudest of all, denying everything. Wellington banged a gavel on the desk and, gradually, the room quietened again.

'That's quite an accusation, lad. Do you have any proof?' he said.

Will had none, but then he thought back to the church steps and Juanita, lying bleeding in his arms. She had said something. What was it? 'evil'...or that's what he'd thought she'd said at the time, but now he suddenly thought she could have been trying to say something else entirely. She had not been saying that whoever had killed her was evil, she had said his name. Deaville's name. He grinned.

'She said 'is name, sir, before she died. I thought at first she said, 'evil' but now I think it was 'Deaville'. She was warnin' me against 'im.'

There was more disruption, and more denials from Deaville, though his face was a pasty white and his eyes held a very frightened look. Wellington brought order again with difficulty.

'That's mere supposition, Mister Tucker, although from what I have heard here today, not unlikely...' Wellington's cold eyes once more bored into those of Paul Deaville, before turning back to Will. 'Why would Lieutenant Deaville want you dead?'

''E's never liked me, sir. Not since Christmas night.'

Wellington looked puzzled and demanded an explanation so Will, red faced, had to tell the story of his liason with Juanita, and Deaville's interruption.

'There is something else, my Lord,' said Richard Camberwell. 'If I may have a quiet word?'

'Anything you have to say that might have a bearing on the case may be said in front of the assembly, Captain,' said Wellington sharply.

'Yes, my Lord.' Camberwell spared Will a sympathetic glance, and Will wondered what was coming. 'I believe that Lieutenant Deaville is jealous of Private Tucker, sir,' said Camberwell.

'Jealous?'

'Yes, sir. The lieutenant has long had designs on my niece, Lady Megan Camberwell. So has Private Tucker.'

There were more murmurs from the watching officers, and even some sniggers, while Will turned red. God, this was embarrassing!

Wellington seemed somewhat lost for words. There was so much more to this case than aiding a prisoner to escape and attempted rape. It seemed that Paul Deaville was probably guilty of much more, and that Will Tucker had maybe done the British army a great service in winkling out the bad apple. He said nothing for several minutes while everyone waited in silence, then, 'Lieutenant Deaville will be imprisoned here in Ciudad Rodrigo until arrangements can be made for his transfer to England. Take him away!'

As the sergeants took hold of his bound arms, Paul Deaville suddenly started to shout. The soldier who was acting as scribe and had just closed his writing case, opened it again in a hurry. 'Yes! It's true! All of it!' Deaville said loudly. 'I wanted Juanita dead! Her mouth was always running away with her and she bedded officers. I wanted to silence her because she knew about Reynard and me. But she was beautiful. I couldn't kill her myself so I got Wilkins to do it for me.' His blazing, maddened eyes stared at Will. 'And we would have got away with it too, but for you. You had to follow her didn't you. I'd told her Captain Shaw would meet her at the church and I was hiding there to make sure Wilkins killed her, then you came. Wilkins ran after he stabbed her, so what could I do? Juanita was talking to you – opening her big mouth yet again – and I thought she was telling you about me so I had to kill you too. But you survived, so I sent Wilkins to the brothel to do the job properly. The bastard got himself killed instead. And you wouldn't even die the other night, damn you! This is all your fault, Will Tucker. All of it! You even love the girl I wanted! I hate you! I hate you! May you rot in hell!'

There was a shocked silence as Deaville struggled to get at Will, his face a twisted mask of rage, spittle dribbling from the corners of his mouth, but the sergeants were too strong for him, and forced him out of the room. The silent officers listened to his shouts until

355

they faded away down the corridor.

When it was quiet again, Wellington turned his long nose towards the assembled officers. 'Well, it seems we do not need further proof and Deaville will certainly meet his end. I have no need of your presence any more, sirs. You are dismissed from this court.'

The officers all left but as Will, pale and shocked by Deaville's outburst, turned to go, Wellington stopped him. 'You will stay, young man,' he commanded. Will, his heart thumping furiously, wondered if he was about to be re-arrested and slowly sat down again.

The room seemed much bigger when everyone had gone. Wellington gave Will one of his rare smiles, sensing his anxiety. 'Young man, it seems you know quite a lot about this case. I would be pleased if you could answer some questions and fill in some details for me.'

Rather over-awed, but eager not to remind Wellington of his own escape from custody, Will did his best to remember details and answer the General's questions truthfully. He finished by relating the meetings he had seen between Juanita and Deaville, and told of over-hearing the two mysterious people on the hillside before the attack on the redoubt. 'They were probably Deaville and Juanita, sir. If you remember, one of 'em dropped a letter, a letter that told the French of our plans. I think if you question Lieutenant Deaville further you might find that 'e wrote that letter. Maybe Juanita dropped it that night after she'd shown it to Colonel Reynard or maybe she only told him about the attack and kept the letter. Perhaps you could match the 'andwritin' with the lieutenant's as proof.'

'I do believe you could be right, Tucker,' said Wellington. he smiled faintly. 'It could be said that the lieutenant was overly careless with his paperwork, wouldn't you say?' Will grinned. suddenly feeling better. Wellington stood up, so did Will. 'Well, I'm pleased that we've found all this out,' Wellington said as he gathered up some papers from the desk. 'I would not have wanted to go on to Badajoz with a traitor in our midst.' His thin lips turned up in another small smile. 'Now, before you go, and although it is probably none of my business, I would like to know if what Captain Camberwell said about you being in love with his niece is true? Or

356

was that mere subterfuge to anger Deaville into telling the truth?'

Will admitted that he felt a great deal for Megan Camberwell. 'So that episode that ended with you being imprisoned in the garrison was brought on by jealousy on your part, was it?' said Wellington. Will's stomach churned again. Lieutenant-Colonel Davenport had said he was not going to involve the army's commanding officer with that offence, but now it seemed that Wellington knew all about it. He braced himself for more punishment. Wellington seemed to read his mind. 'Not much goes on that I am not aware of, Tucker,' he said. 'I believe you also gave Deaville a good pasting when you and Captain Camberwell came upon him trying to rape Lady Camberwell.' Will gaped, horrified. Was he to be chastised for that too? His face took on a mutinous look.

'I'll not apologise for it, m'Lord,' he said stoutly. 'Maybe the other day I was a little 'asty when Deaville and Megan were just kissin', but 'e deserved it this time, and more.'

'I tend to agree with you. And it's all right, lad. You are not the one who's on trial here,' said Wellington quite kindly. 'Though you're damn lucky to have avoided one. I have to admit I was not pleased to hear, after the event, that a private had hit an officer, or that that same soldier had managed to escape from custody, but now I hear the whole story, I can understand your reasons. And after your assistance in bringing Lieutenant Deaville's faults to light, I think I may be persuaded to forget that little episode. This army is mostly made up of Irishmen, convicts, and felons, of which you are one, I believe...' Will grinned. 'Yet...' Wellington continued, 'those same men make up the best infantry in the world. However, if I'm to believe what I've heard here today, Lieutenant Paul Deaville is not one of the best. He's a fool and a traitor, and I can't abide both. The army will be much better off without him.'

Will felt hugely relieved. It seemed he had redeemed himself and was a free man again. Wellington dismissed him, and he walked out of the garrison building with a lighter heart than he'd had for many a day.

That night, as he lay on his bed, he thought over the last day. It had been a good one. Apart from Paul Deaville finally getting his just desserts, he had had a long talk with Richard Camberwell. The Captain had told him that the debt he owed for stealing his purse had more than been repaid, so he was released from servitude.

'If it pleases yer, sir, I'd still like ter work for yer,' he had replied. Not too long ago, he would have shied away from working for anyone for more than a couple of days at a time, but now he found he really did want to continue in the Captain's employ. And not just because it would keep him conveniently near to Megan. Surprisingly, he actually enjoyed it.

The Captain had grinned and said he would be grateful, as Dodge was a rotten cook and it would be good to have some decent meals again. At this they'd both laughed. 'But you will be paid, lad,' Camberwell had continued, 'and when we get back home I'll pay you to look after my horses, if you still want the job.'

Yes, indeed he did. It had certainly been a good day. Will's thoughts turned to the gypsy's stone, and he remembered the prophecies the old woman had foretold when looking in her crystal ball. For Megan two men, one handsome but cruel, the other young and with a knife; himself and Paul Deaville? He remembered the old lady had seen two men in his fortune too, men who would influence his life. They could well be Deaville and Richard Camberwell. And two women, maybe Juanita and Megan. Was she a witch, that gypsy? Witch or not, the lucky stone had saved his life, as had her medicine, and her prophesies had come true.

What was in store for him next, he wondered?

† † †

On a cold day in the middle of February 1812, the British army was on the move again. Sir Arthur Wellesley, Viscount Wellington, sat astride his horse and watched as the army marched past. He himself was staying behind with part of his force to confuse the French, and would start out later. He had won a great battle, the northern route into Spain was open, and the army was heading south. He was confident that the British would win this war, Napoleon would be vanquished, and the threat of invasion by the French on the English people would be squashed. He watched the long, long line of men, artillery, carts and mules, wagons, horses, women, children and cattle file past, and felt an unfamiliar pang of good feeling for them all.

Megan Camberwell rode her horse, Dinah, and felt the cold wind whip her curls back from her face. There was a good feeling inside her too, and it was caused, not by the fact that the army was on the move again, but by the figure she could see marching twenty yards ahead of her, easily distinguishable by the bright hair that stuck out beneath his shako. Will loved her; he had saved her from rape and from a disastrous relationship, and now she knew that she loved him too. It didn't seem to matter any more that he spoke with an accent that used to make her cringe, that he had spent most of his life in petty crime, or that he had been born a bastard at the bottom of her mental social ladder. In her eyes he had climbed to the very top, and she now knew full well that he had virtues many a high-born gentleman did not possess, besides being handsome and so sexually attractive that her insides melted at the mere thought of that smile bestowed on her, or the touch of his hand. She smiled, and urged her horse on so that she could ride beside him, uncaring of the grins from Will's pals who all knew about their new-found love.

Will heard the trotting hooves and glanced sideways with a grin when Megan slowed the horse to match his pace. He knew that Megan loved him now as much as he loved her. In fact, in a stolen moment soon after the excitement of the chase for Deaville had died down, she had told him so, had returned his kisses, and things might have gone a little further if they had not heard Richard Camberwell returning from his duties just then. Her love made him the happiest man alive, and, on top of that, the army was marching again. There were more adventures to be had, and he would be a part of them.

For the army was on its way to Napoleon Bonaparte's biggest stronghold that barred the southern road into Spain.

They were on their way to Badajoz.

Historical Note

To be a Soldier is fiction. However, the story is built around an actual battle that took place during the Penisular War of 1808–1814. During this time, Britain was fighting against France's Napoleon Bonaparte who wished to be ruler of all Europe, if not the world. By 1808, Spain and Portugal were two of the few countries left to be conquered. Spain had earlier been an ally of France but its royal family had been ousted and Napoleon was determined to add both countries to his empire. Wellington was one of the Generals dispatched to spoil the Frenchman's plans.

This was the time of great sea and land battles, when men were pitted against each other with little chance of survival, yet some found army life to be something of an improvement on their existence back home. There, poverty and disease made for very hard times and many, like Will Tucker, found that, if they did not actually enjoy it, the army at least gave them a reason for living. Despite the ever-present dangers, often foul weather, poor food, and boredom, the camaraderie made up for a lot. Being told what to do all the time, men hardly ever had to think for themselves and it is not to be wondered at that those who survived the war often found it difficult to settle back into civilian life with any ease.

Life in the hill cantonments during the winter months of 1811 was much as described in the story and is told in detail by Arthur Bryant in his book, *The Great Duke*. The soldiers made their own amusements and, despite the cold, must have found the time quite relaxing after the hardships of the summer which included the battle of Fuentes de Oñoro and several other skirmishes with the enemy. Some of the details described concerning the hard march from the hills to Ciudad Rodrigo are true. A camp follower did give birth by the side of the road, then carried on walking with her newborn baby, proof that the women who followed the soldiers were equally as hardy as their men. Some men died because of the cold and harsh conditions, and the army certainly had to wade across the River Agueda's freezing cold water.

As to the battle for Ciudad Rodrigo itself, the telling of the assault on the redoubt and digging the trenches is based on Arthur Bryant's description, and that of Roger Parkinson in his book, *The Penisular War*, though there was no warning for the French before the assault, and Will's part in it is entirely fictitious. Colonel Colborne was indeed the officer who led the victorious attack on the redoubt soon after the British Army's arrival.

The attack on the walls, the breaches, and the mass hysteria of the aftermath happened, with General Napier being wounded, and General Crauford killed much as described. Lieutenant Gurwood, the leader of the Light Division's Forlorn Hope, miraculously survived to take the Governor's sword in surrender. The convents used as hospitals must have been ghastly, reeking places, with as many men dying there as during the battle itself, while the citizens of the besieged town surely suffered horribly from the soldiers' depredations.

The reason the British found it relatively easy to take Ciudad Rodrigo was because Napoleon was more concerned at that time with mobilizing a great army to attack Russia, thus paying little attention to what was happening in Spain and Portugal. With the French army scattered, his forces there were in a state of division and indecision. By sending some of Marshall Marmont's men to Valencia, he left Portugal and the border country largely undefended. It was possibly his biggest mistake in the whole campaign, giving Wellington the chance he needed and one of which he took full advantage.

I may have attributed to Sir Arthur Wellesley, Viscount Wellington at the time, far more sympathetic reactions to situations than would probably have been the case. He was known to be a hard, cold man, who thought his soldiers rogues, yet the best army in the world. He treated them with disdain, flogged and hanged without compunction if he thought a man deserved it, yet the British soldiers are believed to have respected, even loved him, and all knew he was the best commander the army ever had.

The rest of the story is pure fiction. There was, as far as I could find out, no 4th Kent Infantry at that time. If there was, or is now, then I apologize for putting them into action where they had no right to be.

Although sometimes dismissed as one of the more insignificant battles of the Peninsular War, the taking of Ciudad Rodrigo paved the way for the British Army and its allies to bring heavy artillery into Northern Spain and thus continue their efforts to expel the French from the Peninsular. More battles were to come, beginning with the siege of Badajoz, more heavily fortified than Ciudad Rodrigo, and a place guaranteed to provide Will Tucker and Megan Camberwell with more adventures.

Bibliography and further reading

The Peninsular War – Roger Parkinson.
Published by Hart-Davis-MacGibbon – London.

War in the Penisular – Jan Read
Published by Faber and Faber Ltd.

The Great Duke – by Arthur Bryant
Published by Collins.

www.ingramcontent.com/pod-product-compliance
Lightning Source LLC
Chambersburg PA
CBHW020838020726
47497CB00005B/1157